"Joël Champetier sports the three essential qualities of the good science fiction writer: a poetic imagination sensitive to the wondrous mysteries of the universe, the ability to ask disturbing questions about that universe and our place in it, and the will to try and answer them rigorously."
—Élisabeth Vonarburg

"In *The Dragon's Eye*, author Joël Champetier imaginatively projects how influences on contemporary Chinese culture might affect the structure of a Chinese colony in the future. His New China is a vividly drawn collage that impacts on all the senses. The novel recognizes the tensions, divided loyalties, and pressures that people who are trying to build a new world from the legacy of one of the oldest, most accomplished cultures on Earth, will face.

"With his first novel in English, Joël Champetier will seem like a newcomer on the Anglophone scene, but with eleven novels in French already under his belt, his skill at building a story to a strong climax is evident."
—*www.scifi.com*

"Need to spice up your reading diet? Add some freshness and piquancy? Expand your horizons into new, exotic territory? Then try Joël Champetier, a genuinely fresh voice, and listen carefully. You won't be disappointed."
—Terence M. Green

"Joël Champetier has a knack for drawing out the unexpected consequences of a seemingly ordinary premise. But he truly excels when it comes to taking them forward to an unflinching conclusion. At which point the reader will often look up, head whirling, and wonder how Champetier managed to make it seem so natural!"
—Jean-Louis Trudel

"*The Dragon's Eye*, Quebecois science fiction writer Joël Champetier's first novel to be translated into English, is a fast-paced spy thriller. As a thriller, *The Dragon's Eye*—originally published in 1991—is more than competent and it moves right along. What lifts it above the average example of its genre, however, is Champetier's marvelously complete rendering of the new world in which its chases and escapes take place. New China is extremely challenging in its difference, and everything about the environment affects people's behavior....The way Champetier subtly implicates New China's environmental context into every action of the novel makes it work as solid science fiction. *The Dragon's Eye* marks the English-language debut of another exciting SF writer from Quebec."
—*Edmonton Journal*

"Combines nonstop action and succinct characterization with a tightly executed plot. A good choice for fans of SF intrigue and futuristic cloak-and-dagger tales."
—*Library Journal*

"Takes the myth of the superspy thrown into a strange world and inverts it. An exploratory journey into a foreign land."
· —*Publishers Weekly*

TOR®

A TOM DOHERTY ASSOCIATES BOOK
NEW YORK

THE DRAGON'S EYE

JOËL CHAMPETIER

TRANSLATED BY JEAN-LOUIS TRUDEL

THE DRAGON'S EYE

Design by Victoria Kuskowski

This novel is a revised and enlarged version of *La taupe et le dragon,* originally published in 1991 by Éditions Québec/Amérique in Montréal, Canada. New French edition published in 1999 by Éditions Alire Inc., Beauport, Canada. The translation is by Jean-Louis Trudel.

This book is printed on acid-free paper.

Edited by David G. Hartwell

A Tor Book
Published by Tom Doherty Associates, LLC
175 Fifth Avenue
New York, NY 10010

www.tor.com

Tor® is a registered trademark of Tom Doherty Associates, LLC.

Library of Congress Cataloging-in-Publication Data

Champetier, Joël.
    [Taupe et le dragon. English]
    The dragon's eye / Joël Champetier.
        p   cm.
    "A Tom Doherty Associates Book"
    ISBN 0-312-86882-0 (hc)
    ISBN 0-312-87252-6 (pbk)
    I. Title.
PQ3919.2.C5225T3813   1999
843—dc21   99-19562
                                            CIP

First Hardcover Edition: May 1999
First Trade Paperback Edition: May 2000

Printed in the United States of America

0 9 8 7 6 5 4 3 2 1

THE DRAGON'S EYE

ONE

UTTER BEDLAM PREVAILED INSIDE NEW CHINA'S STARPORT. A COMPACT mass of Chinese immigrants clogged the corridors of the vast terminal, their exhilaration too great for them to pay any attention to the frantic waving of security guards or the screeching of loudspeakers. Heroically shoving and elbowing his way through, Réjean Tanner extricated himself from the jammed mob and managed to flee toward an area with some breathing room. There, he spotted Commander Wang Zhong, who had kept him a seat on one of the last uncrowded benches.

Tanner thanked his superior, then sat with a sigh of relief, worn out by the nerve-racking atmospheric reentry aboard the shuttle and by the hours spent waiting in the customs line. He massaged his forehead; he felt nauseous, and a hellish headache was splitting his skull open at the seams. After six weeks of interstellar travel, his body was proving unequal to the demands of the local gravity.

Out of sheer habit, he checked his watch. It showed nothing, of course. With a sigh of annoyance, he took off the now useless wristwatch: the ionization of New China's upper atmosphere prevented the orbiting of timekeeping satellites. A locally made watch would probably be his first purchase on New China.

Weariness also affected his superior. The usually stoic Commander Wang indulged in a rare display of petulance:

"Someone should have been waiting, at the very least an agent with a car. I tell you, Bloembergen's casualness verges on insolence!"

An hour crawled by. It was hot. Through the large bays, the orange star splashed with subdued gold the marquetry of the starport's floor, a stylized pattern of intertwined dragons. Wang dozed. Tanner began to feel impatient: how long were they going to stew here?

A small crowd of Chinese immigrants gathered near their bench. A young Han woman positioned herself near Réjean Tanner and, her voice amplified by a megaphone, directed the flow of immigrants to prevent another crush. To make it twice as much fun, she insisted on repeating each instruction in English and Mandarin, with a thick Cantonese accent, as if the megaphone's distortion wasn't enough to almost completely garble her words. Tanner tugged on the edge of her skirt.

"Can't you go and yell somewhere else with that thing?"

The young hostess eyed Tanner scornfully, surprised to find him a large red-haired fellow. A European . . . One who spoke perfect Mandarin. Better than hers, at any rate.

"I'm doing my job," she answered curtly.

Wang urged Tanner to remain calm; it was neither the time nor the place for a scene. They trudged away, wearily dragging their bags toward a quieter part of the terminal. For naught, since joiners were hard at work there, repairing the floor's marquetry and applying a new coat of clear varnish, the particularly unpleasant stink of which boosted Tanner's migraine by an order of magnitude.

They observed through a large bay the thunderous landing of another shuttle. Fifty or so passengers, men, women, and children, exited from the shuttle, thrilled and disoriented, staring at the sky or kissing the cracked concrete of the apron. The shuttle left again immediately in order to complete the transfer of the starship's three thousand passengers.

In a cloudless sky of yellowish green, the sun—Epsilon Bootis A—neared zenith and bathed the floating dust raised by the shuttle's liftoff in a soothing amber light. Farther away, eastward, an industrial park of the Earth Free Trade Area stretched beyond the concrete hangars of the starport. Even farther yet, the sea of shimmering green gold spread outward. Tanner rubbed his neck: hard to find the morning sun beautiful when one was so tired.

"Commander Wang?"

Wang and Tanner inspected the newcomer, a thin Caucasian, fashionably dressed. His pasty-white face made for an almost shocking contrast with his shoulder-length black hair. He held between his fingers a cigarette wrapped in yellow paper. Somewhat foppishly, he touched it to his mouth, then blew with a carefree air a smoke ring toward the ceiling. Tanner blinked, taken aback for a fraction of a second: on Earth, it was rare to find Europeans who smoked. The man inhaled again, then scowled, letting the smoke swirl in time with his breaths.

"I'm Francis Barnaby. I work for the Bureau."

"Well, well, none too soon," grumbled Wang.

Barnaby muttered a vague excuse. He seemed rather amused by the annoyance of the officer. He looked at Tanner:

"And you're the rookie?"

"Réjean Tanner."

Barnaby nodded, his ambiguous smile hard to decipher. His attention turned toward the bay, and as he gestured with a gloved hand he remarked:

"Say, there's that good old Eye . . ."

He pointed east, where a green-tinged dot, so dazzling that a glimpse was enough to hurt one's retina, climbed above the horizon. The Eye of the Dragon: the other star in the Epsilon Bootis binary, a blazing A2 blue-white dwarf. Within all the windows flashed a fluorescing message: DO NOT LOOK AT THE EYE OF THE DRAGON! in English, pinyin, and even old Chinese characters.

Outside, the starport employees stopped whatever they were doing and straggled back inside.

"No more work today," commented Barnaby.

Wang expressed his impatience: he was looking forward to a short rest and a bite to eat. Barnaby gestured for them to follow him, even offering, after a moment's thought, to carry Wang's luggage.

Wang took the lead and they crossed the entire starport, avoiding the immigration queues, walking past the stalls from which wafted the oily smell of fried breads, the sweetish fragrance of sherbets, and the spicy aroma of roasting chicken.

Barnaby was now taking an interest in Tanner's gaberdine. He was unceremoniously fingering the black hems and pinching the fabric.

"So, is this the new rage on Earth?"

"I guess so. . . . I bought it especially for my posting here." Barnaby gestured fatalistically.

"That's the drawback of living on such a remote colony: it's hard to keep up with what's in. . . . pity, though: you won't be wearing it often. First, because it's too hot here. Second, because it's the best way to be spotted by Tewu agents."

"There are Tewu agents inside the EFTA?"

As soon as he closed his mouth, Tanner knew that he'd sounded naive. It was obvious that New China's intelligence service had observers within the free-trade enclave. But Barnaby refrained from making fun of his slip and merely shrugged.

"Of course, in the final analysis, your clothing matters little. For the Tewu, the mere fact you're European will be enough to arouse suspicion—"

Barnaby cut himself off and stopped the two newcomers in front of a bazaar's display.

"I suppose you don't have hats."

"Of course not," replied Commander Wang.

"Simply indispensable. And no shades, either, right?"

He sighed, as if exasperated by their thoughtlessness. He entered the bazaar and bought two sets of wraparound eyewear:

"Not great, but they'll do for today."

He also bought a couple of large conical hats of aluminized plastic.

Outside, even the color of the sky had changed. If a soft green tint still prevailed along the western horizon, the sky shifted eastward to a vibrant electric blue. Tanner tried to spot the burning pinprick of the Eye, but the starport's facade blocked his view of it.

"Put on your glasses and don't look at the Eye of the Dragon," warned Barnaby as he got out his own sunglasses.

"We've already been told."

"You can't be told often enough. The Eye will quickly make you blind if you're not shielding your retinas with glass. Blindness is endemic here on New China. My own eyesight has been deteriorating. . . ."

They walked briskly toward Barnaby's car, down an almost deserted street. Passersby were rare and it was impossible to tell the Chinese from the Europeans: gloves, glasses, and large hats effectively made everybody anonymous.

"I thought the glasses would be tinted," remarked Tanner.

Barnaby whooped with delight:

"I was waiting for that! Newcomers always expect us to be walking around in mirrorshades. I don't know why the media always show us like that on Earth. Maybe because it looks so cool. . . . Of course, our glasses don't need to be tinted; they don't have to stop visible light, but the ultraviolet kind. The glass they use is quite efficient as a rule. As long as you don't stare the Dragon in the Eye—Hell! What's going on here?"

Half a dozen children were playing around Barnaby's car; two of them were even standing on the front hood. Barnaby swore in Mandarin and the kids ran off so fast one even lost his hat. Utterly exasperated, Barnaby shouted for him to come back. The youngster stopped, turned hesitantly, awkwardly protecting his forehead with arms and hands. Scared by the angry tone of the grown-up's voice, the child refused to come closer. Barnaby took out a coin from his suit. He called out more caressingly and coaxed the youngster forward. Tanner was surprised: on Earth, no kid would have fallen for such an obvious trick.

Hard to say if it was a boy or a girl. Eight years old, if that. Beneath the thick black hair and the shades, snot trailed down the face's baby fat. A gloved hand grabbed the coin and slipped it into a pocket. Only then did the kid deign to accept his hat, which he tied on deftly.

"You shouldn't climb on cars," scolded Barnaby.

"It wasn't me."

"What are you doing outside at this hour? Shouldn't you be home?"

The child mumbled a few incomprehensible words. He then asked more intelligibly for another coin and Barnaby told him to scram. Swaggering proudly, the urchin headed back to taunt his friends, who hadn't gotten a coin.

Tanner was amazed: "Children playing without supervision? And not a grandparent or a teacher in sight!"

"This isn't Earth," replied Barnaby disdainfully. "Kids here are a dime a dozen."

He unlocked the door, then shoved their luggage inside the car's tiny trunk.

"Now, get inside quick. You don't have any gloves."

The stubby buildings of the starport vanished behind them as the car traveled down nondescript streets. If it hadn't been for the inscriptions in fluorescing paint, Tanner might have thought he was back in a commonplace terrestrial suburb. The other unexpected detail was the use of the old Chinese ideographic writing, as at the starport.

The trip was short, covering less than three kilometers. Barnaby parked the car in front of the European embassy, a handsome building in violet granite. After a second's thought, Tanner decided the granite was pink, in fact, and that it was the Dragon's Eye which stained it purple. Tanner extricated himself from the narrow backseat. Ignoring Barnaby's assurances that all their luggage would be brought to their quarters, Wang recovered a small aluminum case.

"This briefcase goes everywhere I go."

"Let me carry it, at least," offered Tanner.

Rather grudgingly, Wang accepted.

A liveried domestic appeared. Barnaby returned the keys to him and passed through the large doors of the European embassy, trailed by Wang and Tanner. Two guards immediately challenged the group. Barnaby carelessly flashed his identification. The guards hardly glanced at it, recognizing the agent. They used a sharper tone to ask Wang and Tanner for their papers. But their attitude changed when they saw Wang's black-bordered insignia. With due deference, they returned the documents and saluted.

"Good day to you, sir. Welcome to the European embassy, Commander."

Barnaby guided them through the cool hallways of the embassy, ending up in a well-appointed office where a young Chinese woman sipped a cup of tea while watching television. She reserved a warm smile for Barnaby, greeted Wang and Tanner with a cautious nod.

"So, Siqin, is the old man still there?" asked Barnaby.

The receptionist appeared chagrined.

"No, he left for the restaurant."

"I thought he was going to wait for me here."

"He said he preferred to wait over there, for you and"—she hesitated briefly—"your visitors."

She seemed captivated by carrot-haired Tanner.

"And Jay?" insisted Barnaby.

"They're all at the Quan Ju De. If you hurry, they'll still be waiting to start."

They walked back through the hall. Wang whispered to Tanner:

"What a reception! They let me rot for hours at the starport, me, a ranking officer! And they didn't even wait for me to go out for dinner."

Outside, the large orange sun sank in the west, while the blinding green-hued dot continued to rise. They left the protection of the embassy's porch. The granite facade was almost blue now. Tanner looked at his hand, now tinged an unhealthy shade of purple.

"And keep your hands in your pockets. It's not far, we can walk."

"Is this the noon or evening meal?" asked Tanner. "I can't figure out what time of the day this is."

"Didn't they explain about the eight/six schedule?" replied Barnaby, betraying a hint of impatience.

"Sure, but it's hard to keep it all straight."

"The first step is to forget once and for all that New China's rotation period is eighteen terrestrial hours. Or more exactly, seventeen point nine. Just pay attention to clocks and calendars. Once you're used to it, you'll be able to reckon in terms of 'sectors.' One sector is worth three hours. There are six sectors per rotation period. We work for nine hours, a total of three sectors. We add five more sectors to make up an 'official' day of twenty-four hours. Of course, we're then borrowing two sectors from the next rotation period."

"Don't you take into account the local day or nighttime?"

"In a way, we do. Our week has six 'official' days, the equivalent of eight rotation periods. We set out to avoid exposure to the Eye of the Dragon as much as possible. We always get two working days without seeing the Eye. On the four days when the Eye shines for six of the nine working hours, two are rest days, so that exposure to the Eye is effectively minimized. Of course, we have to shift around the weekend, as the Eye moves in the sky. But right now, you're lucky: the weekend falls on the familiar Saturday and Sunday pair."

"Not simple," sighed Tanner.

"Sure, it is. Forget the theory and just stick to the calendar. Days of the week bear their usual name: Monday, Tuesday, Thursday, Friday, Saturday, and Sunday. No Wednesday. Though mind that this only applies to the Europeans in EFTA. Within New China proper, they do like the Chinese on Earth; they use numbers to identify the days of the week. But they keep the same

kind of schedule. They bloody well have to: it's too hard to ha-
bituate the body to a cycle too different from the usual twenty-
four hours without running into all kinds of problems. . . . Well,
here we are."

Outside, the front of the Quan Ju De—the "Abode of All
Virtues"—was decorated with brightly glowing red, green, and
yellow ideograms, as if transplanted from a historical neighborhood of Shanghai or San Francisco. Except that, here, instead of
neon lights, it was the Eye of the Dragon which made the antique
characters shine.

They left their hats in the cloakroom. Inside, the restaurant's formal atmosphere and red decor, featuring the repeated
motif of a golden dragon, promised comfort and luxury. The familiar smells of garlic, sesame oil, and ginger drifted from the
kitchens. Many families were present, with multitudes of children and a din to match. Barnaby headed for a large table at the
other end of the room, where an enormous European—he must
have weighed at least 150 kilos—was holding court along with a
younger Chinese man, a young Chinese woman, and three kids,
whose ages ranged from no more than ten to less than two. Three
chairs remained empty.

All the guests turned toward the three arrivals. The fat European raised a hand, exclaiming:

"Ah, Francis! What the hell took you so long? We waited,
waited, waited. . . ." He turned toward Wang and Tanner. "I apol-
ogize for starting without you, but you know how it is with
kids. . . . Anyway, you're just in time, we ordered only moments
ago. You'll see: the Quan Ju De has the best food on the island."

Barnaby seemed unimpressed by his superior's enthusiasm.

"In the meantime, let me introduce Commander Wang
Zhong, our esteemed visitor, along with our new agent, Jean Tanner—"

"*Réjean* Tanner," he corrected.

Barnaby introduced the others at the table. The fat one was
Bo Bloembergen, the chief of the European Bureau of External
Affairs for the EFTA, in his late forties, with platinum-blond hair

shining beyond a receding hairline, and a blue gaze peering sagely out of a fleshy face. The young "Chinese" was a Japanese, Jay Hamakawa, short and well muscled, with a brushcut. The young woman was Zhao, Bloembergen's wife, and the three children were theirs: the eldest, Xunxun, then Peter, and finally little Suzy.

A maître d' showed up to take the orders of the three new-comers. Barnaby was unable to settle on a dish.

"Don't spend another hour fooling around with the menu!" thundered Bloembergen. "The duck is fine."

Barnaby expressed his skepticism as to the quality of frozen duck imported from Earth.

"The comparison would be easier if New China consented to sell live ducks to the EFTA," the maître d' replied suavely.

"All right, all right," Barnaby finally decided. "Let's have the duck. With pancakes and soup?"

"Just like on Earth," the maître d' reassured him.

With that out of the way, Bloembergen leaned toward Wang:

"So, Commander, is this your first visit to New China?"

"No, it's my third, as I'm sure your services know full well," replied Wang in a neutral tone.

Bloembergen laughed:

"Don't take it that way, please, I'm just trying to make con-versation." He turned toward Tanner. "And you, what do you think of New China?"

"I've only been here a few hours. Give me a few more to get used to it."

"Of course, of course . . . But still, not too surprised? Is it your first trip away from Earth?"

"Actually, I was staying on Mars. I'll confess the gravity here is stronger than I expected."

"Really? But it's only 0.84 g. Well, I guess that if you were on Mars . . . You'll get used to it soon; it's not like on Colony."

Bloembergen's tone was friendly, which did not prevent him from staring at his new agent with blue eyes as cold as a Mars morning. Tanner looked uneasily at Zhao, Bloembergen's young wife. He was unsure whether the time, the place, or the company was appropriate for a discussion of the secret academy on Colony, where he had gone for advanced training.

Bloembergen guessed the cause of Tanner's misgivings. Turning expansive, he squeezed his spouse and shook her like a cherry tree:

"Come on, now, don't be shy; you can speak in front of Zhao, my sweet meadow flower. She works for us, of course."

The young woman endured the embrace with a wry smile. The older of the two boys explained to Tanner, "Dad is a spy, but we mustn't tell anybody, not even our best friends!"

Bloembergen guffawed and tousled his son's thick black mop of hair. Withdrawing his hand, he overturned a bowl of *hoisin* sauce on the plastic tablecloth.

"Bo!" cried out Zhao as she shrank to avoid getting sauce on her gown.

Bloembergen hastily cleaned the mess with a napkin.

"No problem, no problem!"

The children were giggling. Barnaby and Wang seemed exasperated. Jay was stoic.

"Be more careful, Bo," Zhao rebuked him in Mandarin, a reproving expression on her finely drawn face.

She was beautiful, decided Tanner. Not quite thirty years old, thin, exuding the untroubled serenity of the classical ideal. The unadorned white dress and the black hair falling free on her shoulders—so unlike the overly ornate look favored by fashionable Chinese women on Earth—only emphasized her poise.

"We were saying, Mr. Tanner," said Bloembergen, who refused to let himself be derailed so easily, "that you've mostly worked on Mars."

"In Tselinograd, yes, for two years. I was also an assistant in Intelligence at the European embassy in Beijing."

Bloembergen smiled contentedly. He knew all that, of course.

Appetizers were served, cold, then warm, followed by the skillet-fried duck's heart. Barnaby was mollified: the chef was sticking to the tried-and-true tradition. Protocol was followed to the letter: skin served first, cut into crispy pieces to be slipped inside a small, thin pancake. The duck flesh was served next and eaten the same way. Barnaby was unable to refrain from complaining: the meat was too lean. Bloembergen retorted he should be grateful for the characteristically Chinese fondness for good food, which alleviated the rigors of their exile far from Earth. True to his word, Bloembergen ate heartily, downing the pancakes with the help of impressive quantities of beer. Barnaby almost matched his gusto and Zhao was not far behind. Wang Zhong, ashen-faced with fatigue, took no more than a few sips from his beer. Hamakawa did not drink, and neither did Tanner, who was struggling with a bone-deep weariness and feared alcohol would finish putting him to sleep.

An impassive waiter set down in the table's center a soup made from cabbage and the duck's crushed bones. Tanner withdrew from the fray. The children, quiet at the meal's outset, were starting to act up. Suzy whined, Peter had gone to sleep under the table, and Xunxun kept asking if they would be leaving soon. Zhao whispered a few words in Bloembergen's ear, and the European stared glassily at his guests:

"Gentlemen, you seem tired. . . . So I invite you to escort my delightful meadow flower back to our place, where you have rooms waiting for you. Yours until you find apartments. The three of us will stay behind; we have a few things to discuss."

Wang and Tanner didn't need any more persuading.

Peter was pulled out from under the table. Tanner took him in his arms and carried him to the cloakroom. The maître d' helped Zhao to equip her brood with hats, gloves, and shades. As they were going to leave, Wang glared at Tanner, his face stony:

"What about my briefcase?"

Tanner felt horribly stupid.

"I left it beside my chair."

"I would appreciate it, Operative Tanner, if you went back to get it."

Tanner managed a wan smile and hurried back into the

dining room, still holding young Peter in his arms. A silly mistake, though understandable: he was tired and the dinner had been long. Wang had not seemed overly vexed, but Tanner knew that the commander didn't want to make a scene in front of Zhao. If his superior thought it necessary to hang on to his briefcase, its contents were surely important. Of course, the briefcase was equipped with a secured lock, but Bloembergen probably had the means to make a locked briefcase yield its secrets: X-ray machines, neutron scanners, echogram generators . . .

Feeling extraordinarily foolish under the triple conjunction of Bloembergen's, Barnaby's, and Hamakawa's gazes, Tanner recovered the aluminum case—"I'd . . . er . . . This belongs to us—" then hastened to rejoin Wang, Zhao, and the two other children.

Outside, the show was pure magic. The sun had set and now the Eye of the Dragon shone in lonely splendor overhead. It was the midpoint of the Green Night.

It was called night, but it was a luminous night. Tanner had seen many videos of New China's auroras, he had marveled at pictures, but no recording and no picture could do justice to the fine chromatic gradations of the Green Night. Ethereal veils of yellow, scarlet, and violet snaked across the heavens like jellyfish tentacles, rippled, sliced into each other with an exquisite patience, piled ever upward in layers whose fuzzy contours faded, changed colors, stretched to fray like a fragile gauze torn by a heavenly gale. Then, in the sky, cleared for the space of a few seconds, the most brilliant stars came out shyly. After which new golden veils streamed through it, freshly powdered with immaterial green, cyan, and turquoise, shifting to a medley of argent, fiery red, and deep indigo.

"Don't look at the Dragon's Eye!" snapped Zhao.

Caught in the act, Tanner glanced away. He had barely glimpsed the Eye, but even that was too much for his retinas: wherever he looked, a host of glittering dots danced in front of him. He shivered: Barnaby hadn't understated the risks of becoming blind on New China.

They started walking, with Zhao carrying little Suzy and Peter still sleeping in his arms, while Wang brought up the rear in the company of Xunxun, tired and whining. The heavens did not shine alone; few buildings were without fluorescent ideograms, or window frames, lintels or cornices coated with fluorescing paint. The street was alight with a riot of colors. The pedestrians shared in the gaudy display, especially the gangs of teenagers out for a night on the town, so bright in their fluorescent red and yellow robes and their improbable headwear that they seemed to illuminate the whole street. Even the hats of Zhao and the kids were bordered with luminous stripes. In his European-cut black gaberdine and his nonfluorescing hat, Tanner felt like a shadow among dancers spun from sheer light.

They trudged in silence. Zhao broke it only to encourage Tanner:

"The house is not far, only five minutes now. You can put Peter down and let him walk if he's too heavy."

"No, let him sleep. I envy him."

In fact, Tanner was starting to feel Peter's weight, after the last weeks spent in the spaceship's weak gravity field. Not to mention the briefcase, which seemed to gain mass with each step he took.

Suddenly, tires squealed on the concrete and a horn wailed. Out of nowhere, a car rushed by the small group. Reacting without thinking, Tanner backed away, though the car had not really tried to run them over. He still wasn't used to the planet's gravity, and he fell flat on his back, his shoulders absorbing the impact in a desperate attempt to protect Peter. Zhao cried out, her voice cutting through the fog of his pain and confusion.

Wang bent over Tanner, but the agent was already getting up.

"It's all right . . . I stumbled . . ."

"You're hurt," asserted Zhao.

"Nothing's broken, don't worry."

In Zhao's arms, little Suzy was bawling, scared by her mother's shout. Peter, pulled to his feet by Commander Wang, seemed too dumbfounded to think of crying. Tanner looked around him, still in a daze. Was he imagining those distant shouts? And where had all those people come from, now gathering a few paces away? When Suzy caught her breath to yowl some more, he heard sirens getting closer.

"What's going on?"

Zhao too was nonplussed. Before she could answer, police cars, sirens screaming at the top of their voice, emerged from a side street and braked, the abused tires screeching to a halt in front of a restaurant. A crowd was already forming, as if the building had suddenly emptied; some of the pedestrians without hats or shades were running to shelter in the lee of buildings away from the Eye. Around Tanner's little group, gangs of teenagers converged, joined the growing crowd. They were followed by vans with police markings.

Tanner, his heart still hammering, decided the pedestrians around them, so very ordinary-looking until then, were beginning to remind him of rioters. Zhao, her face blanching with worry, waved for Tanner and Wang to follow her into a dark corner. Standing back from the mob, resolved to defend his companions, Tanner waited.

The police vans stopped in front of the restaurant. Police squads, mostly Chinese, burst out. A loudspeaker ordered in English and Mandarin:

"Get away, there's a bomb in the building!"

Only a few people retreated. More teenagers, afire with excitement, were still rushing up. A minuscule car stopped on the sidewalk not far from Tanner. Inside, two young girls, their faces streaked with fluorescing makeup, goggled at the scene.

"Get back, get back!" yelped the loudspeaker.

A bomb-disposal robot rolled out the back of a van. A bottle arced above the crowd and smacked against the robot's camera. The cheap, plastic empty bounced ineffectively, and the camera swiveled toward the mob. Police officers waded through the crowd to reach the guilty parties. The mass of people heaved, shouts and insults flying on all sides. The policemen caught up with a young Chinese man, who struggled furiously. A girl came to his help, screaming and clawing. More officers ran in, swinging their truncheons. The crowd closed in and Tanner missed the rest of it.

"Please leave the vicinity now," a voice was asking, distorted by echoes and amplification. "You are all in grave danger!"

The rioters showed no sign of obeying. Afraid the situation was taking a turn for the worse, Zhao motioned for Tanner and Wang to follow her down a badly lit alleyway. They met a few groups, but none that seemed hostile. They finally emerged in an almost-deserted street. Suzy was still blubbering, but Zhao seemed to feel better.

"Will you be all right?" asked Tanner.

Zhao smiled weakly.

"Yes. Well, guys, I'd call that a welcome befitting your rank."

"What happened?"

"I don't know. If I'd expected this, I would have called a taxi."

"A bomb threat," speculated Commander Wang. "By the Secessionists, perhaps?"

"I don't know," replied Zhao. "Everything's possible. Let's go, we're almost there; we can speak once we're home. I'm starting to be afraid."

Tanner and Wang followed Zhao silently through almost-deserted streets. The sirens had receded into the distance and the loudspeaker now seemed no louder than the chirping of the insects. As the effect of the evening's jolts faded, Tanner was overcome by a growing sense of disorientation, which the setting did nothing to alleviate. Green Night was ending and Dark Night was taking over. It was already much darker; only a few spires atop the tallest buildings still glowed. New China did not have a moon: for the coming hours, the unfurling of the auroras alone would clothe the stars.

T W O

IN SPITE OF TANNER'S ACCUMULATED FATIGUE, HIS SLEEP WAS TROU-
bled. The weight of gravity on his chest delayed his plunge into
sleep and, thereafter, tormented him with recurring nightmares
in which he suffocated, crushed by slow degrees. The shouting
of children awakened him. He got up and walked creakily to the
window, peering through the slats of lacquered wood. Daytime.
No trace of the Eye, just the orange-hued rays of the sun, already
high in the sky, shining through the mosaic of small glass panes.
Tanner opened the window and let a wave of humid heat into
the room's cool air.

From Tanner's third-floor room, the view over the southern
end of the EFTA was charming. Under the window, the children
played ball in the garden under the watchful eye of their mother,
Zhao. A low stone wall separated the grounds from the street,
used by cyclists and pedestrians—Chinese women, for the most
part, returning from the market with string bags filled with goods,
trailed by bevies of kids neatly attired in red, yellow, or green,
who chased each other, hurled taunts, cried with fury or frus-

trated distress. The older children brought up the rear, bowed by the weight of the bags they were helping to carry.

Beyond the street, the houses spread out, their roofs shining like fish scales: European designs, with stone walls and red tiles on top; modern styles, distinguished by the use of aluminum siding and bright colors; or traditionally Chinese in appearance, with roofs of deep blue tiles with upturned eaves. The overall impression might have been one of clashing architectures if the profusion of palm trees, vines, and plane trees had not melded the varicolored patches into the harmonious whole of a verdant junglescape.

Farther off, there was the sea, also green, but a deeper, opaque green. Its surface gleamed like polished metal, scratched by the wakes of a handful of sailboats. And even farther, beyond the five kilometers of the Ferret Straits, the Blue Tooth coastline—the northernmost thrust of New China's single landmass—shimmered like a mirage. Tanner searched the eastern horizon. . . . No, he could not see from his vantage point the twin dragons of Lengshuijiang. The border town was too distant and the window was facing in the wrong direction.

Someone knocked. A woman—she spoke Mandarin but wasn't Zhao—stated that she'd brought breakfast. Tanner noticed a robe folded beside the bed. The magnificence of the luxurious silk-on-silk brocade made him hesitate: was it really meant to be worn? But he put it on and let a young girl—a round-faced Han, black hair cut short—come in with a lavish breakfast of bacon and eggs. She bowed, announced her name was Yao, and that, if Tanner needed anything, he only had to call, she would do her utmost to satisfy him. Tanner thanked her and she left noiselessly after bowing again.

Slipped between the teacup and the basket of toast, Tanner found a small case, which he opened. He discovered a wristwatch with its own timekeeping mechanism, just like those still worn by the snobs of Earth. With the help of the printed instructions, he managed to figure out what the various numerals, hands, and colored disks were saying. Saturday was just beginning: in fact, it was only 01:12. On New China, hours and minutes were only worth 98.9 percent of those on Earth. But seconds were true to the common standard, so that there were only 59.38 in every minute. The watch also showed that the sun had been up for almost four hours and that the Dragon's Eye was scheduled to rise in less than two hours.

Tanner bolted his breakfast and showered quickly in the bathroom with its jade-green tiling. Under the tepid water jet, he whistled with dismay when he noticed how the backs of his hands were reddened and slightly sore. Yet, his hands had been exposed to the Eye of the Dragon for no more than a few minutes, which had been enough to give him a sunburn—or should he say a "dragonburn"? New China was definitely not the ideal destination for people with sensitive skin.

Tanner dressed, slipped on the wristwatch, left his room, and descended a staircase whose white walls were refreshingly bare, and stepped outside. It felt good to be in the garden. The air was warm, clean, perfumed with the fragrance of flowers lining the foot of the stone wall. Zhao, smiling easily in a pair of baggy trousers and a light blouse, wished him a good day and invited him to have a cup of tea.

"Let's not waste the sunshine; the Eye will be rising in about an hour."

Tanner sat down and accepted the cup of tea. He surveyed the quiet garden, a peaceful oasis set apart from the hubbub of the street.

"Where are the kids?" he finally asked.

"Their instructor took them to school, of course."

"Oh, I thought school was out both Saturday and Sunday."

"Only Sunday, thank God!"

She had a warm and throaty laugh. Pushing back a strand of her long black hair, she asked:

"Were you able to sleep after yesterday's scare?"

"As a matter of fact, I was too tired and disoriented to really be afraid."

"According to the newscast, they did find a bomb, but the

bomb disposal squad managed to defuse it."

"And I feared this would be a boring assignment . . ."

"I don't think you need to worry about that. We're living in interesting times."

The allusion caused Tanner to smile wryly.

"Do you think it was the work of Chinese separatists?"

"New."

"Sorry?"

"Of *New* Chinese separatists . . . On New China, the term 'Chinese' is reserved for the Chinese of Earth, or sometimes for those of the EFTA, in order to distinguish them from New China citizens."

Tanner nodded slowly. He was aware of the right terminology, but not to the point of using it readily yet.

Accompanied by Yao, Commander Wang appeared, the chiseled lines of his face not as deeply furrowed by strain as they had been the day before. Zhao busied herself around him, offered tea, asked if he preferred to sit in the shade.

"No thanks," Wang refused gruffly. "I'll be all right."

A car parked up against the garden's wall. Zhao smiled: it was Jay Hamakawa.

The Japanese, wearing loose-fitting black pants and a red and gold shirt, extricated himself from the tiny car and walked up to the garden's gate.

"It's open," yelled Zhao, gesturing for him to come in. Hamakawa headed for the table, kissed Zhao on the cheek, shook Tanner's hand, and bowed to Wang. More than ever, Hamakawa appeared almost ferally feline, with his round face at once relaxed and distinguished, hair cropped short, his hands square, white, carefully manicured, yet almost frail at the end of the burly forearms, thick with muscles corded like steel cables.

The Japanese operative settled himself comfortably in a wicker chair. Yao brought a second teapot and cakes. Shifting from English to Mandarin, Zhao launched into an impassioned conversation with Hamakawa. Both spoke an excellent Mandarin, with no discernible accent. Nevertheless, Tanner was at first unable to make sense of it. They were talking music, having attended a concert that had impressed them. Zhao dominated the exchange, outlining a complex analysis Tanner could not follow. Hamakawa said little, occasionally nodding and sometimes correcting her or making a point. But his eyes never left Wang and Tanner.

"And you?" Zhao finally asked Wang. "Do you appreciate opera?"

"I don't listen to music much."

"I'm a violinist in a quartet. We're giving a concert tomorrow. Will you come?"

"I don't know if it will be possible," answered Wang after a moment's pause.

"Bo will come. And Jay. And Francis . . ."

"I'm not even sure I'll still be inside the Enclave tomorrow."

"Are you in such a hurry to leave us?" boomed Bloembergen's voice behind Tanner.

Smiling widely, his cheeks flushed, Bloembergen clapped Tanner's shoulder heartily then sat in one of the wicker chairs, which creaked dangerously beneath his bulk. Taking out a handkerchief, he wiped his sweat-covered brow.

"Hot, isn't it?"

Wang cleared his throat politely:

"Mister Bloembergen, I am infinitely grateful for the way you have received me, but—"

Bloembergen shook his head and shushed him theatrically.

"No, no, no . . . We can talk about it later. For now, let's enjoy the sun and taste these cakes so kindly provided for our delectation."

"I don't have any time to waste in the sun," retorted Wang witheringly.

"Yet, we should be taking advantage of its presence," replied Bloembergen, unruffled. "These days, there's so little time to enjoy the sun without having the Eye bother us too. Six hours, not even that. You've just arrived, Commander, you haven't yet lived through the periods when the sun and the Eye share the same degree in the sky and prevent us from ever venturing out without all the accessories."

"On Earth, we believe that if you spent less time sunbathing and as much time on our information network as you spend on your own parallel networks—"

"Please!" interrupted Hamakawa. "We're outside."

He pointed out to Wang a six-story tower, a few streets over, the undulating lines of its tile roof sharply cutting into the white and turquoise froth of the sky.

"The Tewu could be listening in with a directional mike."

Bloembergen spoke toward the tower, in Mandarin:

"If you think we'll mention any secrets here, out in the open, you must believe we're utter fools. No, no: the secret stuff will be discussed inside later."

Zhao frowned:

"Bo . . . Please don't joke about these things."

Bloembergen laughed heartily. Tanner stared at the tower:

"Are there really New Chinese spies in that tower?"

"That one or another," said Hamakawa. "Access to the EFTA is still unregulated. How could we prevent Tewu agents from infiltrating the Enclave?"

"Let's not talk about this here," insisted Zhao.

"And you're perfectly right, my dear meadow flower." Bloembergen pointed toward the east, where the crabapple-green sky was taking on an acid-sharp shimmer. "You're in a hurry, Commander? Well, here's the Eye. I call it the 'Evil Eye.' You got your wish; we'll have to move inside."

They went down into a luxuriously appointed basement, hung in red. Near a fireplace with blue and black brickwork, an immense table with a white lacquer finish spread over half the room. No windows, of course. Zhao took five monitors from a drawer, plugging one of them in front of each chair. Yao came down to ask if anybody wanted more tea. Bloembergen threw his arms up in the air:

"No, no more tea! Or I'll spend the day pissing!"

They sat down and turned on the monitors.

"This computer has no contacts with the local network," said Bloembergen. "Completely autonomous."

Wang nodded approvingly and looked around:

"Francis Barnaby is not coming?"

"Barnaby is a moron," explained Hamakawa as if he were talking about the weather.

"Not nice," said Bloembergen, reproving the Japanese. "The commander only landed yesterday and we're already involving him in our family squabbles. Let's just say that Francis Barnaby doesn't attend all our . . . meetings. But let's speak about you, Commander. I'm not sure I understood correctly the reason for your presence here."

Wang frowned, weighing his words:

"I'm a Black-level unattached operative reporting directly to the European Bureau of External Affairs. Technically, I'm in full command here. What I want: an assistant, someone who knows Lengshuijiang well." He stared down Bloembergen. "My mission is classified Top Secret."

Bloembergen appeared chagrined. "Even for us?"

"Even for you," retorted Wang dryly. "Don't expect flattery from me; the Bureau is more and more unhappy with the work done within the Enclave. The fight against the Tewu is being prosecuted with an unforgivable lack of zeal, and, to boot, our network on the mainland is pitiful. What do you have to say for yourselves?"

Bloembergen, Zhao, and Hamakawa exchanged looks. Wang continued:

"Take Francis Barnaby, for instance. What is he doing in our services if you don't trust him enough to take him into our confidence? Do you suspect him of playing both sides?"

Bloembergen shook his head:

"No. Not Francis, he's too stupid for that. But he's very useful for . . . for certain things."

A shrill stridulation drilled into Tanner's skull. Nobody else jumped, since the alarm was implanted behind his right ear.

"Somebody's opened my suitcase."

Zhao turned to look at him.

"Where did you leave it?"

"In my room."

Zhao touched her monitor. On all their screens, the minutes in progress were replaced with a view of Tanner's bedroom. Leaning over one of Tanner's suitcases, Yao, the young maid, was going through its contents. Nothing to do with girlish nosiness: she was wearing gloves and checked carefully the placement of each object in order to put it back in the same spot, after a thorough inspection. A needless risk for her, since the suitcase contained nothing but clothing and toiletries.

"Foolish girl," Bloembergen observed simply.

"We suspected her," explained Hamakawa to Wang and Tanner.

"What will you do? Interrogate her?"

Hamakawa shrugged. "Not right away. We'll let her have her fun for a few more weeks. Very useful to have such a channel for disinformation. Until the day when our 'friends' realize that we know. Then, we'll have to intercept her before she reaches the continent. Meanwhile . . ."

"Meanwhile, it's really a pity." Zhao sighed. "Yao is the best maid I've been able to find so far."

Bloembergen chuckled:

"Of course! The last thing she wants is to be kicked out!"

Her inspection over, the young spy softly closed the suitcase, carefully putting it back where she'd found it. With trembling hands, she straightened the blanket's folds and started to dust as if nothing had happened.

Bloembergen lost interest in the maid and spoke again to Wang:

"But back to your requirements. You need the help of an expert in New Chinese matters? I'll warn you that it's not easy to cross the border without being spotted. The controls are very strict."

"I'll work something out."

"I see. And when do you want all that?"

"As soon as possible," answered Wang, his tone indicating firmly that the matter was settled.

THREE

THE REMAINDER OF TANNER'S SATURDAY WAS SPENT AT SUPPLIES, where an official from the European Bureau provided him with an apartment, clothing, a credit card, and a weapon. The man reminded him that New China severely restricted the use of guns. Even policemen had to make do with truncheons. Only the military and members of special squads—such as the European Bureau—were allowed to carry weapons. The price of a gun on the planet's black market was astronomical. The bureaucrat turned officious and warned Tanner to take special care of his weapon. If it was ever lost or stolen, he shouldn't expect congratulations from his superiors.

As depressing as an empty flat, thought Tanner as he walked through the apartment assigned to him. The few pieces of furniture were second-rate, and the white walls were dirty. Yet it was so *big*! A kitchen, a large living room, *two* bedrooms with real beds . . . In Beijing or Tokyo, only a millionaire could have afforded such an aircraft hangar of a place. Tanner looked through the window. Outside, the sun had just set and the

Dragon's Eye alone ruled the zenith. Green Night again. He tried both beds, chose the more comfortable of the two, and took from his suitcase a sheaf of disposable paper sheets. He had to read everything before the next day's training sessions.

He put away his purchases, made some tea, tried to find a comfortable position in the threadbare armchair, and plunged into his reading.

The document started with a short history of New China. One hundred and thirty years ago, the discovery of an inhabitable planet orbiting around the orange star of the Epsilon Bootis binary had caused a major commotion on Earth. It was the fifth inhabitable extrasolar planet, a new world, lustily coveted by all. But the Terrans had quickly changed their tune: not only was the new planet relatively distant from the main colonization thrust, but, from the first, the survey results had been disappointing, on three accounts. First, metals heavier than iron, such as nickel, copper, zinc, silver, tin, platinum, gold, mercury, uranium, and the rest, were present only in low concentrations. Second, though marine life was fairly diverse, land-based life was practically absent due to the radiation levels, courtesy of the Dragon's Eye. Finally, the presence of the Eye was, in itself, enough of a disincentive for most would-be settlers.

Earth, or at least the Western powers, had given up. Creating a modern civilization on such a world would be too expensive. And to what end? To live in hiding from the Eye of the Dragon?

Only one social grouping, sufficiently numerous, had expressed interest: the Chinese. Not the Chinese living in the cities, Japanified and constituting a world power, but the Chinese in the countryside, a billion human beings who formed the single greatest homogeneous culture on Earth: quantitatively huge, but politically weak because they were dispersed throughout the rural districts, deprived of modern techniques and financial tools, and weighed down by the yoke of humongous Beijing.

Tanner, until then rather bored by a summary which offered little that was new, could not keep himself from smiling. "*Hu-*

mongous Beijing," indeed . . . The European who had drafted the summary—it *had* to be a European—was betraying his biases.

"At the time, rural China was roiled by dissent. Powerful movements drew their strength from the unfocused desire for a return to the wellsprings of the Taoist and Confucianist teachings which had made China great, before its millenia-old civilization had been hopelessly corrupted by the agnostic and technocratic West and its Japanese lackeys. And Beijing's strict birth control policies were still perceived as intolerably intrusive.

"Colonizing New China required an enormous capital investment for transportation, but especially for biotechnological research. An ambitious genetic-engineering research project unique in its scope was launched immediately to adapt terrestrial plants to the soil of a new planet and especially to ultraviolet levels as much as ten times higher than the normal Earth irradiation. However, rural China was poor. It was necessary to borrow enormous sums, first within China, then from Japan, then from the Europeans.

"In order to keep tabs on the soundness of these colossal loans, it was to be expected that Europe, Japan, and China would infiltrate the leadership of the 'Great Leap.' Indeed, informal agreements allowed data to circulate between the European Bureau, the *diaochabu*—the Chinese agency responsible for gathering and analyzing intelligence—and the ever-efficient Japanese Naicho. Lone wolves will hunt in packs alongside enemies of old if the prey is worth it.

"In *The Art of War,* Xun Zi explains: 'Five kinds of secret agents may be used, to wit: indigenous, internal, double, expendable, and roving agents. When all five are at work simultaneously and nobody knows their methods, they are called "the Heavenly Skein" and they are the sovereign's truest treasure.' "

The rest of the document was printed in smaller type. Obviously, a second writer had taken over. The style was more ponderous, larded with specialized jargon. Tanner often had to read a sentence twice to understand it. He learned how the "Heavenly Skein" of New China's creditors had slowly taken shape, a rather loose skein since it became quickly apparent that the "Great Leap" didn't threaten the security of Earth. In addition, it was not easy to maintain a lasting network on such a distant planet, undergoing accelerated social transformations.

The creation of the Earth Free Trade Area had facilitated the work of the intelligence agencies, but it had also led to the realization of the deep resentment that the New Chinese directed at Earth. The same bitterness existed on each of the Seven Worlds, but the extraordinarily high debt of New China had poisoned the well. Fifty years after the beginning of colonization, the debt had not decreased. On the contrary, it kept increasing and New China was forced to continue borrowing to cover interest payments. Since the election of Xiao Jiping as president, a fellow-traveler of the Secessionists, who were gaining daily in popularity, the Earth secret services had decided to renew their involvement in New Chinese affairs.

The document ended with an overview of the political system. Originally dubbed the Socialist Republic of New China, the highly rigid society conceived by the first settlers had progressively relaxed with the years and effectively transformed itself into a working social democracy within the cities, while the countryside enjoyed a notable degree of freedom, subject only to the constraints of the National Terraforming Plan. The governing party, led by Xiao Jiping, with the able help of Vice President Chen Shaoxing, was opposed only by the moderate and open-minded Peace Party, unfortunately a perennial minority choice, with the support of only about 15 percent of the population.

Yawning uncontrollably, Tanner finished reading. He followed instructions and threw the document in the toilet. The paper disintegrated into a grayish paste. Tanner flushed it and went back to look at the auroras, but he was too tired to appreciate the show and collapsed onto his bed.

✳

Sunday morning. The sun had just set. The Green Night was beginning, and the fluorescent trim of the tiny Japanese car parked on the sidewalk was shining brightly. Bent in half, Tanner got inside, where a tartly sweet stink made him gag. Hamakawa had a cigarette clamped between his lips. Tanner scowled with distaste:

"You too? I'm starting to think that disgusting habit is a prerequisite for immigrating to this planet!"

Hamakawa sucked nonchalantly on the tobacco tube and spewed out rings of fragrant smoke.

"Consider it as training for your new posting. Here, lots of people smoke."

"So I see. Did the Chinese have to bring their vices to another planet?"

Hamakawa breathed out more smoke.

"It's their planet, isn't it? They're the ones who've put in the work and settled it."

Hamakawa drove away, slipping into traffic, weaving skillfully between the fluorescing pedestrians and the buildings outlined in fiery red. Meanwhile, Tanner was pensive.

"That sounds almost like a Secessionist speaking," he finally observed.

"It's hard not to see the justice of some New Chinese claims," answered Hamakawa with a sly smile. "Which doesn't prevent me from asking what's the point of isolationism."

"I would have expected such a remark from a Chinese, not a Japanese," said Tanner bluntly.

"We're much alike, Chinese and Japanese, whatever the New Chinese may think; they see us as China's corrupters, the despoilers of a mythical golden and glorious past. Yet, without the Japanese, would China have gained the technological tools required to settle such a hostile planet? Or would it have bogged down forever in the mire of violence, corruption, and overpopulation which was its lot during the twentieth century?"

It was a rhetorical question. Hamakawa blew out another puff of smoke, then stabbed at the sky with his finger:

"On Earth, the Chinese know how much they owe to the Japanese. But, here, the New Chinese, though they claim to stick faithfully to the old ways, have chosen to ignore the guiding principle of tradition: knowing and respecting the past."

He fell silent, no longer looking at Tanner, a knowing smile frozen on his lips as if to show he didn't mean to be taken entirely seriously.

"You still haven't told me where we're going," Tanner reminded him.

"You're off to your first assignment. You didn't come all the way from Mars just to sit out in the sun!"

Up and down the small streets of the Enclave, the car zigged and zagged. In the end, Tanner was completely lost. Hamakawa handed him a portable screen. Tanner summoned a street map and managed to get his bearings. They were heading toward the Friendship Bridge. But, at the last minute, just as the illuminated muzzles of the Lengshuijiang dragons started to emerge above the skyline, the car turned toward the island's center. Facades adorned with sparkling ideograms paraded past for a few more minutes, then the car slowed near the entrance to a wide esplanade. Tanner recognized an airport.

The two men put on their glasses, hats, and gloves, then left the car. They crossed a vacant lot, walked past the first homes of a housing development—a residential neighborhood, not as exclusive as the one where Bloembergen lived, but still opulent—and reached a public comcabin.

"I'm waiting for a call," explained Hamakawa.

The lazy unrolling of the auroras was a giddy spectacle staged across the vast expanse of open skies, an overwhelming vault streaked and splattered by a crazed artist under which the two men stood obliviously waiting. Not long: Hamakawa pointed out a blinking dot low in the sky. The dot widened into a splotch, then became an oblong and glistening mass, pinned to the diaphanous veils of the auroras.

"What is it?"

"The airship from Nanxiang. The one we're waiting for."

"What do we do?"

"We wait for instructions," Hamakawa answered, pointing to the public vidphone terminal.

"Why use that cabin? Don't you have a portable screen in your car?"

"You're forgetting that good old Eye, playing havoc with radio transmissions."

The vidphone rang. Hamakawa rushed to answer it, spoke in code for a few moments, hesitated, glanced at Tanner, added a few words, then terminated the call.

"I've been called elsewhere. Stay here, keep an eye on the road, and take down the plate number of all the cars that come through, especially black Suzukis. We'll come back for you in about two hours."

Before Tanner could answer, Hamakawa ran to the car, started it up, and vanished beyond the housing development.

Time passed. The airship was still approaching, aglow with fluorescing paint, decorated with gigantic ideograms, as gaudy as a Chinese lantern.

The craft landed. Toy vehicles, festooned with blinking lights, rolled up to the prolate spheroid. Minuscule figures bustled around the nacelle, while other silhouettes marched toward the square shape of the terminal.

During the ensuing hour, a few cars sped through the neighborhood. Tanner duly noted the plate numbers. No black Suzukis, however. With a disconcerting suddenness, the airship's luminosity fluctuated, dimmed, disappeared. The Dragon's Eye had set. For a while, an acid-green glow washed the world's edge, then the dusty grounds of the airport turned into a somber and gray tract of land. The airship was reduced to a dark shape blotting out the auroras, the red, blue, green, golden scratches that scarred the sky from north to south, shuddering, as if a dragon were clawing the heavens to rip out its stars.

Yellow headlights swept over Tanner, brakes screeched, and a van stopped beside him. A shadowy face leaned out through the vehicle's window and an unfamiliar voice called out his name.

"Who are you?" asked Tanner mistrustfully.

"I'm from the Bureau," said the stranger. "Come on, get in!"

A hand slid open the door. Three more people were sitting on the backseat and they squeezed together to make him a place.

"What happened at the starport?" he asked once the van was moving again.

"Nothing," answered his neighbor in Chinese. "The person we were waiting for never showed up."

"What do we do now?"

"For us, the day is over," replied the driver. "For you, I don't know. I've been told to leave you at Bloembergen's."

Tanner knocked. Zhao, stunning in a long black and pink evening dress, opened the door and smiled:

"Ah, Mr. Tanner, you're just in time . . ."

Before Tanner's astonished eyes, she twirled twice, arms gracefully extended.

"What do you think?"

"It's gorgeous," declared Tanner sincerely. "Is it for the concert?"

"Thank goodness, you remembered. I don't suppose you have a tuxedo?"

Tanner was taken aback. "A tuxedo?"

"Old-style formal wear," elaborated Zhao. "For the concert."

"I didn't know I was invited."

"It's not an invitation, it's an order."

Bloembergen emerged in the hallway, stuffed into a black outfit bursting at the seams.

"After all, the only way to make sure the concert sells out is to have all my men there."

Zhao made as if to tear his eyes out, betraying her jitters about the upcoming performance.

"Once and for all, Bo, the Ziegler Quartet does not need your agents to fill a hall!" She turned toward Tanner, adding in mock confidence: "Bo is a boor, and jealous to boot! That's the truth. . . . Well, since you don't even know what a tuxedo is, I guess I better take care of it and see what we can dig up."

Bloembergen gestured for Tanner to follow him. The two men went down into Bloembergen's office in the basement.

"Rest easy, Tanner, I know you don't like music. If I'm insisting you come, it's because Xiao Jiping will be attending the concert."

"New China's president?"

"In the flesh! It's not often that he deigns to leave his palace in Nanxiang. The army and the police are on full alert—and all of us, too, of course. After the other night's bomb scare . . ."

Hamakawa blew in, his forehead wrinkled in annoyance.

"We were misled," stated the Japanese straight off. "He wasn't at the airport."

"A mistake by our informants?" asked Bloembergen dutifully.

"No, impossible. We were meant to take the bait!"

"Who were you expecting?"

Hamakawa sat down and struggled to regain his composure.

"We were supposed to get our hands on Daming Zhenwu! An ex-spymaster of the Chinese *diaochabu,* now working for the Peace Party."

"The opponents of the Secessionists?"

"Yes, yes!" uttered Hamakawa impatiently. "The Peace Party. Our so-called allies!"

Tanner reflected a few seconds.

"I thought the Bureau and the Peace Party were working hand in hand."

"We have a common goal, countering the separatist threat," admitted Bloembergen. "Don't think that means we're working 'hand in hand' with those egg-faces. Far from it. Separatists or not, they're still Chinese, which means they share one overriding interest: themselves."

"The problem," added Hamakawa, his tone distant, "is that the Peace Party leaders don't understand just how Daming

Zhenwu's actions could backfire."

"Bah! Carrying out an assassination on Ferret Island itself would both eliminate an opponent and make the Europeans look ridiculous in the bargain. Why should they hold back?"

"Because that would be going too far. Because they would unite all the other planets against them."

"They don't give a flying *fuck* about the other planets!"

"But since he didn't come . . ." broke in Tanner diffidently.

"The point is, somebody is feeding us false information," explained Hamakawa patiently. "And knows far too well for my peace of mind *what* to give us."

Bloembergen shrugged, as if the whole affair no longer concerned him.

After knocking, Yao entered timidly, holding a gray suit with dark red stripes. The young spy bowed her head in front of Tanner:

"It's the largest we could find, honored guest. Do you wish to try it on?"

FOUR

NINE O'CLOCK. EVENING ON NEW CHINA—DARK NIGHT. AND DARKER than usual: a thick layer of clouds hid even the auroras. The storefronts of the boutiques along Paris Boulevard, washed by a timid though persistent rain, shone like obsidian tombstones when the headlights of Barnaby's car fell upon them. The operative was not very talkative tonight, which suited Tanner. His forehead leaning against the window, he dozed fitfully, lulled by the droning of the wipers.

The car left Paris Boulevard and skirted the Bay of Angels. Ahead, shards of rain-blurred light reflected off the water's surface. The closest lights were those of the concert hall where Zhao was going to play; the farthest were given off by the Friendship Bridge and, even farther off, Lengshuijiang on the continent.

Up close, the concert hall did not lack in majesty. For the sake of originality, or perhaps just to go against the local trend, the European neoclassical look had prevailed over the usual Chinese style, resulting in a double colonnade of white pillars along the facade supporting a massive triangular pediment.

On both sides of the street, cars occupied any available spot. Soldiers in rainproof gear glistening with water patrolled everywhere. A bus the size of an ocean liner slipped into the perilously narrow space left by the cars and parked in front of the entrance, completely blocking the street. Its passengers debarked without undue haste. Trapped between the bus and the cars congregating behind him, Barnaby was swearing impatiently. The bus finally disentangled itself from the incoming concertgoers and cleared out, but Barnaby still had to drive around for a while before finding a free spot, down a back alley.

The main hall gleamed with crystal chandeliers, recessed ceiling mirrors, and costly tapestries. Tanner felt lost in the midst of the tuxedos and evening gowns, as out of place as the soldiers guarding each door. Instead of giving in to the enchantment of the moment and of the decor, he remained on edge, unable to join in the small talk punctuated with outbursts of laughter, unable to share the customary shiver of contained anticipation before a concert.

Barnaby, in a stylish, almost flashy tuxedo—though marred by the darker splotches of a smattering of raindrops—brought him a filled champagne flute from the bar.

"You look unhappy, Tanner."

"I'm wondering what the hell I'm doing here."

Barnaby shrugged: "I've been wondering the same ever since I arrived on New China."

"And I don't know the first thing about this kind of music."

"Perhaps that's for the best. It's not going to be an unforgettable experience."

"Oh? I was under the impression Zhao enjoyed a certain popularity."

Barnaby's bloodless lips curved down to scowl disdainfully.

"Well, sure . . . The Ziegler Quartet is *à la mode*. But it's to be expected: we're far from civilization. Musicwise, it's like this fake champagne: we learn to appreciate what we have."

He clinked his champagne flute against Tanner's.

"To Earth! May we set feet on it again—soon!"

"To Earth," echoed Tanner.

Bloembergen broke through the crowd, followed by Commander Wang. Like Tanner, the old officer seemed to be wondering what he was doing in such surroundings. Nevertheless, he managed a smile for his young traveling companion.

"I thought you were already on your way back to Earth," said Tanner, merely as a conversational gambit, but Wang nodded brusquely, a nettled expression on his face.

"My mission is not going as planned. . . . I can't say more."

"I'm perfectly willing to help," intervened Bloembergen suavely. "But you've left me in the dark."

"Another time," said Wang curtly. "Let's talk about you, Tanner. Are you getting used to gravity again, young man?"

"Not quite. But I can run without stumbling."

"Bloembergen, you're getting an excellent prospect," confided Wang, lowering his voice. "This young man is worthy of his father, Colonel Tanner. Let's wish him as brilliant a career."

The reference to his father startled Tanner. Why was the old-timer raising the topic of his father? Did he think Bloembergen was unaware Réjean was the son of Colonel Bertrand Tanner?

Tanner struggled to remain collected. Wang was only trying to be pleasant. It wasn't the old officer's fault if Tanner hated to be reminded of his parentage. So often, it was to insinuate he would not have risen so quickly without the tutelary protection of his father.

Chimes rang. The concert was about to begin. Tanner followed the crowd into a luxurious amphitheater hung in red velvet. The European Bureau agents did not sit together. Tanner and Barnaby sat in the back. Bloembergen went forward to sit beside Hamakawa, also in a tuxedo, while Wang opted to remain alone, to the side.

Tanner sat and observed the dozen or so ushers who were guiding down the lanes several concertgoers apparently unable to find their seats alone. Tanner asked Barnaby who they were.

"Them? Don't you see they're blind?"

"All of them? But there's at least fifty in this one room."

"Oh, much more than fifty," said Barnaby absently. "But it's not as bad as you think: some of them are still partially sighted. You'll have to learn to expect it. That's what you get for living under the Dragon's Eye."

Tanner was going to remark that you had to be crazy to spend your life on this planet when he noticed many in the house—including Bloembergen and Hamakawa—had turned toward one of the boxes. Tanner looked in the same direction.

Surrounded by an impressive honor guard, dressed in an astonishing scarlet silk mandarin's robe, a Chinese as tall and thin as a reed bowed with a smile to the audience.

"How moving!" jeered Barnaby in a low voice. "Master Xiao honors us with his mere presence."

The president of New China sat down. Around him, four bodyguards continued to stand, their black robes imperfectly hiding heavy-duty machine guns.

"Wonder what's gotten into him," said Barnaby. "What a time to leave the security of his palace in Nanxiang!"

"He misses Western music."

"So they say," answered Barnaby, who'd taken Tanner's joke seriously. "But look over there. No, not there . . . the fourth seat of the seventh row . . . the tall Chinese with black glasses, cleverly passing himself off as blind . . . It's Daming Zhenwu!"

"The guy who didn't show up at the airport? Let's warn Bloembergen!"

Barnaby allowed himself an exasperated clucking of the tongue.

"Our people must have spotted him by now."

Indeed, a female soldier went up to whisper something into Bloembergen's ear. Bo glanced absently toward Daming Zhenwu and leaned to speak into Hamakawa's ear.

"What is everybody doing at a recital of European music?" inquired Tanner wonderingly. "Isn't New China opposed to everything Western, including its culture?"

"The Chinese have always been past masters at reconciling opposites."

"Can't you be serious for a minute? What if Daming took out a gun and shot the president?"

"He can't have a gun, since the entire audience has been scanned. And even if he somehow sneaked one in, he'd be dead before he could pull the trigger. So, calm down, everything is under control."

The red velvet curtain lifted to reveal a small, round platform supporting four chairs and four music stands. The performers emerged from the wings. Applause was sparse, despite the full house. Europeans provided the major share, since the Chinese were traditionally averse to boisterous demonstrations. There was Zhao, holding her violin under her arm, her silken gown shimmering rosily beneath the stage lights. The other two violinists and the cellist were men, one of them a European. They sat down and, without further ado, started playing.

The music was lush, fluid, and stirring, and, much to his surprise, Tanner found himself enjoying it. The back of the seat in front of him held a pocket in which he found the program. The evening's first piece was the String Quartet No. 12 in F ("The American"), Op. 96 by a certain Antonín Dvořák. Tanner had never heard of him. He noticed the date of birth: 1841. The music was truly ancient! Three more works would follow the "American" quartet, and Tanner recognized the name of only one of the composers, Beethoven, another European of long ago.

From the nimble fingers of Zhao and her colleagues flowed a melody now vivacious, now more pensive, and the first movement ended with an energetic crescendo. A pause of a few seconds ensued. Zhao plucked a fiber that had sprung from the tip of her bow, then nodded toward the three other members of the quartet. They launched into the second movement.

If the first movement had pleasantly surprised Tanner, the second confirmed all his past reservations regarding ancient music: it was slow, whining, utterly boring. His attention drifted away from the four players and settled again on Daming Zhenwu, whom he was seeing in profile. The man from New China might have been handsome once, but old age had carved wrinkles around the mouth and blurred the chin's outline, lending to the coarsened features an air at once wise and malevolent. As soon as he formed this opinion, Tanner was amazed to see the spy, upon hearing the first chords of the movement Réjean had judged so dull, smile and yield himself wholeheartedly to the music. Tanner also tried to concentrate and open himself to the archaic harmonies, but the soothing plaint of the strings was too powerful a soporific for him to resist long.

A sharp elbow nudged him awake. Barnaby leaned close and whispered:

"Tanner, you're snoring!"

Around them, a few Europeans glared scornfully at Tanner. The young operative hunched his shoulders, definitely wide awake now.

Once the movement was over, Barnaby added sotto voce:

"Good God, if this puts you to sleep, wait till Beethoven!"

Tanner was unable to respond: the third movement broke over them with renewed vigor. Tanner twisted to see if Daming Zhenwu was still as appreciative. But the spy's seat was empty. He had seized the short interval between the second and third movements to rise discreetly and leave the room. Tanner reported his observation to Barnaby, who did not seem alarmed:

"Don't worry, we're following his every move. He's just behind us—"

Around them, there were angry shushing noises. Tanner turned to look, ignoring the indignant glare of several spectators. Standing with his back against the red velvet hangings, near one of the doors, Daming Zhenwu was still listening, smiling, his arms crossed on his chest. Not far from him, a youthful soldier in a nervous sweat was keeping his eyes on the spy, his hand stroking a compact machine gun. The tension that had begun to fill Tanner relaxed a bit: what could the New Chinese spy, subjected to such close surveillance, hope to achieve?

Daming Zhenwu raised his face toward the presidential

box—like Barnaby had said, he didn't move like a blind man, in spite of his stereotypical dark glasses—and then looked the young soldier in the eyes before nodding solemnly.

The young soldier swallowed. At any other time, Tanner would have understood—and acted—faster. However, twice in the same evening, he had disturbed the concert. For a few seconds, an instinctive diffidence prevented him from grasping what was happening in front of his eyes. Daming Zhenwu left the concert hall, followed by several soldiers and operatives in mufti. The young soldier, however, did not budge from his spot. His jaw clenched, he kept on listening to the concert for a few seconds and then raised his machine gun toward Xiao Jiping's box. . . .

Tanner straightened, his limbs suddenly sluggish. His hand sought his holster, just as he remembered that he was disarmed. A chalky lump blocking his throat, Tanner flung his arm toward the soldier. The spectators facing him frowned. Tanner yelled out . . .

His shout was lost in the full-throated fury of the unleashed machine gun. Designed for combat at close quarters, it was a small-caliber weapon with a high firing rate. The deadly stream of buzzing lead hornets splashed the parapet of the president's box, tore through the red velvet, started a rain of plaster debris and wooden shards. The aim improved, the bullets rising higher and scything through a bodyguard, who toppled over the parapet and crashed among the spectators below. Xiao Jiping and the three other guards had ducked and disappeared, probably hugging the floor. Deprived of a target, the maddened soldier continued to spray the box with lead, until another soldier, coming to his senses, cut down his ex-comrade with a short burst of fire.

The soldier crumpled to the ground, but his machine gun continued to discharge, blasting an arc of destruction from one end of the room to the other as it riddled the hangings with craters, exploded the chandeliers and the ceiling's white stucco, and, dropping in for a bloody coda, hosed with its last slugs the stage and its four musicians.

The din of an enraged pandemonium filled the concert hall,

shrieks of panic mingling with the outcry of the wounded and the angry shouting of soldiers and secret agents. A trembling hand seized Tanner by the wrist: an elderly Chinese was clinging to him for dear life, his face shiny with sweat as it turned this way and that, his eyes lifeless and unmoving.

"What's going on? Help me, I'm blind!"

Tanner forced him to sit.

"Stay down! There's been an assassination attempt. Somebody will come for you later!"

"Zhao's been hit!" yelled Barnaby.

Tanner swore.

"And the president?"

"I don't know!"

Tanner followed Barnaby toward the stage, but he stopped to help up two old ladies lying dazed on the carpet. He left them on a nearby bench, ordering them to wait for help. The pair obeyed humbly, clutching each other.

Near the stage, two young soldiers shoved their weapons into the faces of Barnaby and Tanner, but an employee of the European Bureau recognized Barnaby and waved them through.

Two of the musicians had been hit: Zhao and the cellist. The latter, his neck pierced by a bullet, lay with his instrument in an impressive puddle of his own blood. Zhao's wound, an ugly tear down the forearm, was not fatal. The violinist was gazing stonily at the ceiling, stretched out on the stage, surrounded by her remaining colleagues, Hamakawa, and Bloembergen. The latter was bawling like a motherless calf, beating his chest, tearing his hair out with bloodstained hands. Hamakawa had to shake him.

"Calm down! She's going to make it; it's not serious!"

He turned to Barnaby and Tanner:

"Is the president safe?"

"I don't know," answered Barnaby.

"Well, go and find out! Do I have to tell you everything?"

Barnaby bit back a retort. He jumped down from the stage, signaled for two men in ill-fitting rented suits to follow him.

Bloembergen yelled to a soldier:

"A doctor! Get me a doctor!"

"The ambulances are coming, sir!"

"Isn't there a doctor in the room?"

"The only one we could find is at the president's side," stammered out the soldier.

Bloembergen closed his eyes, caught his breath, finally looked again at the soldier:

"Is the president wounded, then?"

"I don't know . . . I'm not sure . . ."

A European woman in an evening dress hailed Bloembergen:

"The Earth officer—Wang—has been shot!"

Tanner flushed: what a nightmare! With Hamakawa, he hurried to the side of a body stretched on the carpet. Wang was conscious. Under the tuxedo, drilled through by a bullet hole, the right side of his chest was red with blood, soaking through the white dress shirt. The old officer tried to say something, but Tanner was unable to make out the words through the hubbub.

"Don't speak. Do you have trouble breathing?"

Wang nodded.

Tanner unbuttoned the tuxedo and the shirt. The wound was nothing spectacular, just a little round hole near the nipple, hardly bleeding anymore. Tanner gently slipped his hand under Wang's back, ascertaining there was no exit wound.

"Can you breathe better now?"

"No."

The old man's breathing was growing more labored. Willing his touch to be as delicate as possible, Tanner felt the abdomen and tapped the sides of the rib cage, trying to hear through the noise.

"You know what you're doing?" asked Hamakawa.

"I just finished my first aid refresher course."

"What's the problem?"

"I'm not sure. Might be a pneumothorax—air getting inside pleural tissue, around the lungs."

"Is it serious?"

"I hope not."

But Wang, his breathing wheezing in and out with increasing difficulty, lost consciousness. Tanner grew fearful:

"The pneumothorax is squeezing the lungs! We've got to cut a hole to let the air out of the pleura."

"Cut a hole?"

"He's choking! When the ambulance comes, it'll be too late. I need a knife with a sharp point!"

A soldier lent him a military dagger with a razor's edge. Tanner rapped several spots on Wang's chest, chose the one that rang hollowest, and placed upon it the tip of the dagger. The skin resisted initially, then yielded. Wang's whole body arched up and his breath rattled out. The knife's tip had pierced the outside of the pleura and the imprisoned air burbled out, mixed with a bloody froth. Instantly, Wang started breathing again, in greedy gulps at first, then more evenly, stopping only to utter disjointed words as he slipped into delirium.

The ambulances finally showed up, allowing Tanner to leave and refresh himself. When he left the concert hall, he blinked. Through the wide glass bays, the warm rays of the morning sun were shooting off the mirrors of the vestibule. For a second, Tanner felt lost again. Morning already? He glanced at his watch. But no, it was still Sunday evening: it was only twenty minutes past twelve. Not an hour had passed since the concert's start.

In the washroom, Tanner cleaned his hands and face, then rinsed as best he could his soiled shirt sleeves, and finally scraped off the reddish clumps stuck to his soles. He returned to the concert hall, now almost completely deserted. Hamakawa was seated in the last row, silent, his eyes staring at nothing in particular. Under his jacket, the white shirt was spotted with dried blood. He seemed tired, and thoroughly displeased.

"Any news about the president?" asked Tanner.

"He's unhurt. That bloody fool was way off the mark. Probably too psyched up to shoot straight."

"And Bloembergen?"

"He went with Zhao to the hospital."

The tone Hamakawa used to answer did not invite further questioning. But Tanner asked nonetheless:

"Are you all right?"

"No, not at all." He got up suddenly. "Come with me. Let's go home."

"I'm not going home with Barnaby?"

A cruel grin flickered on Hamakawa's lips.

"For the next few hours, Francis is going to be very busy."

"Avenging tonight's assassination attempt?"

Hamakawa threw him a look which meant that it was too obvious to mention.

"We can discuss this elsewhere."

Hamakawa's car fled the swirling chaos of official vehicles: police cars, army trucks, ambulances, taxis hired by reporters. Again they followed the Paris Boulevard along the Bay of Angels, all the way to the residential neighborhoods on the southwestern tip of Ferret Island, where Tanner lived. According to the official schedule, it was time to go to sleep, but it was a beautiful day outside. The thick blanket of clouds had been ripped into fleecy shreds, lazily dotting the sky. The golden sunlight was making the sea sparkle. Tanner's eyes picked out houses in the shadow of palm trees. It could have been the picture of a tropical paradise on Earth. But the sky was blue green, the sun was too large and too yellow to be his sun, and—in how long? three hours?—the Dragon's Eye would cast its baleful gaze above the horizon, providing the inhabitants of New China with a blinding reminder of the obvious fact they were indeed on another planet.

Hamakawa stayed silent until they reached Tanner's apartment. Once inside, he grabbed Tanner's forearm with his hand:

"Zhao's wound has enraged Bloembergen. He sent Barnaby and other operatives to take out everybody who's suspected of being a New Chinese spy. We're talking of a hundred people at least. I've tried to reason with him, but it was useless. These deaths will be . . . gratuitous. Worse than that, in fact. Zhao's blood price is going to upset our entire counterespionage effort, reshuffle the cards of a game whose rules we're still learning. And of course this will inflame tensions within the Enclave and on the mainland. . . . I was supposed to be a part of the hit squads. I refused. For a moment there, I thought Bloembergen was going to have me arrested. But no: he ignored me and gave his orders to Barnaby. I don't know what this will mean for me within the Bureau. . . ."

Tanner went back to his flat. He was still too worked up to sleep. He walked back and forth, thinking hard. Then he left, emerged onto the sun-flooded street, and found a public comcabin. He was going to call Bloembergen's home when he remembered Yao did not work on Sundays. He checked the databank, which had three listings under Kui Yao. One of them lived in the same neighborhood as Bloembergen. Tanner dialed the number. Yao appeared onscreen, her hair tousled, her eyes puffy with sleepiness. She frowned. Tanner was not sending her his image, a flagrant breach of the usual courtesies.

"Who is it?"

Tanner didn't bother with preliminaries:

"Bloembergen has ordered the killing of all Tewu agents within the EFTA. There's still time enough for you to hide, but, if I were you, I'd run back to Lengshuijiang as quickly and as discreetly as possible."

She attempted, vainly, to camouflage her dismay:

"I . . . I don't understand."

"The fun and games are over, Yao. We know all about your doings. Run, and don't look back! The men from the European Bureau are probably on their way."

The young woman looked in mute appeal toward her left. The screen darkened, but the link was not cut off. A man was

whispering questions to Yao in an uncommon Chinese dialect—
Minnan?—which Tanner did not understand. They jabbered for
a few moments. Voices were raised. Yao was fretful, while the
man remained skeptical. Yao, now wide awake and deeply scared,
appeared again. Her chin not quite convincingly defiant, she
challenged him:

"Why are you warning me?"

"Because I'm against needless killings!" answered Tanner
exasperatedly. "Now, scram, you little fool, and take your lover
with you before it's too late!"

He cut the link and walked slowly back to his apartment,
still stunned by his own deed.

The vidphone was ringing when he opened the door. He ran
to accept the call. A pretty Chinese woman in a white smock
appeared. She was calling from the hospital: Commander Wang
Zhong was asking for him.

"He wants you to come alone," specified the clerk.

Tanner sighed. He was starting to feel tired and would have
liked to get to bed. But he couldn't just ignore a summons from
his superior, even if the old man no doubt wished only to thank
him for saving his life.

Commander Wang Zhong turned his head toward his visitor. His
face was lined and ashen. His welcoming smile was weak and
uncertain. He tried to lift his head in greeting, but his smile then
twisted with pain.

"Please," said Tanner swiftly. "Don't tire yourself."

Wang breathed out a ragged sigh.

"So, I owe you my life, young man."

"You might have pulled through without me."

"Don't be modest. At my age, I've seen death often enough
to recognize it when it shakes my hand. . . . But it wasn't just to
thank you that I—"

A cough brought on a scowl of suffering.

"You shouldn't speak."

"And yet, I have much to tell you. But you're right, I won't—" He coughed again. "I won't speak anymore."

Wang reached out toward his portable screen, a highly sophisticated model sitting on the bedside table. Tanner handed it to his superior. The fingers of the old officer darted deftly across the keyboard:

In any case, what I have to tell you is not for all ears. Read this carefully, because you'll only get to read it once. . . .

FIVE

AUTUMN IN BEIJING. THE OSAKA/SEOUL/BEIJING SUBEXPRESS EMERGED from the ground and, the pneumatic brakes sighing deeply, stopped along the glass-enclosed quay of the terminal. Wang Zhong made his way through the milling mass inside the vast halls of the station and went outside. The sky was still making up its mind between freezing rain, snow, and hail. Small icy pellets mixed with raindrops peppered the skin of Wang Zhong's face and neck. He turned his back to the wind and hugged his raincoat closer to him.

A white limousine drove up to the taxi stand. A door opened. A middle-aged European woman, tall and thin, with short hair, motioned for him to join her. Wang tried to hide his surprise when he recognized Lison Robanna. He hadn't expected his contact in Beijing to be a high-level official in the European Bureau of External Affairs. Rumor was casting her as the potential replacement for the current Bureau director, who was getting old and whose decisions were increasingly disputed.

Wang slipped in. A gust slammed the car's door shut. Lison

Robanna stretched out a small and shapely hand. Wang hesitated, then wrapped it in his own wet and half-frozen paw, and shook it. Robanna jumped, startled. Her laughter pealed forth, gently derisive:

"Commander Wang! Whatever prompted you to wait for me in the rain?"

"After three hours on the subexpress, I needed some fresh air, even if it was a bit wet."

The limousine left the station and proceeded to roll down Quianmen Street at a majestic snail's pace, past the buildings whose mediascreens were veiled by the rain, blurring the clash of primary colors favored by the ad designers.

"Do you know who I am?" asked the European Bureau executive secretary, still smiling.

Wang explained what he knew of her. She nodded, satisfied. On the way, they remained silent. The limousine turned into old Taoranting Park, practically deserted, and parked with its hood nudging a stand of black yews dripping with rain. Lison Robanna asked the driver—European, which was almost unheard of in China—to go out for a walk. The man glanced uncertainly at the weather outside, but, without uttering a word, he put on a windbreaker and went out into the rain.

"What you're going to tell me now must be pretty important if you're asking the poor guy to risk pneumonia."

Lison Robanna nodded slowly, then paused, her forefinger pressed to her chin as if she was gathering her thoughts.

"It's become a cliché to lament the ineffectiveness of our data-gathering services on New China, right?"

"The New Chinese don't like Europeans," said Wang, shrugging. "The Chinese *diaochabu* is slightly more successful, but it only helps us grudgingly, and every time it's like pulling teeth."

"What about the Naicho?"

"Bah! The Japanese are doing good work, but they're only a handful." Wang hesitated. "I assume, ma'am, that it was not to complain about the performance of our network that you subjected me to three hours on the subexpress—"

"The situation is not as dismal as most people think. For instance, did you know that we have a mole within president Xiao Jiping's own circle?"

Wang did not answer.

"The mole is Chen Shaoxing."

Wang nodded slowly, properly impressed.

"Indeed. Chen Shaoxing, the president's right-hand man. This has not been divulged to our EFTA branch. In fact, there are fewer than ten people on the Seven Worlds who know this. You are now part of a very select group of people, Commander Wang."

"I appreciate your confidence. How did we manage to infiltrate one of our agents so close to the president?"

"In a way, it was very simple," explained Lison Robanna smugly. "Chen is an operative reporting directly to Sir Walter Fenwick, the ex-director of the European Bureau. Chen was chosen because he was a relative of Xiao Jiping—a young cousin, once removed. It's not the first time we've turned to advantage the powerful family ties of the Chinese. Chen was barred from ever contacting our agents operating out of the Enclave, regardless of his reasons. On the contrary, he was a sleeper who would not be reactivated before it became necessary, even if decades passed. While he remained a sleeper, his mission was to gather as much data as possible on the circles of power within New China; therefore, he was to cultivate as wide a social network as required. We never dreamed Xiao Jiping would notice this young cousin, so earnest and bent on learning, and that he would make him his right-hand man, his trusted henchman, even his confidant! Less than forty-eight hours ago, the head of the Bureau received one of the few coded messages Chen dares to pass along from time to time. The status quo is breaking down on New China. The border between the Enclave and the mainland is closed. In a few months, Xiao Jiping will announce a stop to payments of the interest on the debt. He's even thinking of annexing the Enclave, which he calls a den of spies."

"He's right enough about that," smirked Wang knowingly.

"Well, the Enclave will soon number two more. You will go to New China as soon as possible in order to contact Chen Shaoxing, who will hand over to you all the information that he's collected these last few years about Xiao Jiping and his en-tourage. This mission is classified Top Secret; we don't want to endanger Chen's cover. You must not rely on anyone; not even our agents within the Enclave must be allowed to learn what you are doing."

"You mentioned two agents."

"You know as well as me that Bloembergen, the EFTA Bu-reau chief, is incompetent. We would already have replaced him with Jay Hamakawa—I assume you've heard of him—but he has also been judged incompletely reliable. Brilliant, sure, but an in-dependent thinker, and a bit of a rebel; we suspect him of sym-pathies for the New Chinese. We're thinking of sending in the son of Colonel Tanner. He's amazingly proficient in the requisite languages and his loyalties are rock solid."

"He's rather young."

"I'm not saying he'll replace Bloembergen overnight. Tanner is not aware of our intentions concerning him, so he'll have a couple of years to demonstrate his abilities."

Lison Robanna delicately pushed a button recessed in the armrest. With a muffled hum, the window lowered, letting in a whiff of cool, damp air. She called her driver, who rushed back, got in, stripped off his sadly drenched windbreaker, and huddled behind the wheel, still shivering.

"Sorry, Ivan. I wasn't expecting so much rain."

"I don't mind, ma'am."

"We were discussing important matters too sensitive even for you."

"No apology required, ma'am."

"We'll take our guest to his hotel. You did reserve a room as I requested?"

"Of course, ma'am."

The rain had turned into snow. The limousine of the European Bureau made its way through the groves of yews, a fine white fuzz outlining their branches, and the driver duplicated his slow progress from before back up Quianmen Street, this time out of cautious respect for the slippery cobblestones.

Tanner took over the screen and typed:

So you want me to contact Chen Shaoxing?

Wang shook his head, took back the screen:

You don't understand. Chen Shaoxing never responded to my message! Why do you think I never left the Enclave?

"What's happened to him?"

I have no idea. We were supposed to communicate through the bulletin board and meet in Lengshuijiang. Given his silence, I was going to cross over to the mainland. But now, I'm wounded. You've got to take over for me!

But Europeans can't move freely within New Chinese territory.

Wang scowled.

Make yourself into a Chinese. I'll send the necessary orders to the EFTA labs for a quick job. And Su450jtg . . .

A sudden spasm tore a bleat of pain from him. He added:

Above all, do not speak of this mission to anyone!

I know next to nothing about the continent. I will need a guide.

Wang pondered the point at length.

I can't trust anybody inside the EFTA. Hamakawa, if absolutely necessary and if he agrees to go with you, but don't tell him a thing before
you're on the mainland.

The arms of the old spy settled onto the bed.

"Now . . . let me rest awhile before I . . . I give my orders to
Bloembergen."

The next morning, Tanner was summoned to Bloembergen's office. The big man did not try to disguise his displeasure with
Commander Wang Zhong's new demands.

"His arrogance knows no bounds! Are we going to disrupt
our entire network because of a wounded man's ravings?"

"Technically, we're under his command," Hamakawa reminded him.

Bloembergen stared heavily at the Japanese.

"You, I'd like you to keep quiet. I've had enough of your
interference."

As she rubbed the bandage swaddling her forearm, Zhao
exchanged looks with Tanner, her gaze made strangely bright by
the painkillers. The incident seemed to have left her pensive and
forlorn.

"Bo, Jay is right."

"Oh, Jay is always right, isn't he? And clever, and daring,
and handsome. You'd make a pretty pair, you two!"

"You're such a fool, Bo," she said, her tone weary.

Bloembergen flung his hands up in the air in defeat:

"You heard it, gentlemen. I'm a fool! Why should anyone
listen to such a fool as me? So, go! Out of my sight, Tanner!
Alone or not, with a couple of my men or ten of them. Just go
and get lost on the mainland, and leave me in peace!"

SIX

THE MAKEUP ARTIST WAS A DIMINUTIVE WOMAN IN HER FORTIES, WEAR-
ing a spotless white smock. Her clear blue gaze detailed his face.

"Any interfaces?"

"No, but I have an alarm implant behind my ear."

"It'll have to go," she said in a tone brooking no dissent.
"Now, get undressed."

Tanner obeyed, only keeping his briefs.

"Completely."

The briefs joined the pile with the rest of his clothing. She
paced around him, studying the tall, muscular body with a face
pinched disdainfully as if she were examining a piece of spoiled
meat.

"Don't like what you see?" sallied Tanner.

"You're a redhead."

"You didn't have to get me naked to see that."

She felt his back, his arms, plucked at the fat layer atop his
stomach.

"How old are you?"

"Twenty-eight."

"Good muscle tone. Nice skin too."

She did not make it sound like high praise. She pulled on the hairs of his thighs. Tanner, taken unawares, let out a surprised squawk.

"Don't be such a baby. You can put your pants back on, if you want. And sit down here."

He had to sit, stiff and ramrod straight, in front of a scanner. The chair revolved several times. The cosmetician then motioned for him to get up.

"You can come and see, if you want."

The screen showed Tanner's face and his torso. The cosmetician pushed a few buttons, adjusted some cursors. The freckles disappeared and the peach complexion of the skin shifted to take on a creamy ocher hue. The hair became black, and the eyes too. The eyelids and the cheekbones inflated, then deflated. The final result was freakish: an Asian, perhaps, but by no means a full-blooded Han. The specialist chuckled:

"It's the best we can do. The one thing we can start on now is the skin treatment."

She had Tanner swallow five large translucid capsules.

He followed her into the back of the workshop, whose centerpieces were an operating table and a dentist's chair. She ordered Tanner to recline on the chair.

"Tomorrow, you'll have lost that fair-skinned paleness of redheads. In two days, your skin will be the same color as a Han. For most whites, skin color is not really a problem. Asians are more readily identified by their facial morphological features, their black hair, and their black eyes than by skin color. But for a redhead, the transformation is obviously more complicated. To retain your new coloring, you'll need to take one of these capsules every day."

She handed him a bag that contained a large number of them.

"Now, please lie down; we'll move on to something a bit more intrusive. . . ."

Tanner's head was immobilized so he could receive an unending series of small subcutaneous injections around the eyelids and the cheeks. Technicians came in to anesthetize a spot behind his right ear in order to extract his alarm implant. The cosmetician reminded him the only implant used by the Chinese was an identification tablet. The alarm would have betrayed him as soon as he'd reached customs.

The operation lasted only a few minutes. Tanner got up, slightly dazed, rubbing a strip of Band-Skin smarting behind his ear. But the torture session was not over yet. As announced, an identification tablet was injected in his arm.

Eye color was modified with tinted contact lenses. A permanent-wear wig was glued to his close-shaven skull. For the eyelashes, eyebrows, and the rest of his body hair, he took a long bath in a special dye mix and came out of it with black hair. Tanner toweled himself while watching his image in a mirror: wet, sheepish-looking, already unrecognizable. He scowled as he tugged on the thick black wig.

"How long will it stay on?"

"About two weeks."

"Six-day weeks or seven-day weeks?"

She smiled curtly.

"Doesn't matter. The maxillofacial modifications are only good for twenty or so days. Let's just hope you'll be back from New China by then. Come back to see me tomorrow, for the passport photo; I'll give you some booster shots. I must ask you to be disciplined: never forget your capsules, one a day, every day. You'll probably have a headache, but don't take a painkiller, please; it could mess up or counteract the maxillofacial changes. Don't scratch yourself. Wash your hair delicately in slightly soapy water, and you won't have any trouble. Every morning, shave carefully, and inspect yourself, cutting any suspect red hair. Most importantly: *always* wear your glasses when the Dragon's Eye rises. The slightest burn of the cornea would make it impossible for you to wear the contact lenses."

Hamakawa, waiting in the lounge, smiled when he saw Tanner.

"Go ahead and laugh, I don't mind."

"Don't be so touchy; I think you look great. Come, we'll go through the garage. I left my car there. From now on, you're going to be a recluse."

The car sped into the night. It was Monday morning and, this time of year, the Dark Night lasted four and a half hours before the sun rose. What a way to start the week, thought Tanner; the Chinese, who liked colorful expressions, had surely come up with an equivalent for the "Monday blues." Dense streams of delivery vans, cars, and street peddlers converged and fought for a share of the road. Vending carts offered fried pastries, fresh litchi, noodle soup, grilled chicken, and steamed corncobs, their mouth-watering aromas mingling in a thousand seductive bouquets. Slowing down traffic even more were the children of all ages who walked to school, a small light clipped to their belt to claim absolute priority over all vehicles. At one intersection, two delivery vans collided, attracting a gaggle of wide-eyed schoolchildren, all of which soon tied up traffic up and down the street. The two drivers, one European and the other Chinese, exchanged increasingly heated insults, the first in English and the second in Mandarin, each grasping enough of the other's taunts to wish to come to blows. Police officers materialized, put an end to the altercation, and dispersed the bystanders, already late for school.

Far above, pink and blue whorls veiled the heavens, as if the skies yearned to take part in the morning show.

"The variety of aurorae is amazing," Hamakawa said after a while. "I've never seen two identical nights. It's one of the major sources of inspiration for New Chinese artists, that and the Dragon's Eye. For the latter, some calligraphers have even invented a new pictogram, which has been enthusiastically adopted in modern writings."

Tanner didn't respond, gazing absently at the dark facades of the buildings.

"Let's go back to my place," he said. "I have to make some calls."

"You've got to live with me until you leave. Don't forget your new identity."

"And my stuff?"

"Everything's been transferred to my place."

Hamakawa turned onto a road heading back north, distinctly less congested. The car skirted the grounds of the spaceport. A blindingly bright star was falling from the sky, cleaving the auroras, preceded by a remote and muffled thunder: a shuttle.

"Do we still leave tomorrow morning?" Hamakawa asked after a while.

"If I get the green light from the cosmetician. And if my Chinese passport is ready in time."

His companion nodded, his attention on the winding road. "Don't worry: everything will be ready."

They cut across Ferret Island, leaving behind them the din and the lights of the starport and the well-to-do neighborhoods sprawling across the southern part of the EFTA. On their right, dark waters mirrored the luminous display of the auroras like a black opal extending all the way to the horizon. This was the Northern Ocean, the planet-girdling ocean that spread over all of New China's northern hemisphere, as well as large parts of the southern hemisphere. In the east, the auroras faded as the sky lightened. The Dark Night was drawing to an end.

Hamakawa's car climbed a hill. In the new light, Tanner was able to encompass in a single glance the entire northern shore of the island: a picturesque jumble of houses and palms hurtling down the slope, coming to a stop only where the port began, thrusting piers of painted timber between the waiting sailboats. Here, in humbler surroundings than in other EFTA neighborhoods, lived mostly Asians, which was clear in any event from the plain houses, simple concrete shells painted in white, sometimes adorned with pictograms around the main doorways, the way it was still done here and there in the Chinese countryside on Earth.

Hamakawa lived in one of these Sino-Japanese houses—square, white, and spare, surrounded by a painstakingly raked garden protected by extensive awnings of UV-proof plastic.

"To enjoy daylight even when the Eye is watching," explained Hamakawa.

On New China, it was a small, unpretentious house. On Earth, only the wealthy owned houses remotely as roomy; in fact, in any city of Asia, only the wealthy owned houses, whatever the size. Tanner was forced to admit that life on such a remote colony was not without a few compensations. Surely, the guarantee of one house per family, even in a city, was, along with the absence of birth control, one of the most powerful incentives enticing immigrants to start on the long and expensive voyage leading to exile from Earth. . . .

Tanner's room faced westward, an austere room almost fit for a monk: a freshly varnished wooden floor, white walls covered halfway to the ceiling with decorative inlays, a rolled-up cotton comforter in a corner, a low table, tatamis. A painting, for meditation. Technology intruded only in the form of a portable screen, a top-of-the-line machine casually left on the tabletop. Near the comforter, four suitcases were piled up. Three belonged to Tanner, and the fourth had been entrusted to him by Wang: it was the aluminum case he'd almost forgotten at the Quan Ju De.

Hamakawa made tea and invited Tanner to follow him into the garden, to take advantage of the sunshine.

Tanner turned down the offer. "I've got a few calls to make."

Closeted in his room, Tanner felt unsettled and tired to the bone, probably as a result of the physioplastic injections. His right cheek itched furiously, but he was compelled to refrain from scratching it. The best way was to think of something else.

He sat on the tatami, legs folded. Turning on the screen, he accessed the directory and looked for the Lengshuijiang bulletin board. However, the EFTA bulletin board was the only one accessible. He asked for assistance. How could one check a classified ad put up on the board of the border town? He was told that individuals were barred from directly accessing the bulletin boards of New Chinese cities; perforce, they had to go through the EFTA board. Tanner, accustomed to the flexibility of the Martian network, fumed impatiently.

He accessed EFTA's general bulletin board and checked the message left by Wang:

> While he was drunk, he entered in a dream the peaceful Kingdom of Sophora, married the king's daughter and became for twenty-five years the governor of the Southern Kingdom. One day, his city was invaded, his wife died, and he was sent back to his native land. Then, he awoke . . .
>
> Li Gong-Zuo

He then asked to see if an answer to the message signed by Li Gong-Zuo had been posted on the Lengshuijiang bulletin board. The answer was no. Tanner scowled: Chen Shaoxing still hadn't responded. Had he foolishly addressed his message to Wang Zhong? To check, Tanner requested a search. But no, Wang had received no mail at all. And on the EFTA bulletin board? Still nothing. And switching to Nanxiang's bulletin board? A warning appeared: accessing Nanxiang's bulletin board from inside the Enclave was forbidden.

Tanner then tried to make up somewhat for his missing sleep. He was awakened two hours later by strange muffled thuds. He got up and exited his room.

In the garden, under a UV-proof canopy, Hamakawa was performing some judo routines on a gymnastic mat. He invited Tanner to join him, and his visitor needed no more persuading. Tanner put on a *judogi*. At first, he was dismayed by the stiffness of his muscles and joints—one more shortcoming to be chalked up to his five weeks in low gravity—but the exercise did him good. Once he had warmed up, Hamakawa smiled and suggested they try a few judo holds.

"Sure, but be careful with my wig!"

Ippon! Five times in two minutes, Tanner hit the ground without the slightest idea how he'd ended up there. No use blaming the extended stay in low gravity; he simply was outclassed.

"Don't be mad, you're a gifted amateur. But I'm a champion."

"I've met humbler Japanese," mumbled Tanner as he struggled to his feet.

"I got my weakness for petty vanity from my European grandfather," answered Hamakawa, a wide grin splitting his feline features.

They sat down for a bite to eat and discussed New China. Hamakawa had studied in depth the history and politics of the planet, but his knowledge of the land was mainly theoretical. In practice, he'd never been farther than Lengshuijiang, the border town.

"After all, it hasn't even been three years since I started working under Bloembergen. But you've told me next to nothing about your mission. How far do you intend to go? Lengshuijiang? Kaifeng? Or straight to the capital: Nanxiang?"

"Come with me to Lengshuijiang and you'll know all."

"Don't you trust me?"

"No."

Hamakawa guffawed.

"I think we're going to get along famously!"

The next day, a stranger stared back at Tanner in the bathroom's mirror. A stranger with a creamy complexion, thick black hair, and black, slanted eyes. He broke out laughing, but the laughter stuck in his throat: his tongue had turned purple!

The makeup specialist examined his tongue and gums with unfeigned interest. She reassured him: it was a perfectly normal side effect of the overly strong initial dose. She felt his eyelids, checked the color of his hands. She was unhappy with the color of the fingernails, and he was forced to soak his fingertips in a syrupy fluid for a quarter of an hour. When they emerged from their bath, Tanner's nails were beige and had turned opaque. Rapidly detailing the rest of his body, the cosmetician pronounced herself satisfied.

"As best one can with a redhead . . ."

She took a picture of him, retinal prints, fingerprints, and a genescan, inserting everything in an authentic Chinese passport smuggled back from Earth. She sealed the document with a copy of Beijing's municipal seal. Tanner subjected the passport to a prolonged scrutiny.

NAME:	*Li Zheng*
SEX:	*Male*
DATE OF BIRTH:	*2292-11-02*
PLACE OF BIRTH:	*Beijing*
COMMUNITY:	*Beijing, Heidian District, Nanping Village*
NATIONALITY:	*Han*
FAMILY STATUS:	*Bachelor*
GENETIC STATUS:	*Free*

"Li Zheng? Not very original . . ."

"It's the best kind: above all, you don't want to be noticed." She handed him a small memory-strip. "You'll find on this a detailed map of Nanping Village, with the name of local officials, just in case you're unlucky enough to meet a fellow countryman. We would have preferred to have you come from a more remote part of China, but your accent is a typically northern one. Any other questions?"

Tanner shook his head. The cosmetician's gaze softened a bit and her voice was almost kind as she wished him luck in his mission.

SEVEN

TUESDAY MORNING. HIGH IN THE BLUE-GREEN SKY, TWO MENACING MIENS rivaled the sun's glare, the nostrils black and flaring, the fangs red, the mane a fiery orange, and the ears flattened against the skull like an enraged cat's. On each side of the Friendship Bridge, the Lengshuijiang dragons, rearing on their clawed hindquarters to tower four hundred meters above ground, glared at incoming visitors, one eye a harsh green white, the other a softer orange.

Tanner shook his head, impressed in spite of himself. Here, at the feet of these gigantic statues, an ill-defined uneasiness stole into him, as if the mere mass of the dragons was enough to infect the boldest soul with fear.

He turned back to shelter under the UV-proof awnings, reclaiming his spot in the lineup beside Hamakawa. Ahead of them, nearly a hundred people, most of them Chinese, had queued up resignedly to cross the border. A now familiar roar was heard behind them. The shuttle bus stopped a few meters away from Tanner, ending another commute between Ferret Island and the New Chinese customs over the three-kilometer-long Friendship

Bridge. A new load of immigrants, businessmen, and visitors got off. Having gauged the length of the lineup, the newcomers swore under their breath before joining it. Its antiquated brakes screeching plaintively, the old Japanese bus turned around, took on a load of EFTA-bound passengers, and headed at a leisurely crawl toward the rolling green hills of Ferret Island.

The line creeped forward. A young man rolled his steaming cart up and down the queue, offering noodle soup, roasted chicken, thousand-year eggs, fried fish sticks, and tea. As usual with Asians, the crowd was noisy. Babies were bawling, while some in the line were watching port-a-screens, making the most of the Eye's absence to catch up on the soaps broadcasted from inside the EFTA. Queue jumpers lounged about as unobtrusively as possible, eyeing the lineup in the hope of spotting a chance to get closer to the border post, but they did not go unnoticed. Nor unmolested: two men, farther forward, started scuffling, but the fight was quickly interrupted by an armed guard. The would-be queue jumper was escorted back to the end of the line, running a gauntlet of taunts and derisive comments.

From time to time, a car would roll past; a hand would come out through the window on the driver's side and casually wave some official papers. The border guard would then salute smartly and open the gate without delay.

Tanner was starting to find it hot. Fortunately, the border post was now only a few meters away. Nestled between the claws of the twin dragons, it was a picturesque building, the walls of red bricks supporting a traditional peaked roof with upturned eaves. Businessmen or other commuters whom the border guards recognized on sight went through quickly. The others, like the immigrating families loaded down with luggage, were sent into a different room.

A uniformed woman, face blank, a cigarette sticking out the corner of her mouth, scrutinized Tanner from head to foot, then glanced at the passport.

"Immigrant?"

"Yes, but . . ."

She handed him back his passport, already losing interest. She pointed with her cigarette toward the door on the right.

"Through there . . . Next!"

In a large green and white room, tiled from floor to ceiling, stiflingly hot and clamorous, the new arrivals joined the throng at the other end, there to be questioned and searched. A long and dusty window overlooked the gleaming waters of the Straits, the converging lines of the Friendship Bridge, and the mossy-backed Ferret Island, receding in the distance.

One of the booths became free and a tall New Chinese man, almost as big as Tanner, motioned him forward. A wide smile displaying his unevenly spaced teeth, the customs agent asked politely to see his passport. He entered the data in an antique computer terminal, then nodded, satisfied. He pointed next to a small plate of black glass connected to his terminal.

"Please put your forefinger here."

Tanner obeyed. The computer buzzed its concurrence.

"Now, give me your right arm."

The official pressed a plastic disk near Tanner's right shoulder. The number of the identification tablet appeared onscreen. The computer buzzed approvingly again.

"Can I see your luggage, please?"

Tanner lifted up his two slim suitcases.

"Is that all?" asked the official, suddenly suspicious.

"The trip cost me all I had," admitted Tanner with a bashful grin.

The man laughed sympathetically.

"My father too was poor when he left Earth. A humble peasant from Qinghai, far from the cities, forgotten by all. By all, except the Fertility Service investigators, damn them! When my mother was pregnant with me, she faced abortion or exile. My parents already had two kids—one kid too many, in fact. They made the right choice, but it was a narrow escape for me!"

Tanner relaxed slightly: the official did not seem overly zealous. He absently searched the contents of both cases. Tanner and Hamakawa had packed carefully in order to avoid raising the slightest suspicion: some small change; well-worn Earth clothes, shopmade; a new pair of UV-proof glasses bought at the starport. To provide an extra touch of verisimilitude, Hamakawa had even added a brand-new pair of Korean dress shoes. The customs officer examined the shoes without bothering to hide his instant longing.

"What a gorgeous pair of shoes! If you decided to sell them, I'm sure you'd get a good price, enough to buy a bicycle, maybe—"

An altercation broke out in a neighboring booth. A man was struggling in the grasp of three policemen, who were dragging him away, quickly and brutally, spurred on by the admonishments of a seething customs officer. Tanner managed to catch sight of the arrestee's face before the group exited from the main room. It was Hamakawa!

"What's going on?"

The official shook his head, dumbfounded.

"I don't know. . . . A smuggler, I guess . . ."

Tanner was dying to run after them, but he contained the urge.

"Where are they taking him?"

The customs officer frowned.

"Do you know him?"

"No. Well . . . hardly. We just spoke a bit in the line. He didn't seem like a crook. . . ."

The official was no longer listening to him, but discussing the case with a colleague. Quickly growing bored with Tanner, he snapped shut the suitcases and handed him back his passport.

"In Lengshuijiang, go to the Immigration Service. They'll give you a temporary resident's permit, until you're officially accepted as a new citizen of New China. You can also exchange your credit card for cash, and you can find out there everything you will need to lead a harmonious and enriching life. Welcome to New China!"

In a state of shock, Tanner recovered his luggage and crossed the long room. Without drawing attention to himself, he headed toward the doorway through which Hamakawa and his captors had vanished. A small anteroom was visible, the walls painted a shade of piss yellow, leading to three locked doors. Should he go through? Supposing he found Hamakawa; what could he do, except be captured? Frustration choked him as he went by the doorway, exiting instead through a large door decorated with *Welcome*'s two ideograms, and finally crossed into New China.

EIGHT

WHAT A WAY TO START OFF A MISSION! TANNER THOUGHT WRYLY.

He was having lunch on the terrace of The Traveler's Welcome: stir-fried pork with peanut sauce, noodles, and *wulong*. To the east, propelled by a motor coughing fitfully, a ferry was making its unhurried way to small Meng Tian Island, off the northernmost reaches of the vast New Chinese landmass. Among the island's congeries of verdant hills nestled comfortably a dozen large family estates dating back to the very first years of settlement. The houses overlooked water with the hills at their back, revealing the Taoist influence of *feng shui*—Air and Water in harmony. The respectfully traditional architecture of the Meng Tian estates explained as eloquently as the two dragons of the Friendship Bridge what visitors and immigrants could expect in New China.

A placid breeze, tinged with the alien smells given off by the marine flora in the Straits, brought relief from the day's oppressively humid heat. Beneath the narrow varnished wood slats of the deck, in the bridge's shadow, sluggish reflections stirred the glassy black surface.

In fact, Tanner still hadn't set foot on the continent. The Friendship Bridge extended a fair fraction of a kilometer beyond the border post, widening to make room for restaurants, souvenir shops, car rental agencies, and stands selling train tickets. Though less than a single Earth year had passed since the border's closure, tourism had come to a standstill. Several dealers had boarded up their shops and moved back to Lengshuijiang, on the continent proper.

But it was lunch time, the restaurant was full, and the lazy marine breeze could not take Tanner's mind off his predicament.

He was taking stock with growing alarm. His plight was deadly serious. Where had they taken Hamakawa? Jay was supposed to retrieve their money, weapons, and real luggage, smuggled in by boat during the night. Tanner had the address, but would the Bureau contact willingly give up their things if Jay wasn't along?

Why had Hamakawa been arrested? Like Tanner, he was carrying a phony passport. Obviously, the border police had been warned. The arrest had been too neat, too quick. But who had betrayed him? Was it Yao, the young Tewu spy? But how could she have known? And why hadn't Tanner himself been apprehended?

And what if it were Bloembergen? kept whispering a small, venomous voice in his head. Unthinkable . . . Yet such high-level double-crossing was not unheard of. After all, Hamakawa had disobeyed a direct order from his superior and refused to take part in the wholesale killing of New Chinese spies. What if Bloembergen feared that the European Bureau governing councils intended to replace him with Hamakawa, smarter, more skillful, and all in all more trustworthy? Betrayal would be one way, however despicable, to get rid of a rival.

It still didn't explain why only Hamakawa's identity had been leaked.

Tanner then pondered his best course of action. Did he dare call the EFTA? But whom could he trust? Surely not Francis Barnaby: the assassin was under Bloembergen's sway. Zhao? She seemed to have taken a liking to Tanner, but she was still Bloembergen's wife. Wang? The old officer was wounded and he knew as little of the continent as Tanner.

As nimble as monkeys, three small boys clambered up on the tile roof and unrolled a large transparent canopy above the terrace. The heads of the dragons were reflecting an electric shimmer, and an acid-green dawn loomed in the east, above the plush pavilions of Meng Tian Island. The Dragon's Eye was rising.

Near the restaurant, Tanner spotted a row of public comcabins. The screens did not accept credit cards, but took only cash. Chomping at the bit now that he had come to a decision, Tanner lined up at a change booth, converting the meager funds on his Chinese credit card into anachronistic coins and bills. He accessed the bulletin board, ascertaining that Chen Shaoxing still hadn't answered the message left by Wang.

Ducking out of sight behind a building, Tanner sorted through his things and threw away one of his suitcases in a garbage bin. He then hailed a taxi parked by the border post. The driver, a middle-aged woman, indicated he should get in. She unplugged the charger cable and coiled it in the trunk. Taking her place behind the wheel, she grinned and asked Tanner, in a thick Hunan accent:

"To the Immigration Service?"

"No. I'm going to the Blue Tooth smokehouse . . . Western Quarter, on the street of Lost Crystals."

The moon-faced driver scowled:

"The Blue Tooth *what?* Don't speak so fast. I ain't from Beijing, me. . . ."

Tanner tried to translate in Hunan, but his knowledge of that dialect was too fragmentary. He scrawled the name on a piece of paper, which he thrust under the driver's nose. She shook her head.

"I only read Chinese."

"But this *is* Chinese!"

"No no no! Not pinyin. I mean *real* Chinese! Like so!"

With her forefinger, yellowed by nicotine, she shaped in the air the two ideograms of *jinwen*. Tanner asked the heavens for patience: the driver was able to read only the old writing! He struggled to remain calm and repeated the address slowly, enunciating each word with care, until they managed to communicate.

Buzzing with an angry electrical whine, the small Earth-made taxi took off, shuddering over the cracked concrete of the bridge before merging with the Lengshuijiang afternoon rush.

Traffic was moving slowly. A dense stream of pedestrians, bicycles, and motorbikes flowed down the concrete roadway. At least, it was dense compared with EFTA traffic; in any Earth city, it would have been considered relatively light. Surrounded by traditional-looking buildings, their brick and concrete facades variously painted but always boasting prominent ideograms, Tanner could almost have imagined he was entering a historical reconstruction of old Shanghai. Only the wide, unswerving streets sabotaged the illusion.

Bluish characters appeared in the vehicle's windows: IT IS STRICTLY FORBIDDEN TO LOWER THE WINDOWS WHEN THE EYE IS WATCHING. The driver slipped on a large set of goggles, and she remarked loudly that her honorable customer should do likewise.

"Aren't the windows UV-proof?" Tanner asked, surprised.

The driver looked back, transformed into an unlikely gargoyle by the grin and goggles.

"You a new arrival, eh? Good advice I give you: wherever you are, always wear your glasses when the Eye is watching you, if you don't want to be blind before you're forty."

Don't worry, old gal, I don't intend to stay on New China until I'm forty, he refrained from saying.

The taxi continued to slalom around pedestrians and motorbikes, far fewer in number now that the Eye was flooding the street with ultraviolets. They left behind the residential suburb to follow the seashore. Along the Straits, Lengshuijiang was not so picturesque. In all the cities of the Seven Worlds, industrial areas were remarkably alike: empty streets, dusty yards and concrete expanses, low buildings covered in aluminum sheeting— bauxite being one of the few ores widely found on New China. Tanner was taken aback by the smoke pouring from the numerous chimneys. He knew pollution abatement regulations were not as strict on frontier planets, but his Terran education still predisposed him to be shocked by such overt defilement of the air he breathed.

"Are we there yet?"

"You think they build a smokehouse downtown? Why not smack down in market square? Don't worry, we getting there. Can't you smell it?"

"Smell it?"

The only smell in the air, inescapably present ever since they'd entered Lengshuijiang, was the same acrid aroma he'd blamed on the seashore flora. Yet, the driver was right: it was growing stronger.

The taxi left the concrete roadway and rattled down a gravel road leading to the seaside. There, like a squat ziggurat, a congeries of superposed brick sheds straddled the shore, one half digging into a strand of chalky soil, the other half extending on stilts over the smooth waters of the Straits. From the ziggurat's pinnacle a citreous smoke rose straight up in the calm air, cowling the Dragon's Eye with a diffuse halo.

Tanner slipped on his hat and sunglasses, paid the fare, but asked the driver to wait for him before heading back downtown. She shrugged and restarted the meter.

"Is your money."

The driver was right: the smell came from the main shack. Not unpleasant once you got used to it . . . partway between freshly mown hay and bergamot orange. But not as sweet, and more pungent. A hint of musk, too . . . Tanner gave up; Earthly comparisons failed to capture the smell's uniqueness. Near the door, a dozen or so individuals were arguing with a doorman blocking the way.

"There's no more room, come back later," the employee was saying.

"We don't have to sit, we can stand!"

"No way! We've already got people up to the rafters. Come back tomorrow."

"But tonight, it's Green Night!" the gang's spokesman insisted indignantly.

When he got closer, Tanner realized they were teenagers. Like their EFTA counterparts, they strove to outdazzle each other with fluorescing kimonos and wide hats flashing confident boasts or challenges—SEX ANIMAL; WOLFLING; IMPERIALS ALL THE WAY! They tramped away sullenly, without sparing a glance for Tanner. The Terran spy did wonder why such a crew of show-offs would want to visit a smokehouse, but the thought was fleeting: the urgency of his need overrode everything.

He knocked, and the doorman—shortish, bull-necked, his head shaved—opened again. From behind him came snatches of music and laughter, faint shouts, the clatter of dishes, and whiffs of fumigant. The disapproving wrinkles of his hairless forehead shaped themselves into an unlikely ideogram:

"Didn't I make myself clear? There's no more room!"

"You don't understand. I must see Jacky Ling."

The doorman eyed him scornfully, up and down and sideways.

"Jacky? What about?"

"It's personal. I come from . . ."

Tanner faltered. Would Hamakawa have used his real name? Or his phony identity as Meng Zhongqiao?

"It's personal," repeated Tanner.

The watchdog grudgingly stepped aside to let him in, then locked the door in the face of yet more teenagers issuing from a cab. The door shook, pummeled by their fists and curses. Unconcerned by the squawking of the outraged teenagers, the doorman beckoned to Tanner, indicating that he was to follow him to the other end of the shed.

Still dazzled by the light outside, Tanner did not react right away, bemused for a few seconds. Inside, the smell whose complex bitterness he had been on the point of liking, outside, thickened into a rank and sharply caustic miasma. Tanner struggled desperately not to cough.

"Well? Are you coming or what?"

"What's this smell?"

"Watergrass," answered the man, puzzled, arching a nonexistent eyebrow.

Tanner managed to follow his guide. He was starting to make out, beneath the rows of naked bulbs, long wooden tables mobbed by young men and male teenagers, most of them bare-chested, laughing, drinking tea or beer, playing card games or Go, seemingly indifferent to the stench of burnt vegetable matter that pervaded the smokehouse. Half blinded by tears, Tanner stumbled over the tiles of a game of mahjong being played on the floor.

"Eh, watch out, ape face!"

One of the mahjong players rose in front of Tanner. Space-black eyes gauged him, and he was shoved backward by the player's muscular arms. The other players spread out, simmering with anticipation. Tanner did not flinch, tensing his muscles, ready and eager, if only to vent his accumulated frustrations by cutting the loudmouth down a notch or two. However, the doorman intervened, lifting the mahjong player by an ear:

"Careful, Liu . . . If you want to come back, you better behave. Be quiet and discreet, quiet and discreet like the partridge watching her nest. . . ."

The youth retreated, seething, longing for a sharp retort that eluded him. He scowled darkly, then squatted and clacked two tiles together impatiently:

"Well, guys? How about another game?"

Tanner sighed, his muscles relaxing. Putting an end to the matter, his guide unlocked a door at the back of the room and stepped aside to let Tanner enter a second room, overly bright and overheated. The stink was even worse. A thick yellow smoke rose from a grill spreading over most of the floor. Above the grill, hundreds of pork and beef quarters hung from hooks, basking in the pungent smoke. From time to time, a young man would shift a carcass, wet a patch of dried-out meat, throw a handful of dried grass on the grill. The herb shriveled on the burning metal, growing thousands of tiny vesicles, which popped and poured out the yellowish smoke.

The doorman asked where he could find Ling. The young man, sweating profusely but still smiling, pointed to the back of the room.

"By the dock."

It was no whim that the building extended above the waves of the Straits. Small boats could sail through the piles and, all the while staying out of the Eye's glare, draw alongside the wharf, there to unload large hampers filled with one of New China's native aquatic plant species. No wonder he had been unable to identify the smell, thought Tanner.

The doorman pointed out the oldest New Chinese man present. His sallow, wrinkled skin made him look a hundred years' old, but his energy belied such a first impression. He was helping two other workers, both much younger, fill large hampers slumped on the wharf with a black and viscous, alien seaweed. Watergrass, no doubt.

The old man noticed the new arrivals.

"Yes?"

"Am I ever glad to see you, Mr. Ling! I'm called Li Zheng, you don't know me—"

The elder's gaze slowly took in Tanner's appearance.

"Because *you*, you know me?"

Tanner looked around with a knowing expression.

"Is there a place where we can talk in private?"

Jacky Ling shrugged. "In my office, if it's not too long."

When they reached the sinister garret where Ling had his office, the old man lit up, as if he needed the cigarette smoke to substitute for the watergrass smoke he breathed all day long. His voice marked by a lilting accent, he asked Tanner what he wanted.

"I'm a member of the European Bureau. I've come to get the baggage which you received last night."

The elder's eyelids rolled down. He drew a puff from his cigarette, blew out a thin cloud of smoke. Sitting down behind his desk, he turned his attention to the messages on his comscreen.

"I don't know what you're talking about."

"It's Meng Zhongqiao who was supposed to show up. But they arrested him at the border."

Ling's head snapped up, but the man stayed silent.

"You've got to help me. I'm unarmed, I don't have any money, and I've got to find Meng Zhongqiao. Do you know where they could be holding him?"

Ling hesitated still. He finally opened the door of his office and motioned for Tanner to follow him. They went down a narrow staircase, emerging in a basement with a hard-packed floor, blasted by the almost unbearable heat from the smokehouse's main furnace. In a corner, a door of planks warped and whitened by the salty air led into a poorly lighted storage room. With a sigh of relief, Tanner recognized the suitcases left along the concrete wall.

Ling grabbed his elbow, his eyes shining, the roar of the blaze almost drowning out his whispery voice:

"The Prison of Noble Repentance, that's where they must be holding Jay. All the political prisoners are there. But don't count on me to help you get him out! You're lucky I'm even letting you have your luggage after what happened in the Enclave. After that . . . that useless massacre!"

He released Tanner's elbow, his immaculate goatee shaking with anger.

"I'm doing this for Jay! For Jay! It's the last time I help out the Bureau, got that? Find yourself another spot to take care of your luggage."

"I'm not in charge of logistics. All I want to do is get Hamakawa out."

The old New Chinese shook his head stubbornly.

"If he's not at the Noble Repentance jail, it's up to you! Take your things and get out! You won't find any more friends of the European Bureau here."

"Last night's massacre was a reckless action initiated by the EFTA's local commanding officer, an action in no way endorsed by the Bureau."

Jacky Ling gestured angrily to cut short a discussion that no longer interested him. He picked up two of the suitcases and ordered Tanner to take the remaining two. Tanner obeyed and followed the old man up a staircase that led outside.

Red and bulging like an obese pasha, the sun was vanishing behind a jagged skyline of industrial buildings. Clouds like ropy clumps hid part of the heavens, but the baleful glare of the Eye still shone through, near the zenith. Jacky Ling glanced disgustedly at the burning dot, dumped the suitcases he was carrying, and ducked back down the stairs. Before closing the door, he looked backward one last time, his wrinkled mien suddenly softened by an expression of regret:

"I . . . Please tell Jay that . . . that I can't go on. I just can't keep on betraying my people."

"If I find him."

"I've done all I can for you."

The old man shut the door behind him.

Tanner stacked the suitcases in the taxi's tiny trunk. The sun had set, and the ever-mutable display of the auroras peeped through rents in the dark clouds. The Eye appeared between two clouds, as if chafing to rule its kingdom.

"Don't look the Dragon in the Eye!" the driver warned him.

Tanner jumped inside the car and shut the door. The aquamarine twilight of Green Night was making the fluorescent warnings within the windowpanes shine with renewed vigor.

"Well? Where we go now?"

"I've been given the name of a hotel." Tanner acted the part of someone racking his brains. "It's not far from a jail . . . the Prison of the Honorable Repentant, something like that."

The driver looked at him askance.

"The Prison of Noble Repentance?"

"I guess so, that sounds about right."

"Several hotels are near Noble Repentance jail, but only one I really recommend: Celestial Repose, if you know what I mean . . ."

They headed back toward downtown Lengshuijiang. Instead of driving by the Friendship Bridge again, they turned on a less traveled road heading south. Tanner checked his watch: the working day was not over yet. Nevertheless, everything seemed to have come to a standstill. Tanner was getting the idea that the continent was even more passionate than the Enclave about minimizing exposure to the Dragon's Eye.

Snarling like overloaded generators, two cars sped by the taxi, close enough to touch, forcing the taxi to swerve to avoid them. The driver straightened out, swearing in every Chinese dialect on New China, shaking her fist at the two receding cars, still swerving from right to left down the street.

"Who are those lunatics?" Tanner asked indignantly.

"Ah, is obvious you just arrived! Is like that every Tuesday and Saturday. Gangs of teenagers, loaded with beer and whiskey, having a big party for Green Night. I say they are public menace! I don't know what the government is waiting for. New China is going to pot. For sure, this never be allowed on Earth!"

"You're from Earth?"

"Absolutely! But my parents, they leave when I was six. All I remember is the excitement of the trip. And the fact there was no Eye in Earth sky. My father is dead now. My mother is very old and blind. Can't take care of the grandkids, and my daughters keep yacking, yackety-yack-yack, because I work. They want me to stay home, take care of the babies."

"How many children do you have?"

She wagged her chin proudly.

"Seven: five daughters and two boys. And eleven grandkids, with more on the way."

For a Terran like Tanner, giving birth to so many children defied understanding. Like many Terrans, he was an only child. He tried to imagine what it would have been like growing up surrounded by three or four, perhaps even as many as five or six brothers and sisters . . . Unthinkable.

The taxi entered White Rose Street, a narrow street brightly lit by an orgy of fluorescent paint. Many pedestrians wore extravagant raiments, and the cars parked at random slowed down traffic considerably. Like Tanner's driver had hinted, restaurants, dance bars, and hotels were everywhere. Some establishments looked like second cousins to brothels, crisscrossed with strings of innuendo-laden ideograms—Chinese was the ideal language for suggestive puns and double meanings. In fact, several women strolling by wore clothing that left little to the imagination, under flowing cloaks made of a transparent, UV-proof plastic. In Lengshuijiang, White Rose Street was undeniably where the action was.

The car came to a stop in front of the somewhat more tasteful facade of the Celestial Repose hotel. The driver threw him a final, quizzical glance:

"I suppose the person who recommended this place told you it ain't the cheapest digs in town. . . ."

Tanner realized the driver was struggling mightily to hold back her questions. Who was this lanky newcomer from Earth, a new arrival in threadbare clothing, with a single suitcase to his name, who went straight to a smokehouse, came out staggering under the weight of new luggage, and asked to be driven to a hotel clearly above his means? Tanner regretted keeping the same taxi. He should have sent it back—and then called a new one to come back from the smokehouse. A routine precaution. One more blunder, minor, perhaps, but he was annoyed with himself, painfully aware of his multiplying oversights. Still, Hamakawa's arrest could not have been foreseen. Even if the near future was far from bright, blaming fate would not help him carry out his mission. Instead, he resolved to become doubly vigilant, prudent, and cunning.

He put on his hat and left the car. Too late now. If the driver hastened to report her strange fare to the police, he couldn't prevent it. He retrieved his things and added a princely tip. The driver thanked him effusively, and then the small taxi dropped back into the traffic's chaotic flow.

Tanner slammed down the comscreen on the bedside table. The impact caused the Lengshuijiang bulletin board interface to waver. Still no answer from Chen Shaoxing . . .

The agent rose from the bed and walked back and forth, fruitlessly going over the day's reverses. He ran himself a hot bath, lowered himself into the nearly scalding water with a sigh of delight, then tried to clear his mind. In vain. How could he rest while his partner was rotting in prison? He got out, toweled himself dry with unaccustomed vigor. He picked up the old comscreen again and asked for the address of the Noble Repentance jail. He was told no such name existed in the directory. Well, perhaps "Noble Repentance" wasn't the real, official name . . .

He asked for a list of all the city's prisons, along with their addresses. He was told there were no jails in Lengshuijiang. Tanner sighed: a typically Chinese response. He called the hotel's reception desk to ask the same question. The low-resolution image showed the receptionist staring at him wide-eyed:

"The Prison of Noble Repentance? It's just across the street, a hundred meters down."

Tanner wondered how come he'd missed noticing the jailhouse. It was the only building not splashed with fluorescing paint, a cube carved out of solid night, a black hole in the midst of a many-colored cityscape.

Green Night was in full swing. The tinkling laughter of young women and the braying of drunks mingled with the multitudinous smells and the random snatches of song straying from the dance bars. Tanner had found shelter from the Eye in the shadowed nook where two buildings didn't quite merge, and he was watching the dark concrete facade across the street. Nobody could have mistaken the building's purpose, not with the bars attached to the windows or the policemen guarding the entrance. Not that the latter seemed to take their guard duty too seriously; in fact, the policemen by the door hardly paid any attention to the people coming in or going out, joking or bantering instead with the prostitutes flaunting their wares right under their noses.

"Oh, you're a big one, aren't you?"

Tanner was hugged by a couple of girls, a young button-nosed New Chinese and a tall red-haired European half-naked under a transparent plastic dress, her nipples shining like two pink night-lights.

"What are you doing all alone in here?"

Tanner realized from her accent and a quick second look that she was not a real European, but a New Chinese girl transformed by cosmetic surgery and a cheap wig. He clumsily disentangled himself from their embrace:

"You're soliciting right in front of the police station?"

The fake European exchanged a glance with her partner.

"Is he for real? Man, why should we care? We're licensed!" She added caressingly: "Oh, but I see, you're new in town, aren't you? Just arrived on New China? What luck, we've got special rates for new men like you."

Tanner opted for candor. "You're right, I'm not from Lengshuijiang and my brother's been arrested, and I don't know what to do. You see, we'd been drinking, just a bit, and we ran into a policeman, and, well . . . Anyway, I think they must've brought him here. I just don't know if I'll be able to pay his bail."

The "European" pouted, chagrined to lose a potential customer. She pointed at the somber mass across the street with a luminous fingernail:

"Just go in there and ask. Don't be afraid, they won't bite. All they want is your money to get him out on bail, nothing more." She came on to him again. "But when you find your brother, come back and see us, both of you! Just ask for New Horizon and Xiu Xi; that's us. We'll do our bit to help your bro forget his troubles."

The two girls tittered. Tanner mumbled: "Well, yes, sure . . . Thanks again!"

The policemen on sentry duty hardly looked at him. Tanner pushed the door open. He found himself inside the hall of the police station. Inside, where the harsh lighting made him squint, Tanner was stopped by a wide counter that separated the waiting area, where he was standing, from the rest of the room, given over to a handful of exhausted-looking police keeping up a steady stream of patter with their counterparts at the other end of old comscreens. Beneath posted notices in English, pinyin, and Chinese characters, at one side of the waiting area, a sad sample of the local population were arrayed on a bench: a prostitute whose face was turning blue with massive bruising; a bald Goliath in handcuffs; a small, tragically hard-faced boy; an old bag lady muttering incomprehensible invocations. At one end of the bench, a huge police officer, practically two meters tall, was keeping a close watch on his charges.

Behind the counter, a policewoman hailed Tanner in Cantonese:

"You, what do you want?"

Tanner pretended he hadn't understood:

"I only speak Mandarin."

"You only speak Mandarin," she repeated in broken Mandarin. "Well, I was wondering what you were after. Don't look at me like a dead fish! Not my fault if you don't understand Cantonese."

An older officer, chewing the butt of a cigarette, leaned over the desk.

"Leave him alone. Can't you see he's lost at sea? Well, boy, what can we do for you?"

Tanner stammered:

"I want to . . . to know what happened to my friend Meng Zhongguo. We'd been drinking and we ran into a police officer . . . I mean, he ran into us, but it's us. . . . Anyway, Zhongguo was arrested, and . . . and I was told maybe . . . maybe he's . . ."

The older officer took out a port-a-screen:

"All right, my boy, don't worry. I'm on it. Everything will be all right. You said your friend is called . . ."

"Meng. Meng Zhongguo."

"Yeah, yeah . . . Meng . . . Meng . . . Sounds familiar, all right . . ."

Ingenuously, Tanner leaned over the countertop to watch the old cop scroll through the registry. The name Meng Zhong-qiao, Hamakawa's cover identity, appeared onscreen. Tanner went frantic, jabbing at it with a trembling finger:

"There, there, that's him!"

"Don't touch the screen! And don't fret like that; we've got all the time in the world. Meng . . . Meng . . . This is the only Meng we've got. But didn't you say Zhongguo? This says Meng *Zhonqgiao*."

Tanner frowned. "Maybe they made a mistake writing it down."

"Are you surprised? With that screwy Terran spelling . . ." threw in the Cantonese woman.

The veteran called up the entrance record. Hamakawa's face stared out of the screen, above the retinal scans and fingerprints. The officer gazed suspiciously at Tanner:

"Is that your friend? A Japanese spy?"

"A spy?" Tanner scowled uncomprehendingly. "I don't understand. That's not Zhongguo; no, that's not him. . . ."

"It's the only Meng in the database," the veteran answered calmly. "So listen well, my boy. Right now, it's Green Night, and when it's Green Night, we've got work up to here and better things to do than taking in a rowdy who's had too much to drink. I bet our officer just took your friend home. Why don't you go back and check? Meanwhile, let me give you a piece of advice:

when it's Green Night, keep away from White Rose Street. It's not a place for good boys like you."

Putting on an air of contrition, Tanner thanked the officer, trying not to overdo it. A shouting match broke out suddenly at the other end of the counter, between a policeman and a young woman who disagreed strongly about the size of the bail being asked for a defendant's release. With bovine obduracy, the policeman kept repeating that such was the amount set for his bail. If she refused to pay, the man would stay in prison; that was all there was to it. Tanner shrugged, unconcerned, and left the station.

As soon as he was outside, Tanner's expression hardened. Hamakawa was indeed being held in the Noble Repentance jail. Cell 704, according to the registry. But what could he do now? He started for his hotel, walking briskly, when an embryonic plan began to take shape his mind. He stopped, pondered it for countless seconds, weighed the pros and cons, then doubled back, heading for the prison.

Just in time: among the motley crowd of merrymakers, Tanner spotted the pink dress and broad, lacquered straw hat of the young woman he'd seen at the police station. She had her back turned to him, striding eastward. He followed her, unsure of the best way to approach her. The young woman slowed down, leaned against a lamppost. She was crying. He made up his mind and came up to her:

"What can I do to make those tears go away?"

The headgear bobbed upward, showing a startled gaze, a turned-up nose, a pair of lips coated in fluorescing red gloss, and round cheeks streaked with tears beneath the large anti-UV glasses.

"Please leave me alone. I'm not a prostitute."

Tanner essayed a sympathetic smile.

"I know. I was at the police station a few minutes ago."

Her forehead furrowed, she slipped a finger under the glasses frames to stop the tears.

"Are you a cop?"

"No, but maybe I can help you."

"Help me?" The woman shook her head. "I . . . I don't remember you. . . . Do I know you from somewhere?"

Tanner felt he was losing control of the conversation. He was not handling this well; the young woman would hardly follow a stranger.

"I'm a friend of your . . ." Brother? Probably not. Husband or significant other? "I'm a friend of your husband."

She shot him a sideways glance. Her lips curled disdainfully.

"I should have known. . . . You're talking to the wrong person. Fuzai tells me nothing."

A few steps away, a group of revelers started bellowing in chorus. Tanner glared at them exasperatedly: the carnival atmosphere was interfering with his concentration.

"Could we discuss this somewhere a bit quieter?" he asked. "Choose a restaurant, it's my treat."

She looked down. Tanner insisted: there was nothing to be afraid of, he wanted only to help them. The young woman wavered irresolutely, then gave in. They could go for some tea, perhaps . . .

In spite of the late hour, the Spring Daffodils restaurant was filled to bursting. Fortunately, they were not left standing for long. An expressionless waiter showed them to a tiny table near the kitchens. Tanner ordered a generous meal, and a bottle of whiskey to go with it.

Tanner curbed his impatience. He could not afford to waste any time on small talk, yet he had to: winning over a young Chinese woman was a delicate matter. Still, he was forced to admit his job could have been less enticing. Divested of her wide-brimmed hat and concealing shades, the New Chinese woman was a decidedly cute one. Aside from the weird, resin-slathered hairdo, her features were pleasingly regular, the mouth was sensual, and the eyes were deep and dark, shining with mistrust.

"You didn't tell me your name."

"Li Zheng. And you?"

"Xun Qingling."

The whiskey bottle arrived. Tanner filled two small porcelain tumblers. Qingling let him clink hers, then drank it all in one gulp.

"Not bad . . ."

The compliment was impersonal, but the young woman seemed to be unbending. Tanner filled the tumblers again. This time, Xun Qingling did no more than gaze at the tumbler, losing herself in the amber fluid.

"So, you're a friend of Fuzai. What do you want with me?"

"I want to get him out."

She straightened in her chair, staring at Tanner. "All you've got to do is pay his bail. Do you have the money? I know I don't."

Should he switch stories? Or stay with this one? Tanner was feverishly weighing the pros and cons.

"Qingling, promise you'll hear me out. . . . I'm not a friend of Fuzai's, but I do want to get him out. So, why am I being so mysterious? And why did I approach you? It's very simple: my brother was arrested and he's still in jail, I'm not even sure in what cell. I want to help him escape, but I need your assistance to learn the prison's layout."

"What?"

Qingling gaped at him, her eyes like a frightened doe's.

"All I want to know is where to find cell 704 inside that building," insisted Tanner. "Do you know?"

She shook her head in negation. "You're mad."

She fell silent when the soup was served. Once the waiter left, she whispered:

"You're fresh off the ship from Earth, is that it?"

"No matter . . . Do you know the layout of cells inside the Noble Repentance jail?"

"How would I know? I'm not a criminal! Anyway, it's a prison for men only."

"Perhaps your husband could help me."

"He's *not* my husband."

She bit her lower lip, having given away more than she intended to.

"Your boyfriend, then?"

She hesitated, then nodded affirmatively.

"Do you think he could help me?"

Her lips tightened into a sardonic smile.

"If Fuzai doesn't know the Noble Repentance jail, nobody does! But why should he help you?"

"Because I'll help you to pay his bail."

She nodded skeptically, as if Tanner were being silly.

"The bail is five hundred yuans, and I hardly have a hundred."

Tanner put down five hundred yuans near Qingling's plate. "Will that do?"

"Are you crazy? Don't show all that money here!"

Her hands shaking nervously, she pocketed the money. She swallowed in one shot the contents of her tumbler.

"That's only an advance," Tanner specified. "I'll be even more generous with anybody who helps me to arrange my brother's escape. It's a risk-free propositions; all I want is somebody to tell me how to find cell 704. Easy money, right?"

The young woman threw him a sideways glance, but she stayed mum.

Two waiters picked up the tureen and the soup bowls, replacing them with half a dozen steaming dishes: stir-fried vegetables, fried carp, glazed duck, lion's head casserole, chicken noodles. They ate. The woman's moodiness did not stand up very long to the effects of the whiskey. She came to life and dug in with a will, as if determined to do justice to the meal. Tanner threw in a few jokes: she laughed. He even asked her how old she was.

"I'm thirteen," she said shyly.

At first, Tanner thought she was kidding him, then he realized the young woman was quoting her age in local years, which made her about twenty.

Outside, it was almost Dark Night. The Dragon's Eye,

eclipsed by the taller buildings, lingered above the horizon. The curling horns of the high-rises along White Rose Street still glowed, adding a surreal scarlet to the powdery shimmer of the auroras.

Qingling tripped on the uneven paving, and Tanner caught her in time to save her from a nasty fall. She tore herself hastily from Tanner's arms.

"I drank too much."

"So it seems. You should be thinking of your boyfriend, who's rotting in jail as we speak."

"Oh, he's used to it!" chuckled Qingling. Realizing she'd said too much, she amended, "Oh, that wasn't very nice . . . Zheng. You're right: let's go and get Fuzai out."

Pan Fuzai appeared in the station's hallway between two policemen. Qingling's friend was thin and diminutive, almost scrawny: the scar he flaunted under his right eye made him look like a small-time punk instead of the ringleader he no doubt fancied himself to be. The cops had roused him and he didn't seem to be taking gracefully his unexpected deliverance. As soon as he saw Qingling, he addressed her sharply:

"What are you doing here? Don't tell me you sprang bail for me?"

"But . . . but, of course!" she answered, her face crumbling.

Fuzai gazed ceilingward.

"I already told you not to waste your money to get me out, you silly fool! How much did you pay now? Two hundred yuans?"

Qingling looked at the floor without answering.

"Your bail was five hundred yuans," said one of the policemen.

Fuzai stared at Qingling, his eyes bulging.

"*Five hundred yuans!* My bail was five hundred yuans and you paid it? What the fuck were you inhaling? Where did you get that kind of money?"

The parole officer asked Fuzai to shut up and sign the exit form. The prisoner refused:

"Give her back the money! Give her back the money and put me back in jail! I don't want to pay!"

"Bails are not refundable," replied the officer. "And I've had enough of your theatrics. Sign the exit form and get out of here! You better remember my warning: next time you come in here, it'll be deportation for you, understand?"

Pan Fuzai angrily filled in the exit form, retrieved his personal effects, and then left the police station, grabbing Qingling's arm. Tanner followed them discreetly. Once they were out of sight of the policemen on sentry duty, the pint-sized crook rewarded the young woman with a loud slap in the face.

"Now, tell me, you little fool! Where did you find that money?"

Qingling gaped, taken aback for a second, then her features contorted like a Fury's mien. She slapped Fuzai, calling him a stinking dog. She tried to hit him again, but he ducked the blow and attempted to land a vicious punch, aiming for her belly. Fortunately, Tanner was waiting for it: he intercepted the wrist just in time and twisted Fuzai's arm behind his back.

"All right, you lovebirds, that's enough!"

Fuzai tried an inept judo hold to get free, but Tanner countered it easily. The young man spat:

"This is none of your business, man! Who are you? Let me go! Let me go right now, or you'll regret it!"

Tanner twisted harder. Fuzai howled.

"You're crazy, man! My arm, you're going to break my arm, you—"

"*Shut up!*"

Fuzai fell silent, his face writhing in pain.

"I don't want to hear another word from you, is that clear?"

Fuzai nodded. Tanner proceeded to explain calmly how he had paid his bail and why. He was looking for a detailed plan of the prison, with a schedule of the guards' rounds, a list of critical entry points—in short, all the specifics likely to help him get his brother out of cell 704. He would not be stingy: he was ready to pay five hundred yuans beforehand, and another five hundred after springing his brother loose.

Tanner released Fuzai. The young man rubbed his shoulder, glancing crossly at Qingling.

"Why didn't you tell me when they released me?"

Qingling sighed theatrically. "If you'd let me get a word in edgewise!"

"The cops might have been intrigued by me paying a stranger's bail. I don't want to attract any attention, got it?"

Fuzai examined the European Bureau operative from head to foot. In his narrow face lit by the wanly glowing auroras, his eyes sparkled craftily:

"Give me two thousand more . . . and I'll go with you. Inside the jail. Fifteen hundred yuans beforehand, and the same afterwards."

Tanner didn't answer right away. The amount didn't matter, but he questioned the wisdom of bringing an ineffectual amateur with him. An amateur, perhaps, but one well acquainted with the prison's interior layout . . . And if this young punk was offering to help, it surely meant that Hamakawa's liberation was possible. Feigning reluctance, he accepted Fuzai's offer. The young man smiled:

"When do we march?"

Tanner thought he could make out a lightening of the eastern horizon. Was the sun rising already? Tuesdays, along the Zero Meridian, on which lay both Lengshuijiang and the Enclave, the sun rose when the night period started. Tanner eyed for a few more seconds the sky turning mauve. The auroras' brightness was waning. His watch was right: the sun was rising.

"Next Dark Night, fourteen hours from now. Come to my room at the Celestial Repose."

"And the money?" asked Fuzai.

"I'll give you the money then."

Tanner returned to his room feeling utterly wiped out. How long had it been since he'd last slept? Yet, Tanner did not close the heavy drapes right away. For a long moment, he enjoyed the quiet, letting the clear morning light daub with gold the room's furniture, almost Japanese in its sparseness: a lacquered wood desk, an unframed mirror, wickerwork chairs. He blinked: he was tired and the contact lenses were beginning to irritate his eyes. He carefully closed the curtains, undressed, stretched out on the bed, and fell asleep instantly.

NINE

IN THE BEDROOM'S CORNER, QINGLING WAS WHIRLING IN A BLACK AND pink evening dress, letting it slide down silkily until it crumpled on the brilliant red tiling. Tanner got closer, tasted her hardened nipples, slipped a hand between her thighs, smooth and warm. Tanner entered her and she panted at first, whispering Chinese obscenities, then arched up, suffocating. She was crying. From the wound in her right side, a bloody froth began to seep out. Tanner withdrew, and blood gushed between her thighs. The floor's flagstone tiles, which he had thought were naturally red, were in fact awash with blood. He was back at Bloembergen's, and Zhao's three children were crying too, locked inside the bathroom. Tanner yelled for them to stop crying, that he was going to take care of their mother. But wait, what was he saying? Qingling wasn't their mother. He opened Wang's aluminum case, took out the cryo-kit, grasped a hypodermic needle, but his fingers were trembling so hard the syringe shattered, each shard lacerating Tanner's fingers like shrapnel. He stared at his bloody hands, amazed the plastic fragments could be so sharp. Someone knocked. It was Barnaby, who wanted to assassinate him to steal his gaberdine. Tanner ran down the stairs slippery with blood, Qingling's head in the crook of his arm. He reached the kitchen, opened the freezer to store Qingling's head, but the freezer was already full of frozen heads, which tumbled out and bounced down the stairs all the way into the basement, producing a clatter of muffled thuds as the thawing flesh smacked hard surfaces. Barnaby was knocking at the kitchen's door, knocking, knocking, knocking . . . The door opened. It wasn't Barnaby, it was a dragon with green and orange eyes, the green eye shining so evilly that all the windows flashed, DO NOT LOOK AT THE EYE OF THE DRAGON! Tanner tried to flee, but he slipped on the flooring now sticky with drying blood, and his legs no longer obeyed him, and he felt the dragon's breath on the back of his neck, and the glare of its green eye—

Tanner awoke suddenly. A weird greenish light was filtering through a chink in the curtains. He checked his watch: Thursday, halfway through Green Night. Tanner whistled, half stunned, half shocked: he had slept thirteen straight hours! Shame overwhelmed him. While he was sleeping to his heart's content, Hamakawa was stewing helplessly in a cell. Tanner banished the burning guilt. He could hardly break into the prison in broad daylight!

He dressed, swallowed a capsule, checked his makeup in the bathroom's mirror, shaved carefully. From one of the suitcases, he took out a thin metal case and opened it. The sight of his tools reassured him. He closed the case and went down for a bite—yesterday's meal was now a distant memory. He took advantage of an automatic change teller in the hotel's lobby to replenish his stock of banknotes.

On the way back to his room, he encountered Fuzai and Qingling, pacing impatiently up and down the hallway. The young man didn't miss his chance to grumble:

"I was starting to wonder if the honorable stranger had stood us up."

Tanner didn't bother answering and let them into his room.

Fuzai wasted no time on idle chitchat:

"Do you have the money?"

Tanner gave him fifteen hundred yuans, plus three hundred for Qingling. She looked at him wide-eyed:

"For me? I thought the fifteen hundred yuans were for both of us."

Fuzai sniffed, unimpressed. They'd get eighteen hundred yuans out of it, that's all. He thrust a covetous hand toward Qingling:

"Come on, give me that! You might lose it, or, knowing you, spend it all on junk."

Qingling ignored him and made a big show of slipping the bills in her pocket:

"They're mine. And what if you're arrested in the course of your little adventure? You're the one who should be giving me your money."

"To pay my bail again? Never! If I'm deported to the Heaven Mountains, at least I'll have my fifteen hundred yuans to keep me company!"

The night was very dark, which pleased Tanner no end. Low clouds hid the auroras, and the thin traffic on Pine Street allowed him to scrutinize without being noticed the south side of the jail, even starker, if possible, than the side overlooking White Rose Street. Fuzai examined the black obelisk, counting the lighted squares of the windows. He pointed to one of the shining squares:

"There. Next to last floor, second window to the left."

"Are you sure?"

He spat. "I know the place too fucking well."

A yellowish glare lit up the cobblestones. A delivery van was driving up Pine Street, followed by a taxi. Tanner and Fuzai waited until the two vehicles vanished, then ran to the first fence, which they climbed as quickly as possible. Fuzai got himself tangled in the barbed wire, and Tanner was forced to double back to help him get free.

Afterward, they hurried down the other side and ran through the night, reaching an emergency exit, which was a simple metal door devoid of a lock or doorknob. Huddled in the shadows, Fuzai and Tanner exchanged looks, eyes shining.

Tanner took out his toolbox from his backpack. He picked out three slim crowbars, each half a meter long. With all his strength behind it, he pushed the thinnest one between the door and the frame. He then hesitated, and sought Fuzai's dark silhouette behind him:

"You're sure there's no alarm?"

Fuzai whispered he was certain. Tanner leaned against the rod—without putting all his weight on it, to avoid bending it—and the door moved away slightly from the frame. Fuzai inserted a second, stouter crowbar in the gap so as to widen it even more. Tanner then did the same with the still stronger third crowbar, straining with all his might. The door being too solid, it was the doorjamb that gave way suddenly, popping a large bolt free from the twisted strike plate. However, the door swung through only a few centimeters before being stopped by a large steel chain. Tanner looked inside through the gap. All he could make out was a small vestibule, with walls of gray concrete. A second steel-clad door still separated them from the prison's inner sanctum.

Tanner fished from his backpack a compact metal instrument that he unfolded, turning it into cutters with meter-long handles. Fuzai looked at him dubiously but refrained from commenting. Tanner needed several tries to make them work. The interstice was excessively narrow and the diamond-edged jaws kept slipping on the hardened steel of the chain. Finally, he managed to grab a link. With a loud crack, the chain snapped.

They slipped noiselessly into the vestibule and closed the door behind them. Tanner started breathing again, his heart knocking against his chest as if it wanted to be let out. The second door was equipped with an alarm system, its wiring obvious—it was meant to deter attempts from the inside, not the outside. With a pocketknife, Tanner carefully stripped off the insulation and clamped the naked wire with the two clips of an analyzer. After a few seconds, the analyzer's screen flashed a green light.

"You can open the door now," Tanner breathed out.

Fuzai was unable to contain himself any longer.

"I've never seen tech like this! Does it come from Earth? Do you come from Earth too? You're a smuggler, right? A spy? This guy we're getting out, he's not really your brother, eh?"

Tanner shushed him, raising a finger to his lips.

"Remember, I still have fifteen hundred yuans for you."

The young man nodded sharply. There was no danger he'd forget.

Tanner breathed deeply and half opened the door.

A corridor paved in gray concrete extended in front of Tanner for about fifty meters, lined on each side with cell entrances blocked by metal bars. It ended at another door. Close by, on Tanner's right, a staircase started upward. The agent opened the door, slowly, very slowly . . . A faint smell of urine pervaded the damp air. It was the middle of the afternoon, and the jail was quiet.

The Prison of Noble Repentance was not a high-security institution; the relative ease with which they'd gotten so far confirmed it. New Chinese justice was swift, and often expeditious. Like most frontier worlds, New China tolerated minor infractions, for which it favored community work instead of imprisonment. For more serious crimes, ranging from swindling to manslaughter, offenders faced an almost automatic sentence. Most were exiled to the new settlement areas: the Heaven Mountains, among the peaks to the continent's south; the Serpent Gulf coast, intended to shift the colonization thrust away from the Ferret Island-Heaven Mountains axis; or the hydroelectric projects of the Very Long Dragon Lake. Child molesters, repeat murderers, and terrorists, on the other hand, were judged promptly and executed in short order. The New Chinese did not consider imprisonment as social retribution but simply as a way of immobilizing the accused before he or she went on to interrogation, judgment, exile, or execution—or just long enough for somebody to sober up.

Tanner ran up the stairs soundlessly, then motioned for Fuzai to follow him. They climbed together to the second floor, an exact duplicate of the first: a corridor paved with concrete, and two rows of cells. Heartened, they kept going.

On the third floor, a prisoner caught sight of them. Tanner tensed. He'd been dreading something of the kind. . . . Fuzai put a finger to his lips. The inmate wagged his chin approvingly, smiling wide, and did not utter a sound. The pair of intruders went all the way to the seventh floor, as silent as shadows. Their hearts beating like mad, from the swift climb as much as from nervous strain, they left the stairwell and walked down the hallway between the cells.

With muffled exclamations and hysterical cackles, the prisoners leapt from their bunks and lined up behind the bars. One prisoner, a tall New Chinese as spindly as a reed, started squealing enthusiastically when he saw them:

"Oh yeah! Splendid, man, splendid! It's Deep Wisdom in person who's come to save us! Yeee-ow!"

His cellmate shut him up with a hard punch to the ribs. Tanner ran the rest of the way to cell 704 and leaned against the bars. An unmoving figure was lying on the bunk, wrapped in a dirty brown blanket.

Tanner whispered anxiously: *"Jay!"* The sleeper set aside his blanket with a start, glancing up at Fuzai and Tanner with a flabbergasted expression. The face was round, the hair long and unkempt. Tanner recoiled as if he'd been slapped: it wasn't Hamakawa! The New Chinese rose, a fist clenched to keep the loose prison drawers from slipping down his legs. His mouth was opening mutely like a carp's.

The yells of the gangly New Chinese echoed again down the corridor:

"It's him! It's the monk's holy rage! Yeee-ow! Yeeeeee-ow!"

His cellmate was thrashing him mercilessly, which only

seemed to make him squeal even louder. Tanner pressed his face against the bars.

"Where is Meng Zhongqiao? Was he moved to another cell?"

The prisoner was gazing stupidly at Fuzai and Tanner, who thought to himself he had seen cows evince more intelligence.

"Zhongqiao? The short guy with muscles like a steroid baby? But he . . ."

The madman's shouts kept Tanner from hearing the inmate's next few words:

"What did you say? I didn't catch that!"

"I told you he's *escaped!*"

Tanner felt like a trapdoor had opened beneath his feet and he was falling down a bottomless pit lined with grimacing faces. He stammered:

"When . . . when did he escape?"

In the cage next door, a short, scar-faced fat man was holding his sides laughing:

"Your friend got away this morning. . . . The swamp bandits have come too late!"

The door at the other end of the hallway was slammed open. A guard with a long wooden truncheon burst into the corridor. He stopped, dumbstruck for a second, then grabbed his whistle and practically blew his lungs out.

"Freeze!" he screamed next. "Stay where you are!"

"Let's scram!" Fuzai yelled as he leaped toward the stairs.

Pursued by the guard's high-pitched whistle, the cries of the prisoners, and the crazy chortling of the madman, Tanner followed Fuzai in scampering down the stairs at a breakneck pace. As they passed each floor, the inmates, already alerted by the hubbub of the floors above, joined in the hue and cry, hooting and hollering as they saw the two fugitives cross their own landing. Tanner and Fuzai had made it only as far as the third floor when the deafening howl of a siren drowned the barnyard uproar.

On the ground floor, they almost ran into three guards who had discovered the break-in. The three men quickly raised their truncheons and blocked the way out.

Tanner swore: he no longer had a choice. He got his gun out, and he threatened the three guards with it. Their eyes widened incredulously. And so did Fuzai's: the young man had never suspected his companion might be armed with a gun! The guards set down their truncheons. The guard who'd been pursuing them showed up at the top of the flight of stairs, out of breath. Tanner backed up against the concrete wall. It was a tricky situation: he couldn't point his gun both ways at once. Instead, he aimed it at the face of one of the three guards, while keeping an eye on the guard in the staircase.

"Don't move, you! Throw away that truncheon, or this one dies!"

The guard faltered.

"Now!"

His voice quavering, the guard in Tanner's sights begged his colleagues not to be heroes and to follow orders. Fuzai retrieved the truncheon as it rolled down the concrete steps and shoved the guard into the three others.

"Now, open a cell and stay there!"

"We don't have the keys . . ."

Fuzai jabbed the man's potbelly with his newly acquired truncheon:

"None of that with me, my friend! You've got the keys and you're going to open a cell, you dogs! Stop shitting me and get a move on!"

It seemed to take forever, but the four guards were finally locked inside a cell. Fuzai and Tanner ran out into Dark Night. They scooted up the fence, wriggled through the barbed wire without a thought for their clothing, and jumped onto the sidewalk. Cars were stopping, the drivers intrigued by the noise of the siren. Silhouetted by a constellation of blinding headlights, six or seven figures advanced toward them. Menacing or simply curious, Tanner didn't try to decide. He pointed his gun in their direction and shouted:

"Keep back! I'm armed and dangerous!"

Uttering cries of alarm, the silhouettes ran back to the safety of their cars. Tanner trailed Fuzai through a maze of dimly lighted alleyways until he no longer knew where he was. Finally, they slowed down and joined the flow of evening strollers. They were back in White Rose Street. A few passersby had their heads cocked: wasn't that a siren over there? Most shrugged. Anything could happen in White Rose Street . . .

Underneath the lamppost, opposite the Celestial Repose, Qingling was waiting anxiously. She leaped joyfully when she spotted them.

"Oh, there you are! I was so afraid, with all those sirens . . . But what happened? Where is your brother?"

Fuzai guffawed hysterically. Tanner explained in a few, terse words how their incursion had turned sour. Qingling uttered a sympathetic "Oh!"

Tanner and Qingling went back to the hotel room. Fuzai would follow in a few minutes, since Tanner would rather the hotel employees not see all three of them together. In the elevator, they were silent at first, until Qingling started laughing, at first quietly, and then broke up into loud guffaws. Subjected to the disapproving glare of the elevator boy, she hid her mouth behind her hand. Still, she kept giggling all the way to Tanner's room. She dropped into an armchair and took off her high-heel shoes. Sighing with relief, she massaged her feet. Then she looked at Tanner, stunning in her glittering black and red dress, her hair flowing loose, now freed from the previous day's coating of resin. Her hand over her mouth, she was still struggling not to laugh:

"I'm sorry, I'm not laughing at you, it's the situation."

Tanner had dropped onto the bed, "I'd laugh too, if I knew where Ha . . . my brother was."

She stopped laughing, sympathetic again:

"You really don't know where he could be?"

Tanner shook his head dejectedly. His mission was turning into a full-fledged debacle. Qingling came to him and hugged him. Surprised by the motherly embrace, Tanner did not push her away. She tried to reassure him: his brother was out; that was the most important thing, now. Tanner hardly heard her, his senses aroused by the soft hand cupped around his ear, the warm body snuggling against his. . . . Seized by a sudden impulse, he kissed Qingling on the lips. She backed away, as if hit by an electric shock:

"It's . . . it's not nice to take advantage of the situation. All I wanted was . . . was . . ."

She fell silent, her lips half opened, her cheeks blushing. Tanner drew her against him again, tasting her mint-perfumed mouth. Qingling did not resist, breathing shallowly. A knocking at the door was heard and Tanner got up hastily, his ears buzzing.

"It's Fuzai!"

Qingling did not budge, unresponsive. She did not seem to understand what had just happened.

Someone knocked again, and Tanner opened.

"Nice to see you, Mr. Li. I hope I'm not bothering you?"

Jay Hamakawa, his nose and forehead swollen, attempted an unconvincing smile, revealing in the process his bloodied gums. He looked like a bum in his soiled clothes, a size too small for him. His gait unsteady, he came into the room. Tanner swore and helped him to sit down. The newcomer's obsidian gaze met Qingling's wide and wondering eyes.

"I'm sorry if I'm interrupting something," he mocked, his voice grating painfully.

"It's not what you think. She's helping me."

Someone knocked again. This time, it was Fuzai, who looked over Hamakawa slowly, from head to feet:

"That your brother? He doesn't look much like you."

"Instead of making inane comments, how about helping me to get him to bed?"

Hamakawa demurred. "No, it's all right. They just roughed me up a bit. . . . I've seen worse. Mostly, I'm hungry. I haven't eaten all day."

"Qingling, run him a hot bath!" Tanner ordered. "And you, Fuzai, go buy food for everybody. Also, bring back some bandages, disinfectant, everything . . ."

"Just call room service."

"Are you crazy? I don't want hotel employees to see all four of us in here. So, get going!"

Fuzai, pouting sullenly, stalked from the room.

Tanner and Qingling helped Hamakawa to take off his soiled rags. When they uncovered his shoulders, mottled with bruises and cigarette burns, the young woman, aghast, tried to catch Tanner's gaze, but she kept mum. In spite of his obvious exhaustion, Hamakawa insisted on taking a bath by himself.

Fuzai returned with a first aid kit, two roasted chickens, and some steamed vegetables. Hamakawa appeared. Freshly washed, dressed in a clean bathrobe, he looked human again. Without a word, he took the plate and chopsticks held out by Qingling, and proceeded to wolf down his meal. Nobody spoke as he ate. Hamakawa placed his chopsticks on the cardboard dish, then placed it on the bedside table. He gazed inexpressively at Qingling and Fuzai, then turned to Tanner:

"We've got to speak."

Tanner took out fifteen hundred yuans for Fuzai, and another three hundred for Qingling.

"That's all for now. I'll contact you again if I need you."

Qingling sighed:

"Are you sure you don't need—"

"No," Tanner stated, then adding less abruptly: "And, thanks."

Fuzai gazed indecisively at the banknotes, glanced askance at Hamakawa, and scratched his greasy mane:

"Well, there's one thing . . ."

"What?" Tanner asked icily. "Isn't this enough?"

"No, that's not it. . . ."

He handed back to Tanner the fifteen hundred yuans and dredged up from the pockets of his pants another five hundred.

Tanner blinked, uncomprehending. Fuzai clicked his tongue, a small, insolent smile splitting his pointy rat's face:

"Two thousand yuans. For the gun."

So that's it! thought Tanner.

"Out of the question!"

"Come on. Your gun's not worth two thousand yuans. You're getting the better of the bargain, I tell you. Come on, I'll settle for just ten bullets, no more."

"That's enough! Take back your money and forget it!"

"Two thousand five hundred!"

"Fuzai, stop," Qingling murmured.

Fuzai grimaced nastily and shoved her aside:

"Leave me alone!"

He took back his money, muttering below his breath. He opened the room's door and looked at Qingling:

"Well, are you coming? They told us to get out, so we're getting out!"

Qingling turned toward Tanner, her face unhappy:

"I'm sorry. It's not—"

"Are you done apologizing?" Fuzai exploded. "I don't give a fuck about these two guys. They can go spit in the Dragon's Eye, see if I care!"

With a last discomfited look, Qingling shut the door, cutting off Fuzai's rant. Tanner turned to Hamakawa, who had hardly breathed a word since coming in. Raising a weary hand to ward off explanations, the other agent said exhaustedly:

"Tomorrow . . . We'll talk about it tomorrow. For now, I just want to sleep. Sleep . . ."

Moving like an old man, he lay down on the bed and moved no longer. Tanner cleaned up the meal's debris, then turned off the lights. A dull glow still managed to seep in from behind the blinds. Tanner walked to the window and glanced outside.

The sun had just cleared the horizon. The upturned curves of the roofs, painted in infinitely many shades of blue, rose against a gray and mottled sky. Along the sidewalk, a handful of prostitutes still strolled idly, the lone dabs of color against a forlorn urban backdrop decorated with sun-fearing hues: dusty green, dark ocher, charcoal gray . . .

All in all, not much of an evening, Tanner decided. He pulled the curtains shut. In the dark, he pulled out his comscreen and accessed again the Lengshuijiang bulletin board, not that he entertained any particular hopes. Still nothing from Chen Shaoxing. He undressed and lay down near Hamakawa's unmoving body. He had trouble falling asleep.

TEN

"WHEN I REALIZED I'D BEEN IDENTIFIED, I STRUGGLED AS MUCH AS POS-
sible to distract them. I was afraid you'd been betrayed too and
I wanted to give you a chance, however small, to get away. When
I saw I was the only one they were after, I stopped resisting. They
took me in an office out of the way and they roughed me up a
bit, but without asking me anything. They weren't trying to make
me talk; they seemed to know exactly who I was. Next, I was
transferred to a jail, but I didn't stay long in my cell. They took
me away for interrogation, started roughing me up again, until
an officer came in, chewed out the ones who had been slapping
me around. He gave me a cigarette, served some tea, did everything he could to make friends. He revealed, very politely and
apologetically, that he knew I was from the Bureau, so it was
useless to try and hide anything, and it was in my interest to
explain what I was doing on the continent. I answered sincerely:
I didn't know anything, I was going to be briefed once I got here.

"You can guess what they asked me next: *who* was going to
brief me? That's when it turned nasty: they left me in my cell,

and came back during the night for another interrogation. Now it was the bad cop, snarling he only believed in physical persuasion, so talking was in my best interest, because I wasn't going to get any tea and cigarettes from him. I told him to spare me his bad acting, I'd seen enough of their bad cop, good cop routine. That made him laugh; he admitted they hadn't been very subtle. So he asked me again the unavoidable question: who was I supposed to meet in New China? What followed was rather unpleasant. They brought me back to my cell; then, early in the morning, I was escorted again to the interrogation room. It was the 'good' guard, with his tea and cigarettes. He was all smiles as he asked me the same questions again, and he didn't stop smiling when he threw the scalding tea in my face and then used my back as an ashtray.

"So I fainted.

"The hardest thing was playing the part without ever reacting, since they didn't buy it at first, of course. Finally, they took me to the infirmary, where I was able to get rid of the guard and the doctor in order to escape. In the street, I came across an old drunk who didn't even realize I was stripping him. He got a deal. At least my prison clothing was clean! Anyway . . . Once I had the appropriate clothing, I begged for small change—let me tell you, people in Lengshuijiang are amazingly tight with their money—and I called hotel after hotel, looking for Li Zheng. . . . So, here I am, without a passport, but with the police and the Tewu hunting for me."

Tanner took over, recounting his share of adventures: recovering their luggage, looking for Hamakawa's prison, getting Qingling and Fuzai to help. When Tanner recounted the preposterous end of their attempted break-in, Hamakawa let out a brief burst of laughter. Then his smile disappeared. He smoked, his gaze frozen, finally breaking his silence:

"Those two New Chinese you met. They know too much. They must be eliminated."

Tanner was taken aback. "No way!"

"Especially the young punk," insisted Hamakawa. "Did you

see the face he pulled when you refused to sell him your weapon? It's really a pity you had to take it out."

"There was no other way—"

"On the black market, a pistol like yours is worth five thousand yuans, at least. That young crook wouldn't think twice of selling out his own mother for that kind of money."

"If he blabs to the police, he'll never get his hands on it."

"Thank goodness! Otherwise, he would have told tales already."

"This is not getting us anywhere," Tanner replied impatiently. "What's done is done. Fuzai and Qingling saw my gun, but I will not kill them in cold blood . . . especially Qingling."

Hamakawa bowed his torso in a caricature of submission. He rose from the edge of the bed and strode—stiffly—to the window. He lifted the blinds.

The cloud cover had broken up. Friday morning. Dark Night ruled. Varicolored auroras shaped like threadbare twisters were sliding across the sky, slow swirls of light moving in oily water.

In the street beneath, brightly illuminated by the headlights of cars and delivery trucks, the citizens of Lengshuijiang, inured to the beauties of the show above them, were attending noisily to their affairs.

Hamakawa turned toward Tanner.

"Well?"

"Well, what?"

"Your turn now to tell me a story. I think I've earned the right to find out what we're doing here, right?"

ELEVEN

HALF PAST FOUR, AND ALMOST LUNCHTIME. THE JUST RISEN SUN WAS drenching the oldest neighborhoods of Lengshuijiang in liquid gold. About three hundred meters before reaching the market proper, traffic came to a complete stop. Tanner and Hamakawa left the gridlocked taxi and continued on foot.

The marketplace was bustling madly, enjoying a five-hour reprieve before the Eye's return. A dense crowd was racing, selling, buying, begging, and insulting one another in every known Chinese dialect. Bricks were being stacked to their right. To their left, the mouth-watering smell of *baozi* was being ignored by a long row of craftsmen sunning themselves as they worked in the open. Some turned out scrimshaw, carving mahjong tokens, doorknobs, and cigarette holders out of plastic or pig bone. Others sculpted candlesticks out of local wood or wove cheap straw hats, offered varicolored sweet-smelling confections, painted or stitched silk fabrics.

Hamakawa halted, uncertain of his bearings. Since his last visit to Lengshuijiang, the market had changed and he could no

longer spot the European Bureau's contact. He asked the owner
of a small shop, a little old woman with a face like a raisin, hiding
behind a pyramid of old screens, scratched coms, and gap-
toothed keyboards. The Happy Pig butchershop—had it gone out
of business?

Batting her eyelids, she turned a half-blind gaze toward Hamakawa. She pointed a trembling finger eastward, explaining the
meat and produce sellers had all been moved to the other end of
the market.

Slowed down by the crowd, the two operatives crossed the
entire plaza lengthwise, all the way to a section where great panels of UV-proof polymers roofed over the neighboring stalls of
meat vendors, fishmongers, and produce sellers.

The Happy Pig, though it was one of the largest stalls in
the market, was almost entirely hidden by the throng of New
Chinese shoppers. Behind the counter of scratched and battered
plastic, three butchers—blood on their hands all the way to their
elbows, cigarettes clinging to the corners of their mouths, seemingly heedless of the sharp directives of the customers and the
excited cries of the hordes of kids—were carving with unerring
swiftness pieces of beef, pork, lamb, duck, chicken, quail, pigeon,
dog, cat, rabbit, pangolin, and kangaroo. The prices, written
down in chalk on a large blackboard, ranged from the reasonable—pork or pangolin—to the extravagant—cat or beef.

"This could take a while," explained Hamakawa. "I'd better
go alone. They don't have to know there's two of us."

Ignoring the customers' protests, Hamakawa cut in, reached
the counter, attracted the attention of one of the butchers, whispered a few words. The butcher motioned for him to come behind
the stall. An old New Chinese man joined the agent there,
greeted him with a circumspect nod, and then took him into the
back shop.

Tanner strolled idly through the market. It ran all the way
to a wharf looking out over Ferret Straits. Dockers were unloading a small freighter, stacking crates of still wriggling fish on the

quay, amid the strident hisses of a steam whistle and the rhythmic cries of the foremen.

"... *lai le ... hui le!*"

"... *hui le ... hang le!*" answered the straining dockers.

Tanner spotted a couple of young New Chinese men who were having lunch in the sun, leaning lazily against a concrete wall.

"Say, where are those fish from? I didn't know they'd managed to introduce them in the sea."

One of the men didn't even turn his head, but the other felt like chatting:

"Those fish don't come from the sea, they come from the fish tanks of the Dreamy Lagoon, down south, along the Blue Point Coast. Bloody clever, man: kilometers of lagoons walled off from the sea, with fish inside. Fish farming, they call it! Yeah, sure they've tried to get some Earth fish to live in the sea, but it didn't work; the fish tasted so bad that even the dogs barfed, man!"

In front of a Buddhist temple, Tanner observed the cleansing rituals performed by a dozen monks. Time having passed, he returned to the vicinity of the butcher shop. Hamakawa was nowhere in sight. At the counter of a noodle shop opposite the Happy Pig, Tanner sat down to a lunch of beer and fried fish. He watched with interest and amusement a customer buy half a kilo of rice a few steps away. No wonder he hadn't eaten any rice since his arrival on New China: the biotechs were still trying to perfect a rice strain able to withstand high UV levels. What little rice was produced on New China grew in greenhouses and its price was correspondingly astronomical. Under the buyer's critical eye, the rice was therefore carefully weighed and paid for to the sound of a deep sigh.

Hamakawa appeared. He winked for Tanner's benefit, then went on his way. The young agent finished his beer, then followed his partner across the market to another restaurant. Though the place was packed, Hamakawa found them two free spots. Tanner sat by his side and Hamakawa whispered, his eyes on the menu tacked up to the wall.

"I didn't want to eat where you were. Our agents might have seen us together."

"You don't trust our own side?" Tanner asked with a wry smile.

"Our little border incident has made me cautious."

"But it doesn't make sense—if the leak originated within the Bureau, how come I wasn't arrested too?"

"When Bloembergen asked me for your cover identity, I didn't give him the real one."

While Tanner pondered the implications of this revelation, a waiter stopped to take their order. As soon as the waiter left, Hamakawa slipped under Tanner's hand a small booklet with a laminated cover. His new passport, in the name of Chang Chung. Tanner leafed through it. Gorgeous work, indistinguishable from the real thing. He handed it back to Hamakawa.

"Unfortunately, only the fingerprint and the code string of the identification tablet match. The retinal prints and the genescans are random borrowings from a stolen database. But it should be enough as long as we're not stopped for an exhaustive identity check."

The waiter returned with beer, noodles, and brochettes. The day was hot and humid, and the air murderously still. The sunsplashed table dripped with honeyed hues. Tanner blinked, suddenly irritated by his contact lenses. He took another swallow of the strange-tasting brew. Hamakawa finished all three dishes before releasing a sigh of satisfaction. He searched his pockets.

"You wouldn't have any cigarettes, eh?"

"That shit you smoke? Give me a break!"

Hamakawa shrugged, deep in thought. Then he looked up, still avoiding Tanner's eyes.

"What do we do now?"

"I don't know," Tanner replied, completely frank. "Why isn't Chen Shaoxing answering? Is it deliberate on his part, or has he met with some kind of mishap?"

"The New Chinese government is housed in Nanxiang. Let's

take the train and try to meet Chen Shaoxing on his home ground."

"When you put it that way, it seems simple . . . But you're right, we've lost enough time here. Let's go get our luggage at the hotel and leave for Nanxiang by the next train."

A taxi as hot as an autoclave let them off in front of the Celestial Repose. They decided to go in separately, Tanner first. Refreshed by the lobby's cool air, Tanner made straight for the elevator, walking briskly. Just as the elevator boy was going to close the door, Qingling rushed inside, breathless, and clung to Tanner's shoulder. She seemed terror-stricken.

"Oh, Zheng, it's terrible!"

Tanner surprised himself with his reaction to Qingling's apparition. Struck dumb and slightly peeved, yes, but also happy to see her again one last time before they left Lengshuijiang. However, the young woman was on the verge of tears, the thin blue dress rising and falling with each breath.

"Qingling! What are you doing here? What's going on?"

"I've been waiting for you in the lobby since this morning. I . . ."

She eyed suspiciously the elevator boy, who made a show of admiring the ornamental arabesques painted on the cabin's lacquered wood. Tanner understood; he could wait until they got to the room. The ride up seemed endless. Qingling huddled against him, and he hugged her to comfort her. The gaudy cabin reached their floor and the impassive elevator boy opened the doors. Qingling tore herself from Tanner's embrace and, after glancing timorously down the corridor, left the elevator's refuge.

As soon as the elevator doors closed, she grabbed Tanner's arm again:

"No, don't go to your room! They could be there!"

"Who are you talking about? Did Fuzai go to the police because I didn't sell him my gun?"

"No. Not the police. Fuzai wouldn't dare."

"Who, then?"

Qingling was glancing right and left.

"Bandits . . . You know . . ."

"They could be in my room?"

"I don't know. I don't know! They talked about it. . . ."

Tanner dragged Qingling all the way to his room. It was no use waiting outside in the hallway, and he wanted to retrieve their things. He smiled to Qingling, flashing his gun: he was the one with a weapon, not them.

She seemed only moderately reassured.

Tanner inspected the lock and door frame. He spotted a few scratches here and there, but nothing obvious. He slid the key noiselessly into the lock, turned, and swiftly swung the door open. The bedroom seemed empty. Tanner looked under the bed and locked the door behind him. Gun still in hand, he opened the wardrobe's door. Except for their suitcases, it was empty. He turned toward the bathroom and was on the point of turning the handle when he was struck by an indisputable recollection: that same door hadn't been closed when he'd left earlier.

"You, in the bathroom! Come on out! With your hands up!"

Nothing happened.

"Get out of there, Fuzai. You know I'm armed!"

The only answer was the roar of the traffic coming through the window. Suddenly, Tanner thought he heard feet dragging and he squeezed the handgun harder. The bathroom door opened slowly, letting through two unhappy-looking New Chinese men: a youthful roughneck with a scraggly beard and a hulking brute, bald, fat, and muscled. What a perfectly lovely brace of crooks, thought Tanner. The bearded one glanced at Qingling with hate-darkened eyes.

"You'll regret it, you little sow!" he hissed between his teeth. "We'll cut up that cute ass of yours till—"

Tanner wagged his gun menacingly:

"Shut up! Come on, now! Let's see your cutlery on the floor! Quickly, now!"

The two New Chinese men threw two knives each in the far corner of the room. Tanner kept an eye on them: they had obeyed much too quickly. They were probably still hiding a weapon or two.

"Isn't Fuzai with you?"

"Which Fuzai do you mean?" asked the young one with the beard bovinely.

"Watch out!" shouted Qingling.

The warning came too late. Two arms seized Tanner by the ankles and pulled him backward suddenly. Tanner yelped with pain as he fell to the ground. With a bold kick, the younger of the pair booted the gun from his grasp. The weapon shattered the mirror and Tanner shouted for Qingling to recover the gun just as the bald one kicked him right in the stomach. Tanner had expected the blow: he tensed his abdominal muscles, but the impact staggered him nonetheless.

Qingling got to the gun, but the youth jumped her. He grabbed her by the hair and threw her to the ground none too gently. Mongoose-quick, she sprang back up, holding a large piece of the mirror, which she smashed to bits in his face. The roughneck howled, clutched his face, and cowered dumbly.

"The gun, Qingling!" repeated Tanner, unable to escape the hold of his two opponents.

' But Qingling didn't move. Rooted to the spot, she was gasping in horror, gazing at her lacerated hand and at the young man writhing on the carpet, his face pissing blood.

As if struck by a battering ram, the room's door burst open. It was Hamakawa. The bald one released Tanner and swaggered toward the newcomer, perhaps hoping to frighten Hamakawa with his mere bulk. He was instantly disabused: Hamakawa set him to counting the carpet's knots with his teeth. The Japanese agent rushed to Tanner's rescue and lifted Fuzai bodily by the hair, as the young hood stammered incoherently.

Tanner had trouble rising. It felt like red-hot needles were stabbing his knees and his sides. Still, he lost no time recovering his gun and only then clasped Qingling:

"Don't cry. It's over . . . It's over now."

Hamakawa shook Fuzai like a rag doll.

"What are we going to do with him?"

Tanner came up to Fuzai, still more stunned than angry.

"You, you're going to tell me where the hell you were hid-ing!"

Qingling pointed to one of the drawers of the chest, sobs still bubbling in her throat. Tanner looked at the drawer unbe-lievingly:

"You should have been in a circus!"

His hands trembled with the urge to *really* test the hood-lum's limberness, but the occupants of neighboring rooms were starting to pile up at the door. The elevator boy appeared. Gaping with amazement, he took in the wounded, the blood, and the damages.

"Don't nobody move," he stammered. "The police has been called!"

Hamakawa sent Fuzai flying against the wall.

"Scram, before you make me puke."

Fuzai didn't need to be told twice. Without losing a minute, the two agents bundled their belongings into the suitcases.

"All right, let's go!" Tanner grabbed Qingling by her good hand.

Through the room's window came an ominous sound, drowning the din of the morning rush: police sirens. Tanner turned toward the small crowd that had amassed in the corridor and he yelled at them to make way. Nobody tried to stop them. Tanner, Qingling, and Hamakawa hurtled down the service stairs.

In the lobby, they spotted an oncoming police squad, waving truncheons. The trio retreated through the restaurant, burst into the kitchen, ignoring the indignant invective of the head cook, and emerged in a narrow alley. They ran from the sickly sweet smell of rotting garbage into the nearest street, losing themselves in the throng of pedestrians.

A taxi was threading its way through gaggles of children

returning from school. Tanner waved at it. The driver didn't appear to see them. Tanner swore: on New China, nobody hailed passing cabs. He strode in front of the vehicle, whose tires crunched to a stop on the painted concrete. They piled inside the small car, deaf to the protesting cries of the driver, whose shift was over—he wanted to be home before the Eye came out! Tanner shushed him by slipping him a fifty-yuan note.

"To the Friendship Bridge, and don't spare the amps! You get another fifty yuans if we make it alive."

"Let me guess," muttered Hamakawa dryly, "you'd always dreamed of saying that, right?"

The taxi took off as fast as it could, hindered by the schoolkids crowding the streets. Tanner examined Qingling's injured hand. It was a bad cut, still bleeding. Bloody streaks marred her blue dress. Inside their luggage, he found the first aid kit bought the previous day by Fuzai. He wiped away the blood with premoistened sponges and then sutured her wounds with Band-Skin.

Just as the first gleams of the Dragon's Eye were showing above the horizon, they reached the Friendship Bridge and disembarked a few meters away from the Immigration Service office. Tanner and Hamakawa argued. It was decided Hamakawa would go to the railway station and buy three tickets for Nanxiang aboard the next train. Tanner and Qingling would catch up with him in half an hour. Hamakawa glowered in the young woman's direction, almost remonstrated with Tanner, but said nothing. He left for the taxi stand, the crowd closing around him.

Tanner took Qingling aside. "We're splitting up because we're too easy to spot."

"Is that also why we're changing cabs?"

"You're learning fast." Tanner smiled. "First, however, I'll buy you a dress. The police will be looking for a lovely young woman with a blue dress, spotted with blood; do you understand?"

Qingling hesitated. "Y-Yes. But . . . what you just said to your friend . . . Are you taking me to Nanxiang?"

"I'm not forcing you to come. But I'm afraid you would be

in danger if you stayed here."

She nodded woefully:

"But I don't have any money, any clothing, anything. What am I going to do in Nanxiang?"

"Don't worry about that, I'll give you some money. You can come back to Lengshuijiang later, or send someone to get your stuff."

She nodded again. "Everything's at Fuzai's place. I don't want to ever, *ever* see him again!"

She started to sob. Tanner hugged her, comforting her again: he was not going to abandon her, not after what she'd risked to warn them.

He found a shop selling women's clothing and picked the first dress he thought would fit Qingling. He went back to Qingling's hiding place near the bridge.

"Now, let's find you a public washroom. Go wash your hands and change. And fast! We've got to catch up with Hamakawa!"

Qingling emerged from her hiding spot and attempted a smile, slightly heartened. Her smile turned into a scowl of disgust as she considered her dress:

"I'll look like a grandmother in this outfit!"

"The main thing is not to be noticed." Tanner sighed.

TWELVE

AT THE TRAIN STATION, TANNER AND QINGLING CAUGHT UP WITH HA-makawa just in time to climb aboard the night train to Nanxiang. The unlikely assortment of cars was decidedly picturesque. The aerodynamic curves of the locomotive and a few passenger cars were recognizably European, but the tarnished metal sheeting bore the scratches of decades' worth of wear and tear. The second-class cars combined bodies of New Chinese make with Earth-made undercarriages. There were no two alike and they'd left the factory decades before, but a new coat of paint had restored the shine of the old roofs with upturned eaves. Bringing up the rear, five brand-new cars, their windows and scoured-aluminum panels proudly gleaming, proclaimed the achievements of the budding New Chinese heavy industry.

The Friday night train was full. Tanner, Hamakawa, and Qingling filed down the narrow gangway, finally reaching the three tiny first-class cabins reserved by the Japanese.

Qingling sat down dejectedly on her cabin's bench.

"It's better if nobody sees us together," explained Tanner.

"The police may have asked the employees to keep an eye out for us."

She understood, but she worried nonetheless.

"I'll see you in the dining car. Just remember that we don't know each other."

Tanner moved into his cabin. He was removing his hat and glasses when the train awoke with a shuddery growl. Lurching ponderously, the crowd along the quay—harried travelers, busy railroad employees, and assorted sellers of hats, shades, noodle soup, barbecued pork, pickled cabbage—started slipping rightward. Speed increased. The quay disappeared, replaced by a series of grimy backyards melting into a blur of black and gray streaks. Here and there, a breach in the darkening wall showed, for a fraction of a second, the pair of dragons of the Friendship Bridge, blazing with the fires kindled by the Eye.

Tanner settled in. As the crow flew, Nanxiang was only six hundred kilometers away, but it would take the train nearly twelve hours to climb up to the high plateau of the Haunted Desert, which, at an altitude of two thousand meters, cut off the Liaodongxiang Plains, north of Blue Point, from the more recent settlements in Jade River Valley. The capital, Nanxiang, stood at the mouth of the Jade.

Someone knocked. A tight-lipped conductor asked Tanner for his ticket. She wrote the number on her port-a-screen. Without adding a single comment, or even glancing at Tanner, she shut the door.

Tanner was awakened by a loud knocking. A grinning cabin boy invited the honorable passenger to come to the first-class restaurant car and partake of the humble evening meal that would be served. Before closing the door, he dropped from wooden tongs a scalding towel drenched in lemon-perfumed water. As he rubbed the stiffness out of his neck, Tanner checked his watch. He had slept almost an hour.

Outside, the grain fields of the Liaodongxiang Plains raced by at an impressive clip, under a hazy sun and ragged clouds up high. The Dragon's Eye, burning on the other side of the train, tinged with an acid green the warm hues of ripening wheat and barley.

Rising from the mirror's depths, a wild-eyed New Chinese man, his hair tousled, startled Tanner. What a face! He'd never get used to it. . . . The agent detailed his new self with a critical eye. In spite of the injections, the nose was still rather long and narrow for a Chinese, and his lips too thin. . . . The upshot was that he bore a faintly Vietnamese air, which, on the whole, he thought rather handsome. He examined his hair roots. No questioning the handiwork there. Only a prolonged scrutiny would reveal that he was wearing a wig. He cleaned his hands and face, gently combed his tangled hair, put on a fresh shirt, and decided he was suitably attired for dinner in the restaurant car.

Many passengers were already having dinner. Visibly peeved, Hamakawa was sharing a table with three rambunctious children. Further back, Qingling glanced longingly at Tanner: she was all alone at a table for four. Not for long: a young and elegant New Chinese man with a predatory smile inquired whether the young lady was expecting somebody. Qingling hesitated before signifying that she had nobody to wait for. In that case, would she be extremely offended if he went so far as to ask her the favor of keeping her company for the duration of the meal? Qingling shook her head tightly. The young man sat down triumphantly.

Tanner bowed in front of the couple, gesturing toward the two spots still available.

"Are these seats taken?"

The young man threw him a dirty look but didn't dare bar him from the available seating.

A lavish meal was served: two soups, five dishes, with beer, wine, and all the tea they could drink. There was even rice.

The young man was a prodigious talker. He had done everything, been everywhere. He knew Earth, Mars, Colony, and he had big business contacts on each, of course. He'd met with many of the world's celebrities, and president Xiao Jiping was even a friend of the family. This last comment caused Tanner to pay him more attention . . . but, no, it was only another of the young man's boasts. The unstoppable windbag was already moving on to other topics.

Pausing in mid-recitation of an anecdote so tedious even he was losing interest, the young man questioned Qingling: what did she do for a living?

"Me? Nothing worth mentioning, really," Qingling answered with exaggerated candor.

The young man threw a scornful look at Tanner, who was choking on his rice. None of which prevented him from resuming his boasting where he had left off.

The monologue of the New Chinese man was becoming as monotonous as the train's slow swaying. Tanner shifted his attention to the countryside: a fleecy carpet of bushes unrolled all the way to the horizon. The train had already left behind the cultivated areas surrounding the northern cities—Lengshuijiang, Yonggui, Yuhang, Ximen—but this fallow expanse was still part of the Liaodongxiang: the land had only recently been seeded. A couple of decades would go by before the layer of arable soil grew thick enough to allow cultivation.

Qingling rose and apologized for leaving so soon, asserting she was tired. Before the young man, interrupted in midflow, found the time to realize what was happening, she had vanished. Tanner quietly finished his meal and got up in turn, politely saluting his table companion. The young man did not respond, morosely sipping his tea. Tanner favored Hamakawa with a cheerful smile, but the other agent was too busy pacifying his table companions to return the greeting.

Back in his cabin, Tanner hardly managed to convert the bench into a bed before a discreet tapping came from the door. Qingling, blushing, slipped inside and carefully locked the door behind her. Her eyes facing the floor, she sat on the bed.

"I'm frightened, all alone in my other room. . . ."

"Please don't be. If anything happens, all you have to do is knock on the partition and I'll come right away."

Qingling tittered and reddened even more:

"You . . . you're not making things easy for me. . . . How often do you think I throw myself at a stranger?"

Tanner hesitated, torn between contradictory impulses: an almost painful urge to embrace her, caress her, huddle in her arms; and the unpleasant suspicion that Qingling had only come to thank him in her own fashion. The young woman misunderstood his hesitation. She got up, avoiding his eyes.

"Forgive me. I thought . . . I didn't want to offend you."

She opened the door. Tanner grasped Qingling's hand and closed the door softly. He gathered the young woman in his arms. Wedged between the bed and the door, they kissed long and hard. Qingling finally withdrew her lips.

"I also came to say you have a rotten sense of fashion," she added, smiling mischievously. "This dress doesn't suit me at all."

"Take it off, if you hate it so much."

The dress slid to the floor. Qingling stretched out on the bed, her slim body arching like a fine statuette of gilded porcelain in the light of the setting sun.

After making love, they remained in each other's arms, nestling in the unmade bed. Rocked by the train's gentle swaying, they let the beating of their hearts ease slowly and they watched in silence as the vanishing sun set the sky ablaze one last time. The train was losing momentum. The plains were breaking up into broad, rounded swells, and the train started to climb the gentle slope leading up to the Haunted Desert.

Qingling sighed blissfully, and stretched lazily. Tanner kissed her left nipple—almost black in the surreal blue-green twilight. She pressed herself against him, her eyes like two ponds of ink, which Tanner's gaze could not penetrate.

"You're wearing contact lenses?"

Tanner was unable to conceal his startlement, but he managed to ask, his tone detached:

"Yes. So?"

"Nothing. You're strange. And your friend too. What are you

doing here on New China? Fuzai . . ." She faltered a moment.
"Fuzai told me you were spies from Earth."

"The less you know, the safer you are," Tanner replied dryly.
In his arms, her warm body tensed: "You're not very nice."

He apologized, kissing the chin's delightful plumpness and
stroking her back.

"Believe me, the little you know is already enough to put
you at risk."

Qingling relaxed, coiled against Tanner with another sigh.
She wanted him to speak of Earth. Was it true the Terrans almost
never ate meat? That it was forbidden to have children? That the
Chinese were second-class citizens compared with the Japanese?

Tanner tried to unravel fact from fiction. Most of the young
woman's preconceptions were overstatements. What she de-
scribed was true enough, but it applied only to Southeast Asia,
not to the whole of Earth. It was still possible to live well in
Europe, for instance, even if meat was indeed more expensive
than in New China. Qingling shrugged: she wasn't interested in
Europe, only in China. Tanner mocked her chauvinism. In that,
at least, she was truly Chinese.

"And you, what kind of Chinese are you?"

"The only Chinese of his kind."

Her face scrunched up and she asked quizzically:

"What does that mean?"

Someone knocked, and they heard Hamakawa's anxious
voice:

"It's Chung. Is Miss Xun with you?"

Qingling tittered.

"Yes, she's here," answered Tanner a bit curtly.

Qingling giggled piercingly.

"Not so loud!" Tanner whispered, pinching her bottom.

Her hand on her mouth, Qingling hiccuped wildly and continued to shake the bed with her laughter. When she calmed
down, she started to fondle him again, whispering in his ear that
if he wanted to try again, she was willing. . . .

Tanner awoke in the thick of Dark Night. He gently pushed away Qingling's arm hooked around his waist, so that he could sit up. He bent and extended an arm under the bed, looking for his cryo-kit. His hand brushed against a rounded metallic surface. He pulled out the aluminum case and opened it on his knees. All the kit's accessories glittered dully in the auroral light, each one neatly secured in its place. He shrugged: perhaps he had dreamed it.

He put back the cryo-kit where it belonged and lay down again, admiring the Haunted Desert and its long dunes sleeping beneath the shifting hues of the auroras. As the years went by, the winds on New China would blow in seeds and spores from the terraformed areas, and the Earth vegetation ruling the plains would mount an irresistible assault on the plateau. However, without human intervention, the process would require centuries.

For many more decades, the plateau's sere immensity would vie for comparison with the austere Martian landscapes.

Tanner swallowed one of the skin-color capsules and went back to sleep.

THIRTEEN

"NANXIANG, THE MOST BEAUTIFUL CITY IN THE UNIVERSE" WAS A NEW Chinese byword. Maybe not the most beautiful, decided Tanner, faced with the city's reality, but surely the most picturesque. Through the train's window, earlier the same morning, he had admired the most famous sight on the planet: the New Riverine Palace, the baroque and unexpectedly sumptuous palatial seat of government. Stuck to the cliffside like an overgrown limpet, the palace overlooked the sensuous curve of the Jade, snaking along the valley's bottom, and an unrolled quilt of green and black terraces, stitched with roads like gold braid—the wealthiest neighborhoods of Nanxiang.

The train stopped in a magnificent station whose facades of red brick were buttressed by beams of *zitan*—which could only be imported from Earth—while the walls inside were paneled with red-lacquered wood.

Tanner, Hamakawa, and Qingling stopped on the station's steps, where the bustle of the travelers just off the train was not enough to mar the peaceful and subdued affluence of the surroundings, redolent of a vanished era. Nanxiang obeyed none of the austere strictures of the Japanese style. The fronts of the most humble shops boasted curlicued woodwork, elegant ideograms outlined in aluminum or lacquer scales, graceful arches, dragons, or delicate, stylized flowers. The roofs, covered with blue or ocher tiles, were often doubled, or even tripled. Beneath each window, flowers and bushes bloomed together, united in a carefully designed tumult of colors. The blithe sunshine of a Saturday morn only added to the shiny perfection of the scene, as bright as a new bauble discovered by a child's eyes.

Turning, Tanner was surprised to see Qingling sobbing silently.

"What's going on? Why are you crying?"

She sighed, wiped her tear-streaked cheeks with the back of her hand. A smile trembled on her lips as she answered, her voice very soft:

"It is true: Nanxiang *is* the most beautiful city in the universe. . . . Sometimes, I wonder why I left it."

"Are you from Nanxiang?"

She shrugged mutely with one shoulder, without answering.

"Don't you have any family to take you in?"

She bit her lip:

"I . . . I'd rather not talk about it. I've lost touch with my family."

Tanner said nothing, though it was an astonishing assertion for a young Chinese woman to make. He gave her five hundred yuans.

"Is it enough to get you on your feet again?"

Qingling gazed downward, looking pained. "So it all ends here and now?"

"We've got to go; we need to take care of some important business."

"I'd rather stay with you. Maybe I could help."

Tanner glanced at Hamakawa. Obviously opposed, the Japanese replied, his tone neutral, that Tanner was the boss. Tanner hesitated, then decided that, no, they couldn't take Qingling in tow. They agreed to get in touch, if need be, through the Nanx-iang bulletin board. Qingling made him swear to call her. Tanner promised, hugged her quickly, then ordered her to get going.

Qingling crossed the cobblestoned street, reaching a stair-case that climbed down to the riverside districts. She turned one last time toward the train station. Tanner had a lump in his throat as he answered her parting wave. Then she dashed down the stairs, soon out of sight.

Hamakawa was glaring at Tanner with half-lidded eyes, like an angry cat:

"I see you haven't completely lost your mind, just most of it," he hissed. "For a moment there, I was afraid we'd be dragging Miss Xun like a hundred-kilo millstone around our necks. Should I understand you didn't just spend the night screwing? Did you go so far as to tell her Li Zheng wasn't your real name? Perhaps you even told her you're not even Han!"

"Calm down. Fuzai suspected we were spies and told her so. She concluded that, if we were coming to Nanxiang, it was for our mission. Do you think she's dumb?"

"And now she'll be chattering about her adventures with everybody she meets! How much time do we have before the word of mouth sends the police and Tewu after us?"

"Why should she talk?" Tanner gestured angrily. "Don't for-get we owe her our lives."

"Because of a mess you yourself got us into. They should have been eliminated as soon as they saw your weapon, like I told you!"

Tanner grabbed Hamakawa by the elbow and dragged him into the shade of a giant red granite statue of the Buddha.

"Listen, Jay. You're not here to hinder me. If you have the slightest reservation about my authority or my competence in this affair, the Lengshuijiang train is heading back soon and you have all the time you need to be aboard. I'll just manage on my own the contact with Chen Shaoxing. Is that clear?"

Hamakawa looked at him steadily, making the moment last, before bowing his head:

"Crystal clear."

"Well? Your decision?"

"Do you really think I would have come all the way to Nanxiang without even visiting?"

Tanner relaxed, smiling, and clapped his partner's shoulder:

"Great! Because it's now I'll need your help the most. Do you know anybody in Nanxiang who could set up a meeting with Chen Shaoxing?"

"I've already thought about this aspect of the problem. I can't answer immediately; I've got to make a few calls first."

"There are public comcabins in the station. Make your calls, and I'll check the bulletin boards again. You never know, maybe Chen will have made up his mind to answer."

"Hope springs eternal . . ."

Chen Shaoxing still hadn't answered. Hamakawa was more successful. They were to meet with a *diaochabu* operative in an hour at the Lanting Zi restaurant—the "Orchid Pavilion."

"A *diaochabu* agent?" Tanner wondered.

On Earth, he had never worked so closely with Chinese agents. Hamakawa smiled:

"We're on New China: you've got to leave behind those Terran squabbles. Here, the Bureau, the *diaochabu*, and the Naicho work hand in hand, like most intelligence services whose countries share identical interests. Sometimes, politics do make things simpler."

They exited the station again. Tanner headed for the taxis, but Hamakawa pointed him instead toward the carriages drawn by magnificent horses, their thick coats a deep black. Before Tanner could demur, Hamakawa climbed on the running board of the nearest carriage and asked the old, wizened driver if he knew the Lanting Zi. The old man nodded sharply and gestured to the broad plaited-leather seats behind him.

"Climb in! Climb in!"

Smiling mischievously, Hamakawa vaulted into the carriage. Tanner climbed in too, not entirely trusting the tosses and squeaks of the abused suspension. The old coachman smelled the air and greeted Tanner and Hamakawa with a yellowed grin: would his honorable passengers bear with him? The Eye was set to rise and he wanted to protect his horse. He cautiously climbed down from his perch and opened a drawer set in the carriage's side. He took out a large hat and oversized shades. The horse placidly let the driver attach the protective gear around its head. The coachman worked skillfully, but in a strange, jerky fashion, his every move a study in emphasis. He favored Tanner again with a view of his ruined dentition:

"Some leave on the hat and the shades all the time. Not good, not good at all! The horse doesn't like it. But one must not forget to put them back on when the Dragon's Eye comes out again, to keep it from going blind like me."

Fumbling briefly, he climbed back up on the carriage with the curiously calculated motions of the blind. Tanner pointedly nudged Hamakawa, who seemed to be amused by the situation. The oldster shouted "Ho!" and the carriage moved off, the hoofs clattering and the iron-shod wheels clanking on the polished cobblestones of Gulouxi Street. Tanner leaned toward Hamakawa:

"Is this a joke? Do they really let blind men drive carriages?"

The oldster turned his wrinkled face toward Tanner, still flashing a wide grin:

"I don't need to see to drive. The horse sees. I just give it directions. I wasn't always blind, and for a long time, I drove carriages in Nanxiang. Now, I've got Nanxiang here."

He smacked his forehead tellingly:

"I keep track of the steps, of the turns. Left, right . . . I don't need to see."

"What happens in neighborhoods you don't know?"

"In the new developments? I ask the passengers to guide me. If the passengers don't know, I ask the passersby. The next time, I remember."

At an intersection, the equipage turned right into a wide avenue, freshly paved with sulfur, sloping gently downward. The almost blinding yellow road surface reminded Tanner of the children's rhyme:

New China is a land of marvels
Of smiling faces and happy revels
All the streets are paved with gold
And the old again feel young and bold
In the marvelous land of New China

Traffic was as dense as on Earth. Bicycles, carriages, and cabs mingled harmoniously along the newly paved street, lined with trees and luxurious gardens almost hiding the stone fronts of a multitude of small shops. A taxi buzzed past the carriage. Scornful, the coachman tilted his head toward the taxi:

"The young ones think they're so smart with their electri-cars! Ha! I still win every competition when it comes to knowing Nanxiang best. I always win! I remind them of the old proverb: 'I've crossed more bridges than you've crossed streets.' And I tell them: 'Me too, when I was young, I had better things to do than protecting myself from the Dragon in the sky. And now, witness my plight: I cannot even feast my eyes on the sweet faces of my grandchildren.' When I'm asked what must be done to enjoy happiness in this world, I say: 'Protect your eyes! Protect your eyes! The Dragon will cruelly punish you if you dare to face its gaze.' But those kids always have something better to do when they should be hearkening to the wisdom of their elders. . . ."

Zipping out from the crowd shuffling along the sidewalk, a street urchin lobbed a small object that fell on the pavement, just in front of their vehicle. The firecracker went off between their horse's legs! The horse reared, the carriage swayed dangerously, and the coachman was too busy getting his animal under control to keep talking. Meanwhile, the boy galloped back to join up with his friends, who ran off, laughing shrilly.

Once he'd finished soothing his beast, the coachman eased his own soul by coming up with some choice insults, but he was still grumbling when he spurred his horse onward again.

The avenue widened. The eastern half of Nanxiang appeared, slanting down to the river, dotted with pointed roofs and striped with the yellow ribbons of roads. Lower down, between the red and blue splashes of tile roofs, glints of sunlight reflected off the Jade.

Across the river, the west bank was steeper, and a hundred or so estates, heaped together like mahjong tiles, displayed more and more conspicuous opulence as they climbed closer to the New Riverine Palace, as baroque and oversized as any architect's hallucination.

Higher up, the ragged edge of the cliff took on an acid-green tinge, while the few clouds scudding through the sky subtly shifted colors. In the street, pedestrians remarked upon these signs, forerunners of the Eye's impending appearance. Children were reined in and rigged with hats, shades, and gloves. Adults proceeded to take the same precautions, including Tanner and Hamakawa.

The Lanting Zi restaurant was a squat building standing in the middle of Nanxiang's oldest neighborhood. One could even spot, among the ancient stone buildings, a few Terran-style low-rises, angular and massive, erected before the imposition of the traditional architectural norms in Nanxiang. The Lanting Zi, with its overadorned gables, its balcony with square pillars decorated with gourmandizing dragons, and its wainscotted walls, was in no danger of suffering the censure of the traditionalists. Above the door, a skillful brush had sketched a few characters:

BE CAREFUL WHEN YOU COME IN
BE CAREFUL WHEN YOU LEAVE.

Pushing the carved wood of the door, Tanner appreciated the wisdom of this advice. He stood on the threshold of a bright and capacious dining room, which would have been even more impressive if the plaster of the walls had been less grimy. However, it was lunchtime and the tightly packed diners avidly wolfing down dim sum dishes did not seem preoccupied with the cleanliness of the walls.

A young girl begged them, in Cantonese, to abide a few minutes, a table would be available soon.

"May we speak to Bai Jingtu?" asked Hamakawa.

The girl hesitated.

"He knows we're here."

She took them to an overheated kitchen where, amid clouds of steam, a small army of cooks was busy stuffing raviolis with pork, duck, or red bean paste, filling bowls with sweet and sour soup, and heaping stacks of wicker baskets in the boiling water of steaming woks. The young girl pointed out a fortyish, short-haired, moon-faced man, his white shirt wet with perspiration, who was supervising all the activity.

"Bai Jingtu."

The New Chinese man stood in front of Hamakawa, whose face he scrutinized, knitting his brows in concentration. Then his lips curled up in a knowing smile, as he nodded smugly:

"Now I recognize you. You cut your mustache, right?"

Hamakawa burst out laughing. "You've got a good memory."

The *diaochabu* agent smiled, sparing a brief glance for Tanner.

"Have you eaten?"

"We've got important matters to discuss beforehand," Tanner replied.

Bai Jingtu studied Tanner, examining him from head to foot. His smile took on a hint of mockery.

"Very poor manners," he whispered. "You'll never convince people you're Chinese if you go around saying such things. Reasonable people know that a missed meal is a meal lost. . . . But seriously: it's lunchtime now, I'm busy. Go and eat—we can't talk here. Go! I'll be with you within the hour, I promise."

With a deafening shout, he called a young man to him. He instructed him to find a table for his two honorable visitors and to be generous with rice and beer, for they were his guests.

All in all, the variety of dishes offered by the Lanting Zi was sadly limited, while the quality ranged from the acceptable, to the unusual, to the most distressing blandness. Hamakawa munched absently on a shrimp-flavored fried dumpling.

"This is not great cuisine, I admit. The main problem is the lack of spices. No lotus, no nutmeg, no mushrooms; they're experimenting with substitutes, but the results so far are disappointing. Peppers do grow north of Blue Point, but they have an aftertaste. And the soy sauce is not great either. With the new enzymes, it can be fermented in less than a month, but that's much too fast. Given their nostalgic leanings, it's surprising the New Chinese haven't gone back to the good old way of making it: one year of sustained fermentation in a cask. If I was Xiao Jiping, I'd pass a law!"

"You've been living too long among the Chinese; you're obsessed by food like them."

"It's true. Food could be considered to be an obsession with them. Don't they say Confucius divorced because his wife was not a good enough cook?"

"If he was so wise, he should have learned how to cook for himself," retorted Tanner.

Hamakawa didn't answer. He drank slowly from the beer tankard, eyes half closed, smiling discreetly as if he were savoring the memory of a joke.

"Sometimes, I wonder if the New Chinese aren't on the right track, if the ancient Chinese society, the very traditional society they're striving to revive here, one hundred fifty light-years away from Earth, is not the ontologically natural way for humans to organize social life."

Tanner frowned. "What are you talking about?"

"Think about it . . . Is it just a coincidence that Chinese society is the oldest and, until fairly recently, the most brilliant continuous culture in human history? How many times has China, throughout history, been invaded by barbarians and put under the yoke, before discovering that not only was its culture unthreatened but also that, in fact, its barbarian invaders were being sinicized, as if they were forced to face the truth that the Chinese lifestyle was the *ideal* way of living in societies.

"Remember the Mongols, who around 1220 took over the empires of the Jin and Sung? What did these conquerors, clearly unsuited to handling peacetime affairs, waste no time in doing?

Well aware that 'You can conquer the world on horseback, but you can't rule it from horseback,' they adopted several Chinese institutions which were, at the time, far more advanced than their counterparts elsewhere: a well-ordered fiscal system, paper money, the competitive recruitment of civil servants, the founding of libraries—going so far as to translate into Mongol the Chinese classics and official histories. Instead of erasing all traces of the vanquished foe's culture, the way the Europeans managed to do so thoroughly in the Americas, Kublai Khan ordered the History Academy—which he'd founded himself—to write the official histories of the Sung, Liao, and Jin dynasties, the three Han-dominated empires fallen under Mongol rule. In the end, a mere fifty years later, the Mongol rulers opted to choose a Chinese dynastic title, that of the Yuan."

"I can't argue with you." Tanner shrugged. "I don't know Chinese history well enough."

"You should learn. It would help you understand the whys and wherefores of things."

"My job is to carry out orders, not to question their validity."

"The right attitude for a good soldier. I predict you've got a brilliant career ahead of you at the European Bureau, even if you're obviously not smart enough to handle command."

Tanner refrained from raising his voice:

"You're playing with fire! I could report this conversation to our superiors."

Hamakawa feigned contriteness:

"True, it's a nasty habit of mine, thinking about the pros and cons of the orders I'm given. No doubt that's why I was exiled to the EFTA, to serve under that Dutch swine!"

Tanner elected to disregard the comment.

Bai Jingtu approached their table, wearing a fresh change of clothing, his hair combed carefully. Had his honorable guests enjoyed their meal? His honorable guests politely lied. Still smiling, he led them up a winding staircase. They followed a corridor paved with white tiles, pushed open a door paneled in shiny wood, entered a small sitting room.

A faint green-tinged light filtered through openwork shutters. The smell of fresh polish perfumed the air. From a hidden speaker came melancholy notes plucked from a *pipa*. The three men sat in comfortable, silk-paneled chairs made from lacquered bamboo.

Tea was served.

In a typically Chinese manner, Bai Jingtu did not come to the point right away. Avoiding the purpose for which his guests had come, he analyzed with them the tea's aroma, shared memories of Earth, lamented the rarity of rice, spoke of the Dragon's Eye and the danger of going blind. The *diaochabu* agent exhibited with understandable pride an intricately worked carpet, imported from Earth.

Tanner was almost beside himself with impatience, but pressing the matter would have been unforgivably rude. Fortunately, there was a lull in the conversation and he rushed to fill it by explaining the reasons for their coming.

Bai Jingtu scratched his chin.

"Yes, so Jay explained. But Chen Shaoxing is a personage of no small stature; one can't arrange an audience with Xiao Jiping's vice president as easily as one would hail a cab."

"All we want to know is where he lives. That might be enough to let us get in touch with him by ourselves."

"By yourselves? Chen Shaoxing lives in the New Riverine Palace, of course. But let me warn you that the civil service keeps a better watch on him than the house cavalry of the kings of old."

"Would it be possible to meet him in his official capacity?"

The *diaochabu* spy grimaced:

"Nowadays? In the middle of the EFTA crisis? Difficult, very difficult . . . May I at least know the reason of this sudden interest on the part of the European Bureau in Chen Shaoxing?"

Tanner exchanged with Hamakawa a look filled with uncertainty. His partner frowned: Chen's cover could not be compromised. The alliance of convenience between the European Bureau and the *diaochabu* was still subject to the ups and downs of Earth politics, too much so for Tanner to present the *dia-*

ochabu with a revelation of this magnitude.

"No," Tanner replied simply.

Bai Jingtu did not seem excessively put out. He pondered aloud, lost in apparent contemplation of his teacup:

"I suppose you don't want to assassinate him? No, that would be far too stupid. For such a meager result, why risk so much? Though . . . though . . . Chen Shaoxing is a much talked-about man these days. His position makes him the heir designate of Xiao Jiping. An important man, no doubt, and his disappearance would result in . . . would result in what? Bah! My mind is too tired to puzzle it out."

Bai Jingtu closed his eyes, sadness spreading over his face, as tranquil as it was duplicitous. Tanner fought to keep his tone civil:

"Whether the channels are official or not, we've got to meet with Chen Shaoxing!"

The *diaochabu* agent threw up his arms.

"Like they say on Earth: you're asking for the Moon!"

"Doesn't he have a place in the countryside where he goes to rest?"

"Several. All very well guarded."

"But perhaps easier to infiltrate."

"True, I admit."

"If he were there . . ."

"Indeed."

Tanner licked his lips. Chinese negotiations were a notorious fount of endless frustrations. Was the *diaochabu* spy ready to help them, yes or no? He resolved to smile, amused in spite of himself by the little man's smiling apathy. Yes *or* no? The question, typically Western in its brutal lack of ambiguity, would never elicit a satisfactory response. A Chinese would be prone to answer yes *and* no.

It was clear that, for his part, Bai Jingtu felt under no compunction to help out Tanner and Hamakawa. However, as a *diaochabu* agent, he was committed to collaborating with his counterparts of the European Bureau. One should not expect the conflict of loyalties to overly trouble a Chinese spy imbued with the ancient Taoist dogmas, according to which contraries should unite and opposites be reconciled. Granted, he would help Tanner and Hamakawa, but he would evince as much inertia as feasible while parceling out useful information as sparingly as possible.

"I'll see what I can do," said Bai Jingtu finally.

The *diaochabu* agent rose and left the room.

Less than half an hour later, Bai Jingtu reappeared.

"I've reached our friends inside the walls. Officially, Chen Shaoxing is on a vacation. He hasn't been seen at the Riverine Palace in at least three weeks. He's not visiting with his family. We've checked his Hunan house: he's not there. We've checked the port registry: his yacht has not budged from the docks in almost a year."

"What are you trying to tell us?" Tanner asked. "That Chen has vanished?"

Bai Jingtu seemed to be sincerely perturbed.

"I don't understand it either."

The three men fell silent, lulled by a flute's soft plaint and the noises of the crowd in the street, beneath the window. Tanner and Hamakawa exchanged a quizzical look. Was it all over already, their mission come to a dead end?

FOURTEEN

THE GREEN NIGHT FESTIVITIES TOOK PLACE AROUND NANXIANG'S PORT, opposite the Lanting Zi. In the capital city, the celebration was clearly more family-oriented than in Lengshuijiang. The docks were overrun by a noisy crowd adorned with hats, masks, and night-glow colors. As if the babies crying and the overexcited children yelling their heads off weren't enough, firecrackers were popping in bursts. At times, the booming of fireworks made the ground shiver, just as the sky brightened with flashes more luminous by far than the distant rippling of the auroras.

Tanner, who had followed Bai Jingtu and Hamakawa half-heartedly, finally gave in to the noisily festive mood. Now that the border between the EFTA and New China was practically closed to non-Han, how many Europeans would henceforward be able to boast they had taken part in the famed revelries of the Green Night—and in Nanxiang, no less!

The three men plowed their way through the crowd in order to reach the riverbanks, where they joined bystanders surrounding a group of teenagers. In the shifting light of electric torches,

the youth drew from the water a net half filled with strange creatures dripping fluorescent sparks. The teens fished out the alien
beings and displayed them to the onlookers. One member of the
group came up to Tanner:

"Don't be scared, it won't bite you."

Circumspectly, Tanner took one of the strange creatures in
the palm of his hand. Like the entire indigenous fauna of New
China, it resembled nothing familiar. Cold and wet, about ten
centimeters in length, the animal was approximately shaped like
a bluish, half-peeled banana, the ragged "peelings" obviously
meant to act as fins for propulsion. Out of the water, the creature
was wriggling helplessly.

"It can endure the open air for hours before dying," explained Bai Jingtu. "At night, I mean. In the sun, they dry out
quite fast. A completely useless beastie. Like most of the native
flora and fauna."

"What if I ate some?"

"As nourishing as plastic. And it tastes horrible. Trust the
Cantonese to be adventurous in such matters: everybody knows
now there's nothing edible on this planet."

"I've seen meat being smoked with herbs from the sea."

"Watergrass." Bai Jingtu nodded. "Yeah, it's the new flavor
of the month. With tea, with meat . . . Some teenagers even
closet themselves inside smokehouses to smell like watergrass for
their girlfriends. Other spices are extracted from aquatic plants:
'black chili,' 'cat's-claw' . . . that's about it. Well, there's also the
'glass buds,' but they should be taken in moderation, they're
rather toxic."

They resumed their desultory stroll along the river. The pier
was lined with luxury yachts, the polished aluminum mirroring
the Eye's incandescent pinpoint and the kaleidoscopic display of
the fireworks; with alga-gnawed, wooden-hulled tramp freighters;
and with sailboats, their fiberglass sides tarnished and battered,
all gathered in a seemingly haphazard jumble. Light showed in
most of the portholes, while laughter and scattered words
reached the strollers on the wharf, letting them know that Green

Night was also being celebrated on the river.

Tanner asked Bai Jingtu if he could recognize which of the craft moored along the wharf belonged to Chen Shaoxing? Bai Jingtu pointed to the end of the pier.

"Of course! It's not very far from here."

"Let's go have a look," Tanner proposed.

The crowd thinned out as they got closer to the water's edge. With his leather-encased hand, Bai Jingtu pointed out a trim white cruiser: Chen Shaoxing's personal yacht. The accommodation ladder was raised, and the ship seemed deserted. Tanner assessed the distance between the pier and the forward balcony. Roughly two meters. He checked that the revelers didn't appear to be paying any attention to them, then took off his hat and his gloves, entrusting them to Hamakawa.

"Hey, what are you doing?" Bai Jingtu exclaimed.

Tanner counted off his steps as he backed away from the edge so that he could gather speed before jumping. Only then did he run and leap above the ink-black waves. He managed to hang on without getting noticed. He stepped over the rail, waving quickly to his comrades: Bai Jingtu was disconcerted, but Hamakawa simply nodded, his inscrutable smile unstirred.

The young spy crossed the deck, entered the cockpit, and reached the door of the helmsman's cabin. It was unlocked. He opened it . . . and stood nose to nose with a young New Chinese man, half naked and frantically swinging a long steel crank. Wide-eyed, his voice hoarse with fear, the man unleashed a deafening yell and jumped Tanner, who was almost taken unaware.

The European spy's reflexes saved him. He crouched just as the crank skimmed his right ear. With a calculated violence, Tanner hit the man's groin with the flat of his hand. His opponent folded, grunting wordlessly. The crank dropped down the stairs, clanging noisily and landing at the feet of a young girl, completely naked and utterly terror-stricken, who vanished with a panicked shriek.

Tanner didn't stop to curse, pushing aside the young man and hurtling down the stairs. He found himself in a plush cabin, appointed with mahogany wainscotting and lacquered furniture, the varnished wood reflecting the single lamp's orange light. Smells of food and drink filled the air. On a low table stood an almost empty whiskey bottle amid the meal's remains. Cowering at one end of the bed, modestly draped in a silk coverlet, the young girl begged Tanner not to hurt her.

Tanner faltered for a second, then checked there were no other exits. He jabbed an authoritative finger in the woman's direction.

"You, I don't want you to bat an eyelid!"

On the verge of tears, she assented.

He went back up the narrow staircase to fetch the young man, who, red-faced, was still cupping his genitals with a look of agony. Tanner lifted him bodily, carried him down, and sat him in a leather-covered armchair.

"Come on, stop whining! It's not broken, and it'll work again one of these days; don't worry . . ."

The young man bared his teeth. "Who are you?"

"I'm asking the questions! So, who are *you*?"

"Zu . . . Zu Zeng."

"Very good, Zeng." Tanner nodded toward the young woman. "I see you're enjoying the Green Night in your own way. . . ."

Zu Zeng ground his teeth, didn't answer.

"I'm not sure the boat's owner would be happy to know his watchman is paying to get laid by whores in the master bed."

Tanner had hit the jackpot: the young man, scandalized, stared at the spy wide-eyed. He opened his mouth, produced an inarticulate moan, gulped, and then protested in a subdued tone:

"She is not a whore. And I'm not a . . . a watchman, like you say. I'll have you know this boat belongs to my father, you . . . you . . ."

He didn't dare finish. Tanner said nothing, dumbfounded: Chen Shaoxing didn't have a son. Had Bai Jingtu—the fool!—identified the wrong boat? He asked incredulously:

"You're Chen Shaoxing's son?"

Zu Zeng opened his mouth to answer, then fell silent, a mix of suspicion and malice flashing in his gaze. However, the girl was unable to hold back any longer:

"He's not Chen Shaoxing's son! This boat no longer belongs to—"

"Don't tell him anything, Tui!" Zeng interrupted, not very convincingly.

"But tell him, Zeng, tell him everything!" she begged him. "Don't you see he's going to kill us if—"

"Tell me what?"

Zu Zeng clamped his mouth shut, a defiant if somewhat unsteady glare in his eyes. Since Tanner was not in the mood for a torture session, he shifted his assault to the weakest link.

"Tell me what?" he asked Tui. "Speak, and I won't hurt you. But if you hide anything from me, I'll be merciless."

"This boat no longer belongs to Chen Shaoxing! He swapped his yacht for the boat belonging to Zeng's father."

"Swapped? Why?"

"I don't know!" blurted the young woman. "We don't know! Zeng's father thought it was bizarre, but he accepted because his yacht was smaller and Chen was a friend, a friend of Zeng's father, and—"

"When did this happen?"

She started sobbing. "I don't know . . . I don't know . . ."

"Roughly five weeks ago," confessed Zeng, his voice tired.

"Where is this yacht? Here, in the port?"

"They set sail the day after the swap."

"For what destination?"

"I don't know, I swear!"

"Did your father know where it was heading?"

"No! Shaoxing didn't want anybody to know. . . . You must believe me!"

"The name of your boat?"

Zeng blinked, unable to answer.

"The *East Breeze*," Tui answered.

Tanner strode toward the staircase, turning back one last

time to glare at the young couple. He assumed a threatening tone to say, his voice low:

"I'm from the Tewu. If I were you, I'd think twice before telling anybody what just happened. Nobody is safe from the Tewu, not you, not your father, not your family, and not her. . . . Do you understand what I'm saying?"

The young man nodded, agreeing emphatically, pale with shame and fear.

"And a great Green Night to the both of you!"

Tanner quickly climbed back into the cockpit, lowered the accommodation ladder, and walked onto the wharf, where Hamakawa and Bai Jingtu were waiting for him. The trio cleared out, melting into the crowd.

Hamakawa, Tanner, and Bai Jingtu were having tea alone in an alcove of the Lanting Zi. On the other side of the lacquered straw partition, the hubbub had not diminished noticeably. Green Night, especially on Saturdays, was an excuse to party very late.

Bai Jingtu cautiously tasted the scalding tea. Clearly, he was irked that an agent of the European Bureau had procured an important piece of intelligence before his very eyes, when his own agents had so signally failed.

"Chen's ruse has caught us off guard," the *diaochabu* spy admitted reluctantly. "But why would he pull such a vanishing act? Was he afraid of your coming? What's the connection between you and New China's vice president? Truly, you are a man wrapped in mysteries."

"My mission is in the best interests of both our countries."

"So, I guessed right: you came to assassinate Xiao Jiping's heir."

Neither Tanner nor Hamakawa offered any comment. Bai Jingtu's smile shifted into a grimace:

"A person slightly less forbearing than me might be offended by such distrust."

Tanner sharply set down his cup of tea on the straw mat, about to deliver a stinging retort, but Hamakawa anticipated him:

"We regret that we cannot repay fully the priceless assistance generously rendered us by the *diaochabu*."

Unperturbed, Bai Jingtu acknowledged the kind words, defusing Hamakawa's sarcasm.

Tanner's stomach churned with impatience. Chen Shaoxing had disappeared, and they were drinking tea and quarreling. But what else could they do? The agents of the *diaochabu* were trying to access the port registries in order to ascertain the destination of the *East Breeze*. In theory, the information was available through the bulletin boards, but the search functions required privileged access or the help of an employee. And, at this time of the day, all offices were closed.

Therefore, he concluded resignedly, they could do nothing but wait.

FIFTEEN

TANNER STRUGGLED UP, UTTERLY LOST. YET, HE'D SLEPT WELL, IN SPITE of the restaurant being right under his bedroom, with revelers streaming in and out all through the night. Nevertheless, waking up was hard. The room was dark, suffocatingly so. He shook himself, half-opened one of the shutters of lacquered wood. A burning red orb was floating above the horizon. The sun was rising? But no, the Dragon's Eye was already blustering near the zenith. Therefore, the sun was setting. Green Night was going to begin. Green Night *again*? Had he slept at all? Why did he feel so strange? Anxiety coursed through his veins: had he been drugged? Why had he trusted that infernal Bai Jingtu?

Panicking, he went through his suitcase, stabbed his finger with a tailor's needle, grabbed his gun, and strode toward the door, ready to shoot. In the shadowy reaches of his room, a sudden motion drew his attention. He aimed his pistol at the shape of a tall New Chinese man, bare naked, who pointed the same gun back at him.

Tanner lowered his weapon: what was happening to him?

Instead of making him laugh, the mistake caused him to shake, shivers crawling down his spine. . . . Was he going crazy? The figure in the mirror returned his bewildered glance.

He took his watch out of his dressing gown's pocket. He was unable to . . . he was no longer able to make sense out of New China's schedule. The indications provided by his watch were senseless, utter gibberish meant to confuse him. Green Night, sectors, Dark Night, the Dragon's Eye, all joined in the absurd whirlwind blowing through his mind. He was losing it, he was losing it . . .

He lay down on the unmade bed, keeping his eyelids closed with his fists, breathing steadily, straining to recover his balance. All newcomers to a planet suffered from disorientation. The stranger the planet, the more severe the disorientation syndrome. Usually, it never progressed further than fits of momentary confusion, though a handful of less resilient travelers had fallen prey to states of paranoid and even murderous dementia. The only real cure was a gradual acclimatization in quiet and restful surroundings.

Tanner had done the exact contrary. He was now paying the price.

When he regained a measure of serenity, Tanner looked at his watch again. It was Sunday morning. Indeed, he had slept. The sun was setting, like every Sunday morning this time of the year. In less than an hour, Green Night would take over. Like every Sunday morning. Everything was normal.

Perfectly normal.

Tanner put on his dressing gown and went to the bathroom.

He scrutinized his appearance: an almost imperceptible red-haired stubble roughened his cheeks. He shaved carefully. He was starting to make out his real hair at the base of his wig, though one had to know where to look. Had the swellings of his cheekbones and eyelids gone down? No, he was getting used to his new face, that was all. He stuck out his tongue: the purplish coloring was gone for good. Still disoriented, he tried to remember if he'd swallowed a capsule the evening before. Forgetting to take one capsule might not be catastrophic, but he was annoyed with the gap in his recollections.

Once he was cleaned up, Tanner examined his mirror image. He was satisfied with his new face: indeed, he was growing to like it. And yet, it had not been made to last. Two weeks, the cosmetician had said. Five days ago—four of which he'd spent on the New Chinese continent. Tanner shook himself: he felt like he'd crossed over months ago.

Tanner and Hamakawa were breakfasting in the small sitting room where they had first met with Bai Jingtu, when their host strode in.

"The *East Breeze* was entered on the roll of Linzi's harbor, and it also appears in the registry for the Shandong locks!" he announced. "By then, it was very close to Ming Lake. Unfortunately, the fiber optics network doesn't reach all the way to Ming Lake, so we've been unable to contact the Daping harbor authorities, but all lakebound shipping goes through Daping. Once the Eye sets, we can try getting in touch by radio."

"Is it possible to know if Chen Shaoxing was aboard?" asked Tanner, though he did not expect a positive answer.

"No," answered Bai as if it was obvious. "Names of passengers are not taken down for a simple transit through the locks. We're not on Earth: here, people are free to go where they will."

Tanner switched topics. "How can we get to Ming Lake?"

Bai Jingtu chuckled. "You're not easily discouraged, I see. That's good. The railway extends as far as Linzi, of course, but then you'll have to go by boat or by airship."

"No road? No railway?"

"The railway is under construction. As for the road, it's more of a trail. One look at a map would make you think twice about taking it, Mr. Li. We're talking about five hundred kilometers of complete desert. Such a crossing should not be attempted on a whim. You would need a car, which you don't have. And rental agencies are thin on the ground in New China, especially in the outlying towns. I doubt that you could prepare such an expedition in fewer than three days. And I'm being wildly optimistic."

Tanner scowled:

"I'm not eager to travel by airship. I'm told the identification checks are extremely stringent."

Bai Jingtu nodded slowly:

"Yes, such a trip is indeed fraught with difficulties."

Tanner and Hamakawa apologetically took their leave: they wished to discuss the next stage of their trip privately. They locked themselves inside Tanner's room. The young agent criss-crossed the room, mutely channeling his frustration into his pacing. Hamakawa sat in a contemplative slouch, the picture of unconcern. Nevertheless, he finally lost patience with Tanner:

"Will you stop that?"

Tanner took out the comscreen from his suitcase and motioned for Hamakawa to get closer. They both sat in front of the screen, while Tanner tapped nervously.

Let's talk via the screen. They must be listening.

Hamakawa nodded; that much was obvious.

Bai doesn't want to help. Could find us a car or boat . . . Doesn't want to. Deliberately unhelpful!!!

The Japanese scratched the tip of his nose. That much was obvious, too.

Airship? typed Tanner.

Hamakawa shook his head, typed rapidly:

DANGER. Would have to show our passports.

Boat, then. Can you handle one? asked Tanner.

Can't be that hard . . .

Tanner scowled.

Hard? Nanxiang to Ming Lake=600+ km!!! A bit far for 2 amateurs!

Hire boat and pilot. We have the money, typed Hamakawa.

Or car? More convenient . . . countered Tanner.

Too noticeable! Roads are bad! BOAT!

Tanner agreed. His partner was right: a boat was the only means of transportation that would allow them to pass unnoticed. Inspiration suddenly struck him. He disconnected the room's comscreen from the local network and plugged in his own, which allowed him to listen through a small earphone. Spotting the tap installed by the *diaochabu* was easy enough and he convinced the device that he was hanging up without making a call. Meanwhile, he got in touch with the Nanxiang bulletin board, to see if Qingling had left him a number. It took him a while to find his way among the numerous idiosyncrasies of the local system, but he succeeded in locating the message meant for him:

For you, mysterious Zheng. Call this number and see if I answer: 34 77 91. Xun Qingling

Qingling's face appeared, blurred by the poor optics, frowning. When she recognized Tanner, she exclaimed:
"Oh, Zheng, it's finally you! I don't know how many morons have been calling me since I left that message on the system!" Tanner typed hurriedly:

I can't communicate vocally. You can speak, I hear you, but I'd rather not speak.

The young woman peered into the visual pickup:

"Zheng? I can't hear you . . . Is that normal? Are you writing all that stuff on the screen?"

Tanner nodded sharply. Qingling, distraught, stammered:

"But . . . I can't read Terran."

Tanner gazed heavenward. Another one who couldn't read pinyin! He shifted part of the screen to a graphic mode and awkwardly started tracing characters with his finger.

Where can we meet?

"Why not here, at the Beautiful Meadows hotel?"

Second question: would you know how to handle a boat on the river?

She nodded, wide-eyed:

"Why, sure. Doesn't everybody?"

The train from Nanxiang to Linzi didn't offer the same amenities as the one from Lengshuijiang. The shiny new locomotive alone was of New Chinese make. Like a prince trailed by tattered beggars, the new locomotive hauled a motley assemblage of old wood-paneled cars on Terran-built frames. The train was rushing through Dark Night, between the Jade and unseen fields, producing an impressive—and, if you asked Tanner, rather worrisome—clatter as it left the bright suburbs of Nanxiang far behind.

It was Monday morning, and the train was full: businessmen, contract workers, farmers returning home with their families after a weekend in the city. There were children everywhere you turned, their parents trying to get them to stay still by feeding them lollipops and yogurt.

Tanner, Hamakawa, and Qingling shared the same perforated metal bench. Opposite them, three sturdy laborers were unashamedly eyeing Qingling up and down. Fortunately, they got off after an hour's traveling, in Dunhuang, a small town built on a bank of the Jade. All that could be seen of it were its lights, scattered like an open star cluster across the valley's floor. Two old crones, chattering in a thick Yunnan dialect, got on, with a bored-looking schoolboy in tow.

Qingling recapped. The ideal choice would be a motorboat, but she wasn't hopeful. Boats running on ethanol were far and few between; it was doubtful they would be able to find one. And even if they did, could they get the amount of fuel needed to reach Ming Lake? Tanner was telling her that money was not a problem, but securing a sufficient stock would be. Ethanol was reserved for functionaries, the police, and the army. Asking for too much was the best way to get noticed.

The ideal second choice was a sailboat with an auxiliary motor. With a bit of luck, the sail would do the job, letting them save on ethanol. If worst came to worst, they could even rent a sailboat without a motor, though that would be tempting fate. What if they were becalmed in the dead center of Ming Lake? Qingling sighed: they should have rented a boat in Nanxiang, where the choice was better.

Tanner didn't bother repeating that he refused to waste two days sailing from Nanxiang to Linzi. The train was much faster. Furthermore, though he didn't dare tell Qingling, he'd been in a hurry to leave Nanxiang, where the whole situation with the *diaochabu* was starting to make him feel antsy.

After calling Qingling, Tanner and Hamakawa had slipped away discreetly, with a note of thanks—cursory but polite—pinned to the bed. They had joined Qingling at the Beautiful Meadows hotel, rising early the next day to get seats on the train to Linzi.

Were they being shadowed? Hard to say, with so many people aboard the train. Why would Bai Jingtu have spared an agent to watch two spies from the European Bureau? Because it was the duty of any intelligence service: to find out what was happening, just in case . . .

Hamakawa boasted he never forgot a face. Tanner was relying on his gift to help them spot any unwanted company.

Stewards appeared, propelling carts atop which teapots and dim sum wickerwork baskets wobbled unsteadily. The passengers ate, the best way to while away the four hours of a tedious night-time trip.

Huddled within a small loop of the Jade River, Linzi sprawled lazily inside those confines, garden plots and houses interspersed in a pleasing jumble. Though most homes respected the ancient architectural traditions, the train went by a cluster of concrete buildings, their polished surfaces turning yellow as the sun rose. In any European suburb, they would have fit right in and they reminded passengers, if necessary, that they had put almost two hundred kilometers between them and the severe strictures of the New Chinese capital.

The brakes whimpered once, the train came to a stop, and the three travelers stepped out in a vast station, square and white, though the austere walls were enlivened by hundreds of gaudily colored posters, splashed with enthusiastic inscriptions denouncing Terran imperialism and calling, sometimes crudely, sometimes with considerable comic verve, for the severing of all diplomatic ties as well as the expulsion of the Enclave's bureaucrats. Some of these *dazibao* preached hate of all things Terran with a frenzied fury. Others expressed concisely the frustration of a people controlled by a world that was no longer theirs. A few, in the guise of intricate poetry, exuded the bittersweet sadness common to those who were exiled forever from their native land.

Qingling noticed Tanner's interest:

"And you, which side are you on?"

Tanner apologized: lost in his perusal of the *dazibao*, he hadn't heard her question.

"What do you think of New China's grievances?"

"I don't like that kind of question." Tanner sighed. "My opinion doesn't matter. I must do my job, that's all."

Hamakawa joined them, carrying the rest of their baggage, and Tanner said no more.

There didn't seem to be any taxis. They asked a young girl selling steamed pastries, and she told them, surprised by their ignorance, that the docks were just behind the station. Everybody knew that!

The docks stretched along the shore, as lazy and languid as the sluggish currents of the river . . . or perhaps not so lazy and languid, after all: a painstaking observer would have detected the manifold interplays between wind and wave, light and shadow, the subtle back-and-forth linking the shifting shadows cut by the rigging of ships riding at anchor and the racing eddies gilded by the morning sun. As the port's size became evident, they decided to separate, leaving Hamakawa at a restaurant terrace with their stuff while Tanner and Qingling went off to look for a means of transportation.

His face unreadable, Hamakawa took over a wooden bench and ordered some tea.

Tanner and Qingling visited the port information office, where they obtained a list of the sailing craft for hire. It was a short list. The clerk explained the listings weren't complete: many owners were content to set up a FOR RENT sign on the deck of their boats instead of going through the port office. Tanner checked the port registry of ingoing and outgoing ships. He found a month-old mention of the *East Breeze*: Chen Shaoxing's yacht had indeed gotten this far.

First, Tanner and Qingling eliminated all the larger craft as well as the more extravagant sailboats. In theory, the financial resources of Tanner and Hamakawa were unlimited; in practice, this far from Lengshuijiang, fund transfers would be complicated and would require a searching examination of their credentials, passports, and implants. Aboard the train, a quick inventory had shown Tanner and Hamakawa held almost 15,000 yuans in cash. It was a sizable sum, but it would dwindle quickly if they needed to buy fuel for a motorboat.

In this respect, unfortunately, Qingling's qualms were justified: there were no motorboats among the craft for hire. The office was provided with a small radio transmitter. Since the Dragon's Eye was not in the sky to perturb radio communications, Qingling was able to call the boats with receivers. Among them, only one seemed to answer their needs, but it was a schooner, much too expensive and requiring at least two experienced crew members in addition to Qingling.

They decided to canvass in person the ships tied up in the harbor. Qingling found a fine little sailboat with rigid sails and an auxiliary motor, exactly what they were looking for. But the little old man basking in the sun as he worked on the hull refused flat out when they revealed their destination. Ming Lake? Too far! He would let his ship go only as far as Nanxiang.

Tanner flashed a few 100-yuan bills. The owner looked at him askance: so the stranger was rich, but that didn't turn him into a sailor to his liking. You needed some seasoning to make the three-hundred-kilometer trip through the Haunted Desert! Putting an end to the matter with a parting scowl, he made it clear he was not interested.

For another hour, Tanner and Qingling made the rounds of the floating labyrinth, in vain. Somewhat disheartened, they walked back and found Hamakawa dozing quietly in front of an empty plate and a cold teapot. The Japanese stretched fluidly when he spotted his companions, a surprisingly self-satisfied smile on his lips.

Qingling sighed as she sat down. She was hot, she was tired, and she was hungry enough to eat a pangolin. They ordered fried noodles and fish. Qingling excused herself and left for the washroom.

Hamakawa, who'd been waiting for it, seized his opportunity and muttered, without budging from his seat:

"We *are* being tailed. One man and one woman. They're sitting behind me: the man is small, something of a charmer, in a gray suit; the woman is wearing a blue dress, glasses, and her hair in a bun."

Tanner spotted them easily; they were sitting nearby. Entirely unremarkable in outward appearance, they were eating without speaking.

"They were aboard the train. At the station, they followed us to the docks. Until then, it wasn't worth mentioning. I started paying attention when, after we separated, I spotted the woman, left all alone in the park over there. And, hey, guess who showed up not five minutes after you returned? The same man. He was tailing you."

Tanner congratulated Hamakawa. "Not a word to Qingling. For now, let them have their fun. We'll see to them later."

When Qingling returned, she related for Hamakawa's sake their fruitless search for an adequate embarkation. Over her strenuous objections, they decided to go on to Shandong by commercial shipping and wait till they got to Ming Lake before hiring a sailboat. Qingling sulked, complaining that they didn't trust her and hadn't really looked yet, that it would be even more difficult to find a sailboat around Ming Lake.

"That doesn't make sense," countered Hamakawa. "There are very few roads around Ming Lake. Most everything is done by boat. Surely, it must be easy to rent one."

Qingling agreed reluctantly that Hamakawa was probably right.

"Now it's my turn to stretch my legs," he said. "I'll go find us a means of travel to Ming Lake."

Hamakawa strode away, walking fast. Out of the corner of his eye, Tanner watched the man in the gray suit. He went through his pockets. What was he looking for? Cigarettes? He was out? Grimacing petulantly, he whispered a few words to his wife. He rose, appeared to take his bearings, then hurried off in pursuit of Hamakawa. His wife continued to sip her tea, gazing drowsily at the docks, the river, and the green billows of the low hills on the opposite bank.

"What are you watching?" Qingling finally asked. "Something strange has been going on between the two of you for the last little while. . . . You're hiding something from me."

"We're hiding *lots* from you!"

"Don't make fun of me. You've been on edge ever since we came back from the docks. You weren't like that this morning."

"You'll know soon enough."

Qingling reddened and hissed coldly:

"If I'd wanted male condescension, I would have stayed with Fuzai."

Tanner gaped at her. "It's for your own protection."

She ground her teeth. "Sure, keep your secrets if you need them to lord it over me, and feel so high and mighty! If that's what you call protecting me, I . . . I . . ."

Her eyes shone with unshed tears. Tanner sighed:

"I'm sorry; I shouldn't have been so abrupt. But you must also understand that I can't go around blabbing my secrets to all and sundry. I'm a man"—he stumbled over the right wording—"with momentous responsibilities."

He sipped a mouthful of tea. "I'll tell you this. We've been followed since our departure from Nanxiang. Don't look around you, but I'm talking of the slim woman in a blue dress sitting over there."

He summarized Hamakawa's observations. He admired her self-control: she never glanced toward the other table. Giving in to a sudden impulse, he added:

"Qingling, there's something else you should know. I'm not . . ." No, he could not tell her that, not now. "My real name is not Li Zheng. And my partner isn't really called Chang Chung. But, right now, it's better for you not to know our real identities. And believe me, this is *truly* for your own protection."

"And your mission?" Qingling asked, after remaining silent awhile. "It's not turning out the way you hoped, is it?"

Tanner laughed curtly. "My mission? No, not at all."

"The person you wanted to see in Nanxiang is gone to Ming Lake?"

"Yes."

"It's the same person you expected to meet in Lengshui-jiang?"

"Yes."

"Why won't he or she see you?"

"I don't know."

"Is it a high-ranking person?"

Tanner laid a finger on the woman's plump lips.

"My turn to interrogate you: in Lengshuijiang, why did you risk Fuzai's anger to warn us?"

Qingling's eyelids fluttered:

"Isn't it obvious? Because I liked you well enough. . . . Because you were kind to me . . . and because . . ."

"Because what?"

"As a way to . . . I'd had enough! You know, life with Fuzai was not exactly loads of fun."

"As a matter of fact, I was wondering how you ended up with a guy like him. And that thing about your family . . . are you angry with them?"

She squirmed in her seat, ill at ease. Her gaze moistened and her throat tightened as she told her story.

The Xun family was neither poor nor rich, but everybody agreed it was one of the most respectable families in the small village of Majitang, east of Nanxiang, on the Jade's banks. Qingling's father, Xun Xiongxiong, had emigrated from Earth when he was young and, ever since, he had thought of New China as his homeland. What his occupation—he ran a small composting and recycling business—lacked in prestige, he made up for in domestic bliss, since he was the master of a large house, and his wife, Fuhua, had blessed him with two boys and three girls: a lifestyle that would have been unthinkable on Earth.

Their firstborn was a son, gladdening the hearts of his parents. The secondborn was a girl, who was named Qingling, a quiet and merry child who grew up to be a proper and beautiful maiden, reared in the pieties and respect of the ancient customs.

According to the *Yi Jing*, the trigram for the eldest daughter is *Xun*: "the wind." This correspondence between the family's name and the symbol associated with their first daughter was noticed by Fuhua, who devoted especial care to Qingling's marriage, starting to hunt prospects for her when she was hardly eight. It would be a memorable wedding, she told her husband. The important thing was not to demand a huge dowry from the parents of the groom, but to seize the chance to widen the family circle through an alliance with a greater one. Fuhua dreamed of high-ranking functionaries, of wealthy merchants, of the select circle of families descended from the first settlers. However, Qingling's mother wasn't content with mere dreams, and she made many trips to Nanxiang, staying with friends or relatives, making inquiries, bargaining.

Other parents, looking for a spouse for their son, visited the Xun family. On such days, the house was clean, the beer and liquor flowed freely, and the supper lasted well into the evening. As unobtrusively as possible, the visitors would study Qingling; coming up on her sixteenth birthday. Certainly, she was pretty and even-tempered. And the dowry was set low, so low that some grew mistrustful: was the young girl hiding a secret flaw? Candidly, Fuhua would reveal her reasoning, managing as she did so to flatter her guests for having been considered.

Fuhua's dreams came true: a rich family from Nanxiang solicited Qingling's hand. To a besotted Fuhua, they explained that their son was enamored of the pretty Qingling to the point of refusing to meet other maidens. The sooner the wedding was solemnized, the sooner their son would find happiness. In addition, the dowry was more than generous, the parents being averse to having it said that their son had found himself a discounted bride.

Qingling marked with sadness the end of childhood, but her parents were happy, so she had to be happy too. She met Ansheng, her future husband, who was neither ugly nor handsome, neither especially smart nor especially dumb, and humorless without being dour. Her mother promised her that, over the years, she would learn to love him.

Qingling said little of the first months of her marriage. If they were happy, it did not last. After almost a year of life together, the couple and both families started to wonder why Qingling still wasn't pregnant.

A doctor was called in. Then a second. Then a third. Their finding was always the same, a terrible one: Qingling was barren.

For the Xun family, it spelled disaster. Ansheng sent Qingling back to Majitang and petitioned for divorce, which was almost always granted in cases of sterility. The disgruntled parents sent a lawyer to the Xun family: since Ansheng's wife was not suitable, the Xun would obviously have to repay the dowry. Fuhua and Xiongxiong protested their inability to do so. The money had been spent, of course, most of it going into the dowry of their second son's wife. The lawyer left, coldly threatening them with legal action on behalf of Ansheng's parents.

Qingling's father, crushed, was unable to believe in his misfortune. Fuhua almost went crazy: her daughter had branded the family with a shameful and indelible stigma. In Majitang, this would never be forgotten. The shame of her barrenness would taint her sisters when it came time for them to marry. Even her brothers would be affected.

When Dark Night came, Qingling fled Majitang and her shattered life. Nanxiang was still too close to her hometown, so she took the train to Lengshuijiang, using up in one go most of the few yuans in her keeping. The ensuing months now seemed like a blur. Devastated, she wandered for weeks without either money or work. One night, she was raped. It wasn't the first time, but the incident was particularly violent and sordid, sending her to the hospital. Faced with her speechless state and generally derelict condition, the staff diagnosed dementia and had her transferred to the psychiatric ward. There, a clear-sighted physician recognized that her seeming insanity was but a mask shaped by unendurable anguish. It was long and hard, but he convinced her to speak again. He then listened just as long and hard.

And then it was Qingling's turn to listen: no, she was not crazy, the ward was not the place for her. A real life awaited her outside, a life that might be worth living. Even without children . . .

The glue holding together the pieces of her cobbled-together life was still fragile, but when Qingling was ready, she moved into a quiet boardinghouse. She found a job in the shop of a ladies' tailor. Every day, the deliveryman of a restaurant next door would bring them lunch. He was small and weedy, but so very funny. He courted Qingling, never running out of fresh jokes, making her laugh. He treated her to lunch more and more often, then one Green Night took her to bed. Qingling felt an emotional upheaval, shot through with many contradictory impulses. The youth—he was called Pan Fuzai—did not mind her sterility. "Children?" He'd shrugged. "Why bother with them?" Qingling had been instantly won over; it was the first time she'd met a boy who desired her for herself and for herself alone.

Her ardor held up for a good year, until the shop owner—a wizened old woman whose half-blind gaze had lost nothing of its original sagacity—delivered herself of a short sermon meant to start opening Qingling's eyes. Didn't she understand that, for Pan Fuzai, she was nothing more than a bed warmer who doubled as a servant? The young man hardly worked, drank his girl-friend's pay, made fun of her in public, spent Green Night at the brothel with his cronies and Dark Night in prison!

Qingling tried to clear things up with Fuzai and get at the truth: surely, those were vicious lies they told about him? Fuzai took her questions badly. He threatened to hit her if she wasn't more respectful. Was it really the same youth who used to bring them lunch, always with a kind word for her? The last remnants of her ardor crumbled when she understood that, bit by bit, Pan Fuzai had been sinking into Lengshuijiang's underworld.

Terrible tales were told to her: Fuzai beating up a prostitute, Fuzai taking part in robberies, Fuzai joining a team of hired muscle to rough up the head of a rival gang. She refused to listen: no, it wasn't true, that wasn't her Fuzai . . . her Fuzai . . .

✵

Qingling drank from her teacup, wiped her cheeks, wet with tears.

"You know the rest."

Tanner said nothing. What could he add to such a sad and alien story? He took her hand, and she smiled at him.

Hamakawa came back.

"Let's hurry. I've reserved a cabin aboard the *Tao Qian,* which leaves for Ming Lake in less than an hour."

Surrounded by small sailboats and long barges designed solely for fluvial shipping, the *Tao Qian* did not lack for sheer presence. It was a neat and trim liner of New Chinese make, gleaming with a fresh layer of red and white paint. To replace the intricate rigging of a two-master designed for the high seas, the ship carried two broad, thirty-meter-high cylinders rising to meet the green skies: Magnus-effect rotor-sails, their dazzling white surfaces adorned with a few ideograms inviting the gods to send them steady winds and calm seas so that the captain could enjoy a long retirement.

The liner's freight was a mixed lot. The bow was open to load bags of cement mix, steel girders, and assorted construction supplies. Hanging over the stern, an accommodation ladder allowed the passengers to climb aboard: most were construction workers or belonged to farming families. Standing out in the line, a tall and slim European, his hair a light brown, was burdened with an unbelievable load of assorted cases and boxes. He was able, through divine intervention, no doubt, to hold out between two fingertips his ticket. It was accepted by the steward, so astonished that he never even glanced at it. Tanner, Hamakawa, and Qingling embarked next. After leaving their baggage—except for the cryo-kit, which Tanner never relinquished—in the hold, they climbed back on deck to take in the sights of the ship's departure.

The whole of Tanner's experience in things nautical amounted to a few hours aboard a small sailboat on Earth. The years spent on Mars or the Moon hadn't allowed him to acquire any additional experience, of course! All around him, the sounds and colors were such as to drive away all thoughts of his mission: bawling children, stewards calling out to each other, cranes stacking containers inside the main hold, stevedores shouting . . . The river's languid eddies were strewn with crystalline shards of sunlight as Epsilon Bootis A neared the zenith. A dry wind blowing in from the west carried entangled within it the reek of garlic cooking, the sting of ozone wafting from the unloading cranes, and the inescapably alien smells of the Jade River itself.

Qingling, leaning upon the guardrail, caught Tanner's attention and showed him their two shadows as they handed the steward their tickets and set foot aboard the *Tao Qian*.

"Don't think about them. And don't look at them."

"What are we going to do?"

"Leave them alone. Or kill them, it depends . . ."

Qingling stared at him, wide-eyed. Hamakawa glared at him reproachfully.

A whistle blared: time to leave. The stern's accommodation ladder was raised. The towering rotor-sails started turning, slowly at first, then faster and faster, emitting a subsonic hum. The electric booster cables were disconnected and the mooring lines reeled in. The rotation speed of the spinning cylinders was still increasing: subsonic at first, their silky roar became audible. The ship moved away from the pier, plowing smoothly into the river's currents. The pier was soon hidden by a forest of bare masts as they passed the sailboats riding at anchor.

Giving into his curiosity, Tanner sidled up to the rotor-sails, held back by a slender barrier. Closer up, he could feel the wind's fluctuations.

"It's the first time I've seen such a device."

"It uses the wind's power much more efficiently than an ordinary sail," explained Qingling, unimpressed. "But it only makes sense on a large ship: you need a motor to make them spin, a computer to control the speed as a function of the wind's strength and direction. Personally, I think it's all too complicated and noisy."

In spite of the presence along the bank of gaudy signaling pennants to direct traffic, the numerous lesser sailboats in the vicinity of Linzi slowed down the *Tao Qian*. Later on, the river narrowed and the liner was slowed down again by the construction of a concrete span to link the Jade's banks. The pennants ordered a full stop: a barge coming from the south had priority.

The rotor-sails spun down drastically. An old barge, propelled by its motor, the sails on its three masts flapping uselessly, slipped carefully between the temporary supports.

The Dragon's Eye chose that moment to rise. On the building site, a whistle marked the end of the workday. The workers, numbering in the hundreds, dispersed. Some clambered down into small boats with electric motors, or in sailing dinghys moored to the scaffolding. Most walked back along the bridge to reach a parking lot filled with a dozen buses. Others headed for the stables to retrieve their mounts, camels or horses. The riders untied the leads, checked the hats and shades of both men and beasts, climbed into the saddles, and trotted off, slaloming blithely between the construction cranes, buses, and pedestrians.

Tanner, Qingling, and Hamakawa sought refuge in the lounge, away from the Eye's ferocious glare. New pennants fluttered: it was the *Tao Qian*'s turn to go through. The growl of the rotor-sails was heard again, climbing an octave, and the concrete pillars were soon left behind.

With every kilometer, traffic became lighter: they were moving farther and farther away from Linzi, and the Eye's glare discouraged casual jaunts. The *Tao Qian* raced southward, the rotor-sails spinning at their maximum rate, benefiting from a steady side wind. The liner left in its wake unoccupied industrial parks, isolated houses, vegetable greenhouses, fish ponds, and, last, endless tracts of cultivated fields growing crops of UV-resistant fruits, vegetables, and cereals. The fertile land gave way to a steppe by turns luxuriant and barren, a wild country dotted with shrubs and brambles, among which frolicked hundreds of goats and sheep almost unrecognizable in their protective gear: simple, boxlike bamboo frames covered with more or less transparent UV-proof plastic. Scared by the liner's approach, a hundred or so plastic boxes ran off, steered by panicked sheep's hooves, and dashed behind a fold of land, after many tumbles and fender benders. The goats, less easily intimidated, merely looked up when the liner passed by and, as soon as there was no longer any cause for alarm, set to grazing again.

Hamakawa, Tanner, and Qingling retired to their cabin, but found it overrun by the baggage of the Caucasian traveler they had noticed earlier. The man was arguing hotly, with a broad German accent, for keeping his cases in the cabin with him, an idea vehemently opposed by the cabin boy.

"What's going on?" asked Hamakawa bluntly. "We asked for a private cabin."

Embarrassed, the cabin boy simpered:

"There are four beds in this cabin. There's only three of you."

"I demand this man and his baggage leave immediately. I reserved this cabin for us alone."

The cabin chief, a gangly and unsmiling New Chinese native, showed up and examined the tickets of everybody involved with a critical eye.

"You didn't pay for all four bunks, Mr. . . . Chang. The enjoyment of a quadruple-occupancy cabin by a group of three people is a privilege, kindly granted by the company when space allows. This is no longer the case: two passengers turned up at the last minute and there are no more bunks available. However"—he cast a side glance of the most subtle disdain in the European's direction—"I could ask another passenger to exchange."

"No need for that," interjected Tanner. He turned to the discomfited traveler. "Please forgive this little misunderstanding, and allow me to welcome you to our modest cabin."

The European's face lightened. He thanked them, voluble in spite of his limited vocabulary, insisted on shaking their hands, and introduced himself:

"Franz Gern, climatologist. I'm studying New China's atmosphere. Especially the long-term variations caused by the orbit of the Dragon's Eye during its two-thousand-year cycle around Epsilon Bootis. I'm going to Shandongxiang, the Ming Lake coastal plains, to observe cyclonic activity. Did you know that when the Dragon's Eye comes closer to New China, the risk of tornadoes increases sharply?"

There was no stopping him once he was on his pet subject and Tanner could not avoid inviting him to share their table for supper, an offer that he accepted eagerly. In the dining room, an acceptable meal was served and Franz Gern needed no one to help him make conversation. He was an inexhaustible fount of anecdotes and explanations of his avocation. Hamakawa nevertheless managed to get a word in edgewise:

"Tell me, Mr. Gern: how have you managed to get so far within New China's territory, considering the restrictions currently imposed on foreign visitors?"

Gern scratched his nose, peeling from a recent dragonburn:

"Oh, but that's because I've been here such a long time. Three local years. Long before all the current trouble. I had an assistant, but he died from a fall from horseback."

"I'm surprised they let you roam about freely."

Gern nodded quickly. "In Nanxiang, they actually served me with a notice of expulsion: I had to leave New Chinese territory within the week." He shook his head, disbelieving. "Just like that! They suspected me of espionage! Yes, you heard me right: espionage. Me, a spy? What a joke! And this idea that I should leave the planet? Just as absurd. I'm far from finished collecting data about cyclonic activity in the plains south of Nanxiang and in Liaodongxiang. In fact, the last few months, it's finally been picking up—"

"So, your presence here is utterly illegal," concluded Qingling.

He faced the young woman, winking mischievously:

"Let's just say I've managed to find a way. . . ."

Tanner lent the conversation only part of his attention. He was watching the couple from Linzi. Their followers were sitting at a small table, facing each other in the shifting shadows far from the huge, oscillating chandelier.

Because of the Eye's presence in the sky, deck activities were postponed. The meal went on and on. Gern bought a bottle of whiskey, complaining about the lack of a nobler digestive, such as cognac or kirschwasser, and all four honored the local product while pursuing a somewhat desultory conversation. Gern's vocabulary was extensive enough, but his clumsiness with tones sometimes rendered his statements incomprehensible, if not completely ludicrous. At one point, he asked Qingling a question and was interrupted by a giggle:

"Did I hear you right? You want to kiss me?"

The European's long, dragonburnt nose turned a darker shade of crimson. He tried again, modifying the intonation:

"Wo xiang wen ni—"

Tanner and Hamakawa burst out laughing. Qingling looked peeved:

"Worse and worse . . . Now you want to smell me!"

Sighing deeply, Gern gave up.

The lighting dimmed. A young singer poured into a long black lamé dress appeared on stage, along with a guitar player, a percussionist, and an organist. She sung a syrupy ballad, though her high-pitched, ethereal voice deserved better. Hesitatingly at first, couples made their way onto the narrow dance floor and unabashedly clasped each other, enviously watched by the majority of male laborers. Others, perhaps offended by the decadent Terran music, left the room with an air of vexation.

Her head turned by the whiskey, Qingling wanted to dance. Tanner stuck to his seat, chagrined: he had never learned.

"So, it's time to learn now," she insisted, pulling on his ear.

Tanner did not let himself be seduced: he was safe in his ignorance.

"And you, Chung?"

A fraction of a second later, Hamakawa recognized his pseudonym. He turned her down.

"What a gang of killjoys!" Qingling sighed.

Gern rose hopefully. "I can dance."

"Great! I thought you only knew meteorology!"

She grabbed Gern's hand and, sticking out her tongue at Tanner, led the scientist onto the dance floor. Setting the entire sky ablaze, the sun finally sank in the west. A green, unearthly half-light filtered inside the dining room, outshone by the pink spots around the dance floor, where Qingling and Gern waltzed, his arm around her waist. Tanner was surprised by the intensity of his admittedly preposterous jealousy: did he really like this young New Chinese girl so much?

"Don't make that hangdog look, you'll make me cry," teased Hamakawa. "Instead of moping after Miss Xun, we'd better take advantage of her absence to discuss the case of our two last-minute passengers. . . ."

Green Night. The deck was deserted. In the sky, the auroras fluttered like trails of sparks struck from a giant's anvil. Modulated by New China's magnetic field, the charged wind streaming from the Dragon's Eye fluctuated, oscillated, burst through the upper reaches of the stratosphere, was blocked again, ripped apart, reshaped itself, crumpled, was reborn. . . . High above, the Eye sat enthroned, overlooking this polychrome effervescence with the scornful detachment of some cruel prince. The river's glistening ribbon mirrored the sky's unrestrained revelry, a sword cut slicing through the desert.

Crouching behind a lifeboat, Tanner and Hamakawa didn't need to wait long. The sound of steps rang above the steady background hum of the rotor-sails. Moving like noiseless shadows, the two men sprang from cover and seized the man by the shoulders and the waist. He tried to struggle, but the European Bureau operatives held him too well. They half dragged, half carried him all the way to the guardrail, then pitched him overboard. A muffled cry, the splash of impact. Tanner scrutinized all he could see of the deck: good, no witnesses . . .

The *Tao Qian* was making good speed, and the spy was quickly left behind. A fluorescent circle bobbed atop the river's subdued waves: had the hat lost its owner? A head popped up, snorting and coughing. Though he took a few seconds to fully come to his senses, the man was soon swimming toward the nearest shore.

Tanner felt relief. He hadn't wanted to kill the spy, just get rid of him.

Followed by Hamakawa, he returned to their hiding place. Time passed. For the first time since his arrival in New China, he shivered. The wind coming from the desert was chilly. An hour passed, but they remained patient, sure that she would show up sooner or later.

Tanner shook awake Hamakawa, who was dozing. Somebody was coming. Small and lithe, moving with hurried footsteps: a woman. Tanner gasped, dismayed: it was Qingling! Hamakawa spat a profanity. Tanner rushed out to grab the young woman and drag her back under cover.

"I *ordered* you not to budge from the cabin!" hissed Tanner.

He could hardly see the trembling lips beneath the hat brim and the large shades.

"But you've been gone for hours! I was worried—"

Hamakawa shushed them; he'd heard something. Tanner moved his mouth near Qingling's ear.

"Don't move! Don't speak! Just don't *do* anything!"

A shape appeared on the afterdeck. She stopped right away, circumspect. She had probably been tailing Qingling and found her abrupt disappearance puzzling. A greenish-white gleam came from her hand: even seen from afar, the dagger seemed to be a sharp and vicious piece of work. She stepped behind a ventilator intake, with only a crescent-shaped slice of her hat, silhouetted against the auroras, betraying her presence.

Tanner cursed the turn of events. Impossible for them to leave their place of concealment: the spy would be sure to spot them. It was a ludicrous stalemate. Were they going to spend all night frozen in place?

Hamakawa tugged on Tanner's sleeve. He laid a hand on the guardrail and gestured toward the river. Tanner didn't understand. Hamakawa got rid of his hat and gloves, slipped over the rail, and hung by his fingers from the bulwark. His feet swung freely above the shimmering waves. Wasting no time, he moved sideways, his chest stuck to the hull, his face twisting with the strain.

Qingling was biting her nails to the quick. Tanner tensely admired one more time the sheer guts of his partner. After a century's worth of effort, Hamakawa was given the all-clear by Tanner: he was no longer in the other spy's field of vision; he could climb back up. Hamakawa did so, expending the last of his strength to avoid the slightest noise. He then slumped to the deck, spent, breathless, clenching and unclenching his aching fists. He got up again, climbed a ladder leading to the top deck. His shape capered across the sky, blotting out the auroras and the soaring pillars of the rotor-sails, before dropping into a crouch just above the ventilator intake.

Tanner emerged from his hiding place and unflinchingly made straight for the spy. The hat's crescent jumped up. Fight or flee? She chose to flee. Like a tiger, Hamakawa pounced on his prey. He was almost foiled: grasping that Tanner's companion could not be far, the woman had been expecting such a move. She eluded her attacker's hold, and the blade whistled through the air, just missing his jugular. Hamakawa tripped. Firmly clutched in a black glove, the blade rose up . . .

Tanner caught her wrist, twisting it, kneed the woman's thigh, and clouted her over the ear. Her body went limp. Almost regretfully, her hand opened and released the dagger, whose point buried itself into the wooden deck. Hamakawa and Tanner mercilessly dragged the woman all the way behind the lifeboat and sat her up beside Qingling, petrified by the scene.

Tanner tore off the spy's hat and shades, jamming his gun against the sweat-covered temple.

"Speak or die! Who are you working for? What's your mission?"

"Where's my . . ." stammered the spy.

Tanner slapped her twice. He had to unnerve her, keep her from thinking.

"Your friend refused to talk. So now he's talking to the fish at the bottom of the river. Do you want to live or die? Answer me! Now!"

Hamakawa pulled her by the hair, adding:

"Answer us! Do you want to live or die?"

"I want to live. . . ."

"Who are you working for? Quickly, now!"

She spat in his face. Tanner feigned anger, and he grasped one of the spy's fingers, bending it backward. He changed his mind: if they threw her overboard, broken fingers might keep her from swimming. Instead, he pressed the end of his gun over her right eyelid. He pressed harder. The woman's breathing grew labored. He increased the pressure.

"You won't have to get old to become blind."

"*Diaochabu!*" she said, her breath rattling.

Tanner slightly relaxed his pressure:

"Under Bai Jingtu's orders?"

"Yes . . . No!"

"Yes or no? Be more specific, and stop wasting our time!"

"The orders came from higher up . . . higher than Bai . . ."

This answer baffled Tanner for a fraction of a second.

"What do you mean, 'higher than Bai'? From Earth?"

She faltered. Hamakawa knotted another turn of her hair around his fist.

"Keep talking."

"From the Enclave . . . inside the Enclave . . ."

"Who inside the Enclave? Names. We want names."

"It was . . . it was Bloembergen, from the European Bureau."

Hamakawa shook his head, a wild grin on his face.

"I can't believe it. . . . The fat son of a bitch!"

"Your mission?" insisted Tanner.

"To keep track of your movements."

"Why?"

He slapped her. Qingling was suddenly unable to bear any more:

"Stop hitting her! Stop!"

"Qingling, this is none of your business!"

Tanner turned back to his victim. He repeated, not as loud: "Why?"

"To find your contact."

"And?"

"Determine his identity. And bring back the information to the EFTA. That's all!"

"Is that really everything? What about us? What were your instructions concerning us?"

Her silence spoke volumes. The two European agents looked at each other: there was nothing to add. Hamakawa released the woman. With his gun, Tanner pushed her against the guardrail.

"We didn't kill your partner, we pushed him overboard. I suggest you leave by the same route—dead or alive, it's your choice."

She rubbed her smarting right eye, and she gazed at the dark waters flowing by. She sighed, then grabbed at her waist. Tanner trained his gun on her.

"Don't try anything!"

She scowled. "I can't swim in this dress."

She stripped, tying the dress around her neck. She was a pitiful and grotesque sight, her cheap underwear faded by the years, her nose bruised, her lean thighs shuddering visibly from the chill. Tanner struggled with an upwelling of compassion. The woman had been instructed to kill him! A midnight swim plus a few hours spent waiting the next day for a boat to pick her up amounted to paltry retribution.

"Come on, get going!"

She climbed over the rail and leaped into the night.

Gern blinked sleepily when they came back to the cabin. He shrugged, muttered something in an indistinct tone, and went back to sleep, the pillow over his head.

Qingling retired to wash up. She reappeared much later, her nose red, her eyes puffy. She snuggled into her bed, pointedly ignoring Tanner.

The European agent glanced impatiently toward Hamakawa. His partner shrugged and pulled the blanket under his chin, motionless. Tanner went into the bathroom, checked his face, swallowed a capsule, and went back into the stateroom. The feeble Green Night glow allowed him to discern the shape of Qingling beneath the covers. He listened, trying to catch the sound of her breathing in spite of the droning of the rotor-sails. He put forward a hand to touch the young woman's shoulder, but he changed his mind and retreated to his own bed.

SIXTEEN

TUESDAY. EVERYBODY GOT UP EARLY TO ENJOY THE SUN. IN SPITE OF the morning's slight chill, the breakfast tables were set up on the sun-dappled deck. When Tanner, Hamakawa, Qingling, and Gern sat down to eat, the ship was trapped at the bottom of a lock, the last before Shandong, according to the steward.

The lock was over ten meters deep. Slowly, the water level rose. Upstream, two donkeys turned a capstan, the door pivoted, and the *Tao Qian* sailed into a newly dug navigation canal.

Breakfast was hushed. Gern did try to get a conversation going by extolling the great weather, but not one of his table companions was in a mood to pursue the topic. The liner went on its way in the middle of a muddy plain hardly touched with any greenery.

The plain turned into a construction site. The rotor-sails slowed down: the steady drone of motors could now be heard. The *Tao Qian* stopped in the middle of nowhere: the canal went no farther.

Amid the excavators and the busily trudging workers some

old Terran buses, their metal bodies turned into lacework by decades of rust, took on the passengers and drove them to Daping over bumpy roads, the motors backfiring every so often. The little town had grown on the shore of Ming Lake, where it overlooked the outlet that was the ultimate source of the Jade River.

The bus rolled down a dusty street lined with houses under construction before reaching the city center, slightly more prepossessing with its park, its town hall in the traditional style, including a blue tile roof, and a harbor thronged with sailboats.

With the Eye in the sky, there was almost nobody standing around the central square. Tanner, Hamakawa, and Qingling bade farewell to Gern, then shared the work. Hamakawa and Qingling were charged with renting a suitable means of travel— surely a boat, if the state of the road leading to Daping was in any way representative of the general quality of the Shandongxiang road network. Meanwhile, Tanner would investigate and find out if anyone knew Chen Shaoxing. Out of the corner of his eye, Tanner observed Qingling's reaction: was she cross that he wasn't taking her with him? He would have bet it was the case, but that she was working hard to conceal it.

They went their separate ways. Tanner spotted a small café, the Daping Tea Parlor, an ordinary bungalow that had grown a gray-brick veranda protected by a canopy of UV-proof plastic. Inside, it was practically empty, except for an old man teasing a cat with a bit of string. When the oldster saw Tanner, he turned toward the kitchen, barking a name. After a minute or so, a chubby teenage girl showed up, blinking sleepily.

"Are you open?" Tanner asked.

A yawn made the mouth of the girl gape impressively:

"Sorry . . . Just the bar. Supper will be served after ten."

Tanner ordered a beer and then sat down near the oldster, causing the cat to flee. He greeted the elder with a respectful bow and, in return, was courteously invited to join him.

"Not too many people in the streets," Tanner observed.

"Everybody's working out of town."

"You spend the day all alone? Like an old tiger?"

"By no means!" chuckled the old man. "Old Mang often comes with me on my morning stroll. And that cur Daocheng just loves to come and prove how much better he is at Go. But, right now, it's *xiu-xi*."

"But you? You're not napping."

"No, no . . . I already have enough trouble sleeping at nights. I'm not like those who were born here. I'll never get used to their crazy schedule."

"So you're an immigrant?"

The old man bowed, lowering his gaze:

"Like you, young man . . ."

"Will you grant me the pleasure of buying you a beer?"

"I must regretfully decline your kind offer. My stomach can no longer stand alcohol."

"Some tea, then?"

"As you wish."

Tanner waved in the general direction of the drowsy bartender, who brought them a steaming teapot and two minuscule cups with a rice-grain motif. Tanner reined in his eagerness, as he always did when doing business with the Chinese—or the New Chinese, who were no different. Experience had taught him not to force the issue. Talking first of the weather if need be, while sharing tea, was the ideal way to strike the indispensable personal relationship—*guanxi*—without which it was useless to ask for any favor. He opened with the usual question: what did the old man think of life on New China?

He sighed. He had no right to complain. Here, people could have as many babies as they wanted, freed from the poverty and daily stress of overcrowding in the old country. Houses were big. And they shared in the bliss of reviving the true and only authentic Chinese civilization, free of the barbaric imperialism of Westerners and of the Japanese!

"Yet, you seem unhappy," Tanner remarked. "Perhaps it is because of the Dragon's Eye."

"Back home, the petty harassment of the bureaucrats was much worse."

"Then why are you so sad?"

"I miss my hometown, my friends. . . . You're still young, you still have a long life ahead of you in this strange and raw land. Myself, I come from another country, and bittersweet memories keep bringing me back to it."

The old man brushed away the tears on his papery cheeks. He savored a mouthful of tea.

"But I'm not blind, I can see you're eager to speak. Come on! Ask me what you want; I'll answer the best I can and you won't have to put up with the rambling drivel of an old fool."

Tanner showed him a picture of Chen Shaoxing.

"This is my cousin. He's my only relative on New China. In Nanxiang, they told me he lived in the Ming Lake area. He would have arrived here aboard a large luxury yacht, the *East Breeze*, for he's a wealthy man."

The elder held the picture at the end of his outstretched arm, blinking. He suffered a coughing fit, spat on the ground. Catching his breath, he looked again at the picture:

"There's so many people coming and going since the construction of the canal. And, every day, new people swell the population here in Daping. But you say he's rich? Rich enough to live on one of the estates of Chengdu Point? Though they tell me most of these estates belong to high government officials . . ."

Tanner tempered his excitement:

"Well, my cousin isn't one of them, but perhaps the people over there will know of him."

"I also hear they don't like visitors, not in these troubled times."

"I'll be careful."

Tanner again donned his hat, shades, and gloves. His gait brisk, he started for the port. He found Qingling and Hamakawa on a floating dock, bargaining for the rental of a sailboat with a young man wrapped from head to foot in a large UV-proof raincoat. While the young woman brought the negotiations to a close, Hamakawa hastily took Tanner aside:

"The *East Breeze* bought supplies here! It then set sail on

Ming Lake, but the people crewing her—a woman and a man whose description might match Chen's—didn't say where they were headed."

"We'll start with Chengdu Point. Some high-ranking government officials are said to have villas there."

Hamakawa clapped his tongue delightedly: things were looking up.

They turned back and found Qingling checking that the ethanol jerry cans were being filled to the brim. She nodded approvingly, then screwed the caps shut. Wasting not a minute, they loaded the jerry cans of fuel, then went to wake up the manager of the general store, in mid-*xiu-xi*, and bought supplies for three days on the lake. Lunch was a quick meal of roast pigeon, after which they moved the rest of their baggage inside the craft's cockpit.

Qingling checked the ship's fittings, and straightaway set to getting the sails up, bombarding Tanner and Hamakawa with the directions they needed, as raw beginners, to help her out. She then hoisted the mainsail, with Tanner contributing by pulling taut the last few centimeters. Next, Qingling hoisted the jib. With the sails set, Qingling stepped down into the cockpit, asking for the attention of both Tanner and Hamakawa. She could steer and sail alone, but it would be easier with a crewmate. Who was willing to assist her? Tanner volunteered. She explained in a few short sentences what she expected of him: he would be controlling the sails while she steered.

When he looked unenthusiastic, she laughed:

"Don't worry. I'll tell you what to do every step of the way. It's easy, you'll see."

The lake smelled like the river, with added touches of iodine, vinegar, and assorted molds. From the west, a sustained wind pushed back those smells and caused the triangular mainsail to knock against the mast. Qingling ordered Tanner to haul on the sail. Once the fragrant wind filled it, the small sailboat heeled, was carried away from the pier, and headed for the open lake.

At the end of a foam-lined wake, the docks of Daping grew smaller. Through the flying spume around the bow, two rainbows crowned Qingling, her body arched forward. The young woman, who had been morose ever since the incident aboard the *Tao Qian*, was coming alive again.

She rummaged through her sailor's kit, taking out a bottle of sunscreen, then leaned over to speak to Tanner with a smile, her shades misted over with spray.

"Cover every bit of your skin not covered by cloth with this screen. On the lake, hats and shades are not enough."

Tanner and Hamakawa obeyed diligently.

Buoys warned of the presence of shoals. With Tanner helping, however awkwardly, Qingling tacked. They turned away from shore, in order to come back once the shallows were passed.

Reflected by the windows of houses too distant to be visible, sunbeams shot through the new greenery growing along the shores of Ming Lake. The sailboat neared land again: a dozen or so houses clustered together to form a hamlet. Most of the houses were still under construction. A few, apparently finished, were no more than shacks.

Nope, they would not be finding any of the promised villas here. And the *East Breeze* was nowhere to be seen. . . .

The sun fell toward the horizon. Tanner shouted to Qingling:

"Green Night soon!"

"So what? The Eye is bright enough to let us sail."

"Yes, but we might not be able to see the *East Breeze*."

"We're still far from Chengdu Point."

"The house we're looking for may be right around the end of the point. It would be stupid to sail right by it in the dark."

Qingling assented. She steered the sailboat closer in, struck sail, and dropped anchor. The hills conjured away the sun, the wind died, and a curtain of purplish clouds slid in front of the Eye and the first stirrings of the auroras. Pitch-black night surrounded them, muffling all noises except the soft lapping of

waves breaking against the boat's hull. Their only light the glow
from a small yellowish bulb, they ate in the cockpit, enveloped
by the heated breath and the smells of the lake at night.

Qingling was being silent again, but Tanner judged this was
more from fatigue than another sulk. He tried to break the ice:
"Better?"

She nodded affirmatively.

"That woman's mission was to kill us," Tanner reminded
her. "We were magnanimous."

"I know. I'm not angry anymore."

She was still eating, the bowl held right under her mouth.
She said softly:

"This woman . . . She said she was from the *diaochabu,*
right? That's what she said, right? But I thought the *diaochabu*
was the Terran secret service."

"China's intelligence agency, not all of Earth's," Tanner corrected. "Anyway, that woman was part of a private vendetta
against us."

"I thought . . . I thought *you* were from the *diaochabu.* Running from the Tewu, getting Chung out of jail, all that . . ."

"The *diaochabu* isn't alone in sending agents to operate here
on the planet. The Europeans and the Japanese also have men
in the field on New China."

"But . . . I thought you were Chinese?"

"And why did you think that? Because we speak Chinese
as well as you? The first step in being a good secret agent is a
facility with languages. I speak Chinese, French, German, and
English fluently. I'm pretty good in Japanese, Cantonese, Vietnamese, Khmer, Korean, and Tibetan. I can understand and
make myself understood in a dozen more Chinese languages
and dialects."

"Yes, but *who* are you working for? And what are you doing
on New China?"

Tanner eluded the first question.

"I must get in touch with an informer. A mole, if you know

what I mean by that. I must collect from him information much too complex and valuable to go through any intermediary."

"But why doesn't he contact you?"

"If only I knew . . ." Tanner sighed.

"Simple: he's sold out," said Hamakawa.

Tanner stretched out on the couch, suddenly tired.

"If he's betrayed us, why did he ask Earth to send an agent? All he had to do was vanish without saying anything."

"Your mole must be a real Han to have infiltrated our government," observed Qingling. "If he's taken the side of his own people, you can't say he's betrayed you."

Hamakawa smiled suavely. "Treason is an ambiguous concept, if Miss Xun is in the mood for philosophy . . . an ambiguous concept apt to beget amazing feats of sophistry. Historically, the Chinese were past masters at coming up with new instances of such convenient self-justification. Thus, might we not equally argue, for example, that New China's refusal to pay the debts owing to the countries of Earth is just as much of a betrayal?"

"These debts are unjust: they only serve to perpetuate New China's economic dependence!"

"Thanks for the slogan. Do you get your lessons in economics from the *dazibao*?"

"Jay, that's enough!" Tanner said, annoyed.

Hamakawa frowned. "Watch out! You called me by my real name."

Tanner shrugged. Considering their situation . . . Qingling stared at Tanner, opened her mouth as if to say something, then pouted, too mad for words. She went down into the tiny cabin and bedded down in one of the two bunks.

"We'll have to keep an eye on that little tart," Hamakawa muttered, "she might well warn Chen."

"She's not a tart. And I'm the one who says what we do next. I'm still in charge of this mission, am I not?"

Hamakawa gazed heavenward:

"Oh, please, it's all right; don't take it like that . . ."

"She won't be warning anyone because, as soon as we spot—if we ever do!—Chen's place, I'll go in alone, armed and cautious. Both of you will stay aboard. If I don't come back, you'll take over and carry out the mission. You know how to use a cryo-kit?"

The Japanese pulled a long face.

"So that's what is inside that damn suitcase?"

His scornful pout said all Tanner needed to know about his partner's opinion of cryo-kits. Tanner clapped him heartily on the shoulder.

"You've been on New China too long. Our experts can get incredible results with this technique."

"If you say so . . ."

The two men then discussed the revelations of the second agent on the *Tao Qian*. What were they supposed to think? That Bloembergen, still thirsting for vengeance, had asked the *diaochabu* to track them down and kill them? Why would the chief of the European Bureau on New China be so relentless? Because he was afraid of their revelations if they made it back to Earth?

But there was Commander Wang. Tanner shuddered: if Bloembergen was behind this assassination attempt, he wouldn't bet a single yuan on the chances of Wang, confined to his hospital bed, at anybody's mercy . . . Tanner couldn't believe it: not only was their mission going from bad to worse, it now seemed his own superiors had put a price on his head. Would he dare set foot back inside the Enclave? But those worries he could put off; he'd think of going back once they'd tracked down Chen Shaoxing.

The clouds thickened, and the last greenish gleams in the sky turned dark. The wind died down completely, and the night air became as dark and close as the inside of a tomb. The two men went to bed: Hamakawa on the second bunk, and Tanner on a mattress laid out on the floor.

A soft hand caressed the face of the European agent.

"Zheng, don't be silly, come here."

The bed was narrow. Pressed against Qingling's warm body, Tanner stayed awake for many long minutes, before his groin understood nothing was going to happen tonight, and he was able to go to sleep.

SEVENTEEN

THEY ROSE WITH THE SUN. IT WAS STILL TUESDAY, A BIT AFTER SIXTEEN o'clock: according to the official schedule, it was the middle of the sleep period. Until they spotted the *East Breeze,* they would have to stick to New China's natural schedule to make use of the nine hours of daylight.

They set off again, the mainsail filled by a faint, hot wind. They sailed up the coast, bypassed unassuming villas, spotted yachts and glided within binocular range. But none was the *East Breeze.* No other boat sailed on the lake. In spite of the clear, chartreuse sky and its dazzling golden disk, it was nighttime and everybody was sleeping.

The wind shifted, blew from the rear, even weaker. The sail almost undetectably swollen, the boat like a mercury droplet on the lake's glassy surface.

With the wind going unfelt, time and space melted into the torrid air. Bereft of reference points, Tanner complained to Qingling: they were no longer moving. She pointed to the slight swell of the mainsail.

"We're moving as fast as the wind: that's why you're not feeling anything. I'll confess that's not very rapid . . . but there's nothing I can do."

"The motor?"

"We have hardly four hours' worth of fuel. If we use it up, we'll be utterly at the wind's mercy."

They kept going at the same snail's pace. Finally, the sail hung dejectedly and the wind died down altogether. Qingling sat down, fatalistic:

"Now, it's true: we're becalmed."

Chafing, Tanner paced the deck, oblivious to the majestic beauty of the bare, rocky upthrusts, tall and soaring like gigantic monoliths along the distant shore. Yellowed grass, bloated cacti, and a few twisted conifers, embittered by the poor, alien soil, clung to the jutting headlands. Trickles of healthier green ran down between some of the capes, reaching all the way to the lakeshore, where they invariably played host to a dock, as well as rowboats, sailboats, or yachts, all perfectly mirrored in the motionless watery expanse.

Tanner used the binoculars. It was fruitless, and he knew it: none of these craft was the *East Breeze*. He glared exasperatedly at Hamakawa, who was meditating, lying in the sun. Qingling hugged Tanner, stripping him of his sweat-drenched shirt. She undressed too, granting him a peerless view of her body, shiny with perspiration. Tanner didn't react, his mind dulled by the heat. With a smile, Qingling tugged at the belt holding his pants:

"Stop moping and join me!"

She hooked a short ladder to the craft's stern and climbed down, disturbing the turquoise mirror. A squeal of surprise escaped her. The water was cold. Tanner finished undressing. He was on the verge of diving after Qingling when he remembered his wig and his contact lenses. Instead, he cautiously went down the ladder and confined himself to doing the breaststroke while keeping his head out of the water. Qingling slapped the water enthusiastically, splashing him.

"Don't do that . . ."

She made a face at him, called him an old grouch, and dared him to catch her. She took off like an otter, fast and supple. She quickly outdistanced Tanner, who was sticking to a steady breaststroke, but she just as quickly grew breathless and was forced to stop swimming. Each time she stopped, Tanner made up some of the lost ground. When he'd be on the verge of catching her, Qingling would set off again, laughing. He finally collared her, when she had grown too tired to continue, while he was just breathing a bit harder. They embraced, shivering.

A long, dark body brushed past them, streamlined like a fish, but propelled by a wreath of fins capped with fleshy bulbs. Tanner tensed, but Qingling's hysterical giggles dispelled his fears. It was common knowledge that New China's fauna never attacked human beings. A sucker groped them briefly, after which the strange creature went on its way, escorted by a procession of similar beings, but all much smaller.

They had strayed quite far from the sailboat, still becalmed, as if glued to a backdrop. Their swim back was more leisurely. When they climbed aboard, shivering despite the oppressive heat, Hamakawa interrupted his meditation, watching them with a smile, then looking at the lake. He undressed and dove headfirst into the aquamarine depths. Soon, he was headed into the distance, beating the water with a powerful crawl.

Qingling took Tanner down into the cabin and started drying him with a towel. She lingered between his thighs, deriding the shrinkage brought about by the cold water. Tanner pulled Qingling to him, toweling her and caressing her, promising the shrinkage would be short-lived . . .

After making love, they were as sweaty as before. They slipped back into the cool water and tried to catch up with Hamakawa.

Tanner checked his watch, still restless. Making love and a second swim, instead of soothing his jangled nerves, had increased his impatience with the motionless boat. The mainsail hung like an old rag, as if the craft were stuck in gelatin. The young agent asked Qingling to start up the motor. Hamakawa frowned, but said nothing. Qingling reminded him their range did not exceed four hours.

"We should be able to reach Chengdu Point in about two hours," declared Tanner, aware that the precision of his estimate was unwarranted.

"But no more than two hours, all right?" Qingling frowned unhappily. "Maybe the wind will rise in the meantime . . ."

"Maybe."

The motor balked, but gave in. Snorting and coughing, the sailboat put an end to its imperceptible drift and moved off, its oily wake rippling across the lake's smoothness.

An hour and a half later, the sailboat rounded a headland of jumbled red rock, split by dark vertical cracks. They came upon a bay whose shore was lined with a multitude of pavilions of all sizes. Was it a single estate or several? It was hard to say, but, in the former case, it would have demonstrated unheard-of opulence. At the foot of the slope, three handsome yachts were moored to a wooden dock painted a deep red. Tanner ordered the motor's stop. Clutching his binoculars, he attempted to decipher the ideograms drawn on the hulls.

His grip relaxed and the binoculars thumped his chest. He shook his head, frustrated.

Qingling was testing the air, an eye on the inert sail. She had never seen such a prolonged calm. His voice weary, Tanner ordered the motor to be restarted.

"We've used up about half of our ethanol," Qingling warned, a hint of reproach in her voice.

Tanner pointed out a ragged headland, outthrust as if to bar their way.

"Let's go past that cape. After, we'll stop, I swear."

Angry to be awakened again, the motor roared. The small craft sailed around the stone point. Beyond, a small bay was home to only one house, halfway up the hillside, its walls a mix

of dark and reddish stones, almost hidden by pine and birch sap-
lings. A gravel path snaked through a poorly maintained lawn,
from the house down to a jetty. Moored to the jetty, a gray and
white yacht that had known better days rode above its reflection
in the still waters. Tanner held the binoculars on it. In spite of
the deck's vibrations, in spite of the distance, two characters
leaped out at him from the rust-pocked hull.

"East" and "Breeze."

Hamakawa knew right away from the expression on Tanner's face. He grabbed the binoculars, his face lit up with a predatory grin. Qingling asked excitedly:

"Do you want me to stop the motor?"

Tanner was perfectly calm.

"No. Let's go on a bit."

Half a kilometer farther on, scrutinizing the clear depths to
make sure the keel didn't hit an outcropping, they came to a stop
as close as possible to a rocky bluff. The anchor, thrown by Tanner, wedged itself in a fissure. Qingling pulled on the chain. With
a muffled thud, the hull met the stone face. From there, the
climb was easy enough and Tanner reached an overhang a few
meters above, admiring the white ellipse of the ship cradled in
the lake's dark green waters. He dropped down a rope and hauled
up his cryo-kit. Hamakawa clambered up to the same rocky platform.

Tanner wagged his forefinger in his partner's direction:

"You watch. From afar. You show up only if you hear shouts
or gunfire."

"I was first in line and I don't get to see the main attrac-
tion?" protested Hamakawa.

"You already know far too much."

"What if Chen refuses to talk? What if he's under guard?"

"I told you: keep watch."

"And me?" shouted Qingling from the sailboat's deck.

"You stay there!"

"And what if something happens to the both of you?"

Tanner gazed skyward without answering. He loaded his

gun with stun bullets. Checked the cryo-kit—out of sheer compulsiveness, since he had done a thorough check in the morning. Checked his watch: still two hours before the Eye's return. No need for a hat, the shades would do. He darted away through the rocky maze, shadowed by Hamakawa.

The rock-strewn slope led them to a crumbling overhang about ten meters above the house. He flopped down on the burning rock, sweating all over. It was so hot! Hamakawa lay down beside him. Below them rose a large stone house, generically Asian in appearance, its outer wall provided with a single, arched entranceway, the threshold flanked by red uprights. All around, in carefully studied disarray, young trees dotted the UV-resistant lawn. Behind the house extended formal and vegetable gardens, some in the open air, some inside greenhouses. Nothing moved. Rising time was at least four hours away.

Steps, unsure and diffident, clattered on the rock behind Tanner and Hamakawa. They turned around as one, guns raised. A couple of goats stared back from under their UV-proof plastic enclosures, as if mildly surprised. They came closer, curious. The two operatives didn't move. Finally understanding their two visitors hadn't come to feed them, the goats resumed their grazing of the tough grass that managed to grow in the rock's cracks.

Tanner signaled for Hamakawa to stay. Hiding his gun under his shirt, he took his case and went down the steep slope. He followed the wall to the entranceway, went through, reached the door of the pavilion, and stayed there for a few seconds, listening. Not a sound. Everyone must be sleeping, he thought. He turned the handle and the door opened.

Inside, the hallway was dark and cool, hung with raw, unbleached linen. Should he enter without further ado?

He knocked on the doorframe. No answer. He knocked louder. This time, he heard an indistinct muttering. Feet brushing the wooden floors. A woman in her early thirties appeared, disheveled, blinking, a wrinkled nightshirt reaching down to mid-thigh. She was dumbfounded by Tanner's presence.

"But . . . Who are you?"

"I wish to see Chen Shaoxing."

She was still, unmoving, as if she hadn't heard. From the doorstep, she could see the dock. Her eyes narrowed as she peered down through the harsh daylight. She looked at Tanner:

"How did you get here?"

"Is Chen Shaoxing here?"

Again, she refused to answer. She backed away from Tanner, her gaze fixed on her naked legs. She muttered that she would see what she could arrange, then vanished down the hallway.

More footsteps, doors opening and closing, whispers. Time passed. Tanner started to chafe. The woman showed up again, hair carefully combed, wrapped in a silk kimono, green and bright. Calmly, though her tone betrayed a hint of anxiety, she invited the honorable visitor to come with her. She led Tanner down a long, dark corridor to a door, which she threw open.

On the other side, light was everywhere, flooding through a large bay window and splashing everything: the white walls, the piles of paper and cardboard, the brush racks, the inks and paints, the easels, the canvases of all makes and sizes . . . and the man, who kept on painting as if he didn't care to know his visitor's identity.

The woman opened her mouth, but the expected protestations never emerged. With seeming reluctance, she withdrew, closing the door behind her.

Chen Shaoxing was fleshier than in his public pictures. Wrinkles had furrowed the once smooth face: beneath the chin, at the corner of the eyes, across the forehead, wherever his worries had left their mark. Still pretending he was alone, Chen picked a slim brush in his rack and dipped it in an inkstand. The ink-darkened brush skimmed the sheet of rice paper in front of Chen, his touch sure and swift.

Tanner shrugged. He was too relieved to finally meet the European Bureau's mole to be offended by the man's indifference. He came closer, peering over his shoulder and admiring a page covered with exquisitely shaped ideograms:

Who shall reproach me, if my soul
This anguish suffers twice?
For the spring sung by all,
I both love and hate:
Glad that so early it comes,
Aggrieved when so soon it goes,
Departing without a word,

Chen paused for a few seconds, as if to come up with a suitable conclusion to the preceding verses. He dipped his brush again in the inkstand and drew the final ideograms:

Yet having come unheard . . .

He set down his brush in a water-filled bowl before moving the sheet of rice paper to a small drying table.

"Do you like it?" Chen asked.

"I don't know much about poetry."

"Your layman's opinion, then . . ."

"It's nice work. They didn't tell me you were a poet."

Chen Shaoxing looked at Tanner, taken aback, then burst into laughter. He gazed at the poem with unfeigned delight, sparing another glance for Tanner. Still laughing softly, he walked over to a well-stocked set of bookshelves and pulled out a book. He leafed through it rapidly, found the page, and placed it in front of Tanner's eyes. The paper's antique surface—such a book might be centuries old!—was covered with minuscule printed characters, framed by a graceful print of flowering tree boughs, with one row devoted to the stanza just written out by Chen. The cracked leather of the cover was gold-embossed with three ideograms: *Dream of the Red Chamber*.

Tanner sighed: Chen was reproducing an excerpt from a classic of Chinese literature—a magnificent and tragic love story from the eighteenth century—as an exercise in calligraphy. Chen's amusement at his expense was understandable. Tanner restored the book to its spot on the shelf.

"As I said, I don't know much about poetry."

"Not even *Dream of the Red Chamber*? Didn't you go to school?"

"I read parts of it. A long time ago."

"On Earth? Which version? The one in pinyin?"

"Yes, in pinyin."

Chen implored the heavens:

"To read poetry in pinyin! What a ridiculous idea! How vulgar! Even worse: fraudulent! In pinyin, he says . . . But wait, I think I must have at least one of those horrors. . . ."

He found a slim book wedged on the topmost shelf, opened it to a page, and passed it over to Tanner. It was a short poem written out in pinyin.

"Translate!" Chen Shaoxing ordered in English.

"Translate?"

"In English!" Chen Shaoxing repeated, still in English. "I'm assuming an agent of the European Bureau would be fluent in English, right? Or maybe you would prefer French?"

"No, English will do."

"Translate, then."

Too disconcerted to refuse, Tanner translated aloud the handful of lines:

A jade staircase, the white dew on it.
The night is far gone, moving step by step, silken shoes
Let fall the crystal curtain

Tanner stumbled over an unfamiliar word.

"*Ling long*," prompted Chen, "it's an onomatopoeia."

Ling long, gaze up at the autumn moon.

Tanner looked at Chen, uncomprehending.

"Wait, you'll see!" exclaimed Chen without giving Tanner a chance to demur. He started going through a stack of sheets and sketches, before digging out a page adorned with graceful, watercolored characters. It was the same poem, but expressed this time by the traditional ideograms.

"Now you'll understand. When you translated from pinyin, you only read the *words*, you didn't read the *poem*. A Chinese poem always comprises three parts: one lyrical, one pictorial, and one philosophical. Transcribing the ideograms as Roman characters ignores the expressiveness suggested by the visual arrangement. Now, let us try to translate this same poem, but starting this time from the original. . . ."

Chen pointed at the first column of characters:

"Nothing to fault in that first part: the literal reading is correct. Let's move on to the second: what is suggested by this detail of apparel, 'silken shoes'? A lady, no doubt. I will make her the subject of this poem. The third part is even richer, pictorially. To speak of rock crystal, the poet used two characters, those for water and limpidity. The next ideogram relies on a triple occurrence of the character for the Sun. Therefore, both water and the Sun appear in the text. Therefore, as a first approximation, I would translate this third part by 'the crystal curtain falling like a cascade'—a secondary interpretation of *zhui*—'reflecting the Sun'—the secondary interpretation of *tsing*. Finally, in the last part, *ling long* lets us hear a tinkling of pearls or beads, while, here, the expression 'gaze up' takes on the additional meaning of 'gazing up in sadness,' a meaning it is often given. Thus, without taking excessive liberties with the text, but using all the information provided by the original characters, I would read:

The jade staircase is bedecked with pearls of dew.
The night is far gone: the lady climbs slowly, step by
step,
Her silken shoes wet with morning's tears.
She turns within, lets fall the crystal curtain,
Cascading down like a sun-visited stream.
And, when the silence follows its clear tinkling,
She gazes up in sorrow
At the autumn moon, shining through.

Chen Shaoxing set the sheet back down on the pile it came from, satisfied with his demonstration. Tanner stayed silent a moment, absentmindedly going through some of the sketches and poems. His voice flat, he said, carefully separating his words:

"We could have discussed poetry in Lengshuijiang, I think. You would have spared me quite a long trip."

Chen seemed to deflate, awakened from a dream. His back sagged and his shaking hand sought the support of his painter's stool. He sat down, suddenly drained, old and gray.

"How is Commander Wang?"

"He seemed on the way to recovery when I saw him last."

"Good . . . Yet I didn't expect he would find a replacement so easily. You seem quite young. He must have a high opinion of you, to send you on such a delicate mission."

"He didn't have much choice."

"That may be so," whispered Chen, his voice going hoarse. "It's strange; I immediately understood from Xingxing's expression that I'd been tracked down."

"So why this whole game of hide-and-seek?"

A weary smile twisted Chen's face. "Why ask such a question when the answer should be obvious? You came all this way for nothing. I will reveal nothing of Xiao Jiping's future policies. I . . . I've quit. I'm done with the European Bureau."

Tanner exaggerated his expression of shock and surprise:

"Quit? In mid-mission? There's a cruder word to describe that."

The insinuation clearly stung Chen.

"Certainly not treason, if that's what you're implying! I've changed . . . I've changed my mind. I understand now that Earth is wrong. The European Bureau is blind if it thinks the Earth can keep New China in an economic stranglehold forever!"

"Come on, Chen! Your position in the New Chinese government has gone to your head. It's time to come back down to earth: you're an agent of the European Bureau, first and foremost. You must tell me all you know about Xiao Jiping's plans. That's all there is to it."

Chen stared at him, wide-eyed. A disbelieving laughter burst out of him, instantly choked off:

"I'm not the one who should come back down to earth, you're the one! You and the European Bureau! And the *diaochabu*, the Naicho, all these meddlers from Earth . . . You're the one who must understand that I *truly* became the vice president of New China, and that I intend, in the future, to devote myself body and soul to that role." He spread his hands beseechingly. "Come on, you are Chinese too—don't you understand what we're trying to do here? We're trying to rebuild China, *China*! Far from the Western barbarians! You say that my mind has been clouded . . . what about yours? You accuse me of treachery! Who's the real traitor here? What should we call a Han who spies for the Europeans?" He spat. "Like you, I *was* a traitor, a spy betraying my own people, my own blood. But I had the strength to change."

"So why did you contact Earth? Why did you set up a meeting in Lengshuijiang?"

Chen ground his teeth, finally getting an answer out:

"Are words really necessary? Xiao Jiping and his radical wing are prone to confusing autonomy and isolationism. Breaking with Earth would run the risk of subjecting our people to the misery they fled from when they lived on Earth. And all this hostility directed against Terran tech is . . . unhealthy. You can't terraform a planet with just hard work and good intentions. I . . . I tried to influence Xiao Jiping along those lines, but moderates are unpopular. Just imagine, they're accused of having been corrupted by Earth." Chen's laughter verged on the hysteric. "But that's just paranoid, isn't it?"

"Does that mean they suspect you?"

Chen Shaoxing offered no reply. His hands shaking, he started to tidy his bookshelves, to screw back on the lids of his ink pots, to wring dry his paintbrushes. Giving vent to his wrath, Tanner sent a handful of brushes bouncing from the wall:

"Answer me!"

Chen's white-hot gaze clashed with Tanner's, but the minister looked down first, pursing his lips:

"You don't understand: I told Xiao Jiping everything."

Tanner stood still, flushed, his ears buzzing, his sight blurring. As if of its own volition, a flat denial escaped his lips:

"You didn't!"

"Though it might devour my soul, I chose shame. . . . Shame. Do you know what that is, as an agent of the European Bureau? It all seems so far now . . . the torments of another life . . ."

His gaze lost itself in the contemplation of his antique paper books. He gestured toward the door:

"You can go. You'll get nothing from me."

"I relieve you and place you under arrest," declared Tanner, his voice harsh. "You will come back with me to the Enclave and face charges."

Chen Shaoxing was nodding, as if saddened.

"I think that's enough," pronounced a feminine voice.

Chen's wife had opened the door, pointing a snub-nosed handgun in Tanner's direction. The young agent cursed himself: he had taken for granted that Chen's wife was not involved, an assumption that might cost him dearly. His own gun weighed against his chest. His hand itched with the urge to grab it, but he fought such an ill-considered move. The woman's finger was clenched around her weapon's trigger.

"Did you come alone?"

Tanner overdid his hesitation:

"One of my men is watching this house."

Chen's wife was unable to restrain a derisive chuckle:

"Wrong answer! If one of your men was really out there, you wouldn't have said so!"

Tanner gulped as if his ploy had actually failed. It wasn't hard to fake dismay, his situation being distressing enough as it was. What was in that gun: stun bullets or real ones? Chen's wife appealed to her husband:

"What do I do now?"

Chen hesitated. Tanner jumped in to plea with him:

"Come on, Chen! Can't you see everything is over for you here? If I don't come back, the European Bureau will expose you!"

"Why should you do that?" replied his wife. "Such a revelation would only exacerbate New Chinese resentment of Earth!"

Tanner was thinking frantically. What was Hamakawa waiting for? He managed to stammer:

"Th . . . Then why didn't Xiao Jiping turn Chen's confession to his advantage by making it public?"

She sighed:

"I've had enough of this . . ."

She pulled the trigger. An unendurable burning spread across Tanner's chest. Dazed and stupefied, he stepped back. He managed to slip a hand under his shirt . . . find his gun . . . try and raise it as he whimpered with pain and frustration. But his arm was completely numb and he dropped the gun. The same paralysis stole his legs and he smashed down on Chen's worktable, splashing multicolored inks in all directions. . . .

The cool dampness of a wet towel brought Tanner back to life. A blazing pain was drilling his skull through and through. Tanner opened his eyes and met the worried and watchful gaze of Hamakawa. Jay helped him to sit up: everything started spinning. . . .

"Careful. You cut your head open when you fell down."

Tanner felt his forehead to assess the damage and found the wound just below the hairline. Biting down, he explored it in spite of the unpleasant sensations. His finger hit bone. His hand was red with blood when he withdrew it. He tried not to worry: head cuts were often more impressive than really dangerous. His left eye also hurt, and he vaguely recalled an ink pot striking the orbital bone. He blinked: well, it could be worse. . . .

"Are you all right?" asked Hamakawa.

Tanner tried to nod affirmatively, but it hurt too much. He

gestured interrogatively toward the bodies of Chen and his wife, stretched out on the ground.

"Stun bullets," Hamakawa reassured him. "I gave them a taste of their own medicine." He pointed at Tanner's face. "You've got a green eye."

Tanner refrained from rubbing his eye. So, he'd lost one of his contact lenses. . . .

"Go and get cleaned up," Hamakawa finally said. "You're a frightening sight."

In the bathroom, trembling with delayed shock, Tanner examined the gash in his forehead. The wig was coming unglued, torn and soaked with blood. He finished the job, wincing with pain. He took his time cleaning himself, refilling the sink several times as the water turned red. He found Band-Skin in the medicine cabinet and dressed the wound. He smiled jeeringly at himself: the green eye, the bulging bandage over his forehead, and the—red-haired!—stubble over his skull, all contributed to make him look half crazy, half thuggish, and entirely too unsettling.

Tanner returned to the sunroom, taking in the blood-spattered devastation of what had been a sanctuary dedicated to art and meditation. His gaze stumbled over the slumbering form of the woman, her beautiful face distorted by a snarl of pain.

Hamakawa bent over the inert body, gesturing fatalistically with his hand.

"She must die."

Melancholy surged within Tanner. His partner was right. Once she regained consciousness, the woman would give the alarm far too soon. Without further ado, Hamakawa opened his gun's clip, replacing a stun bullet with a real one.

"No, I'll take care of it," Tanner protested.

Hamakawa seemed irked:

"You can hardly stand. . . . what do you want to prove?"

"It's . . . it's my mission," Tanner replied weakly.

Ignoring his superior, Hamakawa aimed at the heart of the unmoving woman and fired. Tanner thought that he hoped to die like that . . . without even realizing it.

They took Chen Shaoxing outside. An acid-green tinge shaded the foliage of the nearby trees. Hamakawa found ethanol and went back inside the main building.

The goats scurried away while they dragged Chen through the rocks. Staggering between them, Chen gazed tearfully one last time at his villa. In the green and glistening dell, a thick cloud of black smoke rose from the house. Flames burst through the window frames, flickering like greedy dragon tongues.

EIGHTEEN

IN A FEW CLIPPED SENTENCES, AVOIDING ANY MENTION OF CHEN'S spouse and her murder, Tanner explained the truth to Qingling, starting with the disappearance of his hair and the change in color of his eye. The young woman was sobbing softly, disbelieving.

"A European . . . A *white* European!"

Tanner shuddered, struck by Qingling's scorn as she spat out the epithet. The young woman turned on Hamakawa, daggers in her eyes:

"Are you European too?"

Hamakawa shook his head. "Japanese."

The young woman shook her head mutely. A Japanese! That was even worse! Without either shades or a hat, she rushed outside the cabin.

"Wait, where are you going?"

Tanner emerged into green daylight. Crouching in the low shadow of the cabin, Qingling was sobbing wretchedly. He sat down by her, forced her to face him, but her gaze refused to meet his.

"Well, yes, I'm European! So?"

"You lied to me!"

"At first, I didn't know if I could trust you. Later . . . it was better if you didn't know."

"I thought you loved me."

Tanner hesitated:

"My . . . my feelings don't depend on my race."

Qingling nodded slowly, resigned:

"For you, I was just . . . just a crumb of fun on the side! Like with Fuzai . . . I was silly to believe anything else."

"Don't say that. I love you, Qingling, I love you like I've never loved anybody before."

"I . . . I thought you'd take me to Earth with you. Why did you lie to me? Why did I believe you?"

Tanner gaped at her, open-mouthed.

"But you never said . . . You'd want to emigrate to Earth with me? And you'd change your mind because I'm not the right color?"

"It has nothing to do with skin color," Qingling muttered hollowly. "You're not Chinese, period."

"Is it that important to you?"

"For the children, yes."

"Children? But you told me you were sterile."

"One of the doctors told me I could be cured on Earth." She clung desperately to Tanner. "Is it true? On Earth, could I have children? Tell me it's true! Tell me it's not *another* lie."

Tanner patted the back of her blouse, damp with perspiration.

"It's probably true. On Earth, doctors can perform miracles."

Qingling was crying again, her body jerked by sobs:

"Why, oh why aren't you Chinese? Don't you see that our children would be treated like mongrels by New Chinese immigration? They would never be able to come back, and none of their descendents either."

Tanner didn't know how to answer: like most Europeans,

he had never considered marriage primarily as a means to procreation.

"Qingling . . . Listen to me. I can't get married. And I certainly can't have children. Please fact the facts! I'm a secret agent, a spy, can't you understand that? You want us to get married, buy a tiny flat in the suburbs where you would raise our kids and wait for me to come back from missions, is that right? Is that what you want?"

She blew up, almost raging:

"Yes! That is *exactly* what I want! I want children! I want a husband! Is it so shameful? Certainly no worse than lying, stealing, and killing people! You wouldn't give it up? Not even for me?"

She was sobbing so hard he could no longer make out her words. Tanner could only clasp her to him, and stroke her, his throat clenched so tight he couldn't add a word.

Hamakawa leaned out the doorway, impassive.

"The wind is rising," he remarked softly.

Qingling wiped the tears from her cheeks, avoiding Hamakawa's gaze. She looked at the clouds to the west, forerunners of a storm front rising above the horizon. The wind too was rising, warm and gusty.

"I'll get dressed and bring down the jib. We'll have the wind at our backs and the mainsail alone will do."

"Will we reach Daping before the storm?" Hamakawa asked.

"I doubt it."

With the mainsail up, the sailboat flew with the wind. For the passengers, the relative quiet was only an illusion: the sailboat's bow was slicing through waters stirred by ripples slowly building into waves. A sudden gust ripped away Tanner's hat and sent it whirling into the lake. The warm breeze gave way to a cooler wind. Tanner shivered. Behind them, like a gray mountain rising to conquer the sky, a cumulonimbus blotted out the Dragon's Eye.

Chen Shaoxing, prostrate in a corner of the cabin, paid no attention to any of it.

The wind's velocity increased. Foam horses bestrode the waves. Qingling grew worried and handed over the helm to Hamakawa, ordering him to hang on to it. Then, helped by Tanner, she reefed in the mainsail. Yet, in spite of the sail's reduced area, the sailboat hurtled through the raging waters faster and faster.

Far off, the first lightning flashes probed the nooks and crannies of the oncoming clouds. Drumrolls echoed from one horizon to the other, louder than the wind's fitful whistling and the wet slaps of the waves against the hull.

The rain fell, huge drops coming down like a thick, tepid mantle. Between the torrential rain and the spume hosing the cockpit like machine-gun fire, Tanner, Qingling, and Hamakawa were soon soaking wet.

The towering nimbus cover now spread over the whole sky. All around them, lightning bolts were writhing, frenzied. The ceaseless rumble of thunder seemed to hold their chests in a vise. And then the wind started to turn.

Qingling, who was having a hard time restraining the tiller, screamed to Tanner to strike the mainsail. She could no longer leave her post; the wind had grown too capricious. Tanner grabbed the crank and, unsure of his footing on the slippery surface, started across the deck to reach the boom.

A blinding flash, and then a hellish blast crashed through the storm. A lightning bolt had struck within meters of the small craft.

Half dazed, Tanner didn't hear Qingling's warning shout. At the last second, he caught sight of the mainsail slackening, as the wind shifted from side to side, then filling again. . . . He jumped back down inside the cockpit and the boom brushed the top of his head. The mainsail, swollen by the wind, rushed around before stopping with a crash.

The mast snapped, and the unbalanced sailboat at once

heeled more than forty-five degrees from the vertical. Tanner desperately clutched the door frame, watching more than a meter of the starboard deck cut into the waves. Out of the corner of his eye, he saw Hamakawa clinging to the portside stays and Qingling, welded to the helm, unable to save them. The sailboat was tipping over. . . .

The mainsail had reached the end of its endurance: with a strident ripping noise, it tore from top to bottom. The sailboat slowly straightened.

While Hamakawa bailed out the water flooding the cockpit, Qingling threw the sea anchor amid the roiling waves. She then helped Tanner to hastily roll up the shreds of the mainsail around the boom.

They gathered in the cabin, wet and incredulous. Qingling was shaking her head, repeating that it wasn't her fault, that nobody could have know the storm would be so bad. Tanner embraced her: nobody was blaming her.

The lightning bolts stopped their frenzied dancing, and the ceaseless roar of thunder made way for isolated tremors. The rain lasted longer, then abated. Yet, the light grew even dimmer.

Tanner checked his watch: the sun was setting, it was Thursday morning. Beneath the impenetrable cloud layer, Green Night looked more like Dark Night. They put on dry clothing, ate some cold chicken and biscuits. They said little, Chen nothing at all. The yellow glow of the small bulb revealed even Hamakawa's normally impervious face to be haggard with fatigue.

They went to bed.

Taking advantage of the dark's cosy intimacy, under the cover provided by the rain's patter on the roof, Tanner and Qingling silently made love in the bed's warm shelter.

Before going to sleep, Qingling breathed in his ear: "Whatever happens, don't leave me. . . ."

Tanner caressed her shoulder, her breast, her hip. He held her even tighter against him: he would never abandon her.

Since Thursday combined Green Night and Dark Night, they slept through the entire official day, and only got under way in the evening, as a new day was dawning. The previous day's hot and humid air had been dispersed by the storm winds. It was cooler. A slice of the sun peered over the hills, making the lake sparkle, molding gold leaf around the long, tapering clouds.

Already, the air felt hotter.

Tanner shaved his skull and his cheeks, pondering the reaction of the sailboat's owner when he would see the ripped sail. No way they could compensate him; they didn't have enough money left. He shrugged: perhaps the owner would be understanding. There was also the problem of their new passenger: was Chen known in Daping? It was doubtful, he finally decided.

The storm had had a silver lining, too: the sailboat had surely beaten a New Chinese speed record. They were almost within sight of Daping. The motor was started up and, burning the last of their fuel, they put-putted all the way into Daping harbor.

The storm had raged through town with unaccustomed violence. Even finding a berth was no simple matter: they were forced to go around torn sails floating in the midst of numerous waterborne debris. Qingling managed to slip between a wooden beam ripped from the dock and a small beached sailboat. Everywhere, in anger or resignation, townspeople of all ages were assessing the damages, deliberating, cleaning up. Qingling hailed a young man on the dock and threw him a line, which he graciously secured.

Tanner felt a deeply visceral joy to stand once more on stable ground.

Trailed by a horde of children, the sailboat owner appeared, an incredulous look frozen on his face. He had been certain his craft had foundered with all hands. The torn sail? Was that all! He showed them, crushed against the pier, another sailboat that had belonged to him: its hull was dented, the windows shattered, the sails tangled and mud-spattered.

Tanner interrupted his whining: he could pay three hundred yuans for the sail, would it be enough? The owner's head jerked as if it had been slapped and his eyes narrowed:

"Three hundred yuans? Are you joking? If I can get the sail repaired for as little as a thousand yuans, I'll be the best bargainer of the Shandongxiang Plains!"

"Five hundred yuans," Tanner offered. "It's the best I can do."

The owner almost choked. And the other five hundred yuans, where was he going to dig them up? Not from renting his boat to tightwads like them! His eldest daughter came up to Tanner, and she begged him not to pay any attention to the old fool's grumbling. She took the five hundred yuans, making her father yelp even louder. Taking the other sailors as witness, he asked what grudge the gods held against him, to let his children dishonor him so, his own children. . . .

The onlookers, no doubt used to the scenes of the grizzled sailor, went back to work. None were in a mood to smile.

Tanner, Hamakawa, Chen, and Qingling walked to the Daping Tea Parlor, where they were served supper. During the meal, they noticed in front of the restaurant two of the buses that carried travelers to and from the canal. The buses were empty, and their drivers nowhere to be seen. Tanner questioned the young waitress: where could they find the drivers? Blinking bovinely, the young woman pointed a weary finger toward a table where two New Chinese men were chatting animatedly.

The two drivers greeted Tanner with suspicious glances when he walked up. To hell with *guanxi* and palavering—Tanner asked straight out if one of them would be willing to take them to the canal.

The question did not exactly elicit a wild burst of enthusiasm.

"Our day is over."

"According to the schedule, the last boat will leave Linzi in less than three hours. That leaves us plenty of time to get there."

One of the drivers looked at his watch, stifling a yawn.

"Maybe. But, as I said, my day is done."

Tanner didn't feel like spending another day in this back-of-the-beyond hole. He swallowed some uncharitable comments and struggled to remain polite:

"Are there any other means of transportation than the bus?"

"I'd be amazed."

"I can pay."

One of the two drivers, a tall and spare man with an uneven goatee, raised an eyebrow. How much was the stranger willing to offer? Tanner contained his irritation:

"I'm not a bus driver! Name your price."

The tall and lanky one said casually:

"Two fifty."

Tanner put down two hundred and fifty yuans beside his plate of fried noodles. The driver who had cited such an extravagant fare to get rid of a nuisance was nonplussed. He unhurriedly pocketed the bills and threw a sardonic glance at his companion, who was obviously smarting that he'd, so to speak, missed the boat.

Their driver finished the last of his tea and got up.

"Come with me."

They could not leave right away. The driver wanted to fill up. And since the general store was closed, no ethanol was to be had. The driver left to find the shop owner in order to convince him to sell enough fuel for a return trip to the canal.

The foursome was forced to wait. It was even hotter now than the previous day. Even up north, around the EFTA, it was rarely this hot. The sea's proximity tempered climatic swings. Whereas, in the middle of the continental plain, the summer's extremes made themselves felt unhindered.

Not to mention that the unpleasant smell of a manure plant nearby increased their discomfort by an order of magnitude.

"Come on, my New Chinese friends! Collect your shit!" exclaimed Hamakawa with a spiteful smile. "Collect it and spread it all over your world."

The Japanese turned toward Tanner:

"Did you ever think of it, that men cannot live on a planet if it's too clean, that they must absolutely cover it with their own shit first? Isn't that the case on New China? Where would the National Terraforming Plan be without the use of the excrements produced by people and their animals?"

Tanner and Qingling exchanged quizzical looks.

"I'm surprised no New Chinese poets have ever explored the symbolic aspects of this," added Hamakawa.

"Actually, Wang Feng Wu did write a few satirical pages on this topic," Chen corrected dully. These were the first words he had uttered since their departure from Chengdu Point. He fell silent again, staring vacantly.

Tanner motioned for Hamakawa to follow him outside the bus. The Japanese reluctantly joined his partner out in the sun.

"What's going on?" asked Hamakawa when they were out of hearing range.

"Shouldn't I be asking you that same question? You're behaving strangely, you're not yourself. Are you feeling all right?"

Hamakawa shrugged:

"It's this heat . . . I'm on edge. . . ."

"Is that all? The heat? Chen's wife has nothing to do with it?"

Hamakawa's obsidian gaze shone with an unnerving gleam:

"Do you think I enjoyed killing her?"

The question's tone, heavy with unspoken despair, stunned Tanner. He shook his head: no, he never would have thought such a thing.

"Well, you're wrong," retorted Hamakawa tunelessly. He stayed silent a long moment, before his face lit up with its customary feral smile, at once cruel, smug, and slightly phony. "But don't worry, white man, your faithful sidekick is not cracking under pressure. I shall be as constant as the northern star."

"I hope so," Tanner said, not completely convinced.

They climbed back inside the bus, each thinking his own thoughts.

The driver finally showed up with fuel, grinning at his four passengers on the verge of dying from heat prostration inside the close air of the bus. The vehicle started off. Through the open windows, a trickle of warm air fostered the illusion of a cooling breeze.

They rolled down empty streets, went past abandoned construction sites, rushed by cereal fields withering in the heat and the sun.

Tanner nervously checked his watch. No reason to worry: the last ship bound for Linzi would leave in about two hours, whereas the trip shouldn't take more than an hour. And yet, he was nervous, on edge. . . . Like Hamakawa, the heat was getting to him.

Qingling wiped her brow. "I think we're in for it again."

The young woman was right. In the west, an enormous cumulonimbus, dark gray shading to black, was overrunning the sky. An ashen dusk blighted the landscape, the cereal stalks bowing anxiously. Lightning scoured paler streaks in the granitelike mass, while blasts of an erratic hot wind carried thunderous echoes. The rain furtively held back, letting through only a few heavy drops, bursting on the windshield like insects.

The bus crested a low hill, which afforded them a far-reaching view of the newly sown plains. The sprinkling of raindrops they had received was only a harbinger of the oncoming storm: a few kilometers away, toward the canal, a curtain of heavy rains was devouring the horizon.

This was not a mere storm: from the lightning-crowned base of the nimbus, a dark extrusion grew downward, wavering, as if it scrupled to come into contact with the earth. The extrusion tapered to a narrow tip, stretched like taffy and smashed into the ground in the midst of a cloud of whirling debris.

Uttering an inarticulate yell, the driver stopped the bus. Tanner felt the remaining hairs on the back of his neck bristle. In the air, the sting of ozone aroused a surge of atavistic terror hard to overcome. A tornado! And the European agent would have sworn it was making straight for them.

The driver nervously tried to turn around, but mixed up his maneuvers and finally stalled. And the motor refused to start up again! Flustered, he turned the key so hard he broke it in the ignition. And then stared, flabbergasted, at the grip of his key and the shiny stump of its stem.

The storm front rushed toward the road. Still no rain, but wind gusts scourged the old bus. Tanner left his window open in spite of the dust the wind was blowing in: he wanted to track the whirlwind's progress, a dark shadow bucking wildly in front of the oncoming rain's curtain. Hamakawa went to see the driver: was there really no way to get the bus moving again? Qingling clung to Tanner, scared, her voice climbing in pitch, though it was almost drowned by the wind's howling:

"Are we in danger?"

What did she think? That he was a tornado expert? He'd never seen one before.

The wind grew stronger, and a cloud of reddish dust engulfed the bus. Everything vanished. A noise that should have been too low to be heard, like the grinding of a giant millstone biting into bedrock, overwhelmed everything else, drowning the roar of thunder and the wind's shriek, filling the whole world. Tanner hugged Qingling as a dark and swirling wall hid the air and the earth. The tornado was upon them. . . .

Capriciously, the cyclone veered away and moved off with disconcerting speed, covering its retreat with deafening blasts of thunder. Tanner released Qingling. Where he had gripped her arm, red marks were showing.

The rain took over, torrential. Tanner breathed easier. A close call! But he felt Qingling tighten:

"Look!"

The rain was clearing the dust from the air. A blurry landscape appeared. The storm was not done with them: across the plain, hammered by lightning bolts, two more tornadoes were dancing in the midst of a ballet of lightning flashes.

Hamakawa ordered the driver to open the door and he went out to open the front hood, followed by Tanner, who objected strenuously: "Get back aboard. This is insane!"

"There's got to be a way to get this going without the key!" Hamakawa yelled above the drumming of the rain on the roof of the bus. Tanner, out of arguments, soaked to the bone, climbed back inside the bus.

The two tornadoes did not seem too menacing. In the distance, a third twister formed, slipping southward. Closer to the bus, much too close, the cloud ceiling crumbled to shape a fourth cone, still faltering. The nascent cyclone leaped over the bus, but it was fully formed when it reached the other cyclone, a much larger one. Like copulating serpents, the two coils writhed and melted together, a dark, whirling, debris-filled cloud. The tornado's head slowly moved toward the roadway, but the tip, as if of its own volition, balked, questing in another direction. The tornado stretched, tilted, finally toppling over. . . . A gigantic column of whirling air fell across the road and, like a towering steamroller, surged toward the bus.

Qingling snuggled against Tanner. This time, there would be no escape!

The impact was too brief, too loud, too brutal to be encompassed by human senses.

The vehicle's rusting body shook in the sudden squall of splattering mud and gravel. Stones and branches shattered the windows. The back of the bus lifted up, the vehicle pivoted on its front wheels, and it overturned in the neighboring field, the remaining windows bursting from the sheer force of the impact.

Silence fell—a relative silence, as the wind and thunder still screamed. But the tornado had passed. Tanner got up: he was covered in glass splinters, though he had suffered only a few cuts. Nothing serious. Qingling extracted herself from Tanner's arms. With an expressionless gaze, she looked up stupidly at the seats hanging from the side of the overturned bus. Ashen-faced, Chen Shaoxing stared reproachfully at Tanner, as if he alone were responsible for the entire catastrophe. Toward the front of the bus, the driver was lying inertly on a bed of smashed glass.

Careful not to cut himself on the glass shards, Tanner left Qingling and examined the driver. The man had been unlucky enough to be thrown partway through a window, his head and a forearm crushed between the clay soil and the window's edge.

Tanner checked his pulse, harboring no real hope for the man. . . . He set down the hand on a clump of glass-pierced soil.

"Jay," Tanner whispered hoarsely. His partner hadn't had a chance to get back inside.

Tanner and Qingling crawled out through the shattered windshield. Rain was still pouring from the ceiling of low, gray clouds. Wading through the sodden barley and mud, Tanner and Qingling looked for Hamakawa.

"Jay? *Jay!*"

The storm rumbled the only answer they got. Chen Shao-xing, stumbling, appeared and joined the search. After nearly half an hour, lashed by wind and rain, wet and miserable, they gave up. How could Hamakawa have survived? Either the tornado had carried him away, goodness knows where, or he'd been caught beneath the bus. . . . The thought made Tanner shudder.

Tanner went back inside the bus, tried to extract the driver from his seat. It was useless. Retrieving his cryo-kit and suitcase, Tanner left the bus, leading away Qingling, still too dazed to cry, and a visibly exhausted Chen. The canal was too far off. They had hardly left the vicinity of Ming Lake. Therefore, they walked back toward Daping.

They didn't go far. Chen fell to his knees, breathless, his face taking on an unhealthy pallor. Tanner admonished himself: of course, the old devil couldn't keep up with the pace he'd set. But it was not only exhaustion. Chen's wrinkled face twisted with pain and he suddenly complained of a sharp pang in his left arm.

Tanner had him lie down on the road's wet gravel. He checked the mole's pulse, inspected his eyes more and more anxiously. He started when he discerned the bluish lips, the uneven breathing. With a curse, he unfastened the wet shirt and stuck his ear against the smooth chest. When he looked up, Chen had already lost consciousness.

"What's happening?" shouted Qingling.

Tanner shook his head, unable to grasp this latest calamity: Chen was having a heart attack! It was too much. . . . Tanner kneeled in the mud and cried, the sobs racking a body unused to them. Qingling sat by him and hugged him wordlessly.

Stop bawling! Use the cryo-kit! That's why you've carried it all this way!

The thought lashed Tanner into action, as if Hamakawa himself had spoken. He shook himself, ashamed of his reaction. Chen Shaoxing wasn't dead yet! He rose, lifted the mud-spattered aluminum case, and opened it frantically. He'd lost so much time already!

Qingling frowned when she saw the hypodermic needles, vials, and pressurized spray cans. What was all that? Tanner took her by the shoulders, asking her to lend him all her attention:

"I'm going to try to save Chen's life, but I need your help. Can you help me, whatever happens?"

She brushed aside a strand of wet hair fallen over her eyes. She faltered: what was he going to do? In a few vivid sentences, he explained.

Her chin sagged.

Inside the aluminum case, Tanner picked up a large pressurized syringe, breaking the seal and turning to Chen. The needle, fitted to a long coil of plastic tubing, quested for the carotid. The neck's fat prevented Tanner from aiming accurately; he had to try three times before nailing the artery. A scarlet drop appeared in the plastic tube. Tanner opened the valve: the drop of blood beat a hasty retreat and the syringe started to pump the stabilizing serum inside Chen's head. He ordered Qingling to hold the syringe in place: the fluid would have to flow for at least an hour.

Meanwhile, Tanner took out the vials and instruments from the cryo-kit. The bottom unfolded into a thick, ovoidal, foam-lined bag. He connected a small compressed gas tank to a metal nozzle protruding from the bag, enclosing both in a canvas bag provided with an electronic gauge.

Tanner returned to Chen's side. The mole's breathing was barely audible, coming in snatches, and his pulse imperceptible. Tanner increased the flow of the stabilizing fluid to its maximum value and straddled Chen's broad chest.

"The serum must continue to circulate inside the brain!"

He massaged Chen's heart, no longer feeling his own fatigue, heedless of the cracks of the mole's broken ribs.

A warning light told him the syringe reservoir was empty. Drained, Tanner wiped away the water trickling into his eyes, though fortunately the rain had almost entirely stopped, and he took out from the case one of two blue bottles.

Chen, unmoving, had stopped breathing.

"We've got to hurry," muttered Tanner.

He screwed a stylet-capped plastic cannula to the nozzle of the bottle, giving it to Qingling to hold. He removed from the cryo-kit a spray can and a large scalpel. He tore out the useless syringe. A moment of hesitation, and then he set the scalpel against Chen's neck and attacked the tender flesh energetically. Qingling looked away.

The blood spurted, quickly stopped with a few squirts of the coagulating fluid. The scalpel sliced through the carotids and the cervical veins. Though Tanner continued to spray the coagulating fluid, blood still flowed in abundance. The agent paid no attention to it; he grabbed from Qingling's trembling hands the blue bottle and inserted the stylet cannula into the severed artery. He released the pressurized liquid. Blood drained slowly from the veins and the other carotid, to be replaced by a pinkish liquid. The blue bottle emptied. Qingling handed him the second one, which Tanner plugged into the other carotid.

"Please hold this."

Chen's head was still connected to the body by the vertebrae. Tanner slipped the strong blade of the scalpel between two vertebrae and leaned on it with all his weight. The blade cut through all the way to the wet soil.

He examined the head: the fluid now dripping from the veins and arteries was almost entirely clear. He reversed the head, the neck on top, took up one last spray can with his blood-soaked hand, and sprayed a white foam over the severed flesh. He also filled the mouth, nostrils, and ears with it. Opening the ovoid bag, he plunged the head inside it, smothering everything under a layer of white foam. Then, he firmly fastened the thick bag with a self-tightening clip, tied shut the outer bag, checked the positioning of the small compressed gas tank, and opened the valve. With a faint whistle, the gas inside started to drain from the tank.

Tanner straightened, catching his breath. He exchanged a look with Qingling, stared at his hands dripping with a peculiar red ooze. Only then did he fully realize what he'd just done. He would have wanted to laugh, or perhaps cry, but, of the conflicting emotions huddled within his breast, not even one tried to come out.

Two hours on foot. Luckily, it was no longer raining. Tanner and Qingling reached the outskirts of Daping. Here, the small port town did not seem to have really suffered. Tanner checked the cryo-kit: the coolant from the first tank was exhausted. The temperature gauge indicated 8°C. Not cold enough. He threw away the empty tank and snapped on a new one. He opened the valve. A bit later, the gauge showed 7°C.

They went on. Here and there, a window was broken, a few tiles had flown off, or scaffoldings had collapsed around the houses under construction. Nothing serious.

The city's center and port were a very different sight. Smashed hulls, shredded sails, and masts snapped in half littered the lakeside, amid muddy streaks splashed halfway across the central square. At least two fires were raging unchecked.

Tanner and Qingling made for the city square, or at least what was left of it. They spotted the second bus, seemingly intact in spite of a thick coat of drying mud, still parked in front of the rubble pile the Daping Tea Parlor had turned into. Half a dozen people, men, women, and teenagers, were searching through the ruins. A youth shouted suddenly; he lifted a plank, pointing to a dust-covered hand. Everybody hurried to dig out the victim, but their haste proved unjustified. The body of the second bus driver, encased in plaster and rubble, was carried onto the debris-strewn grass.

An overworked policeman with a handheld radio stopped by to see if there had been anything or anybody to save from the Daping Tea Parlor. He was told this was the third dead body removed from the ruins. Managing to catch the attention of the policeman, Tanner asked if there was any way of getting from Daping to the canal.

The policeman faltered, confronted by this tall, strapping fellow, his head shaved and his face slashed, his clothing spattered with blood, and loaded down with luggage.

He confined himself to gesturing impatiently toward the ruins:

"Don't count on the driver. He's dead. I don't know where the other bus is."

Tanner explained the other driver had died at the wheel of the second bus, on the northern road. The policeman nodded. Many people were dead. Which did not solve Tanner's problem:

"How can I get to the canal, then?"

"What for? The canal itself is blocked by mudslides and debris."

"But I've got to be in Nanxiang as soon as possible!"

The policeman blustered angrily. "Instead of thinking about leaving, you should help us clear away the rubble!"

Tanner looked again at the bus, immobilized, unused. Beside it the dead and the wounded were being laid out, apparently at random. The people digging up the rubble wore nothing to identify them. Tanner even saw children, age, eight or nine, who were helping to remove the smaller debris. He looked for stripes on the policeman's shoulders, but he realized this wasn't an officer.

The European agent pointed to a particularly wretched trio: an old lady with a bloody gash across her forehead who cradled a howling baby in her arms as she attended to a younger woman with a broken leg.

"Why aren't these victims identified?"

The policeman was taken aback. "They . . . they didn't tell me anything about that."

"And the rescuers too aren't badged. And what are children doing in there? It's dangerous."

"But we can't control everything! We're overwhelmed!"

"Where are your headquarters?"

"The chief of police is dead," explained the policeman. "Fuzhi, the second in command, was on duty at the station when the tornado struck. He's wounded."

"Don't you have a central command post? Communications?"

"We have five radios. We relay information as needed, from one policeman to the next."

"Your disaster relief plan is totally inadequate! There's no excuse for this utter chaos!"

Tanner felt the policeman was about to weep: "But we don't know what to do!"

The European agent sighed deeply.

"You've got to establish a central command post, a communications system, an identification system, a security team, and a transportation system. Where can we put a command post? Is the hospital untouched?"

"The nearest hospital is in Tanzhou, thirteen kilometers to the north. I don't know if they've been hit."

"Aren't you in touch with the hospital?"

"No."

"You should be in constant touch with the hospital. Send one of your men there with a radio. . . . No, send a civilian. You need all your men here. Where can we get power?"

The policeman pointed to the town hall, behind them. Except for some missing tiles, the building seemed unscathed.

"The town hall has a generator."

"It will be our headquarters."

Tanner strode resolutely toward the town hall, with Qingling and the bewildered policeman hard on his heels.

"Tell all your agents that, henceforth, they will be reporting here. You will be in charge of communications. Also, find all the doctors, nurses, and other people with medical training. One of your men will be the head of the security team; tell him to requisition a vehicle. . . ."

Still firing off instructions like a machine gun, Tanner burst into the town hall's council room. The mayor was nowhere to be found. Two councillors—dealing with a mother carrying a howling baby—greeted them circumspectly. Tanner pointed to one of the councillors with his finger:

"You! Call everybody and tell them the town hall is now the headquarters for disaster relief operations. One of you, under the head of security, will requisition all the equipment needed by the rescuers and doctors, making sure that everything is accounted for and that no looting happens. The policeman with me . . . what's your name?"

"Zuo Fushan."

"Zuo will be in charge of communications. All messages concerning the emergency plan must go to him!"

The oldest councillor present protested shrilly:

"Emergency plan? What emergency plan?"

Tanner struggled to answer without blowing up:

"The emergency plan we're currently implementing!" *And making up as we go along.* "We'll need blankets, fuel, and medical supplies—and anything else required for first aid, as determined by the chief of our medical team . . . as soon as we have one."

Stunned at first, the Daping councillors were soon delighted to obey someone who seemed to know what he was doing.

Three nurses and a doctor showed up. The doctor was appointed chief of the medical team, with a radio-equipped civilian as assistant. The medical personnel had to stop running everywhere, asserted Tanner, it would be up to the civilians to pull out the wounded from the rubble. A nurse protested: without a doctor's supervision, the civilians might cause irreversible damage to the most seriously injured by pulling them out, and some of the wounded still trapped might require immediate care.

The doctor interrupted him: Tanner was right, there were

too few of them to justify dispersing their efforts. Care had to be rationed: all the wounded would be brought—by civilians—to headquarters, where triage could take place.

Volunteers soon turned up in droves. Eager teenagers were set to identifying the rescuers with hastily cut plastic armbands. The wounded were classified according to four categories, each with its corresponding colored armband: green, for superficial wounds; yellow for serious injuries that did not require immediate attention; red for emergencies; and black for the dead or the dying.

"We'll need UV-proof tarps to cover the wounded as soon as the Eye rises. And, please, keep the children away from the ruins."

Tanner realized he was still holding the cryo-kit. He called over Zuo Fushan. Was there a freezer in the building? Zuo scratched his head: probably. Tanner and Qingling followed Zuo downstairs, where they found a small working freezer. Tanner disposed of his cryo-kit, then turned to Qingling, who seemed totally exhausted.

"Stay here and get some rest."

He then said to Zuo that nobody was to touch, under any circumstance, the item inside the freezer. Tanner thought for a moment the policeman was going to click his heels and salute.

"I'll see to it personally!"

They went back up. A young girl presented him with a bright yellow hard hat, adorned with the broad black strokes of a clumsily painted ideogram: *Boss* . . .

They got in touch with Tanzhou hospital. It was overwhelmed, of course, and the accent of the person he was speaking to was impenetrable. Tanner called over the doctor and handed him the radio: it was his job to deal with it.

Waves of wounded were coming in now. Fifty at least filled the hallways of the building. The doctor and the nurses bustled around the ones with red armbands, while volunteers gave first aid to the walking wounded. A load of those with serious injuries—yellow armbands—were sent to Tanzhou aboard the bus.

Since they no longer had to fear the Eye's malevolent stare, the victims with black armbands were left outside.

A sudden hubbub broke out near the improvised morgue. Tanner ran to intervene. A woman and two indignant young children were insulting the young security guards, and casting stones at them. He interposed himself:

"What's going on?"

Tears were shaping muddy runnels through the woman's soil-encrusted cheeks as she hiccuped with pain and outrage, her hand held out toward a hideously burned human shape lying in a stretcher. In spite of the black armband knotted around one blackened limb, the injured man moaned and shuddered slightly. The woman gathered her breath to wail:

"He's not dead! He's not dead! Take care of him, you wretches!"

"He's too badly burned," Tanner firmly explained. "We can't waste the time of the doctors and valuable drugs on a dying man."

The woman flew at him, hysterical. The security guards were forced to hold her back and throw her out. Two young parents were now grappling with Tanner: it was a terrible mistake, their son had been put in the morgue, but he was not dead yet, he could still be saved! They dragged Tanner to the bedside of a four-year-old boy. The mother started to caress the bloodied head, though the neck muscles were already rigid, and mumbled incoherent words of comfort.

Tanner struggled with a moment's dizziness. So many dead children. It was impossible to grasp. He called a guard over:

"Double the guard here! Throw the parents out! Nobody must come here, or we'll lose control. There'll be time later to mourn the dead."

The rescuers were now wearing hats and shades. Was the Eye rising already? Tanner checked his watch, incredulous, then looked at the green-tinged sky. Could it be so late? A teenager brought him a bowl of noodles and boiled carrots. Tanner thanked him, went downstairs to see how Qingling was doing. By a pile of wet clothing, the young woman was sleeping on the bare concrete floor, rolled up in a blanket.

Tanner didn't dare wake her. He found a chair and sat down for the first time in hours. He gulped down his meal. Weariness fell upon his shoulders like a mantle. He gazed at Qingling's bare foot sticking out the end of the blanket; he would have liked to get rid of his wet shoes, like her. He thought of Hamakawa to stop feeling sorry for himself.

Hamakawa . . . He was unable to believe he was dead. . . .

Tanner shook himself. He was going to fall asleep on his chair. He got up and climbed back to the main floor. Zuo Fushan spotted him first:

"I've found an all-terrain vehicle. How about requisitioning it to transport the wounded?"

Tanner, alert once more, weighed the implications of the policeman's find. A vehicle . . . He congratulated Zuo: where was this mechanical marvel?

Gunfire interrupted his reply.

"What was that?"

Zuo smiled, embarrassed. "I assume they're warning shots meant to scare away looters."

"You assume? Why don't you speak to your security?" asked Tanner, pointing at the radio.

Zuo frowned, perplexed. He lifted the radio in the palm of his hand and thumbed open a channel, from which issued a stream of crackling and shrill whistles.

"The Eye just rose," he replied simply.

Tanner swallowed a curse. As if they didn't have enough trouble, the Eye was now perturbing radio transmissions. He returned to the topic of the gunshots:

"So you have guns here?"

"Only two rifles," answered Zuo defensively. "For emergencies. Don't forget, many criminals are expelled from northern cities and sent here to take part in the colonization effort."

Tanner raised his hand without questioning him further:

"Very well . . . but let's try not to alarm the whole town."

They set up a courier network, with long-legged young boys

and girls in charge of relaying messages. Communications with Tanzhou hospital could not be restored as easily, but, the last they'd heard, the skeletal hospital staff had the situation more or less in hand.

Tanner turned again to Zuo:

"Finally, we never did go and see that famous vehicle. . . ."

They walked through the corridors of the town hall, careful not to stumble over the wounded—so many children!—stretched out on blankets spread over the tiled floor. They went outside. On one side of the building, under a makeshift tent, a bunch of teenagers chattered excitedly as they cut rectangles of about two square meters out of a large sheet of UV-proof polymer, which would be used to protect the victims still trapped in the rubble.

Tanner followed Zuo beneath a gallery. Away from the Eye's glare, a rugged four-wheel-drive truck of Terran make crouched in the shade. The small van was not new: the vehicle's body was tarnished and dented, the windshield cratered by gravel, the tires crusted with mud. Sitting impatiently at the wheel, the European driver seethed as he waited. Tanner had no trouble recognizing him: it was Franz Gern, the meteorologist they had shared a cabin with aboard the *Tao Qian*.

However, the scientist did not identify the head of the relief operations.

"So?" demanded Gern, glowering at Tanner. "You're the boss? When will you let me leave with my van? It's European property: you have no right to requisition it!"

Zuo ordered him to shut up. Tanner preached moderation: this was an emergency, the van would be restored to him afterward. Didn't the honorable foreigner wish to help these poor people? Gern's breath whistled out between his teeth: yes, he was ready to help them, but in his own way, by studying the meteorological conditions.

"Treating the injured is all well and good, but would it not be better if tornadoes could be predicted with the help of a proper climatological model?"

Tanner conceded the point, but it was a bit late for prevention.

He rushed downstairs to retrieve Qingling and the cryo-kit. The young woman was awake, dressed in an oversized—but dry—change of clothing donated by a pair of helpful teenagers. Tanner and Qingling embraced, as the two young girls tittered shyly. Next, the European agent recovered his cryo-kit, glancing with instant satisfaction at the temperature: −12°C. That should do for a while.

They returned together. Gern had a good memory for faces, after all: he recognized Qingling. He looked again at Tanner and made the connection:

"You were on the liner, right? What happened to your hair?"

Tanner gestured exasperatedly. "Must have been the wind!"

He handed over the direction of operations to Zuo, who watched him prepare to leave with misgivings.

"Where are you going?"

"Don't be afraid, I'm just making an inspection tour. In any case, you've got the situation well in hand, am I correct?"

"Er . . . yes, of course, but—"

"See you later, then!"

Tanner climbed aboard. Qingling followed, throwing him a befuddled glance. The van's motor started up with a smooth and forceful growl, answering Tanner's wishes. Mechanically, the truck seemed to be in flawless condition.

"Where are we going?" asked Gern mournfully.

"What kind of range can you get out of the fuel onboard?"

"Almost nil," Gern said with a scowl. "I've got hardly any left and everybody refuses to sell me some."

"I'll take care of that. How much do you need to get to Linzi?"

The European's jaw dropped.

"Linzi? Across the desert?"

However, before Tanner could explain, Gern laughed:

"*Gut, gut!* It looks like we understand each other, after all. That's where I wanted to go. At least two other cyclones were seen farther north. I wasn't thinking of going all the way to Linzi, actually, but I'm always ready to help out. As long as I have the fuel . . . and as long as I can stop along the way to make observations."

Tanner almost retorted that he was in charge, but he kept his mouth shut. Why alienate Gern with disobliging words when the man was feeling so friendly? There would be enough time later to make him understand who was, indeed, the boss.

With a noise of grinding gears, the van set off. They passed the bus coming back from Tanzhou and parked near the general store, where a couple of husky fellows, under a policeman's supervision, were distributing the precious fuel.

The policeman recognized Tanner and he reacted with due diligence. He unquestioningly parceled out a hundred liters of ethanol. The odorous fluid was poured into the tank. There would be enough left to refill the tank later on. In any case, confirmed Gern, it was enough to reach Linzi. Moving cautiously, the truck came back through the city square, avoiding a group of rescuers carrying wounded wrapped in UV-proof blankets. Standing in front of the town hall, Zuo Fushan, his police hat colored red by the Eye's rays, saluted uncertainly. Tanner saluted back, adding a faint "Farewell!" under his breath.

The policeman's attention was diverted: a breathless young girl ran up to him. He listened carefully, asked a few quick questions. Out of sheer reflex, he grabbed his radio, before remembering that the Eye was scrambling communications. He raised his gaze to the Eye, whispered a curse, then followed the young girl inside the town hall.

A horn blared twice: Gern's van was preventing the bus loaded with more wounded from going back to Tanzhou. Tanner pointed north.

"Let's go," he said simply.

NINETEEN

TANNER DREAMED OF WINDS, SAILS, AND BLOOD. HE DIRECTED HIS weapon at the heart of Chen's wife, getting off a shot. But she wasn't dead; she walked over to the bodies of Qingling and Hamakawa, stretched out on the ground. With a large scalpel, she slit their throats. The stabilizing serum dripped slowly from the severed arteries. Chen's wife invited Tanner to lie down, still holding her bloodied scalpel. Tanner fled, but the cryo-kit kept bumping into everything and slowing him down. He went down a staircase slippery with blood. He was back in Bloembergen's place. The door burst, rammed open by his pursuer; a Lengshuijiang dragon wedging its black snout between the broken planks, its green eye shining malevolently in the room's darkness. Behind it, the Enclave was blazing . . .

A sudden jolt of the van awakened Tanner, his head cushioned between Qingling's warm thighs. A soft hand caressed his shaven pate.

"Did you sleep well?"

"No," he grumbled, rising from the backseat of the van.

"One nightmare after another . . ."

Qingling embraced him to reassure him. Then, it was her turn to curl up in the hollow of the seat, her head using Tanner's thigh as a pillow.

The state of the road surface discouraged any impulse to go faster. A dark desert stretched all around, searingly desolate in the metallic dusk. The Eye had just set, and so Tanner had slept almost four hours, as he might have guessed from the stiff muscles of his shoulders and neck. The road—more of a trail, in fact—extended northward, as straight as a ruler. Far off, the Jade River briefly mirrored the clouds, daubed with the fading colors of dusk, and then a very dark night fell upon the world, the clouds above smothering all sources of light.

They spent hours watching the trail scamper beneath the front bumper, fleeing from the twin light cones of the headlights. Tanner took over from Gern at the wheel. Fluffy fissures cracked the opaque cloud veil, and the desert grew slightly brighter as dim auroras danced above, milky, shapeless, so wraithlike the stars shone through them.

Breaking with the surreal ambiance, Gern dictated into his port-a-screen a description of the auroras, characterizing them with the help of a specialized and necessarily obscure jargon. He noted the time, the temperature, the atmospheric pressure, as well as the equatorial coordinates of the Dragon's Eye.

The trail turned terribly bumpy, and the van slowed to thirty kilometers an hour. The suspension whined as if on the verge of death and Qingling almost fell from her seat, which put a definitive end to her slumber. Gern spotted something on the road, *oohed* with glee, and asked to stop.

Though he entertained the idea of refusing, Tanner finally gave in:

"Oh, why the hell not? I was beginning to feel like a piss."

The shaking stopped, the motor fell silent. They went out into the night's cool air, stretching with out-and-out delight. An unexpected tang floated in the desert air, a mix of salt and tobacco. Tanner relieved himself, then joined Gern, who was examining the trail and the surrounding desert with a pocket light. In spite of himself, Tanner was intrigued by the researcher's behavior.

"What are you looking for? Do you hope to find signs of life this far from the terraformed regions?"

"You'd be surprised by the distances some seeds can cover," answered Gern without interrupting his searching. "Earth plants can now be found as far away as the Kang Islands, in mid-ocean, a thousand kilometers from the nearest land. But that's not what I'm looking for. In fact, I'm looking for . . . this!"

Something sparkled in the desert sand: Gern aimed his lamp's beam on a small, translucent creature, approximately hand sized, not unlike a crumpled plastic bag. Half jellyfish, half squid, it was wholly dead.

"Here's another . . ."

Now that they'd learned how to spot them, they found a multitude of similar animals, of all sizes, lying shriveled in the dusty gravel. The phenomenon that had stranded them in the heart of the desert was surely recent, since the largest creatures were still moist and sticky. Qingling joined them, her curiosity piqued by their comings and goings:

"But those are crystal fishes! What are they doing here?"

Gern gestured westward with his hand:

"They came from the river."

"I don't doubt it," retorted Qingling. "But they surely didn't make the trip willingly!"

"No. They were transported by a tornado."

"Another tornado?" exclaimed Qingling, incredulous. "It's a damn epidemic!"

"You said you were working to establish the meteorological model of New China?" inquired Tanner.

"That's right."

"You want me to believe that after more than a century, nobody's done it yet? I would have thought a proper survey had been done *before* the colonization."

"New China is different: the Dragon's Eye introduces a perturbing factor, with a cycle of two thousand years. So far, only a small fraction of a single cycle has gone by since the arrival of the first automated probes, which means that hard data is scarce. We've had to resort to computer models, necessarily incomplete and meant to be corrected by accumulated experience. To give you an idea of their failings, the models never predicted cyclones in the Jade basin. Historically, which means for the last fifty years or so, tornadoes were in fact extremely rare around here. Until these last few years, when tornadoes have become increasingly common and murderous . . ." He shook his head, frustrated. "*Ach!* If only we could put weather satellites in orbit without having the Eye destroy them . . ."

"Is it really impossible to manufacture satellites able to stand up to the stellar wind of the Eye?"

"Impossible? Not at all! But very difficult and expensive. And the payoff would be meager, since most of the time, the data would not be able to punch through the ionosphere. Unless they used lasers, but those would require more power, making the satellites even more expensive. The New Chinese government has other priorities. . . . Bah! If this planet had been perfect, they would never have given it to the Chinese."

"Let's go," Tanner said. "We still have several hours of driving before we reach Linzi. Do you want me to drive?"

Resolved to endure, their backs increasingly bruised by the vehicle's jolting, they pushed on. A vermilion dawn revealed a vista of rounded dunes, rust-colored. As the sun rose, the salmon-pink horizon blurred. The van's grimy interior turned into a sauna redolent with the stench of their sweat. The windows had to be opened to avoid suffocation. The water flask was empty. Soon, they started feeling thirsty. And hungry . . .

Tanner checked the cryo-kit: the temperature of its contents was getting dangerously close to zero degrees Celsius. He connected his third and last container. Whistling faintly, the gas expanded and cooled the interior. Once the small tank was empty, the internal temperature had dropped to almost −8°C. In theory, thanks to the stabilizing liquid, the brain could undergo thawing, but it was far from desirable.

They pushed on.

Far ahead, splinters of green indented the rusty horizon. Forlorn dandelions and sickly brambles sprang up alongside the road. A cocoa palm. A dead yucca. And then, the outbreak: in a few kilometers, an authentic jungle sprang from the desert sands. The road, its surface improving noticeably, snaked between two walls of vegetation for another fifty kilometers before reaching the first human habitation since they'd entered the desert, three hundred kilometers farther south.

They halted. It was a general store, a prefab cabin hastily put together, unremarkable and poorly maintained. Qingling stepped out of the truck, quickly wilting in the humid heat:

"Don't tell me we're going to have more twisters."

Tanner took off his sweat-drenched shirt, shrugging fatalistically:

"Why not? We should be used to them by now."

He went to knock at the door of the store. Was anybody home? He knocked again. Still no signs of life. His patience sapped by the heat, he kicked the door near the handle. The frame cracked. A second kick and the latch tore away from the frame.

The reek of rancid soy sauce and moldy food sweetened the cabin's air. Amid the dry goods and sundry groceries, Tanner found water bottles, uncapped one, and gave it to Qingling. She poured the crystal-clear water down her parched throat, but drank too fast, choked, managed to curse between two hiccups, and then started to laugh while still hiccuping. Tanner drank next. Qingling uncapped another bottle and, with an ecstatic groan, let the water stream down over her hair, coarsened by dirt and grit; over her face, reddened by the heat; over her outsized blouse, wet with perspiration.

Tanner explored the shop further. With a shout of joy, he

discovered shoes and socks. His boots were still damp, and so he jubilantly threw them away, putting on new socks and shoes, delighting in the simple luxury of dry feet. His second major discovery was a functional freezer in the back shop. Tanner ran into the van to retrieve the cryo-kit, under Gern's mystified gaze.

"What's in there?"

"You don't want to know."

They took out enough frozen meat and sherbet to squeeze the cryo-kit inside, then set the temperature to its minimum setting. Qingling opened a box of rose-flavored Popsicles and passed them around. Gern took the popsicle and looked around guiltily at the dusty back shop.

"What will the owner say if he surprises us here?"

Tanner shrugged, uncaring.

"We'll pay him for what we took, what else?"

"We broke the door."

Tanner opened a fridge and took out a green-furred peach, a wrinkled cucumber, and a plate of tofu with dry, crumbling corners. He estimated these perishables had been moldering for at least a week. The prospect of meeting the proprietor was unlikely, Tanner deduced. Gern changed topics, aiming his Popsicle at the freezer:

"Looks like that bag is pretty valuable."

"Extremely valuable. We'll wait as long as we need to for it to be thoroughly frozen."

Gern got up to examine the freezer, especially the electrical plug.

"We could take the freezer with us. I've got the motor powering a 220-V generator. Didn't you notice the outlet behind the bench?"

Tanner threw him an astounded glance:

"Couldn't you say so earlier?"

With Gern watching worriedly, Tanner and Qingling managed to rearrange the meteorological gear in order to fit the heavy freezer in the back of the vehicle. Tanner whistled happily: the problem of cooling the cryo-kit was solved for the rest of the drive. He climbed behind the wheel again, Gern sitting beside him, but he had to look for Qingling, who was frowning, as if she was listening to something:

"Are you coming?"

She shushed him, hand in the air, head cocked to listen. Tanner heard it too: a buzzing in the sky, getting closer . . . The shrill buzzing grew louder, became a roar filling the entire sky. A craft as sleek as a raindrop burst above the clearing and disappeared just as fast, humming angrily. Two more jetcopters raced after the first, just as oblivious to Gern's truck. . . . Oblivious? Not quite: the buzzing suddenly split in two, with a lesser chord shifting pitch. It was easy to guess that one of the copters was doubling back. Tanner grabbed the wheel, then released it. Trying to flee was absurd. They couldn't outrun a jet-propelled aircraft. Cutting down its still considerable speed, the menacing snout of one of the jetcopters appeared again, came to within fifty meters, swung around the van and its passengers while raising a cloud of dust. Tanner had no trouble recognizing the white ideograms painted on the green camouflage of the fuselage: *New China*.

An army helicopter.

Uninteresting! decided the occupants of the noisy aircraft. The humming of the blades deepened, blowing grit into the eyes of the three travelers. Like a giddy ladybug, the helicopter whirled as it rose. The jets screamed, ripping the air, and the jetcopter returned to its path above the jungle canopy. The roar of the jets abated, reduced to a distant hum, which finally vanished into the silence.

Disconcerted, Tanner, Qingling, and Gern discussed the encounter. They had all recognized the insignia of the New Chinese Army. The army? Here? And the aircraft seemed to be making for Linzi. Or perhaps for Nanxiang, the capital, suggested Tanner. They agreed on one point: the incident was worrisome, especially in the context of the last few months.

Tanner got the van underway again: more than ever, he wanted to get back to the Enclave.

The forest made way for tilled fields, dotted with pointy-roofed farms and crosshatched with rows of trees in order to keep the still thin and fragile soil in place. Peopling this bucolic landscape, thousands of farmers were taking advantage of the Eye's absence to care for their precious harvests. The Jade sparkled briefly between the low hills in the distance. Nestled in a loop of the river, Linzi itself appeared.

Tanner drove through town, parking the van in front of the train station, and got out, watched at a prudent remove by passersby. Between their Terran-made truck, their ratty and disheveled personal appearance, and the presence of an actual European, the little group could not hope to pass unnoticed.

They divided up the work. While Qingling and Gern bought new clothes, Tanner would purchase train tickets for Lengshuijiang.

In the washroom, Tanner almost jumped when he caught sight of himself. With his green eye, the dawning red-haired stubble on his skull and cheeks, his mud-spattered and faded clothes, his Band-Skin dressing, and the blood-crusted slashes on his right cheek, he looked like a beggar of indefinite race. He washed, shaved carefully, found a cleaner shirt in his suitcase, and swallowed one of his last skin-color capsule. There, he was less scary now. . . .

Nevertheless, he noticed that the facial modifications were starting to wear off. His eyelids were almost back to their original size. If only he could have camouflaged his green eye again! He cursed the cosmetician who had forgotten to include spare lenses. But who could have foreseen such a string of disasters?

Tanner sighed: it was all over now. He had tracked down Chen Shaoxing, for better or for worse. He could now take the train to Lengshuijiang and get back to the EFTA. Where he would have to confront Bloembergen. Therefore, his trials were not over yet. With an impatient sigh, Tanner postponed thinking about it: he would have all the time he needed during the long train trip back. He faced the mirror again, as if to probe the intentions concealed by his bicolored gaze. Another gaze, ink-black, occupied his thoughts. Qingling . . . Always Qingling.

Did he really intend to go back to Earth with the young woman? Actually, he would no doubt be unable to return to Earth that easily. Hadn't the European Bureau of External Affairs posted him to the EFTA so that he could take over from Bloembergen? Of course, he didn't have to accept that position. But what would the Bureau say? What would his father, the famous Colonel Tanner, say?

Seized by a sudden fit of righteous anger, Tanner paled: they could all go fuck themselves! He'd had enough! Enough! He recalled a clear voice saying, in between sharp sobs: *I want children! I want a husband! Is it so shameful? Certainly no worse than lying, stealing, and killing people!* Qingling, at least, yearned for a real life. What did the Bureau offer except the emptiness of an existence spent obeying orders?

Tanner exited the washroom, leaned against a newly plastered wall, his face hot, a burst of heat blazing through him. He reached a decision, so easily he felt dizzy: once he was back on Earth, after handing over Chen Shaoxing's head, he'd resign from the European Bureau. A feverish anticipation of deliverance seized him by the throat. There, he thought, almost weeping, it's done. . . . It's over.

He knew he would not change his mind. Not after Qingling. Not after Jay's death. He remembered his life before, but was it really *his* life, this ceaseless rush of places, faces, trips, orders to carry out without even understanding them at times. All of it jumbled together like a handful of pictures scattered by a gale.

Tanner put a stop to the whirlwind of memories. Still leaning against the wall, he drank in the subdued elegance of the Linzi train station, its sleepy shops, its clamoring *dazibaos*, its employees waxing the floor. He savored the smell of ginger and fried dumplings, the whiff of paraffin from the floor polish, the faintly ammoniacal pungency of the *dazibao* ink. He filled his ears, one last time, with the sounds of shoes slapping on the tiled floor, with the laughter and jeers of the station workers, with children's cries, with the almost subliminal flute and violin music coming through the speakers.

He walked slowly toward the ticket booths. It was over. . . . It was over for good. But, later, he would think of New China with affection. His memory would drape a decent forgetfulness over the squalor and the sleepless nights, the blunders and the murders, while lending a magical aura to visions of the past: the effervescence of the Lengshuijiang marketplace, the New Riverine Palace, seemingly afloat on the morning mist, Qingling's gilded body reclining on the train's bunk, a swim through the limpid waters of Ming Lake, the friendship of Jay Hamakawa . . .

The counter clerk dipped her red-striped cap, frowning as her face expressed her lack of understanding.

"*Wo budong!*" she grumbled with an awful Cantonese accent.

"Two tickets for Lengshuijiang," repeated Tanner in Cantonese.

The employee shook her head negatively:

"Nanxiang!"

"Yes, with a stop in Nanxiang, but I want to go on to Lengshuijiang."

Tanner refrained from grimacing: was the railway network so anarchic that travelers were forced to stop in Nanxiang to arrange the next leg of a trip? The employee jabbered a few more unintelligible words.

"Sorry, I didn't catch that. . . ."

"There are no more trains for Lengshuijiang!" shouted the employee as if Tanner was deaf. "No more trains! Don't you know it's war?"

"What?"

"War! War!" she proclaimed at the top of her voice. "What

hole did you just crawl out from? Don't you know our valiant troops have invaded Ferret Island to kick out the Terran scum?"

Tanner stepped back as if he had been slapped:

"No . . . No, I didn't know . . ."

He hurried toward a comscreen to connect with the Nanxiang bulletin board system, the high-pitched voice of the woman still screeching in his ears. *War! War!* So, the fears of Lison Robanna, the executive secretary of the European Bureau, had indeed come to pass. Tanner allowed himself a disenchanted scowl: wasn't it to prevent such a rebellion that he had been supposed to get in touch with Chen Shaoxing? Was he too late, then?

"Mister! *Mister!*"

The clerk was shouting herself hoarse trying to attract his attention, her upraised hand waving the tickets he'd bought and forgot on the counter. Tanner, much to the amusement of the other travelers, hastened to retrieve his tickets, stammered his thanks, and rushed back to the bank of screens.

The bulletin board told him little more than the few words of the ticketseller.

Thursday afternoon, Xiao Jiping, until then president of New China, had dissolved the presidential state with the accord of his ministers. New China would henceforth be known as Imperial China, with Xiao Jiping self-proclaimed as its new emperor, the first of the Xiao dynasty. The first edict of the new emperor was draconian: it officialized the break off of diplomatic relations with Earth, canceled all reimbursements of the debt, and declared the Enclave part of the imperial possessions. At the same time, the New Chinese Army, now known as the Imperial Army, had invaded the EFTA.

Nervously tapping the screen's surface, Tanner explored all the nooks of the system, ultimately sparse with additional specifics: censorship was probably responsible. It was revealing that Europe, Japan, and China were no longer mentioned as politically independent entities. The bulletin board's official line spoke only of "Earth." There was nothing, however, that might lead him to believe the EFTA had fallen to the invading troops. Which meant that it was still holding out—or at least that the European military base covering the northern reaches of Ferret Island was still inviolate. Tanner regained his usual confidence. For a few chilling moments, he had truly wondered how he would ever make it back to Earth. Now the problem was slightly less insuperable: he had to reach the Enclave.

Gern and Qingling appeared. She ran toward him, unrecognizable in a very staid red and white outfit, almost traditional—not at all what she was used to wearing. She threw herself in Tanner's arms, distraught:

"Zheng, did you hear? It's terrible!"

"I know. I just read it on the bulletin board. . . . And all the trains go no farther than Nanxiang."

"How will we get back to Lengshuijiang?"

"Do you think my van could be useful?" asked Gern.

Tanner threw him a knowing look:

"I thought you were going back to study your tornadoes?"

Gern wiped the sweat on his freckled brow:

"Circumstances have changed. Don't forget I went down to Ming Lake against the orders of the Nanxiang bureaucrats. And I'm easy to spot, am I not? You can't understand, Mr. Li, how it feels to be white in such circumstances."

"You'd be surprised. . . . But let's get back to your proposal. You're offering your van to get us to Lengshuijiang? Is there a trail through the Northern Desert?"

Qingling and Gern exchanged looks. The woman shook her head negatively and the European's shoulders sagged.

"Anyway, we would be much too noticeable," added Tanner. "You can do what you want, but Qingling and I will take the train to Nanxiang. There, we'll play it by ear. However, if you'll let me give you a piece of advice: get rid of the vehicle before it gets you into trouble."

Gern pummeled his forehead, unable to decide:

"Do you know how much it cost to import that vehicle by space freight? And I'd leave it like that, for anyone to pick it up?"

"A retreating army sometimes has to abandon its artillery. We won't be doing any worse."

"Give me ten minutes," Gern said, devastated. "I've got to recover my notes and some of my gear."

"All right, but make it quick!"

TWENTY

THE TRIP TO NANXIANG WAS UNEVENTFUL. THE TRAIN WAS STILL UN-comfortable, but there were few enough passengers that Tanner, Qingling, and Gern were able to lie down on the fiberglass benches and get some sleep, uneasy though it was.

"Ten minutes to Nanxiang," sputtered a loudspeaker. They rubbed their eyes, stretched, gazed outside. As Green Night drew to an end, the first lights of Nanxiang shone in the dark. As if scared away by political uncertainty, the auroras had made themselves scarce. The uncommonly bare night sky allowed the stars to shine unhindered.

Tanner checked the cryo-kit: −9°C. Its long stay in the van's freezer had brought the temperature down, but it was bound to start increasing again soon. Qingling snuggled against him, begging for a measure of comfort. He fondled her, kissed her, promised her that everything would turn out for the best . . .

The bright lights along the quays of Nanxiang's sumptuous train station swept by their window. The brakes squealed and the train stopped. Qingling pointed toward the almost deserted main hall. Scurrying like khaki green ants, soldiers were setting up a barricade across the pink granite expanse, leaving only a narrow passage through, right by a plastic table. It looked most definitely like an identity check.

Tanner swore, a thousand mad ideas flashing through his mind: staying aboard the train, jumping off on the other side and fleeing down the tracks . . . Calm down, he admonished himself. What was he afraid of? His passport would check out. But Qingling no longer had a passport. And what about Gern? He ran the greatest risk. Tanner threw the European a quick glance, worry overwhelming him. And what if the soldiers also went through their luggage? He rose, leading Qingling by the hand. It wouldn't help to fret uselessly.

It was indeed an identity control. The drowsy passengers complained for form's sake when they were told to line up, but the display of the soldiers' firepower cut short any extended remonstrations.

The soldiers in charge of the control itself painstakingly checked every element: passport, retinal prints, identification implants. They were thorough but behaved correctly; there were no scenes, no useless brutality. It was Tanner's turn. Courteously, though coldly, an official asked for his passport. Tanner handed it over. Meanwhile, a female soldier subjected him to a retinal scan. A picture was taken. An identification recorder was pressed against his upper arm and the implant's code appeared on the screen. He was brought back in front of the official, who seemed unhappy, his gaze going from the passport's photograph to Tanner's face.

"If the retina and the implant didn't check out, I would have taken you for an impostor. What happened to your hair?"

"I'm from Ming Lake. I was hurt during a tornado strike, and they shaved my head to treat me."

The official seemed to relent.

"So, you're a victim of those tornadoes we've all heard about? But what are you doing in Nanxiang?"

"We've come—with my wife here behind me—to get my eye

examined by a specialist." He pointed to his green eye. "Look how it's become discolored since my accident. It's gotten so I can hardly see out of it anymore. The doctors in Tanzhou can't figure it out."

The official came up to Tanner, examined his eye:

"Indeed, how strange. . . . Do you know the doctor Jing Yu, near the Park of Memories? He's a great master of the art: he took care of my mother, who's almost blind, and now she sees well enough to babysit our children."

Tanner bowed respectfully.

"I shall follow your advice most gladly and speedily."

"Very well, now move along," said the official, handing back Tanner's passport. "Next! Your wife, you say? You can stay, but she's got to answer our questions."

The soldiers did not treat Qingling's lack of a passport lightly. She was required to give the names of her parents and her citizen's identification number, which she luckily knew by heart. The implant in her arm confirmed her assertions, but the official still reminded her curtly that she would need to get a new copy of her passport made as soon as possible. Qingling's voice fluttered tremulously: she had lost everything in the tornado strike, and now they were going to war with those horrible Terrans. It was terrible, absolutely terrible!

The official smiled at her, comforting.

"Don't you worry. The Terrans won't get to Nanxiang. Remember, we're here to protect you."

Tanner and Qingling, released, walked all the way to the terminal's doors. They stopped, made as if to check the contents of their baggage, and observed Gern's reception. . . . As could be expected, the European caused a sensation. The official went through each identifying document backward and forward, subjected Gern to a barrage of questions in an unfriendly tone. The meteorologist was finally let through, but two soldiers escorted him straight to one of the lacquered wood benches lining the station walls. All three sat together, Gern hardly daring to gaze forlornly in Tanner's direction.

Time passed. The soldiers conscientiously identified the last passengers. Once the routine checks were over, Gern was brought back to see an official, who was discussing the case with his superior via his port-a-screen. The conversation went back and forth. Ever more probing questions were put to Gern, and the arguing resumed between the two functionaries. Finally, the checkpoint's official berated Gern at length, with the scientist nodding helplessly. His baggage was searched mercilessly. Additional questions were asked about the strange scientific instruments he traveled with.

Tanner's nerves were on the verge of snapping. With every passing second, he was afraid the soldiers might come and ask what he was waiting for. . . . But no. The official finally returned to Gern all his documents, along with a card that was pinned to his chest and the recommendation that he keep the card always in evidence.

Shaking nervously, Gern hastened to pack again the scattered contents of his suitcases. He then walked unsteadily toward the main exit, without looking at Tanner and Qingling. The couple waited for a few more minutes before leaving the station under the scrutiny of the soldiers' eyes.

Beneath the sky's starry dome, Gulouxi Street stretched in front of them, deserted, almost unreal in the yellow glare of the sodium lights. When he spotted Gern's abandoned suitcases on the sidewalk, Tanner felt sheer panic rise up in him. Where had the European gone? Retching noises emanating from behind some ornamental shrubbery answered that question. Gern, kneeling on the lawn, was vomiting. Tanner asked if he needed any help, but Gern shook his head; he was already feeling better.

Tanner derided him gently: "I would have thought the nerves of a tornado chaser were made of sterner stuff."

Gern reappeared, weaving unsteadily, his skin almost waxy in the sodium vapor light. He managed to produce a sketchy smile:

"As a matter of fact, I found those soldiers more frightening than a tornado."

"What do we do now?" asked Qingling. "I'm scared."

Aboard the train, Tanner had pondered the next step in their trip back. The prospect of again asking Bai Jingtu for help was not a cheery one, but did he have a choice? He was their only contact in Nanxiang. Of course, the *diaochabu* agent had not been very cooperative, but recent events had surely strengthened his solidarity with fellow Earth citizens. And the inn would allow them to eat and sleep before the next day dawned. Qingling was right: they were so tired they were no longer able to think logically.

A sleepy taxi driver dropped them off a few blocks away from the Lanting Zi. Determined to be cautious, Tanner had given a phony address in the restaurant's vicinity: the building was real enough, but it had no connection he knew of with Bai Jingtu. They trudged the remaining distance to the Lanting Zi. All the lights were off, except a night-light above the door, throwing pitch-black shadows at the feet of the gallery's pillars.

It wasn't locked. They entered. The great dining room was dark, almost deserted with the exception of a couple of youths washing the floor. Friday night was almost over, the Green Night festivities had come to a close only three hours earlier, and the washing up wasn't done yet. Cooking smells, as well as the stink of stale beer, started Tanner's stomach growling. But they were more sleepy than hungry. He headed for the counter, where a young girl—she couldn't have been more than fourteen—sat by the till. She spared a dumbfounded look for Gern before asking how many rooms they wanted.

"A room for three," answered Tanner. "I'm a friend of Bai Jingtu."

The young girl threw him a distraught glance. What had he said?

"I'm a friend of Bai Jingtu," repeated Tanner. "Is he here?"

The young girl's gaze grew even more frightened. Before he could move, she vanished behind a faded cloth curtain. Tanner swore under his breath: was the little goose going to wake up Bai Jingtu? A few overexcited whispers warned him before the drape was pushed aside by a mature woman wrapped in a silk nightgown.

"What do you want?"

Her tone was bluff but not defiant. Anxious, rather.

"A room for the night."

"Didn't you mention Bai Jingtu? Do you have any news of him? I'm his sister—talk to me!"

The same tone, at once insistent and beseeching. Tanner and Qingling exchanged looks of surprise.

"There must be a misunderstanding. I'm a friend of Bai. I thought he was here."

The woman sent the teenage girl to bed. She stared wonderingly at Tanner, Qingling, and Gern—especially at Gern.

"Jingtu has been arrested by the police. The Imperial Police, that's how it's called now. I thought . . . you would know. You're friends, you say? What kind of friends?"

She mouthed the word *diaochabu*. Tanner nodded affirmatively. She stared again at Gern, still incredulous:

"A European here? Are you crazy?"

"He knows nothing of our activities."

"Then, he must leave here immediately."

"He helped us out in a matter of importance. We're tired. We'll leave tomorrow morning."

"No, I want you to leave now!"

"Then, call the police," Tanner challenged her, pointing to the comscreen.

Her black pupils flashed thunderbolts, but she unhooked a key from a rack and motioned for them to follow her. She brought them to a small room, where a single bed was set by a dark wood wall. The two men left the bed to Qingling and stretched out on the floor, too tired to complain. Nervous tension kept Tanner awake until he identified the object of his unease. The cryo-kit! He considered alternatives: he was not eager to part from the precious article in his keeping, but did he have a choice?

Bai's sister, however suspicious, finally agreed to open one of her freezers: if it was a bomb or something equally fishy, why would a stranger insist on storing it in such an incongruous place? Tanner climbed back to their room and lay back down on the floor instantly swept under by the rising tide of his weariness.

TWENTY-ONE

MEIWANG, THE TEENAGER WHO HAD WELCOMED THEM THE NIGHT BE-
fore, brought them soap, towels, and a hearty breakfast. The
dozen or so cold dishes—leftovers from the previous day, obviously—came with chrysanthemum tea.

"There's a toilet upstairs, but be careful: my mother doesn't
want your Caucasian friend to be seen by our customers."

Tanner went down to check on the cryo-kit. His mind at
ease, he returned to the bedroom and kissed Qingling, still half
asleep.

"Feeling better?"

"I think so. What are we doing today?"

"Many things!"

Basking in the pristine sunshine of a Saturday morning,
wolfing down the improvised breakfast, Tanner regained much of
his customary drive.

Tanner, Qingling, and Gern dressed. Bai Jingtu's sister reappeared, overcome with worry, wringing her hands—no, no, they
could not stay with them forever. What if somebody caught sight

of a European on the premises? She already had enough worries
since her brother's arrest. Taking care of the restaurant claimed
all her attention. And she knew nothing of her brother's activities. . . .

Tanner tried to allay her anxieties:

"Don't worry, we have no intention of overstaying our welcome. However, in order to leave Nanxiang, we need some information. I'd like to meet an agent of the *diaochabu* or of the
Japanese Naicho."

She looked at him wide-eyed, aghast:

"Not here, not here! The police are watching us!"

Tanner noticed she hadn't rejected the possibility of such
an encounter, but that she was merely afraid for her own safety.

"The faster you set up a meeting, the sooner you'll be rid
of us."

She opened her mouth to protest, then bowed her head,
defeated. Her voice muffled, she asserted that she'd try to arrange
something, then abandoned them in the small room.

The sun rose like an orange in an apple-green sky. Tanner
and Qingling, lying against each other on the narrow bed, doze
fitfully, soothed by the sound of Gern's footsteps as he went
round and round to lull his apprehensions.

Almost three hours later, the corridor's floorboards creaked
as other steps were heard. Meiwang, the young niece of Bai
Jingtu, came in with mirrorshades hiding her eyes, gloves, and a
hat. In one hand, she carried Tanner's cryo-kit; in the other hand,
she held out a farmhand's protective helmet.

"We're going out. The Eye is rising."

The farmhand's helmet was for Gern. The wraparound
cowling and reflective visor lent the meteorologist a faintly cy-
bernetic air, perfectly fulfilling the helmet's object. Nobody could
have guessed he was European. Tanner and Qingling made do
with old hats and scratched shades.

They followed Meiwang outside, walking all the way to the
sun-flooded docks just as the first rays of the Eye, peeking over
the horizon, struck the city.

"We'll take a taxi," explained Meiwang, "but not in front of the restaurant."

Meiwang had arranged for a taxi to pick them up near the docks where Chen Shaoxing's old yacht was still moored. The foursome managed to pile inside the car.

"Huainan," said Meiwang to the driver.

The driver grimaced.

"Huainan? On the West Coast?"

"Yes. And we're in a hurry," she added imperiously.

The driver looked at the three passengers crammed on the backseat. He seemed surprised that the youngest was giving the orders. Muttering that his own children showed more respect for their elders, he headed for the Jade.

It was Saturday, market day. On the bridge, traffic was slowed to a crawl. The population had taken advantage of the morning's first few hours to do their shopping. Now that a green radiance pervaded the sky, everybody was going home. Tanner soon saw a bright side to the congestion: an identification checkpoint obstructed the bridge, but the soldiers manning it, considering the hour, were waving most people through in order to avoid backing up traffic. The driver, however, was getting worked up, honking and yelling: "Where did he come from?" "Move your ass!" "Get it in gear, fatso!" Tanner was cringing and asked him to tone it down—the maniac was going to attract the unwanted attention of the soldiers if he kept on like that.

And so it turned out. When a delivery truck sneaked in front of him, the driver put on such a show, honking and hollering profanities, that one of the soldiers marched toward the taxi, menacingly unlimbering his machine gun. Stressing his words with a shake of his weapon's barrel, he yelled at the driver to shut up and get going.

Ignoring the Eye, the driver leaned out the window, shouting at the soldier:

"What? You're telling *me* to shut up?"

Meiwang blanched. Qingling's nails dug into Tanner's forearm. This madman was going to ruin everything!

The soldier reached them, anger darkening his face behind the full UV-proof visor. He rammed the blunt end of his weapon through the open window, right under the driver's nose.

"Yeah, I'm telling you for the last time to shut your yap!"

With a scornful grimace, the driver pushed the weapon's tip back out the window.

"Watch out with that thing; my goodness, you're going to hurt yourself! Oh, my ancient ancestors! Don't tell me the army is hiring mental defectives nowadays?"

The soldier was unable to contain himself any longer. He burst out laughing and stretched a gloved hand to tousle the driver's hair.

"Why not, if monkeys get to drive taxis? Good old Lu! Always the soul of courtesy when you're behind the wheel, I see!"

The driver was laughing too now.

"And you, they got you a job fit for your abilities, I see: directing traffic!"

"And you can tell I'm doing a good job!" The smiling soldier waved at the congested bridge. "Look at the result!"

Still laughing, the soldier stepped back and let them pass. The driver was still chortling over his little bout of playacting. He winked at Meiwang, teasing: "Nothing to it, kiddo! You didn't have to be scared; that was just my cousin!"

"Very funny," replied Meiwang dryly. "Can we go to Huainan now?"

"Come on, don't give me that look. If we can't have a bit of fun—"

"You'd better watch the road; you just missed that grandmother!"

The driver just started laughing again.

The driver avoided the west bank's estates: since the attack on the Enclave, traffic was severely controlled in their vicinity. Instead, the taxi turned upriver, where the cliffs melted into gentler slopes, yellow roads snaking up to the plateau that bordered the Bay of Flowers all the way to the extreme northern tip of the White Tooth. They bypassed the magnificent sight of Nanxiang's upper town, and reached in no time at all Huainan, a village no less picturesque. The rugged stone houses rose on the edge of the precipice. Nailed to the cliff of blue-gray stone, a multitude of wood and aluminum staircases slanted down to a narrow, rocky beach from which docks jutted this way and that over the greenish depths of the Bay of Flowers.

The taxi's trip ended in the middle of the small village, in front of a half-built inn. Meiwang waited until the vehicle was out of sight, then led the three fugitives to one of the staircases bolted to the cliff. She started going down. Under his helmet, Gern swore audibly. A tiny cry of terror escaped Qingling's lips. Even Tanner felt his heart leap into his mouth: the cliff face fell vertically over more than two hundred meters. Suddenly, the staircase seemed much too fragile and rickety to take their weight. . . .

Meiwang, the sea breeze whipping her long black hair, encouraged them:

"It's perfectly safe, come on!"

Laughing at her own terror, Qingling clutched Tanner's arm.

"Okay, let's go! But hang on to me!"

The climb down was dizzying: the steps creaked, the handrail was loose, and a raw, salty wind gusted cruelly. Still, faced with the grandeur of the sight, exhilaration soon replaced fear. The sky was endless, spotted with clouds. The tranquil mass of the rocky headland, the rainbows wavering in the warm, briny drizzle, the fragrant wind, the outflung strands of the Bay of Flowers, the foam-lined waves rushing in, all came together in an unforgettable vista. Tanner was almost disappointed when they reached the docks.

"They'll come and get us," said Meiwang.

They bided their time for a while before a man in shades, but hatless, showed up. He argued with Meiwang—his words

carried away by the breeze—and then motioned for them to follow him. Without waiting for more, Meiwang started the climb
back up. Tanner ran to catch up with her. He thanked her and
her mother, and Bai Jingtu. If he made it, he would never forget
their assistance.

Meiwang stared at him, then shrugged a shoulder. Without
uttering a word, she darted up the steps of wet wood.

They followed their new guide through a maze of docks,
climbing aboard a timeworn two-master with rigid sails. The deck
was slippery and dirt encrusted, as if abandoned. Their guide
knocked on the hatchway door. On the other side, somebody
shouted, "Who goes there?" in Chinese. The man identified himself. A latch was pulled, and a Chinese man of mature years,
holding a huge, old-fashioned revolver, let them climb down in a
moldy-smelling gangway.

They followed the narrow gangway, finally entering a common room as run down as the rest of the ship, its portholes cur-
tained shut with rough cloth. There, in the yellow glow of two
electric bulbs, sitting on benches of dull plastic or old steel
chairs, or on the fiberglass flooring, a dozen men and women,
some of them wounded, gazed at the newcomers with eyes slitted
by circumspection.

The old Han pointed to the dilapidated hold and its forlorn
occupants, his round face split by a proud grin:

"The Naicho welcomes you aboard the *Glory of the Ancients*!"

A few passengers still had the heart to snicker.

The man with the gun—more or less in charge—was called
Tsukura. He was not Chinese but indeed Japanese, an agent of
the Naicho in Nanxiang. Like all the passengers aboard, he was
fleeing Nanxiang to get back to the EFTA.

Tsukura addressed Gern:

"The European Bureau showed a lot of nerve, sending an
agent this far on the mainland."

Guessing the reason for the confusion was not hard: naturally, Tsukura had assumed the only Caucasian in the bunch was

the European spy. Well, well, Tanner's disguise was still holding up! He introduced himself—as Li Zheng—and his companions. All he said about his mission was that it was classified Top Secret.

Tsukura allowed himself a sardonic grin:

"Now that the EFTA is falling to the New Chinese foe, I wonder what's the use of keeping it secret."

"How soon are we leaving?" asked Tanner, eager to change the subject.

"When Green Night begins. You're very lucky the message from our dear Mrs. Bai reached us in the middle of this debacle."

Tanner pondered Tsukura's answer.

"I still can't believe our luck. You waited for us. Why?"

"You would rather have stayed in Nanxiang?"

"Of course not. But I didn't expect such heroism from the Naicho."

Tsukura pulled a disappointed face.

"Your distrust saddens me. However, the situation forces me to be candid: you're aware of what's happened to the Enclave, right?"

"Actually, no. Is the Enclave occupied?"

"Maybe . . . It's unclear. But surely not the whole of Ferret Island; I'm sure the European military base is still holding out. But the New Chinese will capture it sooner or later. Meanwhile, all foreigners are being evacuated; they've been at it for several days, but there won't be enough room for everybody. Now, Mr. Li, the last Japan-registered spaceship left two days ago. The only ships left at the base are European freighters. And who's going to get priority? Surely not Japanese agents like us. I'll admit we were getting pretty desperate. It was then a message from that dear Mrs. Bai held out unexpected hope for us: a *diaochabu* agent was asking her for shelter and seeking for a way to get back to the EFTA. Nothing very exciting about that, as far as it went. But what did we also learn? One of the companions of this mysterious operative was Caucasian! Could it be the famous spy sent by the European Bureau on a Top Secret mission on the mainland, as we learned through an infiltrator eavesdropping on

Bloembergen? And so it struck us, obviously, that if we brought back this strange spy, we might deserve a bit of room, however small, aboard the European freighters."

"What makes you think I'm that valuable?"

"Well, however it turns out, we had to try our luck," asserted Tsukura with an ingenuous smile.

Tanner glanced mutely at the cabin's moldy walls.

"Are you sure this old barge won't sink halfway there?"

"Don't look a gift horse in the mouth," answered Tsukura in English. "Though in our case, we should say a stolen horse . . . I admit it's not a looker, but its back-up motor will considerably shorten the trip to Ferret Island."

As soon as the sun disappeared, the remaining able-bodied agents of the Naicho hauled on the rigid sails. The briny-tasting wind moved the old ship away from its mooring. A few moments later, the large auxiliary motor was brought into play, its full-throttle growl deafening the passengers and shaking the aged fiberglass partitions.

Tanner fled the noise, donning again his hat and shades to climb on deck. Thanks to the motor, the ship was making good speed. The bow parted deep, black waves, and the deck was soon drenched, glistening in the eerie light of the Dragon's Eye.

The trip was harrowing. In the course of their desperate flight, the Japanese had concentrated their procurement efforts on motor alcohol, not food. They were forced to share biscuits and tepid water, the only supplies laid in by the Naicho agents. In addition to the physical hardships entailed by the dirt, the noise, and the primitive sanitary facilities, they also felt the strain of having to deal with the wounded.

One of the injured, a woman in her forties, struck with a bullet during the evacuation of the Naicho headquarters, died agonizingly, her breath rattling for an unbearable half hour. Her companions seemed to be at the end of their tether, so Tanner and Gern offered to dispose of the body.

With as much decorum as possible in the circumstances, they found an unused sheet, rolled the body inside, and, after a short prayer by Tsukura, dropped the shroud into the fragrant waters of the Bay of Flowers.

Green Night was ending. Tanner and Qingling closeted themselves in one of the tiny cabins and, in each other's arms, dozed fitfully for a few hours. Orange sunshine finally brightened the cabin. They stayed entwined, lying side by side, sharing memories and dreams. Tanner revealed that he was resolved to resign from the Bureau as soon as he made it back to Earth.

"And me?" asked Qingling.

"You're coming with me. Isn't it obvious?"

Without a word, she hugged him with all her might.

Dark Night, Monday morning, two o'clock. . . . Beneath the dark purple auroras, the first handful of lights of Ferret Island floated atop the inky sea. Tanner had more or less expected gunfire, explosions, fires, helicopters buzzing through the sky, and dropping bombs. Instead, everything seemed quiet. But he refused to delude himself: things *had* changed. Normally, the EFTA would have put on a dazzling display of neon and electric lights. It wasn't exactly a blackout, but . . .

To starboard, by comparison, the lights of the Lengshuijiang suburbs spread along the horizon, their reflections swimming through the dark waters of the Straits like a weird new marine fauna.

Now that their destination was in sight, Tsukura faced another hurdle: the radar of the European base. He ordered the motor stopped. The silence hung heavily, after all the hours spent enduring the motor's clangor. As if they were afraid of being heard, the sailors now whispered their commands. They jumped if the fickle wind made the rigging creak. Then, clouds sailed between the auroras and the ocean. The darkness became nearly absolute: it was now impossible to see one's outstretched hand. The lights of Lengshuijiang and Ferret Island became the only reference points in the night.

Above Ferret Island, a series of blinding flashes startled everybody on deck, followed a few seconds later by the roar of multiple blasts; salvos of gunfire, muffled by the distance and the rumblings of the sea. Floodlights turned on. Tanner regretted losing his binoculars. He would have liked to see more.

In the night, Qingling's voice was like a velvety caress:

"I was beginning to hope all this talk of war was only another rumor . . ."

Tanner stretched out his hand, brushed a bare arm. Qingling came to him, hooking him by the waist. He nuzzled her tangled hair. She sighed:

"I'm hungry."

"Me too."

"What shall we do if the base is abandoned?"

"I don't have the slightest."

In spite of the cool composure he maintained for Qingling's benefit, anxiety was torturing Tanner's stomach as much as lack of food. They had to get there as fast as possible, Chen Shaoxing's head would deteriorate past any possible usefulness. The last time Tanner had checked the internal temperature of the cryo-kit, he'd been dismayed to find that the gauge indicated 5°C. He'd been told that up to 10°C, at least for a short while, there was still hope. The cryo-kit still hadn't reached that fateful temperature, but when were they going to find another freezer in order to bring down its temperature? Tanner was surprised to find himself hating the cryo-kit and its grisly contents. He shook himself: why give a fuck for the ghastly device? All that mattered now was Qingling, and saving both their skins!

The wind had practically exhausted itself. The aging hull no longer creaked, the threadbare sails no longer knocked against the masts. The only sounds: the lapping of the lazy waves rippling across the sea, the pounding of footsteps on the deck. A silhouette blocked the view of the scattered lights on Ferret Island.

"Can we afford to come any closer?" asked Tsukura.

Tanner did not blame the Japanese for his eagerness; he too looked forward to setting foot on the island. But he vetoed the suggestion.

"If the Europeans think we're New Chinese, they'll fire on us for sure."

"Then we must abandon ship. And try our luck on the island. But we only have a small lifeboat, built for six. We can pile in nine to ten people, maximum. But surely not fourteen! We'll have to make two trips."

Tanner tightened his hold on Qingling:

"We won't make two trips. Let's lower the boat, get all the people we can aboard, and the others will swim."

Tsukura didn't answer. One of his lieutenants observed they were rather far from the coast.

"It only five kilometers," countered Tanner. "It's no great feat if one can cling to the boat to rest from time to time. I'm volunteering, of course."

Almost invisible in silhouette, Tsukura did not react, absorbed in mulling over the alternatives.

"So be it."

Tsukura went back down below to tell his companions what had been decided.

They lowered the lifeboat. Tsukura was the first to go down, in order to receive the wounded. Suddenly, he tripped and fell headfirst into the boat, which almost capsized. He rose, swearing and rubbing his neck. He made light of his misstep: nothing broken! They would just have to be more careful; the hull was slimy, and he'd slipped on algae scum.

The three wounded were brought down, and Tsukura settled them more or less comfortably in the hull's bottom. Then, it was the turn of Gern and three agents who had never learned how to swim. Tanner, with his pocket light, swept a narrow beam over the embarkation and the slow swells of the obsidian sea. Though it was already overloaded with eight people in it, the small craft still floated easily.

Behind him were left Qingling, two women, and two men.
"Qingling and the ladies. The others will swim."

Qingling protested: she didn't mind a five-kilometer swim.
Tanner pulled her to him, kissed her, and looped a rope around
her waist.

"It's not gallantry. You're not as heavy as the men, that's
all."

An intense light set the horizon aglow for a brief moment,
a dull roar following a few seconds later.

"Hurry!"

Qingling, then another woman. The boat sank dangerously
lower. Tsukura, his every move carefully calculated, clambered
back aboard the *Glory of the Ancients*. One last woman made up
the boat's complement. Tanner threw down to them their weapons, the cryo-kit, and a pocket light.

Equipped with a single oar and a suitable plank, the boat-
load set off from the *Glory of the Ancients*, bound for Ferret Island. Tanner, along with Tsukura and two other Naicho agents,
dove into the waves. The sea was warm, almost like a bath. In
spite of their precarious situation, it was a relief to leave behind
the filth of the old sailing ship. Shifting to a powerful breaststroke, Tanner caught up with the boat in order to assure Qingling that everything was fine.

Propelled by the uneven strokes of the paddlers, the boat
made quick headway at first. Not a word was uttered. The lights
of Ferret Island might appear set at a perfectly fixed remove, but,
as the interminable minutes passed, as the hour mark was
reached, it became obvious that the boat had progressed. Still,
the boat wasn't setting any speed records, and Tanner found it
easy to keep up with his economical breaststroke.

However, one of the Japanese, either a poor swimmer or
simply worn out, was falling off the pace. More and more often,
he needed to cling to the boat to rest, slowing it down. Qingling
murmured that she could switch places with him.

"I forbid it!" hissed Tanner. "You'll overturn the boat!"

"Everybody stay where they are!" added Tsukura. "And not another word!"

After half an hour at this tortoise's pace, they had to face the facts: the Naicho agent had reached the end of his endurance; he was going to drown. Qingling renewed her offer, which could not be turned down. Without a wasted motion, she slipped smoothly into the sea. Recovering the Japanese agent was a more involved and riskier undertaking. Their hearts stopped, once, when it seemed the boat might capsize, but no. . . . The Japanese lay down with the wounded, weeping with shame and weariness.

They resumed their progress. Tanner had long ago exhausted the questionable charms of his predawn swim when, faraway on Ferret Island, a dazzling blast erupted in the night sky, daubing the low hills with an unreal yellow-orange light. With a moment's lag, the sound of a muffled explosion ran above the rolling waves, counterpointed by the sharper cracks of grenades going off and the chittering of machine-gun bursts.

The flare fell back to the ground, but not before Tanner and his companions discerned ahead of them, outlined against the fading reddish glow, several ominous-looking ships, veiled till then by the utter lightlessness of Dark Night.

Tsukura swam toward Tanner.

"Did you see?" he asked, breathless.

"Yes."

"Friend or foe?"

"New Chinese, for sure."

"How did they slip under the radar?"

"I don't know. Maybe sabotage back at the base."

"Did they see us?"

"I don't think so. They were backlit by the rockets, not us."

"What are they up to now?"

"Nothing good."

Noiselessly, they neared one of the New Chinese ships, which could be detected only through the periodic occultations of the island's lights. Their nerves taut, close to the breaking point, they came within fifty meters of the vessel, as silent as a ghost ship, before passing it.

The swimmers, who hadn't eaten a bite in over thirty-six hours, were beginning to weaken and to let themselves be towed by the lifeboat. Tanner too was beginning to shiver. Struck by a sudden inspiration, he asked them to throw him the cryo-kit. It was as he thought: the thick plastic foam bag made a passable lifesaver.

Letting the sluggish pace of the boat get to him, Tanner whispered that he was going ahead to reconnoiter the spot where they would land. Tsukura's voice, ever more hoarse with fatigue, burst forth in the dark to endorse his idea. However, Qingling protested.

"Don't go away. I'm scared."

"Don't worry."

"Th . . . then, I'm coming with you."

"No!" replied Tanner impatiently. "You're safer here."

Helped by his makeshift float, the agent left behind him the pitiful boat and lost himself in the night. He swam . . . Inhale. Exhale. Inhale . . . He swam, blundering for centuries through the sea's cool currents, its subtly rancid smell, its salty bitterness, its endless liquid shudderings. . . .

His hand hit bottom. He staggered to his feet on a slippery mat of seaweed, trembling with fatigue. He stumbled forward, water up to his waist, fighting to stay upright, his back bent and his breath wheezing out. . . . He collapsed on the beach, oblivious to the sharp pebbles bruising his rib cage. There, emerging into the rustling stillness of a warm night on an alien planet, Tanner caught his breath, happy to be back on Ferret Island. All his senses on the alert, he listened, but he heard only his own breathing. He watched, but all he saw were phosphenes dancing an illusory ballet to the beat of his blinking eyelids.

A series of muffled snaps, not far off, startled him. A dozen luminous trails arced up toward the local zenith before popping and blazing a furious red, shining so bright it hurt the eye.

The blood-red flares showed ten or so New Chinese three-masters, reduced to the size of toys by the distance, dotting a sea as shiny and lifeless as a plastic sheet. Much closer, a minuscule vessel, a mere lifeboat, was making with desperate haste for the shore, overloaded with Tanner's stunned companions.

Instantly, coming from the hills, gunfire shattered the quiet. The bluish-white streaks of tracers ripped through the red night. *Qingling!* Tanner didn't even hear his own yell in the din. Bullets whistled by. He threw himself to the ground, observing incredulously the immense, murderous outburst.

The target wasn't their boat, but the New Chinese ships anchored farther off. Beneath the ceaseless barrage coming from the island, the passengers rowed steadily. The New Chinese ships, deluged with bullets, responded with rocket fire. Ineptly aimed, the rockets landed haphazardly, their wasp like buzzing almost drowned by the shrieking of the tracers. Explosions blasted the sea, the beach, the hills. A second ship was firing now, not just rockets, but also shells of lesser caliber.

Erupting not far from Tanner, a deafening concussion almost knocked him out, dusting him with a short-lived rain of sand grains and wood chips.

The inevitable occurred. A rocket slammed into the ocean, exploding far enough to spare the boat's passengers direct injury, but when the resulting wave reached the overloaded craft, the passengers couldn't help it being swamped.

Tanner ran into the water, slipping on the treacherous algae and splashing seawater in all directions as he righted himself. He yelled, "Qingling!" to hold together his crumbling composure. If he'd yelled twice as loud in her ear, in the midst of this hellish din, she wouldn't have heard a thing. But there was still hope: his companions were swimming toward the shore. And they weren't far now—they could make it, they could make it! Qingling was a good swimmer. She was almost there!

Flame blossomed and scattered bits of the lifeboat in all directions, dazzling petals uncurling high in the air before spreading over the waves among which Tanner's shipwrecked companions were dog-paddling. The shock wave reached him, slapping his forehead. . . . He blinked, half blinded. Overlaid with incendiary fuel, the sea itself was burning. In front of the blazing edge, four swimmers propelled themselves frantically forward. They were so close now! However, the sheet of flame was spreading over the roiling surface, catching up with the slowest of the four and hugging him in its deadly embrace. . . . Another swimmer in turn was too slow. . . .

The two survivors—Qingling and a Japanese!—reached the seaweed beds, but they still had water up to the waist, and the fiery curtain was upon them.

"Dive! *Dive!*" yelled Tanner, the words tearing out of his throat.

TWENTY-TWO

DAWN WAS BORN AS AN IMPERCEPTIBLE DILUTION OF DARKNESS, HINTing at the twisting branches of plane trees and the languid curves of palm leaves. The black sky then turned indigo, streaked with pink and purple highlights. It had now lightened enough for Tanner to guess that the vegetation surrounding him was green. The European Bureau agent, squatting in a small copse, moved forward to a better vantage point. From there he spied one of the more modest EFTA neighborhoods, apparently deserted in the pale morning light. A faraway siren cracked the silence, then got closer: a khaki and green van sped through the empty streets, its siren ululating all the way. As soon as the van turned the corner, people emerged from the houses, forming on the street a sparse and anxious crowd.

Tanner nearly shouted gleefully: the van bore the logo of United Europe!

He beat his way back through the tall grass and almost stumbled over two bodies stretched out in the underbrush. Qingling bucked and twisted, dismay flashing in her frightened doe eyes. She sighed.

"You scared me."

"The Enclave is still free!" he exclaimed.

Qingling bit her finger, tears of joy in her eyes. Nabeyama's head lifted up; he attempted to smile though his face was ashen with pain. He asked about the noise they'd heard.

"It was just the curfew being lifted," explained Tanner, jubilant. "Let's go! Come, we'll just flag down an army car to get to the base!" He looked at the Japanese agent. "Can you walk down to the street?"

The three survivors hadn't escaped unscathed from the blazing sea. Most of Qingling's back was burned, down to the top of her thighs; though her injuries were superficial, they were too painful to let her sit. The burns Tanner had suffered on his hands while putting out the fires consuming their clothes were also inconsequential, even though they did hurt and reduced his dexterity. Nabeyama, the Naicho agent, had been less fortunate. He'd been swimming with nothing on his feet, and his right foot had struck a puddle of burning jelly. . . .

Nabeyama looked at his swollen foot, blackened and covered with bleeding, sand-encrusted blisters. He gulped hard.

"I can give it a try. . . ."

Helped by Tanner, Nabeyama got up. Balancing on his unharmed foot, he carefully put some weight on his right leg. The blood drained from his face and Tanner thought he was going to swoon. Nabeyama leaned again on Tanner, his body racked by sobs of pain. He found his breath and managed a washed-out smile.

"If I'd had anything in my stomach, it would have been worse."

"We're not stopping now! Just lean on me for a few meters and our troubles will be over."

Qingling grimaced with pain when she got up, holding the cryo-kit. The saltwater had damaged the temperature gauge, but

Tanner didn't need it to guess that the temperature had climbed above 10°C a long time ago. But he wasn't going to abandon the cryo-kit now.

Taking small steps as they went down the hill, they broke from cover and reached the street. Pedestrians couldn't help noticing them, but the rare passersby lowered their gaze and changed sidewalks, as if they were plague carriers. Others retreated inside their homes. Through a door opened no more than a slit, the wheezing voice of an old man startled them.

"Are you all crazy? Hide yourselves! If the Europeans see you, you're dead!"

"We're not New Chinese—"

The door slammed in Tanner's face.

"They think we're survivors from the New Chinese ships," whimpered Qingling.

Her words brought Tanner back down to earth: he also looked like a Han! Indeed, just how were they going to prove they were not New Chinese? He regretted not having found the time to warn of his impending return. But how was he supposed to have pulled off such a feat? He would have needed to start thinking about it in Linzi. As a matter of fact, in all the running around, he'd forgotten to do so. Now, it was useless to cry over it.

"I hope our men will ask questions first and shoot later . . ."

Looking at Qingling and Nabeyama, he regretted the wisecrack; they already had enough to worry about. There was precious little he could do now, except get rid of his remaining contact lens. Tanner left Nabeyama holding up a wall and, with his trembling, soiled fingers, he managed to remove the minuscule plastic disk.

They resumed their hobbling gait.

Reverberated by the concrete walls, the distinctive whine of an electric motor rose behind them. A patrol halftrack with EFTA insignia soon rushed past them. Just when it seemed those inside had overlooked the strange trio, the vehicle braked sharply and stopped. A blond head leaned out a side window. Orders were barked. The heavy vehicle backed up, blocking the way of the three pedestrians.

The halftrack was still moving when a door opened, letting out three soldiers armed with machine guns. Two were Caucasians and the third was Asian, but all three wore the battle dress of the Enclave's military base.

The leader's order echoed like a whip crack: "Hands up, and face the wall!"

"Don't shoot! I'm an agent of the European Bureau," Tanner shouted in English.

The blond soldier pushed him brutally against the wall, then also pushed Nabeyama. The soldier's boot knocked against the foot of the Japanese agent, who crumpled on the sidewalk, yelling in agony.

"Watch out, he's wounded!"

"You, the hairless jackass, eyes to the wall!" squawked the blond one. "And you too, cutie!" With the business end of his gun, he shoved Qingling in the back. The pain made her clench her teeth, while Tanner summoned the tatters of his self-control in order not to fly at their throats. He turned his face to the wall and growled, still in English:

"I'm an agent of the Bureau! Of the European Bureau!"

"You're asking me to believe that, egg-face? You're still wet and burned, you stink of napalm, and you're trying to tell me you weren't part of the landing party?"

Tanner was searched roughly, the soldiers finding his passport, his weapon, his wad of wet bills.

"Look at all that money!"

"You don't understand: I'm not New Chinese! I've got green eyes, damn it!"

The leader waved the sodden passport under his nose.

"You've got New Chinese papers. How do you explain that?"

"They're fakes produced by the EFTA branch of the Bureau!"

All three soldiers chortled openly. Their New Chinese intruder had an answer to every question! The blond one turned toward Qingling:

"And you, my pretty? What do you have to add?"

Qingling didn't speak English, so it was in Mandarin that she begged the three soldiers to spare their lives.

"What about that?" said the soldier with a ferocious grin. "Here's one who doesn't try to make us believe she's European."

He started searching her, lingering around her breasts and between her thighs, as his companions smiled lewdly. He even slipped a hand into her pants. She winced and moaned with pain. The other soldiers hooted and jeered:

"Eh, pisshead, get away; you're just too rough with the ladies!"

The blond one lifted the back of her blouse and showed them the skin bruised with angry red blotches.

"It's not me. She's the one whose ass got burned!"

The other soldiers snorted derisively:

"Hey, cutie, what were you *really* doing during the firefight?"

"My goodness, she just lucked out: guess who the girls call when their ass is hot for a real man!"

"Look into the bag!" interjected Tanner, his rage choking him. "It's a cryo-kit! A *cryo-kit!* Do you at least know what that is?"

"You, the blabbermouth, I told you to shut up!"

"Will you *at least* get in touch with Bloembergen? You know who Bloembergen is, right? Fucking hell, will you at least *call your superiors?*"

For a long and crazy second, Tanner really thought one of these soldiers, brought to the edge of frenzy by combat stress, was going to silence him forever with a bullet through the skull. Fortunately, the blond soldier's shell of arrogance crumbled slightly when he mentioned Bloembergen and the cryo-kit, and the righteous, red-hot rage emanating from Tanner apparently did the rest. The patrol leader blinked several times, then ordered his young Asian comrade to call up a superior.

The young man jumped back aboard the halftrack. After a few minutes on the com, he stretched out his torso through the window to deliver the handset to Tanner.

"It's for you," he said, visibly crestfallen.

Tanner hugged Qingling, who was sobbing silently, and he took the handset with all the dignity he could muster under the circumstances.

"Yes . . ."

"Tanner, is that you?" asked someone whose voice was raised to be heard above the noisy background.

"It's me. Who's speaking?"

"It's Francis Barnaby. Hell, can't you tell anymore?"

"Is Commander Wang there?"

Tanner's question earned him an incredulous cackle.

"You old devil, it is you! And in a rush as usual . . . Good God, Tanner, where have you been?"

"That's a matter between me and Commander Wang."

Barnaby's chuckle turned condescending.

"In that case, you're a bit late, my friend. Your dear Commander Wang scampered out of here by the first available ship. I'm the boss now, old sod. For the duration, anyway . . ."

Tanner kept silent, then shook himself. It was neither the time nor place for drawn-out explanations.

"Listen, Barnaby, we need an ambulance here. I've got two wounded with me. And a cryo-kit, if you know what I mean . . ."

"Right, I get the picture. . . . Don't worry, an ambulance is on the way. Let me speak to the patrol leader, will you?"

Tanner gave over the handset to the blond soldier, considerably less sure of himself now. The soldier listened, replying with no more than the occasional "Yes, sir" or "Certainly, sir" before returning the handset to his comrade. He then saluted Tanner somewhat hesitantly.

"We're ordered to protect you while we wait for the ambulance, sir."

"Good. That's better."

"I . . . Can we help you, you and your"—he hardly dared to

glance at Qingling and Nabeyama—"you and your companions? I . . . We're sorry for the misunderstanding, sir. It's a war zone here, sir."

"That's all right, soldier." Tanner sighed. "Don't overdo it."

For Qingling, still huddling against him, he summarized in Mandarin what had just occurred. The young woman did not seem that reassured. Still, she whispered in a tiny voice that she was thirsty.

"Oh yes . . ." echoed Nabeyama hoarsely, still crouching on the sidewalk. "Water! And, please, please, don't touch my foot again."

"You heard that?" barked the patrol leader to his companions. "Water, on the double! And watch out for the casualty's feet."

The eagerly expected ambulance arrived, escorted by an armored vehicle. The ambulance itself was a civilian vehicle—dotted with a few bullet holes—but the two medics who took care of Qingling and Nabeyama were in uniform and seemed utterly competent. Qingling's wounds were not as severe as those of the Japanese, but, since she couldn't sit down, she was also put in a stretcher, on her stomach.

The medics hastened to tie down the stretchers inside the vehicle's back. As soon as the doors were closed, the ambulance sped off, rolling between the two military vehicles along the deserted streets of the Enclave. Tanner, sitting opposite the medics on a jump seat, held Qingling's hand while one of the men carefully cut away her clothes to assess the damage.

"It's over," whispered Tanner to the young woman as she lay prone. "We're safe now. It's over."

The sudden feeling of relief and security which overwhelmed the agent, now that they were safely ensconced within the ambulance, brought tears to his eyes. He asked the medic for Qingling's prognosis.

"I've seen worse. As always with burns, the greatest risk is from infection. Her life is not endangered, don't worry. In a specialized burn center, she'd come out of it with hardly any scars.

But at the base infirmary . . . Well, we'll do our best."

Tanner translated into Mandarin the explanations of the medic. Qingling didn't say a word, but she was no longer crying and she appeared to be somewhat reassured.

"Your friend only speaks Chinese," observed the medic with a knowing grin. "And the other is Japanese. But you, I bet you're a European under that makeup job."

"It's a long story."

"I see. I don't know who you are, or what you were doing at the other end of the island. But we've been promised a promotion if we bring you back alive."

"I hope you get it," answered Tanner curtly, his tone conveying clearly that the medic would have to content himself with knowing no more.

It was hard for Tanner to orient himself from inside the cab. All he could see, as he twisted his neck every which way to catch sight of the road, was that the convoy had left the residential neighborhoods and was following a roadway bordered with industrial buildings. One of the buildings had burned down not long ago, judging by the smoke that rose up amid the twisted and blackened beams. The medic explained that the EFTA hospital— the one where Wang had confided in Tanner—was in the hands of New Chinese troops. Now, the infirmary of the Earth military base had to serve as a makeshift field hospital for the Europeans and their allies.

Tanner spotted a control tower above the treetops. The road followed a high fence topped with barbed wire and the convoy slowed down to enter the military base proper. The access road was spiked with vicious-looking steel blades and its approaches were swarming with soldiers, some of them in armor. The guards at the entrance parleyed briefly with the driver of the armored vehicle. The steel blades sank beneath the roadtop and the way was clear.

As the ambulance entered the precincts of the military base, a world-ending roar set even the air inside the cab to vibrating.

"What is it?" asked Qingling.

"A shuttle taking off," explained Tanner. "The starport is right behind us."

The ambulance stopped in front of an anonymous building that was part of the military base. Under Tanner's watchful supervision, Qingling and Nabeyama were transported to a room with a high ceiling and echoing walls—a gymnasium, deduced the operative when he noticed the colored lines on the ground and the large glass bay that afforded the adjoining cafeteria a view of the room. Dozens of beds filled the entire floor space, almost all occupied by wounded. A visibly overworked nurse signaled for the medics to follow her.

They crossed most of the room, the air alive with human heat and the muffled rumbling produced by the sufferers packed within. Near the far wall, the nurse assigned to Qingling a bed whose mattress was covered only with a transparent plastic slipcover.

"Don't you have any sheets? Come on, she can't—"

Motioning impatiently, the nurse waved off Tanner's protest.

"I'll bring her some after I've taken the other to the operating room. I can't do everything at once!"

"Sorry," said Tanner, though the rebuff left him feeling both sheepish and irked. He struggled to remain calm: everybody was on edge.

He shook Nabeyama's hand. The two men hardly had a chance to wish each other good luck before the Japanese disappeared in the direction of the surgery.

Tanner and the medic helped Qingling to get up. With a wink of complicity for the New Chinese woman, the medic stripped off the sheet from the stretcher and laid it on the bed. Qingling smiled as she pronounced one of the few English words she knew:

"Thanks!"

The two men were helping Qingling to lie down, covering her as best they could with the folded sheet, when a couple of newcomers came up between the rows of beds. Both of them were European and wore dark suits.

"Réjean Tanner?"

Tanner recognized the two men. Agents from the European Bureau. He nodded briskly:

"That's me."

The agent who'd spoken pointed to the bag at Tanner's feet.

"We've also been asked to bring back a cryo-kit."

"That's indeed the item in question."

"I'll leave you," said the medic, taking away his stretcher. "My best wishes to your young friend."

"Thank you. And good luck with that promotion!"

"Barnaby asked us to bring him the cryo-kit," repeated the Bureau operative. "And you too, Tanner."

"I'm coming."

Tanner clutched Qingling's hand. She'd been listening to the unintelligible exchange with an anxious frown. He kissed her on the temple and told her he had to leave for a little while. The young woman immediately started sobbing, her hand squeezing Tanner's with desperate force.

"No, don't leave me! I beg you, don't leave me alone."

"Come on, there's no reason to be afraid. We're on a military base. You are now surrounded by a million soldiers. Nothing can happen to you here."

"Don't leave me! You swore you wouldn't abandon me."

"My poor Qingling, I'm not abandoning you. I've got to report to my boss, that's all. I'll be back in five minutes."

"You've got to come with us, Tanner. Now."

"Hell, guys, let me catch my breath here!"

Qingling's hand was trembling more than ever.

"Oh, Zheng, Zheng . . . Don't go. I'm so afraid."

Tanner kissed her cheek and nose, spattered with tears. Faced with the extremity of her terror, he made light of the young woman's candor, opting to laugh rather than cry.

"Come on, Qingling" he whispered in her ear. "Let go of my hand now. Be reasonable. I'll be back right away. . . . Right away . . ."

Subjected to the exasperated gaze of the two agents from the Bureau, Qingling finally released Tanner. The operative hastened to pick up the cryo-kit and turn toward the two men.

"Gentlemen . . ." His voice broke. "Gentlemen, let's go."

Francis Barnaby, the interim head of the European Bureau on New China, awaited his three agents on one of the underground levels in a large white room, noisy, stiflingly hot, and crawling with officers and personnel from the military base. When he saw Tanner coming toward him, he broke off his conversation with an officer and crossed his arms theatrically. Smoldering under his long, disheveled black hair, his eyes burned with the fixed stare of a man on the verge of a nervous breakdown. Barnaby scrutinized the face he was having trouble recognizing.

"Bloody Tanner!" he finally erupted with excessive good cheer. "So, it is you! I can't believe that noggin of yours . . . You showed up just in time, let me tell you: the last transports bound for Earth will be taking off in less than four hours."

In spite of everything he'd seen and been through, Tanner was taken aback. He hadn't imagined the Enclave's situation was that desperate.

Barnaby stretched out a hand for the cryo-kit.

"We've prepared a liquid nitrogen bath for . . . for your gizmo . . ." He faltered an instant, a sardonic smile on his lips. "Who's the poor sod? Hamakawa?"

"Hamakawa? No, no . . ."

Tanner shook his head, suddenly dizzy. Evidently, Barnaby had no idea of the identity of the person whose head was inside the cryo-kit. In fact, since Wang's departure, Tanner was the only person on New China able to appreciate the importance of what he was holding in his hands. A tech came up and relieved him of his burden. Tanner watched the cryo-kit be taken away with a mingling of relief and deep unease. He shook himself again. He was so tired . . . Damn, he was tired!

"And Bloembergen?" he nevertheless managed to ask. "What happened to him?"

"I told you. He's dead."

"Sure, but in what circumstances?"

"The circumstances were bizarre, to tell the truth. He was killed in his bed. With a shot to the head. Bang, point-blank! Brain juice all over the wall. Probably a New Chinese commando."

"And his wife? Zhao? The kids?"

"Disappeared. Kidnapped." Barnaby let loose a high-pitched chuckle. "This may disappoint you, Tanner, but right now, I couldn't care less. We've got other fish to fry. If you need to go to the john, now's the time, because we're hightailing it out of here and saying good-bye to this bloody planet!"

Tanner's heart started pounding in his chest.

"Wait, Barnaby, I'm not alone. Two of my mission partners are coming with me."

"What? Who?"

"A Naicho agent and a . . . a woman who works for us."

Barnaby scowled:

"The Naicho? I don't give a damn for the Naicho! And who's this woman?"

"A New Chinese. Who works for us. Her knowledge of the mainland is invaluable."

"Yeah, right! She wouldn't be your main squeeze, too, by any chance?" jeered one of the agents who'd come for Tanner and who added for Barnaby's benefit: "They were hugging and calling each other pet names. I thought we were going to spend the whole day waiting for them."

"She's coming back with me to Earth. End of discussion!"

Barnaby's eyes widened:

"Oh no, Tanner . . . Oh no, no, there's no way at all we can take your little girlfriend! Space is severely limited. It's quite a shortage. . . . Please realize we've just had our arses kicked—literally into orbit. The Enclave will hold out just long enough to let everybody ship out, and then it's going to be everyone for himself, the usual end of the empire scenario, believe you me!"

A burst of such intense rage filled Tanner that a spell of dizziness almost made him fall. One of the agents held him up.

"Hey, watch out! Calm down a bit."

"He's hysterical. Somebody call a doctor."

"I do not recognize your authority," Tanner managed to croak as he regained his focus. "I'm working under the direct orders of Commander Wang. You can . . . you can all bug out like scum-sucking rats. But I won't leave without Qingling!"

Barnaby came closer, a nasty smile flashing his very white teeth. He stroked Tanner's cheek with a show of phony sympathy:

"But, my poor Tanner, I'd be quite happy if you stayed, believe me. And that lemon-face we've had to push out to make room for you would be even happier. However, I'm sure you had a thoroughly enjoyable trip in New China and that lots of people on Earth will want to hear all about it."

Tanner yearned to rub out that smug smile once and for all. Before he could throw a punch, Barnaby's assistants caught his arms. Tanner struggled furiously and succeeded in escaping their grasp. He dashed across the room, shoving aside officers and other personnel as he came through.

"Get him!"

"Don't shoot! Don't shoot!"

"Shit, what's going on?"

Tanner knocked back the door in front of him and took off down the main corridor of the base. In his state of near exhaustion, only desperation lent him the strength to outdistance the two agents of the Bureau after him. And only instinct guided him through a series of identical hallways. Tanner ran and ran, knowing just how ridiculous and absurd his flight was, since he was heading for the infirmary, for Qingling, and his feverish mind, drunk with despair at the prospect of leaving his beloved behind, nevertheless understood that Barnaby's men knew he was coming this way.

But he couldn't stop running. And running. Hysterical laughter bubbled up from his burning lungs, fighting to erupt from his aching throat. Of course he was running! Wasn't that all that he knew how to do? What else had he done ever since the beginning of his mission? Running with no idea of where he was going. Like now. He was lost. He no longer knew where he was. How could it be otherwise? They were all alike, these gray hallways. . . . All alike, these drab and astonished faces watching him go by, tearing down the corridors like a madman.

Yes. Like a madman.

He was hardly running anymore when the agents behind him jumped on his shoulders. He fell and didn't offer any resistance. He didn't resist when they handcuffed his hands behind his back. Above him appeared Barnaby, along with a woman in a medical uniform.

"He's a tough guy," explained Barnaby. "What can we give him to get some peace around here?"

"Two milligrams of isofarate should calm him down."

"Give it to him!"

Once more Barnaby caressed the stubble on Tanner's cheeks:

"Come on, Tanner, relax . . . A little sleep and you'll be on your way to Earth."

"Don't do it," Tanner implored. "Take me to the infirmary. Let me at least tell her—"

His shoulder twinged. Compressed air whistled out. Tanner cried. A cold torpor ended his wretched sobbing, and it all vanished into a dry, icy darkness.

TWENTY-THREE

IMAGES FROM THE PAST, ECHOING WITH ALIEN SOUNDS, ETCHED WITH the acid tints of nostalgia. . . . Qingling, in the Spring Daffodils restaurant, her eyes shining, almost glowing, the red pleat of her lips kissing moistly a tiny porcelain tumbler. Qingling, stunned by their first, almost accidental kiss in a forgotten hotel room. Qingling, naked on the train's bunk, her nipples upraised with desire, the setting sun burnishing with gold her body as it yearned to be caressed. Qingling, on a sun-drenched restaurant terrace, her throat clenched and her gaze liquid, telling the strange and sad story of a useless life. Qingling, at the helm of the sailboat, a frail silhouette against the reddish background of the sharp-edged peaks serrating the shores of Ming Lake.

Qingling . . . Qingling . . . The memories were already losing their living immediacy. He could no longer hear her high-pitched laughter, the chanting of the Lengshuijiang stevedores, or the wheezing of the steam brakes, just a faraway and confused rumbling. He could no longer recapture the vivid sights of New China: the smoldering Dragon's Eye and the faces glowing with fluorescent makeup, the blackness of ink on rare rice paper and the redness of shed blood—the vibrant colors had turned intothe faded hues of an old print forgotten in the sun.

Soon, now, he would have but a mere handful of floating images, gray and blurry. And the silence of deserted places.

Tanner started: Lison Robanna's secretary had just said something.

"Excuse me . . ."

The young woman was staring at him, her eyes green and translucent.

"Are you feeling all right?"

Tanner shrugged, his annoyance clear:

"Yes! I was thinking—"

"Ms. Robanna is now expecting you."

Tanner went down a long hall hung with ornate wallpaper, past a wide window overlooking Geneva. Nothing had changed. The sky was the same blue—perhaps a shade too blue for a visitor just back from New China—as the narrow end of the lake. White peaks rose atop the horizon. The sun shone quietly above the untroubled panorama, unchanging, of the old European city.

The office of the new director of the European Bureau of External Affairs was spacious, modern, comfortable. Seated behind a large desk of real wood, Lison Robanna was gazing vacantly into space, plugged into the network. She gestured absently, inviting him to sit in one of the overstuffed, leather-covered armchairs. Tanner obeyed.

Robanna spun out her conversation. It was rather irritating to face a person absorbed by the network: the vacant stare, the subvocalized whispers . . . Tanner contained his impatience: he was no longer in New China. Did he really expect the director of the European Bureau to have tea served?

Robanna's head pitched forward and she rubbed her reddened eyes. She seemed tired, as if she hadn't slept in years. She focused on Tanner, arching her eyebrows questioningly:

"Forgive me. I don't remember your name."

"Réjean Tanner. I'm back from New China to report on—"
She interrupted him:

"Yes, of course! I just accessed your file. You were supposed to contact Chen Shaoxing in New China, but he died, crushed under a bus or something like that?"

"Perhaps you're confusing him with my mission partner, Jay Hamakawa. Because Chen died of a heart attack."

Lison Robanna nodded affirmatively:

"Yes, that's right, I see it now. . . . Please forgive my distraction, but I'm no longer responsible for your case file. I doubt you can imagine the disarray in our services since the New Chinese troops took over the EFTA. Everybody's shouting, everybody's asking for an explanation, everybody wants my head on a platter. . . . I'll have to tack skillfully if I don't want to earn the dubious distinction of being the shortest-lived director at the helm of the Bureau!"

"You have my sympathies."

Tanner's sarcasm verged on outright insolence, but the director was no longer listening, in any case, dragged back within the network. She grimaced, giving her instructions in harsh whispers: "Well, find somebody in charge!" "He has no right to butt in!" "Handle him! It shouldn't be hard, he's a fool." "Don't tell me that! I want plausible deniability."

Her gaze found Tanner again. She sighed.

"Our services are being restructured. If I summoned you, it was to introduce you to the person who will oversee from now on our operations on New China. He should be here at this point; today our lab boys are due to start extracting usable data from Chen Shaoxing's brain." She smiled as if struck by a fresh idea. "In fact, perhaps we could join him downstairs? Have you ever witnessed a memory extraction?"

Tanner hesitated imperceptibly:

"No . . ."

An elevator took them far belowground. They passed a

maximum-security checkpoint before going down a long, featureless hallway provided with ancient luminescent ramps. At the far end, a door opened automatically. On the other side was a cloakroom, harshly lit by mercury bulbs, with stainless-steel gurneys upon which were piled smocks and trousers made from blue-green paper. They put on the sterile garb, donned plastic caps and filter masks, and Tanner then followed Robanna through a maze of narrow hallways.

The extracting room resembled both an operating room, insofar as it featured the same surgical gowns worn by technicians and ambiguous smells, and a flight control room, a function of the abundance of screens of all kinds. Five figures in blue-green smocks surrounded a long case of transparent plastic, brilliantly lit, inside which Chen Shaoxing's head—or what was left of it— bathed in the stabilizing serum.

At least, that's what Tanner supposed: it was hard to make out the face through the mess of probes and assorted feeding tubes. Furthermore, the cranium was exposed, bolted in place with small plastic screws, and pierced with newly cut openings through which dozens of minute yellow electrodes passed to penetrate the brain's wrinkled mass.

Lison Robanna caught the eye of an individual engrossed by the proceedings.

"Here's the new Bureau chief for New China; I believe you already met him on your previous mission: Francis Barnaby."

The one-time assistant to Bloembergen shook Tanner's hand limply, while his perpetually bored face went so far as to shape a vague smile. He corrected Lison Robanna:

"It's not called New China anymore, dear director, but Imperial China. No matter, we are indeed acquainted, Tanner and I."

Tanner said nothing. During the trip back, after the hyperspace jump had brought them to within a three-week journey of Earth, he had spoken not once to Barnaby.

The new chief pointed a hand at the floodlit case and its unsettling contents:

"So, Tanner, that was the objective of your *Top Secret* mission. . . ."

He underlined the two words with an irksome superciliousness.

"His death was an accident."

"Hmmmm . . . So I understand," Barnaby admitted as if it were of no consequence. "Whatever the case may be, you brought back the most important part of him."

"Have you been able to obtain anything?" inquired Robanna.

"They're working on it."

The techs moved on to the next stage in the operation. A remotely operated scalpel with an ultrasharp edge cut through the stub of spinal cord sticking out from the neck. The scalpel withdrew, and a second remote applied with extreme delicacy, flush against the clean cross section of the spinal cord, a small, square plate gleaming with iridescent hues. A flat cable connected the plate to one of the largest holographic memory computers Tanner had ever seen.

"This little plaque you see there is a neuro/cyb interface made specially to order," commented Barnaby. "The holocomp will be trying to communicate with Chen Shaoxing through it. Each one costs about thirty thousand euros. It's so fragile we have to work underground to shield it from cosmic rays."

Minutes passed. The techs were watching their monitors, subvocalizing from time and time more incomprehensible directions.

"When are they going to start?" Tanner asked.

"It's begun," stated the head technician. "The holocomp activated the communication protocol as soon as the neuro/cyb interface touched the spinal cord. However, right now, it's too early to say if Chen Shaoxing will be able to communicate."

Tanner shuddered:

"You're trying to make him . . . conscious?"

The tech scowled and gestured dismissively:

"Conscious? The word has so many connotations. . . . I'd

rather say *functional*. A person in a coma, for instance, is not conscious, but their brain is still functional. Incidentally, with a similar apparatus, doctors can communicate with comatose patients."

"But will he realize what's happening to him?"

"Everybody has their own opinion as to that."

"What's yours?"

The technician glanced quickly, embarrassed, at Lison Robanna and Francis Barnaby.

"Does it matter? He's dead anyway."

"His personality can't be transferred into the memories of the holocomp?"

This time, the man laughed openly:

"There's a myth that's hard to kill! No, no . . . The holocomp will only let us communicate. A man's personality can't be transferred into it, let alone maintained within it. At least, not yet . . . Still, this whole discussion is moot: in this case, it looks like we're not getting through. The synaptic link has been established, but it looks like there's nothing beyond the basal metabolic functions. I'm afraid the brain was imperfectly preserved."

"The freezing wasn't continuous," Tanner confessed.

"I know, I read the report. But the tissues didn't seem to be that severely damaged—"

"Try pain!" Barnaby interjected impatiently.

"Pain?"

The technician coughed:

"Yes . . . Sometimes, with the help of the holocomp, the stimulus of a sharp pain can 'awaken' the personality. But it's a last resort."

"We're down to that or nothing," insisted Barnaby. "Try it."

The technician glanced in Lison Robanna's direction, but she was connecting again to the network. He ordered a short pain pulse two seconds long. On the screens, the curves jittered during the specified duration. Once the pulse ended, the sensory output curves returned to normal.

"Still no response. Yet, as you saw, the pain registered."

"Try again!" commanded Barnaby.

"I know what I've got to do," replied the technician, miffed.

He ordered three pulses, stronger than the first. The sensory output curves jumped three times. Still no response. An oscillating pain with a ten-second period was induced. Subjected to this quasi-abstract torture, Chen Shaoxing's face remained unperturbed.

"Uh oh!" the tech suddenly exclaimed, exchanging looks with his assistants. "Something is happening. . . . Yes . . ."

Tanner could make nothing of the data and output curves flashing on the screens, but it was nevertheless obvious that the cerebral activity of Chen's brain had changed drastically. Some curves plummeted, while others climbed out of sight. About twenty lights went from red to green.

"We've got him!" muttered the tech nervously. "Hurry up with your questions; he's not stable. It better be always the same person. A person he knows."

"Go ahead, Tanner," ordered Lison Robanna. "You're the only one who spoke to him."

"If you can, speak to him in Mandarin," added the tech. "It's his mother tongue. We must do everything we can to make it easier for him. Speak normally: the room is wired."

Tanner gulped, rattled by the responsibility he suddenly felt weighing down his shoulders. He'd learned how to conduct an interrogation. Still, the unreality of the situation, the strangeness of the fluid-filled case and the oppressive room whose walls were plastered with screens and monitoring equipment all the way to the ceiling interfered with his concentration.

"Chen?" he finally asked. "Chen Shaoxing? Can you hear me?"

There was no answer, only the whisperings of the techs exchanging instructions, the muffled clickings of the pumps, the hum of the ventilation system.

"Chen? Can you hear me?"

"He hears you," muttered the tech, pointing to a screen, which bore him out. "Don't repeat a question if you don't get an answer. You must find another synaptic pathway."

"Chen Shaoxing, Réjean Tanner here. If you can hear me, answer me."

"Who are you?"

The three abrupt syllables, uttered with the clarity and neutrality that characterized artificial voices, left Tanner at a loss.

"Answer," prompted the tech. "You mustn't waste the connection."

"I'm . . . I'm Réjean Tanner. I'm the agent of the European Bureau sent by Commander Wang to contact you. Do you remember me?"

"No."

"Do you at least remember Commander Wang?"

"Wang . . . Wang . . . Wang . . . Wang . . . Wang . . ."

The tech signaled for Tanner to intervene, to say something, anything.

"Wang Zhong, yes!"

"Wang Zhong . . ." There was a pause several seconds long. "I remember . . . I remember Fenwick . . . Sir Walter Fenwick . . . Is that you, Walter?"

The tech and Lison Robanna nodded frantically. Barnaby looked puzzled for a moment, but Tanner remembered Wang's account of his meeting with Robanna and the role Fenwick had played in planting Chen as a mole within the New Chinese elite. In fact, Fenwick had been a frequent visitor to Tanner's childhood home, being a good friend of Tanner's father.

"Yes, it's me," said Tanner. "I'm Walter Fenwick. I'm glad to speak to you again after all these years."

"What's going on, sir? I . . . I can't see you."

"You . . . You're back on Earth, Chen."

"On Earth. That's impossible."

"Yes, you're back on Earth, Chen. You've completed your mission, and now we'll debrief you."

"That's impossible, sir. I didn't complete my mission. I betrayed the European Bureau. I betrayed the confidence you all placed in me."

"That doesn't matter, Chen."

"How can you say that? I betrayed you . . . I betrayed you
. . . I betrayed you . . ."

"But we know that you regret your choice, Chen, and that
you will make amends by revealing all that you know."

"Ah. I regret having betrayed you, Sir Walter. Ah. Ah. After
all the Bureau had done for me. Ah. Ah. Ah . . ."

A quick glance at the head technician and Tanner understood that the weird series of "ahs" corresponded to sobs, repro-
duced with inhuman detachment by the holocomp.

"Chen? Listen to me, Chen! Stop thinking of your betrayal.
I . . . I forgive you, Chen. Now, answer my questions. Do you
think you're able to answer?"

"Yes."

"Bloembergen!" whispered Lison Robanna in Tanner's ear.

"Chen, speak to us of Bloembergen. You know who Bo
Bloembergen is?"

"Of course. Why do you ask me that? What's happening to
me, sir?"

"I'm asking you that because we suspect Bloembergen of
being a double agent. The New Chinese got to him, didn't they?"

"No."

Tanner traded quizzical looks with Lison Robanna. He remembered being on the deck of the *Tao Qian* and interrogating
the spy that had been tailing them. Hadn't she confessed that it
was Bloembergen who had ordered Tanner and Hamakawa followed? Had she been lying to get them off her back?

"It wasn't Bloembergen who leaked the identity of my agents
when they crossed the border?"

"I don't know. Bloembergen . . . We had . . . Xiao Jiping . . .
We had a mole inside the European Bureau headquarters. It
wasn't Bo . . . It wasn't Bo . . . It wasn't Bo . . . It wasn't Bo . . .
It wasn't—"

Tanner cut him off.

"Who was it?"

"I don't understand, sir. I feel . . . I'm not well, sir . . . I don't feel well . . ."

"Who was the mole?"

"Where are you, sir? I can't see you. I'm scared, sir . . ."

"Answer my question, Chen. What was the cover identity of the mole infiltrated within our EFTA headquarters?"

"It was Zhao, sir."

"Zhao?" Tanner couldn't help exclaiming. "Bloembergen's wife?"

"She allowed us to foil your best-laid schemes from the beginning. She also organized the fake assassination attempt on Xiao Jiping."

Tanner, Barnaby, and Lison Robanna shared knowing looks.

"Why a fake attempt, Chen? Why this whole masquerade?"

"To distract you from our preparations for the invasion of the EFTA . . . I am so deeply ashamed that I betrayed you all, sir. When I learned your emissary, Wang—I remember him now, Wang Zhong—learned that he had survived, that the bullet meant for him had only wounded him, my doubly treacherous soul rejoiced . . ."

"They thought it was a stray bullet," Tanner managed in a forlorn voice.

A long silence ensued before the voice, still horribly calm and detached, rose again from the speakers of the holocomp.

"And my wife, Walter? Is Xingxing with you?"

"I . . . No, she's not here."

"Where are all these horrid images coming from, sir? I'm remembering better now. I remember the flames. I recall Lake Ming, the storm. But you weren't among us, sir . . . Xingxing . . . Ah. Ah. Ah. Ah. Your men murdered her, sir . . . The flames, I remember the flames . . . Why? Why? She had nothing to do with all of this . . . Ah. Ah. Ah. Xingxing . . . Xingxing . . ." A long silence. "And I'm dead too, of course . . . Ah. Ah. Ah. You're interrogating my corpse . . . Ah. Ah. Ah."

This time, the interruption seemed even more abrupt, matched with general havoc on the screens. Almost all the green lights switched over to red. While the other techs subvocalized instructions at a headlong pace, the chief turned toward the three observers.

"We've lost him."

"I can see that," said Barnaby. "Now, get him back."

The tech nodded sadly.

"When they're sufficiently awake to appreciate their own condition, we almost always lose them for good. We call it the 'lucidity crash.' "

"Try anyway."

"If you want, but we'll be wasting our time."

"Do it."

Half-heartedly, the techs got back to work. During the ensuing hour, various combinations of pain stimuli were tested, each one more intense than the last. The output curves would writhe furiously over the entire screen, but they never secured the slightest reaction from Chen Shaoxing. In the end, "to see if they got anything at all," the head tech selected the highest pain setting and continuous input for fifteen minutes.

"That way, at least, I get to go to the can."

After this final attempt, which also failed to produce any results, Barnaby disgustedly ordered an end put to the experiments. Lison Robanna had had to leave; more pressing matters required her attention. The technicians disconnected the holocomp, looking bored, and pushed into the adjoining cold room the cart with the box containing Chen Shaoxing's head.

"What are you going to do with the head?" asked Tanner.

The technician pursed his lips:

"We rarely get a brain in a transitional state like this. The holocomp has made contact, even after the 'crash,' but nothing more . . . It's intriguing. We'll look into it again when we have more time, perform some experiments, stuff like that."

The man added the bizarre gurney to the end of a row to-
taling a dozen more, each with its own pinkish ovoid bathed in
stabilizing fluid. The thick steel door whispered shut, pivoting on
impeccably oiled pistons and hinges.

The three men were the last to leave the extracting room.
Having disposed of their used garments, the technician invited
them to go out for a meal.

"The one disadvantage of this line of work," he remarked
good-humoredly, "is that you can't have lunch on the job."

Tanner didn't answer. He was walking behind the tech
and Barnaby, scowling darkly, staring vacantly at their backs.
He felt utterly empty. For his part, Barnaby emitted an incredulous sigh:

"Zhao . . . When I think that, all this time, Bloembergen's
own wife was torpedoing our initiatives. Zhao! 'She's working for
us,' he'd say. 'My sweet meadow flower,' indeed! She really had
us going, his sweet meadow flower. Tanner, do you remember
her performance the evening of the murder attempt? Amazing
that nobody caught on."

Tanner groaned vaguely.

"Bloody unbelievable, I say," Barnaby continued. "To think
she was getting humped by that fat swine Bloembergen all these
years. Imagining the two of them in bed together is already grotesque enough. But to think she didn't love him, that she was
doing it *for the cause* . . . Good God, she even gave him three
kids!"

"The perfect cover," said the tech. "She's living proof,
wherever she is."

Finally noticing Tanner's silence, Barnaby waved a hand in
front of his face:

"Come on, get a grip, old sod! The extraction, right? The
first time, it's always rather affecting. Don't worry, you'll see lots
more, and some even worth waiting for!"

"Yeah," chimed in the tech. "Especially if you work under
Barnaby!"

The two men laughed.

"I resign."

The elevator door opened and they got in. Barnaby scratched his ear, frowning:

"What did you say?"

"I said I won't work under you. I quit. I'm leaving the European Bureau of External Affairs."

Barnaby's limp face developed the indulgent frown one might put on for a talk with an unreasonable child:

"Now, see here, you can't leave the Bureau like that. You've got to give yourself a chance, forget about this slightly unsuccessful mission."

"Slightly unsuccessful, indeed," repeated Tanner with a manic grin.

"There will be other missions. Don't worry: under my command, you'll get the opportunity to pay back those fucking lemonfaces."

Tanner too was laughing now, a harsh laugh that set the others' teeth on edge.

"No thanks, you can have the pleasure."

"You're bitter. Aren't you confusing a simple post-mission letdown with the kind of life-changing experience that really calls everything into question?" pontificated Barnaby. "You've got a two-month vacation coming to you: take it and get some rest, relax, get laid—"

"Please spare me the usual bullshit!"

Barnaby fell silent, raising his eyes heavenward. The elevator door slid open, letting the trio walk out into the posh lobby of the government building. There was a nip in the autumn air outside, and workmen were busy adding glass panels to improve insulation in time for the first snows. A young woman crossed the lobby, hobbled by her long, narrow dress but skipping charmingly, late for the evening shift.

As they exited into a small, bustling street, Barnaby and the tech exchanged a last look with Tanner.

"Very well, Tanner. I see you're still angry at me for what

happened back in the Enclave. Let's be reasonable, now . . .
What happens in the field should stay in the field. What would
you have done in my place? It would be a great shame if this
misunderstanding affected our relationship . . ."

Tanner started to walk off, struggling to contain a fit of
hysterical laughter:

"You're an even bigger asshole than I thought."

"All right, all right . . . We'll discuss it when you've calmed
down."

"Go fuck yourself!"

Barnaby called out to him:

"Don't you even want to know what happened to your little
New Chinese crumb?"

Tanner walked back toward the two men.

"What are you talking about?" he growled.

Barnaby loosed a brief, self-satisfied titter:

"Well, well, so she was your girlfriend, wasn't she? Your
report was so—how shall I put it?—evasive about her that it was
almost touching. Wait, let me remember the phrase you used . . .
'A native auxiliary in agreement with our goals,' wasn't it? 'Native
auxiliary' . . . Rather droll, isn't it?"

"What do you know about her?" growled Tanner.

"Relax, relax . . . I don't know anything about her, nothing
at all. Sorry, Tanner, I didn't mean it. But it's your fault, too, old
sod. You looked so riled up I thought for a moment you *really*
intended to quit . . . Well, see you later!"

Barnaby, still sniggering, motioned for the tech to follow
him. The two men left Tanner behind.

He walked alone for an hour or so in the city's busy streets.
The wind was cool, like a balm on his burning face. He followed
the stone wall overlooking Lake Geneva, facing the Jet d'eau, the
majestic fountain spouting its white plume as in centuries past.
He sat on the cold, rough concrete. From the depths of his memory, the exquisite characters of an antique poem fluttered
through his mind:

Who shall reproach me, if my soul
This anguish suffers twice? . . .

Tanner rose, walked slowly toward the shops of the old city center. Perhaps he could find *Dream of the Red Chamber* somewhere . . .

ACKNOWLEDGMENTS

I wish to thank the following people, who encouraged me and helped me at various points with the research, the writing, and the correction of this novel:

Dominique Balavoine, René Minot, Christian Roussel, and Élaine Piquet, experts on China; Maher Jahjah, Élisabeth Vonarburg, and Francine Pelletier, who read and critiqued the first draft; Dr. Hubert Watelle, sailing aficionado and my advisor on the topic; and my father, Raymond Champetier, who proved to me with the help of the Stefan-Boltzmann law and the blackbody equation that the Dragon's Eye could not put out as high an ultraviolet flux as is shown in the novel!

The translation of a Chinese poem, in Chapter 17, is a scene inspired by the book *Sagesse de la Chine* by H. van Praag (Verviers: Gérard & Cie, Marabout, 1966). The poem was excerpted from Li Po's *Livre de Jade*, in a French translation by Judith Gautier.

Many details of this novel were inspired by a reading of *Kang Sheng et les services secrets chinois* by Roger Faligot and Rémi Kauffer (Paris: Laffont, 1987).